Heartlines

Shireen Magedin

AUSXIP PUBLISHING

Print: 978-0-6456326-4-4

Edited by Rosa Alonso
Cover Design by Mary Draganis
Interior design by AUSXIP Publishing

AUSXIP Publishing
www.ausxippublishing.com

ABOUT HEARTLINES

I am very pleased to present to you the third book in my *Journey's Trilogy*, which I have called Heartlines. While it was a unique pleasure to write it, I would like to think that I could address social issues that affect people nationally as well as internationally through my books. In Heartlines, I have touched upon a poignant, and yet relatively covert, concern. The media has started to speak about it, and there are a few NGOs that are doing exemplary work, but there is so much more that I feel we can do about the social disease of child trafficking. While well-to-do people and celebrities have the money to pay exorbitant fees to adopt a child on the black market, thus creating a niche, children will continue to be ripped away from their families. To give the adoptive parents their due, their objective is usually to bypass red tape, but very few are unaware that the children they have welcomed into their homes might not be orphans at all.

On a more sinister side, the demand for child pornography on the dark web grows day by day, and this situation is more devastating than that of the children who are adopted into loving families, albeit illegally. These practices are disturbing and sometimes life threatening, as the children invariably die of disease, drug addiction, suicide, and even murder. Therefore, creating awareness about the social issue of children being taken from their families is imperative and should be treated seriously.

Heartlines follows Sarah and Tanya on a journey where they track international child smugglers whose specialty is to pick up children in areas that have either been hit by natural disasters like earthquakes and floods or ravaged by war. Very often, the children's families can't be traced because they are thought to have died amidst these tragic events.

The route taken by the duo was based loosely on a route that my parents, bitten by the wanderlust bug, followed not once or twice, but three times. My siblings and I were blessed to be dragged along, and we got hands-on education as my father quizzed us mercilessly whenever we passed through a town or country. Believe me when I say it was a lot of fun, and I am happy to have incorporated some of our experiences for you to read in Heartlines.

DEDICATION

*I dedicate **Heartlines** to both of my parents.*

Just like with Lifelines and Bloodlines, I dedicate my third book, Heartlines, to my parents, whose wanderlust took us to many corners of the world. I would also like to dedicate this novel to my siblings, Yusuf and Janie Soomro, with whom I had so much fun on our journeys. I hope we can have more soon. To my daughter, Sharmeen, and my son, Nadir: thank you for your patience and love.

ACKNOWLEDGMENTS

I have come to realize that the best part of writing is when the author, in this case me, is encouraged by people who are so much more experienced. I cannot thank Taylor Rickard enough for her kind words and nudges when she would take the time from her busy schedule to read my chapters. Rosa Alonso, you have been an editor extraordinaire and have polished the manuscript till it shone. For that, you have my heartfelt gratitude.

Alison Slowski and Mariam Bally (along with Aunty Crystal), you are amazing and have always had my back as beta readers.

Last but not least... what can I say about Mary Draganis? She has been there all along encouraging me, and I can't say how much it thrills me that I can call myself an author because of her. Bless you.

Sarah and Tanya's Journey

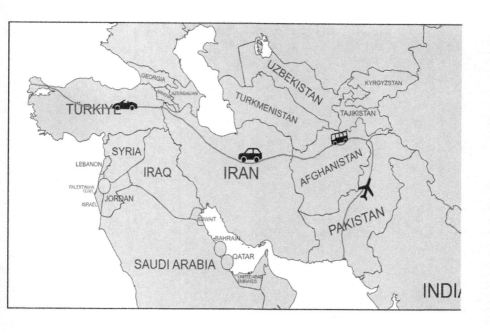

PROLOGUE

"Every single minute matters, every single child matters, every single childhood matters." ~ Kailash Satyarthi

SARAH CROUCHED IN THE CRUMBLING DEBRIS trying to be as quiet as she could. She was hiding under a solid oak table in the rubble of the house that had been destroyed just a few minutes before. In her haste to find cover when the initial explosions started, she was able to gather two of the orphan children from the village clinic where she was working. The two little girls and Sarah had taken refuge in the relatively undamaged basement. She had ducked in there because the basement was in one of those old school buildings that were built with multiple strong archways reinforced with steel, and she had been told by the village chief that it had survived the multiple earthquakes and continuous aftershocks from the random explosions from enemy fire. It seemed sensible at the time to hide there, and for a short while after the noisy explosions and the ominous grating of the underground stones while the earth moved, it was extremely quiet. The only noise she then heard was the sound of dripping water from the destroyed pipes and the skitter of the crumbling concrete that was still shifting even after the explosions had stopped. She had to keep quiet and hoped the children wouldn't make a noise. She was terrified because she suspected that the house hadn't collapsed only with enemy fire—she had an inkling that there was foul play as well.

Suddenly, Sarah heard voices coming from above. She cocked her head to catch what was being said to gauge whether the "rescuers" were friends or foes. She didn't want to shout out to be saved just yet. From the heavy footsteps, it seemed like there were men moving around above her. As they came nearer, she could finally make out what they were saying and realized that the men weren't benevolent rescuers. *Oh, God! They had found her!* The men were talking in Pashto, a language she recognized but wasn't very fluent in. She could just make herself understood with a few words and sign language while she worked in the relief camp near Battagram, deep in the tribal areas of the North of Pakistan. She knew she was trapped. Not only in the basement, but also in this no man's land where she had accompanied Tanya and her team to work undercover as a relief doctor in this war-ravaged part of the world. Their goal was to hunt for the child traffickers and slave traders that had descended in the area like vultures picking the spoils after the devastation due to the lethal disaster.

There was already talk in the village that many children whose parents had died in the war were missing, and just that morning, after a series of strong missile explosions, a busload of college girls had disappeared from the nearby city. Apparently, the disoriented and frightened girls thought that the bus they sat in was their usual transport, and since they were told by their teachers to go home to their families immediately, they boarded it without any thought. They just wanted to go home, to safety, little realizing that the driver wasn't their usual one. Only God knew where he had taken the poor girls. There were a lot of orphans in the village and Sarah hoped that they were safe and didn't fall into the clutches of the predatory men she could hear walking above her.

Sarah tried to get her bearings in the gloom. She was worried because there was no way out since the rubble had covered the only exit from where they hid. Moreover, she now had responsibility for two more innocent souls. She needed to be careful. Any mistake on her part could cost them their lives.

Sarah hoped the baby would remain asleep. The poor mite had exhausted herself with her crying jag when the noise around her scared her. The loud sound of the rubble falling had drowned her cries. To keep her hands free and to tend to the other little girl, a toddler, Sarah had tied the baby to her chest with a long cotton scarf. The toddler clung to her side, whimpering softly.

"Shh! We don't want the bad men to hear us!" She whispered as she hugged the little girl closer.

The toddler, already wise for her years, nodded even though large tears were forming in her eyes and her lower lip quivered in fright. But she knew that this lady, the doccy, would help them and keep them safe, so she stuck her thumb into her mouth and snuggled closer to Sarah while trying her best to keep quiet.

The baby started to wake up and move about. Soon she was wriggling restlessly against the bindings and, just as she was poised to let out a cry, Sarah remembered that she had her pacifier in her pocket, and quickly stuffed it in in her mouth. She hoped she would be diverted with it, at least for now, but she knew it was near both of the children's feeding time and she hoped that the evil men looking for them would be long gone before they had full-blown hunger tantrums.

"I hope Tanya can find us soon," she muttered to herself. She reached up to touch the pendant that she always wore around her neck. It had a special homing device it, and once activated, she could be tracked from within the radius of one kilometer. To her dismay, in the frantic rush to run for cover and hide, it must have fallen down and she couldn't feel it around her neck anymore. She felt a frisson of panic. How would Tanya find them now?

She knew it was still daytime since there were weak rays of light streaming between the debris near the grimy window. The basement was dimly lit by the dusty rays and had an ominous gloom, but maybe the light would be enough so that she could look around to find and activate her pendant.

"Where are you?" she desperately kept repeating to herself as she blindly groped around her. She couldn't do much with a two-month-old baby in her arms and a two-year-old toddler clinging to her like a limpet.

Sarah's eyes were getting accustomed to the dark, so she squinted to have a better look around her unwanted dungeon. She saw that the basement had been used as a storage space by the men. No wonder they wanted to access the place, even if it was ruined.

"Come, get up quietly. Don't make a noise. We are going to see what's over there," Sarah whispered to the little girl. Moving around with the girls clinging to her was difficult, but it was a necessary evil, because she was worried they might start crying if she went even as far as other side of the room without them. They seemed to be drawing comfort and strength from Sarah's presence.

She tried to be quiet, until she noticed that the men's shouts and their footsteps had faded away. With relief, she stopped worrying that their small shuffling sounds would attract attention.

Making her way to a cupboard that had fallen from the force of the tremors with its doors facing upwards, Sarah gingerly opened them hoping that the hinges didn't squeak too loudly.

To her delight, there was what seemed to be a treasure trove there—bundles of candles, boxes of matches, and best of all, canned food and condensed milk. This was a gift from heaven. Now she had the means to look after the children without them creating a ruckus when they were hungry, and they could wait in relative comfort till they were finally rescued.

Sarah lit a candle and had a closer look at her surroundings. The basement didn't look so ominous in the light. It was only by holding up the lighted candle that she saw that her hand was shaking. She hadn't realized how scared she was, but now the adrenaline rush was diminishing and she was feeling the effects. However, she had to try to harden her heart so that she could be brave for the two little girls she was tending to. She scanned the floor for her pendant, not really hopeful that she would find it, but she had to try. After scrambling through the rubble and shining the fast-diminishing candle in every possible crevice, she finally saw a muted glint of silver from under a small pile of stones. She quickly picked it up and saw that though dusty, it seemed undamaged. The clasp had become loose, but that had happened a few times since her brother had damaged it a couple of years before. Pressing the hidden switch that activated the homing device, she looked affectionately at the pendant that her partner Tanya had given her to commemorate their tenth anniversary. It was shaped like a stethoscope tied together with tiny silver handcuffs. She loved it and vowed to either have the clasp properly fixed once she was home again or get a new chain for the pendant. She was lucky that she found it under the rubble, and hoped that the homing device embedded in it was still working. She definitely expected it to. After all, it had been made by MI6 and was supposed to be able to weather all sorts of situations and stress.

The baby was now getting restless in her arms. Sarah patted her gently to comfort her and shuffled towards the cupboard once more. She chose a tin of condensed milk and a sealed bottle of water. Rummaging further in her treasure trove she found some sterile latex gloves. She used one of the matchsticks to make a hole in one of the fingers and poured in a mixture of condensed milk and water giving it an acceptable consistency for the baby to suck upon. After closing the top of the glove with a tight knot, Sarah put the pierced finger into the baby's mouth and looked down at her in affectionate satisfaction when she started to suckle greedily.

The toddler looked on and finally glanced at Sarah with a silent plea in her eyes. Sarah understood immediately and prepared another glove with a thicker consistency of the milk. Soon she was also happily sucking on the glove like her baby sister. As she sat back, trying to relax, Sarah realized that she hadn't had anything to eat in the last twenty-four hours either. Her stomach just then took that opportunity to growl like an animal. When she looked once more at the stores in the cupboard, she saw tins of baked beans and vegetables. She was relieved that every can had a tab to pull them open, so she didn't need to have a can opener, if there was one at all. It also meant that the canned goods were fairly new, since tabbed cans had only come to this part of the country recently.

To her surprise, Sarah found a mattress propped against a nearby wall. It was dusty because of the debris, but at least she could put the children down when they finally went to sleep. Her arms were starting to get tired and just the thought of putting the baby down on the mattress made her feel much better.

Sarah's watch showed that it was going to be night soon, so she pulled the mattress onto the floor while still holding the baby as it suckled on the makeshift nipple. Giving it a perfunctory sweep with her hands, she gently put her down after she spread the baby's blanket on the mattress. The baby rolled to her side and promptly fell asleep while still drinking her milk.

The toddler also lay down without Sarah telling her to do so. She was exhausted; she fell asleep right away.

Now that the children were comfortable, fed, and asleep, Sarah had time to think about their predicament. She closed her eyes and focused on Tanya. She tried to summon her partner telepathically. She hoped that they would be found by friendly people instead of the ones that had started the lethal hostilities in the village. She was still a bit disoriented and couldn't really pinpoint whether the damage was due to the explosions themselves or the strong aftershocks. The men had been looking for her, and she knew from the little she understood that they were not friendly at all. They knew that she was "meddling" with their "business." Moreover, Sarah had valuable merchandise with her—the two children. They wanted them back, and Sarah wasn't sure whether they would let her live. It seemed that her cover had been blown and this was one of the dire consequences. Thanking all that was holy, she was relieved that the men had left for now and hadn't persisted in looking for them. Maybe they thought that they weren't alive anymore and planned to come and dig them out later.

"Tanya... I need you. The babies need you. Come rescue us." Sarah closed her eyes and repeated the sentences as if they were a holy mantra. Now she just had to sit back and wait.

CHAPTER 1

"Love is such a powerful force. It's there for everyone to embrace—that kind of unconditional love for all of humankind. That is the kind of love that impels people to go into the community and try to change conditions for others, to take risks for what they believe in." ~ Coretta Scott King

SIX DAYS EARLIER...

Sarah

Life couldn't have been better, in my opinion, but I knew I shouldn't say that—I might jinx it. Whenever I mentioned that I was at peace and content, something would pop up and shatter our serenity, so it was better that I didn't voice these thoughts and feelings out loud. Was I superstitious? Of course, I was. How could it be possible that I have extra sensory abilities and not believe in coincidences and karma?

Since our adventures in Pakistan three years before, we had lived in relative peace. My brother stayed in England and his family had grown to include little Natasha. She was adorable and the apple of her aunts' eyes. Her elder brother Daniyal was now going to nursery school and looked so cute when he went there every morning clutching his Mickey Mouse lunchbox.

I looked up as I was writing my diary and saw the love of my life walk into the room. She had a slightly annoyed look on her face, but I knew she was just exhausted. I had an inkling that dealing with slavers and child traffickers was affecting her more than she admitted.

"What are you doing?" asked Tanya with affectionately indulgent smile. "Ever since you got that laptop and learned about the internet, you have been online nearly every day." While munching on a pear, she looked over my shoulder to see what I was doing.

I laughed and flipped the cover down. "I was just writing my daily diary. I promise I will show it to you one day, but not now. I am still learning how to handle this machine, so things are still a bit sketchy."

Tanya laughed and pulled me up and hugged me. It was gratifying that we still had that spark in our relationship even after nearly fourteen years together. I loved this brave agent of mine and I knew she loved me, too, because she showed me every day with her gestures and her words. However, it was her smoldering looks that were even more proof that she loved me, and I couldn't help but love her back. There was no doubt whatsoever in my heart.

"You are home early today, my love," I said as I looked up into Tanya's beautiful dark eyes.

"They gave me the day off. Actually, they told me to take the rest of the week off, so I came home immediately. We have so little time together on normal working days that this extra time is like a gift."

"Oh, that's wonderful!" I exclaimed. "Shall we go away for the weekend? We could take the ferry to Calais and spend the weekend in Paris!"

"I was thinking more in the lines of spending a couple of lazy days in our hammock in the garden. The weather is wonderful and we both need the rest. You have just finished a week of night duties. You do look exhausted, love."

"You are right, but it would have been fun." I was mildly disappointed, but I put my head on Tanya's shoulder and sighed. I was aware that both of us had been working hard. Tanya had just come back from Tajikistan two days before, where they caught a notorious white slaver who was selling the local girls to the Middle East. I looked closely and saw the strain on Tanya's face. At that moment I felt a strange energy coming from her and realized that there was something else bothering her.

"What is wrong, Tanya? What aren't you telling me?" I asked gently while cupping her cheek with my right hand.

She covered my hand with hers and gave a low chuckle. "I can never hide anything from you, can I?" She turned my palm up and kissed it gently, but she had a faraway look in her eyes. It was as if she was trying to solve a puzzle and wasn't quite sure of the solution.

"Let's order a pizza and have an early night. I will tell you what's on my mind. Just have a bit of patience, dear heart. I need to think things over." With that, she walked over to the sofa and sat down, deep in thought.

"Well, I am here whenever you are ready to talk." Picking up the pizza menu from above the fridge, I bustled over to the phone mounted on the kitchen wall and dialed the pizza place. "Is marguerita pizza with extra cheese and olives okay? Or would you like something else?" Tanya was set in her ways where her pizza was concerned, but I still always asked. She might surprise me one day.

"No, no, that's okay," she said distractedly. There really had to be something wrong because there was no repartee or banter. This wasn't good. I had a sick feeling in the pit of my stomach and my hair started to stand on end. My intuition kicked in...

Tanya

"Have you heard of the earthquake that has devastated the north of Pakistan, India, and Afghanistan?" asked my new boss, Mr. Humphrey. Then, almost to himself, he mumbled, "Of course you have. You are the most informed person on my team."

"I have, sir. Not only has there been a lot of damage, but I hear the fatalities are more than a hundred and fifty thousand people." I was concerned what the implication of this natural disaster would be to my department in Interpol. I had been assigned to liaise with British and South Asian agencies to stop child smuggling and slavery, and to help repatriate young girls and children who were kidnapped and taken against their will, sometimes by their own families, to Pakistan to be forced into marriages. This earthquake would be manna from heaven for people who wanted to traffic young women and children.

"Agent Kareem, I am aware of your exemplary results in bringing traffickers to justice. However, I would like you to go undercover this time. I believe that people who are picking up the children in the earthquake areas are part of a powerful international conglomerate. Our department wants to catch the head of the organization. Just going in and hauling the local perpetrators to justice would not be enough." He huffed out a deep breath and passed a hand over his thinning hair in frustration.

"Many international and local relief agencies are landing at Karachi airport and are traveling to the north of the country to establish relief camps for the survivors," he went on. "The Pakistani army is collaborating with everyone who is going to help the people there and ensure that they can work safely."

"That's nice," I murmured politely, wondering what it had to do with me.

"I want you to go to the affected areas undercover as a relief worker," said Mr. Humphrey. "I also want your partner to take leave of absence from her hospital and go with you."

"Sarah?" I was suddenly more attentive. "Why her? We have many doctors in our agency that are properly trained in field work!"

"For one, she is a pediatrician. We would need her skills if any of the children are ill or injured. Regrettably, our doctors in the agency are more comfortable with adult medicine, so given the circumstances, it is a good idea to recruit her for this crucial mission. Sarah is also familiar with that area of the country as well as the colloquial languages. It would take weeks for us to train someone to match Sarah's skills." Humphrey looked at me pointedly as he talked, as if I should have realized what they wanted from Sarah instinctively.

"But, sir, she has her own work here in London; she can't just drop everything and go. She isn't an employee of Interpol. Have you forgotten that? We can't just order her around!" I was starting to get annoyed. It was my job to face danger on my assignments, but to deliberately throw Sarah there was something I would draw a line at.

"Of course, I know that she is not a member of our organization," he said, visibly irritated with me. I could see that he was on the verge of losing his patience. "I have read her files and have seen that she has volunteered to work in disaster areas before. People know her—she is well known to some of her medical colleagues who will also be volunteering, since the same teams usually go to areas where they are needed, and they have developed a camaraderie. Even though it's been a while since Sarah has done such work, we believe she would fit in very well, and no one would suspect her to be part of the Interpol team. I have already talked to her boss, Professor Bingham, and he has agreed to let her have paid leave of absence for up to six months. Additionally, she will be getting a handsome retainer from us." Humphrey looked sternly at me, annoyed that I was being contrary. "Go home, take a few days off, and talk to Sarah. We will train her in the basics and then send the two of you off. The silver lining in the cloud for you is that she will be at your side most of the time. I don't want either of you to engage with the smugglers. I just want you to get enough evidence that would lead to whoever was in charge, and then come back home. The rest will be up to the local law enforcement agencies."

I gave a low growl of frustration. I knew that Sarah would be upset that Interpol went behind her back to her boss without asking or informing her. I was annoyed, so I could definitely foresee what she would say when I told her the news.

Mumbling under my breath, I picked up my briefcase and stomped out of the office. I caught a fairly empty train to go home—maybe I should always travel home earlier to avoid the rush hour...

As I walked home from the station, I passed a flower shop. I considered buying my wife some flowers, but decided against it. Sarah would immediately catch on that I was trying to get her to do something that she might not like.

I reached the gate of our house and admired the small garden in the front. Sarah had planted a border of roses along the low wall and they were just starting to bloom, but for the first time, I was reluctant to go inside. I knew I couldn't hide my concern from Sarah.

I murmured a short prayer and walked into the house. There she was, sitting in the sunny conservatory. The sun was glinting off her auburn hair making it shine from within as if with fires of its own. She looked so beautiful sitting there at her new computer, frowning in concentration as she tried to figure out its complexities. Since she hadn't yet noticed me, I took the opportunity to just enjoy looking at her. She was my life, and if anything happened to her, I would be devastated. Moreso if I was the one leading her to disaster. How could I even broach the subject to her?

I picked up a pear from the fruit basket on the dining table and casually walked over to where she sat, making my presence known. Sarah looked delighted to see me home earlier than usual, but I was still distracted, no matter how hard I tried to act normal, and of course she caught that immediately.

"What is wrong, Tanya? Why are you upset? Tell me. You do know that I worry about you. Especially when you go on your assignments." Sarah looked at me with such love in her eyes that I just had to tell her. I couldn't hide anything from her – ever.

"They are sending me on another assignment," I said tersely.

"What is it about this assignment that is upsetting you? You go on assignments all the time." Sarah was understandably confused.

"Remember we saw the news about the earthquake in Pakistan? Well, they want me to go there undercover with a relief agency. Apparently, children and young girls who have survived the disaster are being picked up by alleged smugglers and are not heard of again. I have been asked to gather intelligence that would lead us to the ringleaders. Interpol believes that this is not a local operation. They have some information that it might be part of an international network..."

"How horrible for the children! They must be so scared!" Sarah had tears in her eyes. "I wish I could do something. Maybe even be part of a medical relief camp to help the sick and injured children."

That was my cue! Sarah had made it easy for me, but I still hesitated. I didn't want to put her in danger, and those people were unpredictable.

"What is it, Tanya? Tell me. You should know that my intuition is buzzing like a top." She laughed uneasily.

"Interpol wants you to come with me. They want you to work as a medical relief worker while keeping your eyes and ears open for anything that you might find strange. They also think that as a qualified pediatrician, you would be able to assess the condition of the children when we find them, and give them medical care if it were required at the time."

"But what about my job? I can't just drop everything and go with you!" Sarah frowned at the thought.

I looked shamefacedly at her. I tried to speak but somehow couldn't get a coherent word out. How would she react to my department's meddling?

"Aha!" she exclaimed. "What have you done, Tanya? Out with it!" Sarah tried to look annoyed, but I saw the hint of a smile on her lips.

"I am so sorry, Sarah! This was handed over to me as a fait accompli. Mr. Humphrey has already talked to Professor Bingham and has requested a paid leave of absence for you. In addition, he has arranged a stipendium that will be paid to you by Interpol, so there won't be any loss of income for you. As a matter of fact, it would be quite a bonus." I tried to make light of the situation, but Sarah just stood there listening to me bluster without saying a word. I was starting to get anxious. I held my breath while waiting for the storm that I thought Sarah would be unleashing on me, but then she took a deep breath and smiled.

Sarah giggled. "Will I get one of those agent IDs? That

would be so cool. Tell Mr. Humphrey if he gives me one, I will go with you to Pakistan."

Provisional Agent Sarah of Interpol was born in that instant, and despite my misgivings, she was raring to go. Of course, she would want to be where she could help children; I should have known.

CHAPTER 2

*"The smallest act of kindness is worth
more than the grandest intention."*
~ Oscar Wilde

SARAH

I had a feeling of melancholy and strange déjà vu when we
arrived at Karachi airport. The only difference to my
previous visit was that most of the passengers disembarking
from the planes were relief workers from all over the globe.
The amount of equipment and medical paraphernalia that
everyone carried was mind-boggling and, in a sense,
gratifying because we knew that this was all for people who
actually needed medical care. I felt proud that I was part of
this worldwide confluence of medical professionals and

volunteers. Even though we did have a hidden ulterior motive in going to the disaster-struck areas, I was certain that I would be applying my medical skills there. No matter what, I am a physician, and I will never forget that.

As we exited the crowded terminal, I tried to look over the heads of the teeming crowd by standing on my toes. I was under the impression that either my brother or my father would pick us up, but there were no familiar faces to be seen. It seemed my family had disappointed me once again. I thought that things were going well since our last visit. Ammi was still being her usual self, of course, but I had reconciled with my brother Azaan and my Baba. Why weren't they there?

I was about to say something about this to Tanya when she turned to me and said, "We will be picked up by the Interpol liaison agent here in Pakistan. Remember we aren't on a holiday, so don't be sad that no one came to pick us up. I know what you are thinking. Don't worry; we will see your family once we have finished our mission and are on our way back home."

I nodded in agreement, but I still felt a bit sad that I wouldn't see my family just yet. Tanya was right—we had to focus on our assignment. There was no time for personal sentimentalities. Children were being spirited away, and it was up to our team to gather enough data to stop the criminals who were preying on the innocence of childhood.

Just as I turned to answer Tanya, an official-looking jeep swept into the VIP lane of the airport and stopped with a flourish in front of us.

"Most probably our liaison here," said Tanya as she tried to look unobtrusively through the darkened windows of the car. It was strange that it just stood there and no one seemed to move or come out of the car. We looked at each other in surprise. Maybe this wasn't our guy?

We were about to turn away when a well-dressed man stepped out of the car and started to shout in an angry voice while pointing at us. "Tanya! What are you doing here? How can you have the audacity to show your face in this town? You are a black mark on the honor of our family. You should go back to whatever hellhole you have crawled out of!"

Who in heaven's name was this boorish impolite imbecile? I thought of even more derogatory words in my mind, but before I could say anything, Tanya grabbed my arm and gave it a squeeze, as if she wanted me to be quiet. I, on the other hand, wanted to scratch that man's eyes out for being so rude to Tanya.

"Sarah," she said quietly, "I would like to introduce you to my elder brother, Shahnawaz Kareem."

The man kept on abusing, blustering, and gesturing while Tanya got paler by the moment. A curious crowd had gathered around the car and were trying to find out what the commotion was about. Tanya didn't say a word. For starters, it would have been difficult to get a word in, and it would likely develop into an uncouth argument. She just stood there with her head held high. With dignity and poise.

All of a sudden, mid-tirade, Shahnawaz started to cough and clutched his chest. He let out a dreadful moan and fell face down in the mud. It must have rained the day before, and there were a lot of muddy puddles, which meant he didn't hurt himself as much as he would have if the ground had been dry.

I examined him for a pulse and checked whether he was breathing while yelling to the crowd to stand back.

"Tanya, get the airport medics. They will arrange for an ambulance," I said to my stunned partner.

Shahnawaz's pulse was very weak, hardly discernable, and he wasn't breathing. I started CPR immediately. I had to if I wanted to save his life. No matter how horrible he was to Tanya, he still was a human being and her brother. I used a muslin cloth to cover his mouth to give a few rescue breaths and continued with the chest compressions. Every thirty compressions I would stop, check for a pulse and breathing, and then give two rescue breaths if required. After what seemed like an eternity, I felt his pulse get stronger and he started to take a few breaths spontaneously. By that time, the airport ambulance had arrived and a paramedic took over the CPR from me since I was getting very tired. Once they were certain Shahnawaz was stabilized, the paramedics took him away to the nearest cardiovascular institute.

Someone put their hand on my shoulder to steady me as I shakily got up. As I tried to focus on my surroundings, I heard the crowd start to clap. They were acknowledging that I had saved a man's life. It was nice to be acknowledged, but that was what anyone with basic knowledge of CPR would have done. I looked up to see who was helping me and I was thrilled to see Inspector Razia, one of our dearest friends and one of the bravest policewomen we knew standing next to me. As soon as I was on my feet I was engulfed in a big hug.

"It is so good to see you, Razia! How are the twins? They must have grown a lot since we last saw them!" I was babbling and not even embarrassed by it.

Razia laughed. "Slow down! All is well. The children are

nearly young men now and they keep talking about the nice time they had with you and Tanya when they visited you in England."

I turned to look for Tanya and couldn't see her anywhere. Razia understood who I was looking for and told me that Tanya had hopped onto the ambulance just as it was pulling away from the curb. We were to meet her at the hospital. We climbed into Razia's official jeep and sped to the hospital. I didn't think about Shahnawaz. I knew I had done all that I could for him and it was up to the cardiologists now, but I was worried about Tanya and how this unexpected encounter was affecting her.

Tanya

Even though we were back in Pakistan for an official Interpol assignment, it was nice to land in Karachi. The crowds at the airport were as flamboyant as ever, and we had to fight our way through people laden with flowers and garlands to welcome their visitors from abroad. I had been told that our Interpol liaison would pick us up, but I never got the person's name; I was just told that they would show me an ID when we met.

Sarah looked upset as she scanned the crowd for a familiar face. I had forgotten to tell her that her family wouldn't be at the airport. We were there on an official assignment and we had to stick to the standard operating parameters if we were to be successful. I had just told her that we would be meeting her family after we had completed our mission when a jeep bearing the dual badges of the Pakistani police and Interpol stopped in the VIP lane in front of us. It had to be our ride.

There was an uncomfortable pause when there was no movement from within the car. Then a painfully familiar figure burst out of the jeep and started to rant and rave at me. I couldn't believe my eyes. Shahnawaz? My brother was the Interpol liaison? When had he joined the police? I was stunned for a moment, and then I tuned out his voice and let his hateful words bounce off me. I didn't care what he said because he was the one making a fool of himself. My only concern was that he didn't attack Sarah.

Suddenly, I saw him fall down while clutching his chest, but the seriousness of his condition still didn't register with me. Sarah had to shout at me to get me out of my "zone". I ran to the airport medical center and called out the nearest medic. "Please call an ambulance! There is a man lying on the curb and he's having a heart attack!"

The medic phoned for an ambulance and told me to calm down and take a seat. I was impressed with how efficient their clockwork procedures were.

"Is there anyone with the patient?"

"Yes, my friend Sarah has started CPR. She's a doctor. Please hurry up; he needs to go to the hospital immediately." I was beside myself with worry. Even though we hadn't parted amicably all those years before, he still was my brother, and I didn't want him to die.

The ambulance came within a few minutes and was directed towards where Sarah had laid Shahnawaz on the ground and was calmly counting the chest compressions that she was giving him.

While I looked on, someone tapped me on my shoulder. I whirled around and was very happy to see Inspector Razia, one of my dearest friends. They must have called her as well —If a senior police officer had died on her beat, she would have been responsible.

"What is going on, Tanya? Why is it that whenever we meet, you and Sarah are knee deep in trouble?" she said with a smirk.

"Our Interpol liaison officer turned out to be my brother. I don't think anyone told him my complete name. I am known as Agent Kareem at work. It is quite a common name, and it must have been an unpleasant surprise for him to see me standing there, waiting for him. He started to rant and rave until he had what looked like a heart attack."

Razia was shocked. She knew my history and how much my family hated me. "Has he lost his mind? He is supposed to be on official duty, and even though he doesn't like you, he should not let that affect his work."

"Please, do me a favor," I said while looking at Sarah, who was still busy with the paramedics. "I am going with the ambulance to the hospital. Can you bring Sarah along with you?"

Razia looked at me in disbelief. "After all he has said, you still want to go with him?"

"Shahnawaz is my brother and there was a time when I was very close to him. No matter what happened at the time, I still love him. I will not let the bad memories eclipse the good ones. Not when he needs someone." I couldn't believe how much this incident had affected me. "I will find you and Sarah once I know that he is comfortable. I guess it would also be up to me to bite the bullet and call my parents." I was dreading that because I knew that would only end in more abuse, at least from my father.

This was also a big hiccup in our mission. "I wonder who our Interpol liaison will be now. I hope that whoever they assign to us will be more pleasant than Shahnawaz Kareem," I said dryly.

I left Razia and hopped onto the already moving ambulance. The medics were not happy with that and wanted to stop to let me off, but once I explained that I was Shahnawaz's sister, they allowed me to ride along with them.

As I sat on the bench that was parallel to the stretcher where my brother lay, his face almost completely covered by the oxygen mask that was pumping the life-saving gas into his lungs, I felt sad as I pondered over the fragility of life and how much of it is wasted by hating people for following their own dreams and beliefs. Shahnawaz and I were siblings. We had loved each other once upon a time. God help me, I still didn't resent him or bear a grudge towards him, but our society imposed its taboos on different values and perceptions and individuals like Shahnawaz chose to follow those taboos like lemmings to end in ultimate destruction. His hate reacted so negatively on his body that now he was helplessly lying on the stretcher, just pulled back from the brink of death by Sarah. I found that ironic.

Once we reached the hospital, Shahnawaz was taken to the cardiac care unit, or the CCU, as it was called. It was up to me to get him registered and sort out his particulars. I had searched his pockets and found his wallet, which had his national ID card and his police ID in it. Being a government employee, he was eligible for free health care, so it was easy to get him admitted into the hospital. As soon as I finished with the paperwork, I talked to a doctor who was just coming out of the CCU.

"Doctor, my brother Shahnawaz Kareem has just been brought in. Can you please tell me how he is now?"

"Oh, yes," said the doctor, whose name tag showed that his name was Dr. Shahid. "He is stable and we have sedated him for now. Whoever was responsible for giving him CPR at the time of his heart attack did an exemplary job. They saved his life."

"That was Dr. Sarah Shah, a friend of mine. We just landed from London, and he was supposed to pick us up. He was lucky that Sarah knew what to do."

"Yes, he is definitely a lucky man," said Dr. Shahid with a smile. "You can go in for a few minutes, but we don't allow any of the patients' attendants to stay in the CCU. Once he is shifted to the ward, he will be allowed one person to stay with him."

Shahnawaz looked so frail lying there in the hospital bed with all the wires and pipes allowing him to stay in this earthly plane. 'Hmm...' I thought wryly that I was starting to think like Sarah.

I stayed with him for a few minutes. He continued to sleep and wasn't aware that I was at his bedside. Now I had a difficult task—I had to call our parents. Theirs was the only phone number that I knew, and I didn't want to riffle anymore in my brother's wallet. Unfortunately, I didn't even know if he was married or had children. A wave of sadness washed over me, but I had to be brave. I couldn't leave him alone in the hospital.

I walked out into the massive lobby of the hospital and saw Sarah and Razia waiting for me near the reception counter. Sarah rushed over once she spotted me. She gave me a reassuring hug and kissed my cheek.

"Have you talked to your family yet?" She asked me. I could see her compassion for me in her eyes. She knew how difficult that would be for me.

"Not yet," I answered. "But now that you are here and I have moral support, I can take anything that's hurled at me."

Sarah and Razia followed me to a bank of telephones that were set against the wall in the far side of the lobby. All of them were occupied by frantic relatives letting their families know about their loved ones. We had to wait for a short while until one was free for us to use.

I dialed my parents' number from memory, hoping they hadn't changed the number. The phone rang a few times and then was picked up. I recognized my mother's voice, but I could not get a word out because all the emotions and the pain from the past years flooded back and choked me. Without even realizing it, I started to cry.

"Hello, hello!" said my mother. She heard me crying but wasn't sure who was on the line.

"Who is it?" I heard my father shout in the background.

"I don't know, but it seems they're crying." My mother sounded scared and confused.

"Give me the phone. I told you not to bother with crank calls!" My father spoke to my mother in his usual rough and derogatory manner. I felt the old anger bubble up, the same emotions that I used to feel as a teenager when my father would be disrespectful to my mother.

"Ma!" I was able to croak out before the phone was snatched away from her.

"Tanya! My child!" she cried out.

"How dare you say her name in this house?" I heard the sound of a slap and a whimper. I swear if I had been anywhere near the man, I would have ripped his arm off. The bullying needed to be stopped. Maybe I would be able to do something for my mother later. After all, I was now older and stronger, and I had the law to back me up.

"What do you want?" shouted my father into the phone. "I am hanging up and I don't want you to bother me or your mother ever again!"

"Wait! Abba!" I shouted desperately.

"What is it?" His voice sounded even more repulsive than before. "You have ten seconds to speak and then lose this number."

"Shahnawaz has had a heart attack. He is in the cardiovascular institute." I spoke as fast as I could. I didn't want him to hang up before I could give him all the information. "He has been admitted into the CCU, but they will shift him to a regular private room once he has stabilized. He is sleeping now, so I am leaving. Please tell everyone who needs to know that he is in the hospital."

With that, I quietly put down the receiver and turned to Sarah. I was usually the strong one, but it was such a relief to put my head on her shoulder to cry. And cry I did. For the years of pain and grief because my family rejected me, for my father's abuse towards my mother and I, and most of all, for my brother, who I loved but who wouldn't acknowledge me. It was heartbreaking to realize that I had to creep away from the hospital like a criminal in case I aggravated his condition.

CHAPTER 3

"There had been moments when she felt he had almost forgiven her. She would always remember those moments."
~Jane Austen

SARAH

Even though I knew how Tanya's parents had treated her, coming face to face with a part of her past was nearly as painful for me as it was for her. I had never seen my tough, brave partner cry as if her heart would break, and that shattered my composure for a while. In the rare moments when Tanya talked of her family, she used to shrug off her feelings. It had been over twenty years since she had had any contact with her family, so I thought she would be able to handle the emotional implications of their abuse. It seemed that their hate for her had festered deep rather than settling down and healing. What sort of people were these? They were ostracizing their own flesh and blood without realizing what a genuinely nice person Tanya was. If we hadn't been there, Lord knows what could have happened to Shahnawaz —while there would have been many well-meaning souls trying to help, by the time the airport medics arrived, it would have been too late. I refused to be coy here. We saved the man's life, and the least one should expect would be a thank you or a kind word.

"Tanya, love, let us go to Razia's place. We can have a short rest and then we need to plan what we need to do now, given the situation." I tugged on her arm wanting to lead her away, but she jerked her arm away and dried her face on the tissue that I had just handed her.

"Razia, take Sarah with you; she must be tired after our long flight. I will wait here till my parents come, and then I will join you once I am reassured that Shahnawaz is not alone."

Razia looked puzzled. She knew the abuse Tanya had suffered from her parents, and yet she still wanted to stay back.

Tanya shrugged. "He is my brother. No matter what has been said and done, I want to know that he has someone there with him. Hearing the vitriol in my father's voice was extremely disturbing, but I do want to see whether my mother is all right. I heard my father slap her while I was talking to them." She took a shuddering breath and continued. "My mother has always been bullied and physically abused by my father. She was always too scared to say anything. Being of the generation where divorce was looked upon as a taboo, she didn't want to leave him. What would she have done with three children, with only a basic education and no solid job experience? My father knew that, and he would shamelessly take advantage of her time and time again."

Razia and I looked at each other and nodded in silent agreement. We understood what we had to do.

"We love you and we aren't going anywhere. We will stay with you. I need to be with you. I want to know that you are all right," I said.

Though she didn't say anything in reply, I saw the shimmer of tears in her eyes, and she held on to my hand as if she would never let it go. I hugged her, not caring that we were in a country where public displays of affection were frowned upon. I wanted to convey my love and support for her as much as I could. She needed to know that I was there for her in every possible way.

"What was the name of the doctor who is looking after Shahnawaz?" I asked.

"Dr. Shahid Abbas."

"Shahid!" I exclaimed. "He was in my surgery group when I did my house job. I know him very well. Let me go and find him. As a doctor, I know where to look for the attending physicians, and I am sure there must be some of the staff who still remember me from my house officer days."

"I was sure you would know someone here," said Razia with a smile. She remembered the times when I was so involved in my house jobs that I hardly had time to see her or Tanya. It was an extremely busy time. But then, that was part of the strenuous training that is required to hone the medical students into competent doctors. No doubt I loved it.

"Would you ask him about my brother?" asked Tanya. She looked frazzled and there were worry and tension lines around her mouth and eyes. It pained me to see her suffer like this. Even though she always had a tough policewoman's exterior, the people close to her knew she was compassionate and caring.

I walked towards the doctor's lounge and saw a few nurses and housekeeping staff that I recognized.

"Dr. Sarah!" shouted a nurse called Nadira. "When did you come back from England?"

Nadira was one of my old work friends and I liked her. She used to be on duty when I had my night shifts, and we had many midnight picnics together in the ward. She knew about my relationship with Tanya and always mentioned her when she sent me New Year's greetings with her annual letter by email.

Nadira came out from behind the counter where she was working and hugged me.

"Nadira! How wonderful to see you! I didn't know that you had started to work in the Cardiology Unit."

"My transfer to this ward is very recent. Actually, I have been here for only a week, so I am still orienting myself with the ward's procedures." She self-consciously adjusted the scarf which was part of the nurses' uniform and smiled happily at me. "How long are you here for?" she asked. "Knowing you, you must have joined one of the relief teams that are going to earthquake-stricken areas."

I laughed. I was surprised that she had remembered my

penchant for volunteering my medical services whenever they were needed.

"How clever of you," I mocked her gently. "Yes, I am going up north with an American organization called Relief Inc. They are sponsoring doctors and nurses to go and work in the areas devastated by the earthquake. They promised that they would take care of our meals and accommodation. That way we can concentrate on our work without worrying about our basic needs."

"I wish I could go with you, but I had a baby six months ago and I don't want to leave her with strangers." Nadira had a wistful expression on her face. "But I know that you and your team will do an exemplary job. Bless you!"

"Congratulations! You told me that you were married. The photos you sent with your email were gorgeous—such a beautiful bride, but I didn't know you had a baby!" I was genuinely happy for my friend and, although I wanted to talk to her a bit more, I was in a hurry and wanted to catch Dr. Shahid before he went off duty. I said my farewells to Nadira and resumed my trek to the doctors' lounge. When I knocked on the door I didn't get a reply, but I heard some strange sounds coming from within the room. I turned the knob on the door, peeked in, and saw Dr. Shahid sitting on a chair with his head nestled on a pillow that he had put on the desk in front of him. His snores escalated in volume and then stopped when he had a small bout of *apnea*. That was when a person needed to be woken up since the oxygen supply to the brain diminishes at that point.

"Shahid, wake up..." I gently shook his shoulders and he woke up almost immediately. It was a trait you only see in doctors like him or me who are on the job for twenty-four hours and have night shifts. Even when we are asleep, we are subconsciously alert.

"What? Who? What is the emergency? I didn't hear the phone ring?!?" Shahid was understandably confused. He squinted at me and then picked up his glasses and put them on.

"Dr. Sarah!" He was surprised to see me. "Where did you spring from?"

"We have a patient here and I came looking for you because we wanted to know his status."

"Was that the patient that came from the airport? They said that a doctor had performed CPR on him. Was that you?"

"Yes, that was me." I smiled. "Could you tell me what his condition is and how long will he be staying at the hospital?"

"Come along. I will show you. Doctor to doctor. Anyway, as he was first your patient before you sent him off to us, there really is no issue of patient confidentiality. He is sedated at the moment, but I will show you his charts and what the consultant has written in them about his present and possible future treatment."

As we walked together to the CCU, I waved to Tanya and Razia when I passed them in the waiting room. I stepped behind Dr. Shahid into the little room that acted as a barrier foyer where the medical staff would put on sterile shoe covers, gloves, and gowns. The CCU was quiet and everyone talked in hushed tones. The only sound that pierced the almost cathedral-like atmosphere was the beeping of the cardiac monitors affirming that the patients they were attached to were still with us.

Walking over to the third patient from the left, I

recognized Shahnawaz. In the frantic rush of giving him CPR and then supervising his transfer into the ambulance, I hadn't had a proper look at him. His hair had flopped over his forehead and he looked much younger now that he was in repose. I could see that he had the same cheekbones and forehead as Tanya. There was no doubt that he was her brother.

Dr. Shahid took Shahnawaz's file from the pouch hanging at the foot of the bed and showed it to me. We discussed the investigations that had already been completed and the possible outcome of the *angiogram* that would be done once Shahnawaz had completely stabilized.

"From the *echo cardiogram* and the *ultrasound*, we noticed that there are a couple of blockages in the coronary arteries and that he would need *angioplasty*." Dr. Shahid frowned a little as he looked at the reports.

"How dangerous is that for him?" I asked. I had heard about this procedure, but since it didn't overlap to my specialty, I hadn't given it much thought before.

"No, not dangerous at all. This is an exciting and new procedure that opens the clogged arteries of the heart," Shahid explained.

"You mean he will need surgery?" Tanya would be so worried. I needed to get as much information as possible so that I could reassure her that Shahnawaz was in capable hands.

"That's the beauty of this new procedure." Dr. Shahid smirked. "You *have* been out of touch!" he teased me just as he used to when we worked together.

"Hey! I am an eminent pediatrician! I have my own stuff to do." I gestured dramatically towards myself. "I can't fiddle around with adult medicine anymore! Anyway, if the procedure is not major surgery, then what is it?"

Shahid smiled at my enthusiasm. "The surgeon uses a tiny balloon catheter that is inserted from the major vein in the leg and threaded into a blocked blood vessel of the heart to clear and help widen it to improve blood flow to the heart. It is often combined with the placement of a small wire mesh tube called a stent. This stent then helps to prop the artery open, decreasing the chance of it narrowing again."

How fascinating! Adult medicine, especially cardiology, had come a long way since I had dabbled in it oh, so many years before.

After talking to Dr. Shahid, I was satisfied that Shahnawaz was in capable hands. I thanked and said goodbye to my colleague and went to look for Tanya. She was in the same place where I had left her. I had never seen her so upset and vulnerable. This unexpected incident had affected her quite deeply. It shook me to the core to see her so hurt, but I reminded myself that I had to be the strong one this time. Tanya needed me to be her support in every way.

"Tanya!" I called out. Both of my friends looked in my direction. One with hope in her eyes and the other with relief written all over her face. Poor Razia...she was as upset as we were.

"Your brother is resting and stable. I have seen him myself." Sitting down next to Tanya, I took her hand in mine and stroked it reassuringly. "They have to do a few tests and then they probably will go ahead and perform an *angioplasty*." Seeing the puzzled looks on both of their faces, I smugly explained my new-found information to them.

Tanya was relieved that her brother was out of danger, and she hugged both me and Razia. I felt her desperation and pain as she held us, and I prayed to all that was holy that I would be the same pillar of strength for Tanya that she always was for me. Now we just had to sit back and wait for her parents to come.

Tanya

What were the odds that my own brother was our Interpol liaison officer, and on top of that, that he collapsed due to a heart attack after a very vicious tirade when he saw me? I was shocked how much this whole situation affected me. I didn't realize how deep the old wounds were still buried within me, waiting for a trigger to enable then to bubble up once more. Just hearing my mother's voice brought back a flood of memories. Good as well as bad. My brother and I used to be so close; we were like twins. We wanted to wear the same clothes, sleep in the same room, and eat the same food. He was my big brother, and I adored him. With the innocence of childhood, I was confident that he would always be there for me when I needed him.

My father still was as angry and hateful as that fateful day when he threw me out of his house when I was only eighteen years old. It might be common in the west, but it wasn't something that was done in Pakistan. A daughter lived with her family until she finished her education or was married off. I wasn't brought up like my western counterparts to be independent at that age, and I don't know what I would have done if my aunt hadn't taken me under her wing at the time. With her support I was able to go to college to educate myself. I competed and won every scholarship possible and, thanks to the contents of the little bundle that contained money and jewelry that my mother covertly handed to me as I left my parents' house, I could ultimately go to university and have a respectable career. It was a long and painful journey, but I had my Sarah and good friends like Razia that had shown me time and again that my chosen family was dearer to me than those people related to me by blood.

My inner child burst out of where I had confined it for so many years and I couldn't help myself. I put my arms around Sarah and Razia and cried as if my heart would break. I knew it was futile to expect to be reconciled with my genetic family, and after that telephone conversation with my father, I lost hope to even have a short conversation with my mother.

"Your brother is in good hands." Sarah rubbed her thumbs on my hands as she held them. I knew she was trying to reassure me, but I could not stop my tears. It seemed that the grief I had bottled up for years was just flowing out of me.

"We can go as soon as I see someone arriving to see my brother." I hiccupped sadly.

"Are you hoping to have a glimpse of your mother?" Sarah's tone was sympathetic. I would have been so embarrassed if she mocked me, but her love and her understanding was a balm to my frazzled nerves. I nodded and took a deep breath. Shahnawaz was stable and the family was on their way. We had a mission and we needed to focus on that. I didn't want to be embroiled in family drama, but it seemed that we were sucked in whether we liked it or not.

I saw many people standing or sitting around the massive waiting hall. Some had smiles on their faces and others were hugging each other and crying just like I had a few minutes earlier. We blended in, all the while acknowledging a strange camaraderie that develops when people come together in stressful situations. Just like sitting in the waiting room of a CCU in a major cardiac care hospital.

We were just about to sit down when I saw through the glass doors of the hospital a chauffeur-driven car arrive. The driver hopped out and helped someone from the car while another person walked around it and aggressively barged into the hospital as if he owned it. It was my father. It was so typical of him to march ahead and leave my mother to meekly follow him. He looked much older than when I had last seen him. His hair was almost completely white, as were his neatly trimmed beard and moustache. I peered over his shoulder and saw that my mother still had that cowed look on her face that she always had whenever he was with her. When did she get so old? She looked almost fragile. Her face was marred by the deep lines of worry that were etched permanently into her face. I wanted to go over and smooth those lines, hug her, and tell her she need not be frightened anymore, but I knew that was illogical. I tried to be unobtrusive and fade into the woodwork, but my father's sharp eyes found me, and he resolutely walked over to us with a thunderous expression on his face.

"Tanya!" he shouted angrily, causing many heads to turn towards us. I cringed because I realized that our family's dirty linen was about to be aired very publicly.

"What the hell are you doing here? We don't want scum like you near us!"

My mother finally caught up with him and started to pull on his sleeve.

"For Allah's sake, be quiet. We are in a public place! Please..."

My father shook her off and she stumbled. She would have fallen if Sarah hadn't caught her in time. I leapt forward and hugged my mother as if my life depended on it, and I was gratified that she hugged me back. "I missed you so much, my Tannu," she whispered into my ear before her husband roughly pulled her away.

"I don't want you polluting my family with your perverse beliefs. Go away and don't show me your face again!" He was now getting red in the face, and I was worried that he might join my brother in the CCU if he kept that up. I put my hands up in a conciliatory manner and started to walk towards the exit with Sarah and Razia. We weren't needed there anymore. We had done what was required and now we had to get on with our lives, but the inner child in me kept asking that pertinent question...why don't they love me? I was the same person before and after coming out to them; I was still their daughter. Bigotry and narrow mindedness always defy logic, however, and there was nothing I could do about that. At least not then.

We wanted to escape the negativity and unending abuse of that horrible man. We could hear him continue his tirade even though we had moved away. I looked back and saw that my mother, now the recipient of his ire, was crying. I felt my heart break, but then Sarah reached out and held my hand. Pulling back my shoulders and holding my head up high, I kept on walking. Just as we were about to exit the hospital, we heard someone call me.

"Ms. Tanya! Please wait!" It was Dr. Shahid. We waited while he hurried over to us. He was quite handsome, and the white coat flapping around him as he walked briskly towards us made him look like the epitome of a young and successful doctor.

"Dr. Sarah told me that Shahnawaz is your brother..." he said while trying to discreetly catch his breath.

"Yes, he is. Is there a problem?" I looked towards my still blustering father, who was standing at the other end of the room, and pointed him out to Dr. Shahid. "We are leaving now, but that man over there is his father. If you have anything to say about Shahnawaz's medical condition, you can tell him."

Dr. Shahid looked disdainfully towards the ranting man. "My patient is now awake, and he is specifically asking for you." He leaned forward and read Razia's ID badge. "He also said that you were to come to see him as well. I think he mentioned that he had something official to say to you, and he refuses to rest until he has spoken to the three of you."

Wondering what Shahnawaz could possibly say to us after all of the nonsense he had said before, we reluctantly let ourselves be led by the doctor into the CCU to stand at my brother's bedside.

"Your father tried to follow us in," Sarah whispered to me. "He wasn't very happy when they stopped him at the door."

I cocked my head and listened. I could hear the loud and strident protests from my father. I grinned in glee.

"Let's see what Shahnawaz wants and then we need to get out of here. We need to focus on why we came to Pakistan." I shrugged and tried to keep a calm demeanor even though the encounter with my family had cut deep into my psyche. "As it is, no one wants us here anyway."

Sarah squeezed my shoulder and brought my world back into balance.

Shahnawaz was propped up in the bed with the cardiac monitors still beeping, and he had an oxygen cannula in his nose. He looked smaller, different from the man who had verbally attacked me at the airport.

"*Bhai*, the doctor said you wanted to talk to me." I stood in the doorway waiting for him to speak. I didn't want to step any closer. He stared at me for a while, and just as I had decided that this was all ridiculous and was ready to leave the room, he spoke.

"Whether you like it or not, we have a mission to complete. You are here to collect data on the kidnapped children and the smugglers. Nothing else. Do you hear me?"

My hackles started to rise. I knew my job and I had my orders. Who was he to speak to me in that way?

He must have noticed my outraged expression because he quickly changed tactics and spoke in a neutral tone. "Listen, this mission is crucial. We need to be vigilant and now I can't come with you, so I would like to talk to Inspector Razia's superiors to allow her to go with you. It might take a few hours until the paperwork is complete, but you could wait until tomorrow before you leave for the earthquake-stricken areas."

I looked at Razia and Sarah in surprise. This was actually an ideal situation. Having someone we knew and trusted with us on this mission was a big advantage, especially on an assignment of such epic proportions.

Razia and I nodded in agreement. "Tanya and Sarah can stay the night at my place, and I will go to the police headquarters early in the morning to get my orders from the Inspector General." I could detect the excitement in Razia's voice. She loved field work but had to slow down once the twins were born. That time when she accompanied us to Parachinar was in an unofficial capacity.

"So, Interpol..." said Shahnawaz looking at me. "Kareem is a fairly common name, so I didn't realize I would be picking you up from the airport. It was a big shock to see you standing there."

"No doubt," I agreed sarcastically.

Shahnawaz gave me a sharp look but didn't say anything. He turned towards Sarah. "Are you the doctor who saved my life?"

"Well, I did perform CPR until the ambulance arrived," said Sarah with a shy smile.

"Thank you," Shahnawaz said simply. He held out his hand towards Sarah. I was surprised. After all the series of events that had led to him here, he was trying to be reconciliatory. Maybe this heart attack reminded him of his mortality and the time limits that we have on this earth. I was happy that he thanked Sarah. There might still be hope for him.

"Tanya, I still don't agree or accept your lifestyle, but you are an adult, and it is your prerogative how you live and love. My only regret is that I listened to Abba's hateful tirades

49

about you and that I let you go when our parents told you to leave. I was your older brother and I should have taken care of you."

You could have knocked me over with a feather... My brother was apologizing to me! I just stood there with my mouth opening and closing like a fish. No words came out.

Shahnawaz laughed wryly. "You had better go now. I am very tired, and I still have to endure the parental unit." He winked at us to show that he was joking. "You all have a lot of planning to do before you leave. Best of luck." With that, he shook hands with all three of us. I saw the strain this was taking on him, but he held up well. I wanted to say more, but Dr. Shahid realized that his patient was looking exhausted, and he firmly but politely started to herd us out of the room.

We crossed my parents as we stepped outside. Hatred radiated from my father, but I ignored him. I walked to my mother, stood for a moment in front of her, and then, on an impulse, stooped down to hug her petite frame. "Thank you, Ma, for everything," I whispered into her ear. "Your gift helped me move on in life."

I felt my father's hands roughly trying to pull me off my mother. I turned around, looked him straight in the eye, and said, "If you punish Ma for that hug, I swear I will do the same to you!"

I walked out of the hospital and into the parking lot with my head held high, but unseen to the cruel psychopath, my tears were streaming down my cheeks. It was just Sarah's presence that kept me grounded. And I thanked God for that.

CHAPTER 4

"Plans are nothing; planning is everything."
~ Dwight D. Eisenhower

SARAH

Sitting down in Razia's cool living room, away from the blistering heat of the day, was like coming home. I had always felt comfortable and welcome with her family, and I knew that Tanya felt the same. After a much-needed shower and a sumptuous meal, Tanya, Razia and I sat down in the study and brainstormed. We had to plan everything meticulously. The people we were after were ruthless and had been smuggling women and children for years. They would obviously be aware of every twist and turn in the legal system. We had to be clever and stay a step ahead of them as much as we could.

"Let us put on the television and see what the local news is saying about the earthquake. Maybe we can get an idea of what to do." Tanya sounded frustrated and I could see that she was nearly at the end of her tether. The day had been stressful and emotional for her, and she hated to feel so discombobulated.

"Since Shahnawaz is out of the picture, we have to gather as much information as we can and then act accordingly. Dr. Shahid has categorically said that he didn't want us bothering his patient with work related problems, so we are on our own for now." Razia switched the television on as she spoke.

The familiar introductory tune that heralded the Pakistan television news blared out as soon as the screen sprung to life. We were just in time to listen to the headlines.

"Now the latest on the earthquake," said the monotonous newscaster. "Relief agencies in Pakistan fear children separated from their families in the post-earthquake chaos are at risk from human traffickers and childless couples." We looked at each other in surprise. It was quite a coincidence that they were mentioning the same issues that we wanted to gather intel about.

"Thousands of injured children have been flown by helicopter from the areas worst hit by the earthquake which devastated the northern areas of the country. Many have been admitted into the Pakistan Institute of Medical Sciences (PIMS) hospital in Islamabad. The director there has ensured that a police officer is posted outside the ward they have been admitted in, and security guards are vetting visitors at the hospital entrance. These stringent processes were put into place after the hospital authorities reported that there were repeated attempts to abduct the children." The newscaster shuffled some papers as the screen changed to show a video of the injured children in the ward.

She continued with a voice over as the camera panned the ward overflowing with patients.

"An unknown number of children arrived at hospital unaccompanied because their parents are either dead or lost, and aid agencies fear there are few safeguards to prevent strangers from snatching them. The local spokesperson for UNICEF said that it is a worrying situation and that they are urging the government to put strict measures in place to make sure the children are safe."

All of us listened carefully to the bulletin hoping to get as much information as possible from it.

"The Prime Minister has ordered that all earthquake orphans are to be registered and taken into protective care. None will be put up for adoption for now since the International Committee of the Red Cross will try to reunite them with their families over the coming months." With that, the newscaster shifted to another topic.

We started discussing the situation and brainstorming what we could do to go forward. There were a lot of scenarios that could be pursued, but we had to be systematic and logical.

"We need to go to Islamabad and meet with the Interpol representative there. He can take us to meet the people in the federal committees who are responsible for the prevention of child trafficking. Let us not reinvent the wheel," said Tanya.

"You are right; they would have information about the

people involved and we could request them to share the processes that are already in place," agreed Razia as she jumped up to make a phone call to her colleague in Islamabad. "However, instead of us exposing ourselves and going to the officials, I will ask my colleague, Inspector Akhtar, to do so. He is discreet and will respect that we have to be incognito if we want to be successful."

While Razia was busy with the phone call, Tanya and I sipped our tea and looked over the plans we had already jotted down. So far, they seemed haphazard, but it was like putting together a puzzle and I was sure that in the end we would have a complete picture.

Just then Razia's maid, Bashira, came into the room and set a tray of snacks in front of us. She always made the most delicious *pakoras* and *samosas*. I glanced up at her to thank her and noticed that she was sweating profusely and looked very pale. All of a sudden, she swayed and fell down with a loud thump. I couldn't catch her in time, but at least she didn't hit her head on anything as she fell down. The strange thing was that she was unconscious before she reached the ground. I jumped up to examine her as fast as I could. I noticed that she had lost weight from the last time we saw her a few years before, but she didn't look all that ill when she served us breakfast in the morning.

"Bashira! Bashira! Wake up!" I said, lightly slapping her cheeks. "Tanya, please sprinkle some cold water on her face." Her pulse and respiration were strong, so she didn't need CPR. She also didn't have a fit, therefore I needed her to wake up so that I could assess why she had fainted so suddenly. Bashira opened her eyes within a few minutes and seemed confused as she looked around.

"You fainted just now," I told the bewildered woman. "How are you feeling?" I rummaged through my bag for my torch and my stethoscope.

"I really don't know what happened," said Bashira. Even though she was now conscious and sitting up, she still was extremely pale. Her conjunctivae were nearly white, indicating that she was severely anemic.

"Have you had anything to eat today?" asked Razia. She was understandably concerned because Bashira was like a family member. She had been her maid and the twins' nanny since they were born.

"I forgot..." mumbled Bashira. "I didn't have time to eat, so I put my breakfast aside for later on."

"You have had a busy day; you need to eat. Otherwise you will feel ill if your blood sugar drops." I noticed how her eyes shifted away when she was asked about her meals, so on a hunch I asked her the pertinent question. "For how many days have you been skipping your meals?"

Bashira looked startled and then suddenly burst into tears. Razia put an arm around her to comfort her while I patted her hands. She cried for a short while and then hiccupped before she spoke again.

"My husband lost his job because he became a drug addict and was high most of the time. His employers obviously didn't tolerate that. My children are hungry, so I take my portion of the food home to feed them. Please don't be angry with me." She looked anxiously at Razia.

"Of course I will be angry with you!" Razia was appalled. "You should have told me that you are having problems. There are always a lot of leftovers, and you could have taken them with you!"

"I didn't want to bother you, and to tell you the truth, I was ashamed."

"There is nothing to be ashamed of. You are part of this family, and that means that you are to be healthy and happy as long as you work here. From now on, you will take the leftovers home to your children. I only wish you had told me before you became so weak and ill. I was wondering why you were getting tired so quickly since you used to be so energetic before."

"I will write a prescription for multivitamins and iron for you. Please make sure that you take the tablets, and see that you eat three square meals every day." I rooted around in my bag till I found a pad and my pen.

"Give the prescription to me," said Razia holding out her hand once I had finished writing it. "I will send the driver to the pharmacy right away and Bashira can take the first dose after she has had her lunch."

"Can you bring Bashira a sweet drink please? She probably fainted because of her low blood sugar, then she can go and have her meal." Razia nodded and fetched a bottle of cola from the fridge. She made sure that Bashira drank it all, then helped her get up on her feet and escorted her to the kitchen, where she ate her lunch under Razia's stern eyes.

"Well, that was a bit of excitement," laughed Tanya. "You always seem to attract the strangest of medical dramas and I am so impressed how you handle things thrown at you with such aplomb."

I tried to smile at Tanya's compliment, but I still felt as if there was something else that was going on. My intuition was buzzing, and all of a sudden, I stumbled and fell against

Tanya when I felt a deep emotional pain twisting my innards. It was pulling me down, so deep that I had to make an effort to concentrate and get out of that horrible void-like sensation or it would have devoured me mentally as well as physically. I jerked away from where I was sitting and went to stand by the open window to gulp fresh air into my lungs as I tried to center myself. Tanya came over to put her arm around me.

"What is wrong, love? Are you getting some of your vibes again?" She looked worried, and if I looked like I felt at the moment, it must have frightened her. Since I still didn't have the strength to say anything, I just nodded and sunk into her embrace while resting my head on her shoulder. With unspoken consent I could tap into her energy and draw strength from her. When I finally felt that I could manage to function normally again, I went into the kitchen and looked at Bashira very carefully this time, trying to gauge her emotional situation rather than her physical well-being. She was wearing a long-sleeved tunic and I hadn't noticed earlier that she was holding one of her arms stiffly by her side. When I touched her this time, I felt her pain hit me once more, but this time I was ready and I shielded myself from the psychic onslaught.

There was something evil that was sapping the energy of this hapless woman, and it wasn't only the abuse that she was getting from her husband. My energy was being sucked into a dark void just by standing near Bashira. If that evil was not vanquished, she could lose her life, and so could I now that I was caught within the evil morass. I tried not to show that I was scared, but I felt my body break out in goosebumps and the hair on the nape of my neck stood on end. The muscles of my back felt as if I had been flogged. The pain was excruciating. What had happened to Bashira? Who was so malicious that they wanted her dead?

"Bashira, did anyone recently give you a *taweez*? A protection amulet?" I tried to look for one on her person as discreetly as I could while I waited for her answer. It was just a wild guess, but that was the only explanation I could come up with.

"Yes, how did you know?" She looked confused. "My mother-in-law gave me one a month ago and said I should wear it where no one can see it, and all of my marital and financial problems will fade away. She said it was from a well-known mystic who lived near her village."

"Where is the amulet? May I see it?"

Bashira fumbled with her bra strap and unpinned a small square amulet that had been covered with black leather. It was about two centimeters square and looked quite innocuous. I held my hand out to take it from her and I immediately wished that I hadn't. As soon as the amulet was in my hand, the feelings that I had before returned with a vengeance. I nearly passed out and had to hold onto Tanya to prevent myself from falling down. This was pure evil!

I gave the amulet back to Bashira and looked at her with dread in my eyes. "Where is your mother-in-law from? Where does she live?" I could hardly get the words out; my tongue felt thick, as if it had been numbed by a local anesthetic at the dentist's.

Tanya looked worried and held me up so that I wouldn't fall. She guided me towards a chair and made me sit down, and then fetched me a sweet drink.

"My mother-in-law lives in Banaras Colony. She visits us

once a week and makes us eat some weird sweets. She insists that they are blessed and good for us, but when she leaves in the evening, we all feel sick. I don't know if the sweets were cursed or if she had added poison to them."

"Banaras Colony? That is where a lot of fake spiritual healers and sorcerers live. They are rumored to practice black magic and can disrupt households and even kill people with their amulets and spells!" I remembered reading a lot of graffiti on the walls advertising spiritual healing of relationships, erectile dysfunction, and piles. Hidden in plain sight within the graffiti were also advertisements for sorcerers who promised to bring back cheating husbands or kill enemies.

"Why do you think your mother-in-law wants to get rid of you? You have been married for five years now and you have two lovely children. What can she possibly achieve by getting you out of the way?" Tanya asked. Even though she had seen a lot of evil in her police career, Bashira's plight seemed to touch her deeply.

"My husband and I fell in love and got married in spite of her not consenting to the union. Since my father had died when I was young and my mother didn't earn enough to give me a large dowry, I entered the marriage with just the clothes that I had with me. My husband used to be a good man and he told me that as long as we had each other, that would be enough. But his mother is greedy. She wanted him to marry a girl from her village whose father was well off. She had been promised a hefty sum of money if her son married that girl, but my husband refused that arranged union and married me instead." Bashira sighed and took a sip of her drink before she continued. "Now that you have told me about the amulet, I believe that the change in my husband could have also been caused by it. Believe me when I say that I love him, but it's becoming more and more difficult to live with him."

I turned to Razia. "This amulet has to be thrown into the sea. That is they only way it can be neutralized, so that the harmful effects can wear off from Bashira and now me as well. Can you please arrange that? I am worried that it might affect others too."

Razia nodded and rummaged in her cupboard until she found a lead box in which she told Bashira to put the amulet. She then called her driver and gave the box to him.

"Drive to Clifton Beach and throw the contents of this box into the sea. Please go onto the pier to make sure that it floats away into deep waters." The driver nodded and left. He was from a village in Punjab and knew about amulets and curses, so he did not question the strange task.

Once the amulet was out of the house I already felt much lighter. Bashira also seemed to perk up. But there was one more task that I had to do before I could relax. I had a feeling that this wasn't over yet.

"Please roll up your sleeves," I asked Bashira. She looked at me with fear in her eyes and shook her head, but I insisted that I wanted to see her arms. Even though I had suspected it, we were all appalled when she reluctantly rolled her sleeves up. There were bruises all along both of her arms. I lifted her tunic from the back and we saw similar welts, cuts and bruises that were probably inflicted with a stick. All three of us stared in horror. I had tears in my eyes when I imagined the pain that this poor woman had endured, so I reached out and gently hugged her.

"If I don't step in front of my husband, he will beat the children in his drug-induced rages. I have to protect them," she whispered.

"I told you that if your husband was violent with you again, I would arrest him and throw him into jail!" Razia was beside herself in anger.

"No, please, no! He is the father of my children. What will they do without a father?" Bashira held out her hands towards Razia in a beseeching gesture and then started to wail loudly.

"You are the one working until you are exhausted. You take your share of food home to feed him and the children, and yet you are on his side?"

"Razia Bibi, even if he is an addict, I still have a husband. The people in my area will not leave me in peace if I kick him out and live alone."

"You know that I have empty servant's quarters behind my house. There are two rooms and a courtyard with a private entrance. I have offered it to you many times. You will be safe there since it is in the police colony's compound. I will go with you this evening and fetch your children. They will have enough food to eat and will be able to live with you without having to worry that their father will beat them."

Bashira was silent. From the various expressions flitting over her face we knew that she was seriously considering Razia's offer. Finally, she sighed deeply and nodded. "All right, I will take your offer and move here with my children. I want them to know love and have a good education so that they become upright citizens when they grow up. They can't do that when they live in a violent home. Thank you."

"Good. We will go and get your children and whatever

else you need from your place as soon as the driver gets back from Clifton."

That was exhausting, but I was happy that Bashira and her children would be safe at Razia's place.

Tanya

I was irritated. I hated going forward on a mission without proper planning and information. That imbecile Shahnawaz was supposed to have had the information we needed and relevant procedures in place since he had been working on them for a while now. Sarah, Razia, and I had just been recently brought in and we desperately needed to know what was going to happen. It was just a fact-finding mission, but we needed to know where to go without being obtrusive. I was categorically told by my boss that we had to remain incognito. We were grasping at straws by trying to get information from news bulletins and that made me extremely uncomfortable. Or maybe Bashira's amulet was affecting me as well, I thought with a derisive smirk.

Razia returned from her errand. She looked worried and it seemed she wanted to say something to me but didn't know how. She kept opening her mouth to speak, then she would shake her head and look away.

"What is the matter?" I asked her, hoping she would tell us what she had learned from Akhtar in Islamabad. Whatever he had said had made her uncomfortable.

Razia sat down with a frustrated huff and looked at us

for a few moments without saying anything. Then she took a deep breath and started to speak.

"Akhtar was quite a font of information. Besides telling me where we needed to go and that Interpol would be sending someone to meet us in Peshawar, he had some disturbing news. Apparently, about a year ago there was a break at the central jail and one of the two inmates that escaped was Dr. Farooq."

"How did that happen?" I jumped up and started to pace up and down the room. Just knowing that Farooq was out of jail was enough to increase my stress level. Even as I prayed that we wouldn't have anything to do with him, I instinctively knew that somehow we couldn't avoid him.

"Why weren't we told about this?" Sarah sounded worried. If Farooq knew that she was back in the country, he would try to make her life miserable again. He had been hounding her ever since he was an intern and worked with Sarah at the same hospital. Then her parents had arranged a marriage between him and her without her consent, and to force the issue, he had kidnapped his sister and nephew, who happened to be married to Sarah's brother, Adam.

"What has Farooq and his jail break got to do with our assignment?" I asked Razia.

"That's one of our major hurdles. Our intelligence agencies have said that when Farooq escaped, he avoided the authorities by hiding in the mountains up north. There are a lot of hiding places there so anyone who knows the area well can hide there for years and not be caught. Now they have confirmed that he is the liaison in Pakistan who smuggles women and children over the border to Afghanistan en route to the Middle East and Europe."

"From feckless doctor to dreadful smuggler, how the arrogant have fallen..." Sarah was upset, but we had a clue to work on now, although it was a small one. We knew that Farooq was from Parachinar, so we would have to send a scouting party there to see whether there were any covert routes over the mountains into Afghanistan that were being used by the smugglers. In the meantime, we needed to be closer to the sources—the earthquake zone.

"Akhtar has faxed all of the material that he could gather in this short time to my home office. That includes whatever information the federal offices were willing to give him." Razia shuffled a stack of faxes that she had with her. She handed them to me saying, "We need to study every little detail no matter how unimportant it might seem right now. Every bit could be helpful."

"How did Farooq escape from prison? Wasn't it a supposed to be a maximum-security facility?" Sarah asked.

"According to Akhtar, Farooq and another inmate had appealed for a shorter sentence, and they were in court for the review of their cases at the time of the escape. Farooq's cousin had bribed a security guard who smuggled a razor, a switch blade, and a change of clothes into the men's room and hid the bundle under a washbasin. The two men, on the pretext of using the facilities, found the bundle and shaved their heads and beards, changed their clothes, and walked out unnoticed. Though it hasn't yet been proven, the policemen who were supposed to guard them while they were in the men's room were also allegedly bribed to look the other way. They are still under investigation by internal affairs."

Trying to shake off our feelings of dread, we pored over

the faxes late into the night. We needed to be well versed with all of the information provided before we travelled in the morning. It was decided that we wouldn't take any papers with us in case we were found out, so we needed to rely on each other to remember as much as possible. Razia had arranged for an early flight to Peshawar, where we would be met by the NGO, Relief Inc., that was hosting us while we supposedly did volunteer medical work. They would be driving us to Abbottabad and then onwards onto the earthquake zone.

"Do you have a special permit for your gun?" asked Razia.

"Yes, I do. It's endorsed by Interpol as well as the Pakistani Federal government," I answered while pulling the card out of my wallet to show her.

"What about you, Sarah? Do you have a weapon as well?" Razia looked at Sarah, who made a disgusted face.

"I refuse to carry a weapon. I will leave that to the both of you," she said firmly. It was an old argument that I had with her, and from her tone of voice I knew that she was firm about not carrying a weapon. Ever since she had been shot by Farooq on her last visit to Karachi, she had developed a phobia of guns. I couldn't blame her—it was a painful time, emotionally and physically. She tried counseling, but so far there had been minimal help. She was steadfastly stubborn in her aversion to any weapon.

I sighed in frustration but conceded the argument to her... this time.

CHAPTER 5

"There is a spiritual obligation; there is a task to be done. It is not, however, something as simple as following a set of someone else's rules." ~ Terrence McKenna

SARAH

At last we were on our way to the airport. Razia's driver maneuvered skillfully through the morning rush hour traffic of the huge metropolis of Karachi. I looked out the window with a touch of melancholy. There used to be a time when I drove through this colorful melee myself, extremely stressed to reach work in time. The most dangerous road hogs were the colorful minibuses that were commonly used as public transport. They blatantly flouted traffic rules and never stayed in their own lanes. Each bus in itself was a work of art. "Did you know that the artwork on Pakistan's buses and trucks is renowned world over for depicting South Asian animals, celebrities, and religious icons? The glow in the dark paint and stickers transform the highways and cities into strange kaleidoscopic processions, especially at night." I sounded a bit pompous while telling my friends this tidbit. "I attended an art seminar in London and their main focus was this form of art. I was surprised how interested the participants were." I kept looking out the window to try to identify the motives and the couplets written on the fast-moving vehicles.

"Look! They have even painted the pillars of the bridges with 'truck art'! It is such an innovative idea to prevent unwanted graffiti artists to leave their untidy scribblings there!" I was fascinated by the depictions of the history of Karachi that the art students at a local college had painted on the pillars.

"The new mayor's mandate is to clean up the city and create a positive visual impact. Therefore, you will see a lot of these artworks, especially on the main road to the airport." Razia was proud of the project since she and her sons' school had also volunteered in the cleanup drive. "Our group has pledged to plant over one hundred thousand trees around the city this year and another hundred thousand next year. We want to make Karachi a garden city just like it was in the 60s and 70s." I heard the enthusiasm in Razia's voice. This project was definitely close to her heart.

"The city would be even more beautiful if the trenches and gutters that have been dug by the roadside for pipes and wires were covered and properly finished," Tanya grumbled.

Her mood hadn't lightened since the day before. In her opinion, we weren't prepared enough for our journey and the tasks ahead, and I knew that irritated her. I think she was also still upset about the altercation she had with her family and the surprising fact that her own brother was the local Interpol agent. What annoyed her most was that Shahnawaz hadn't given us much information.

I leaned over and gently squeezed her shoulder. She reached up and held onto my hand. I could feel her frustration and I tried to calm her down by caressing her hand with my thumb. I felt her relax to some extent, but I knew that her level of stress and anxiety was still high.

"Let us see what your Interpol colleague has to say when we reach Peshawar. I am sure they will have some information that we can use." Tanya scoffed, but I felt her relax a bit more under my touch.

Razia watched us with an amused expression on her face. "Lighten up, Tanya. You do realize that you land on your feet all the time, right? If I didn't know that you were human, I would definitely think you were a cat." She laughed at her own joke. After looking at her incredulously for a beat, Tanya found that funny and started to laugh as well.

The flight to Peshawar was supposed to be two and a half hours from Karachi, so we all settled into our seats and tried to occupy ourselves. Tanya pulled down the meal tray in front of her and used it as a desk as she went over her notes. Razia was fiddling with the monitor in front of her, trying to find a movie that would catch her interest. She finally gave up and settled down with a game of Tetris.

I tried to find a comfortable position and go to sleep, but no matter how much I tried, the realm of Morpheus evaded me. There was something strange happening on the plane, and my senses were not letting me ignore it. Though I had helped a lot of people with my ESP, there were times when I just wanted to be left alone, but then, how could I refuse to save a life? I didn't know who needed my help though. I looked around and everyone seemed to have settled in their seats. Some had their headphones on while others were trying to nap. Where, oh where, was the intense negative energy coming from? My hair was standing on end and my stomach clenched with frissons of dread. I had a feeling that I had to find out what it was as soon as I could—it was a matter of life or death.

"Something is going to happen. I feel it," I told Tanya.

"Hmmm, all right, carry on, carry on..." She was so distracted that she didn't even listen to what I was saying. I turned towards Razia, but she had fallen asleep and was quietly snoring as she leaned against the wall near her window seat. I was squeezed between the two of them and my feeling of disquiet was increasing by the second.

Under the pretext of using the bathroom, I got up from my seat, squeezed by Tanya, and started to walk down the aisle. As I moved forward, my internal buzzing increased to the point that I felt a sharp pain in my abdomen.

When I reached seat 9-C I nearly passed out. I held on to the back of the nearest seat as a wave of evil and despair washed over me. The plane lurched and I had to use both of my hands to hold onto the seat as my body twisted around with the momentum.

"I am so sorry," I said to the passenger that I had jostled. I was about to move on when I looked closely at the man sitting there. He was a young man—about twenty years old.

At a first glance, I thought that he was just scared of flying, but there was an almost wild look in his eyes. It wouldn't have been noticed by anyone else, but since I was looking for something out of the ordinary I could tell that there was something wrong with this man.

"Are you all right? Shall I get the attendant? Do you need anything?" I tried to speak calmly because I didn't want to spook him. Somehow, I felt it was important not to rile him up. He was wearing one of those jackets that sports hunters use, with many pockets all over. It was then that I noticed that he had a strange pen sticking out of the top pocket. I hoped I was wrong, but it looked just like one of the pen pistols that we had seen in Darra Adamkhel when we passed through the arms manufacturing town three years before.

"No, no, leave me alone! I don't want anything!" he brushed me off rudely.

I knew then that this man was the source of my disquiet. I was sure that he planned to use that pen, but I didn't know when and how he intended to do so. I put up my hands in an apologetic and conciliatory manner and straightened my back. I avoided eye contact with him in case he was alerted to the fact that I suspected what he was up to, and I forced myself to slowly walk back to my seat, even though I wanted to run as fast as I could. This was something that I had to share with Tanya and Razia. I couldn't handle this problem on my own.

"Listen to me." I had to have Tanya's complete attention. With a grunt of annoyance, she tore her eyes away from her papers and looked at me with a slight frown.

"What is it? Can't you see I am busy?"

"I need you to listen to me very carefully." I spoke in a low voice because I didn't want to be overheard and cause unnecessary alarm amongst the passengers. "Let's wake Razia up. I need to talk to both of you. It's a matter of life and death."

Tanya became more attentive instantly. She knew I wasn't a person who would use such words lightly or create panic unnecessarily.

Razia woke up as soon as I shook her shoulder. She wiped the sleep out of her face with a wet wipe and looked curiously at us.

"What is wrong? Why are you looking so nervous?"

"Yes, this had better be worth disturbing me," said Tanya, still in a bad mood.

"We need to tell the air marshal that there is a man with a weapon on the flight. I just saw him on seat 9-C and I believe we need to act as soon as we can. All the lives on board could be at stake, even ours."

Now I had their complete attention. I told them about my intense feelings of dread and how I had walked along the aisle until I found the man. He needed to be taken into custody and his weapon confiscated. I still wasn't sure what he intended to do, but my feelings of disquiet were increasing and I was on the verge of hurling my breakfast into the barf bag in front of me.

"Are you absolutely sure that it is a pen pistol?" asked Tanya. "We don't want to cause panic on the flight. Also, if we startle the man he might begin to shoot randomly, and anyone near him would be in mortal danger."

"I am sure it is a pen pistol. Remember the ring-shaped triggers that the pens had on top of them? The ones that you had to pull back before you could fire the pistol?" I was getting annoyed with all these questions, but I knew that Tanya wanted to be certain that we were in danger before she reported the situation to the captain and the air marshal.

Tanya stood up quietly and went to the front of the plane, where she talked to the air hostess who was just about to wheel the meal trolley into the aisle. After a short but terse conversation, the woman turned towards the intercom, but Tanya stopped her and showed her badge. Then both walked towards the cockpit to talk to the captain.

I trusted Tanya and I knew that she trusted me and my feelings, but I was scared. This was a hair trigger situation, and the outcome would depend on how it was handled. Terrorists had no conscience. Their families were paid handsome sums if they blew themselves up or put themselves in dangerous situations. They were given false promises of paradise. Their ultimate goal was nirvana, and they didn't care who they took along with them. After all, they had been brainwashed and were not educated enough to think for themselves. They would never realize that what they were doing was a sin and paradise was not on the cards for them. Never ever. Suicide and murder were the ultimate crimes in any religion or school of thought.

I sat back in my seat and gave Razia a worried glance as she also got up and started to walk towards the cockpit when Tanya gestured to join her. I closed my eyes and started to pray fervently that we would manage to avert a disaster.

Tanya

. . .

I didn't like feeling out of sorts and I knew I was taking my bad mood out on Razia and especially on Sarah, who had been the epitome of patience with me. She understood how I felt and was humoring my bad behavior. My family issues aside, I really wanted us to be as prepared as possible before we reached our destination, so I went over my notes many times until I was nearly cross eyed. I wanted to be sure that we hadn't missed anything. Sometimes even the smallest factoid could be significant. Therefore, as soon as the plane took off, I immersed myself in those papers while grumbling and cursing Shahnawaz for his inefficient and incomplete data.

After a while, I noticed that Sarah had started to fidget in her seat and seemed visibly upset, but I erroneously thought it was my attitude that was upsetting her. I wasn't yet prepared to talk to anyone, even to Sarah, so I let it go. I actually heaved a small sigh of relief when she got up to go to the bathroom. Don't get me wrong, I loved her more than my own life, but before our mission I wanted to concentrate and immerse myself in its preparations. Any slip up could cost us our lives, and that was a price I was not ready to pay.

I was engrossed in my work and didn't notice how much time had passed, but it felt like Sarah came back to her seat almost immediately. There was that expression on her face, the one that meant she had had one of her premonitions, or 'feelings' as she called them. With a sigh, I put down my papers and turned to her. I realized my grumpiness was unprecedented and I tried to give her my complete attention to make up for it. What she told us was not only shocking; it was downright frightening.

"There is a man who is sweating profusely and looking

very anxious and jumpy in seat 9-C. I was accidently thrown towards him when the plane lurched and I noticed that he had one of those pen pistols in his pocket. You remember we saw them in Darra Adamkhel? You said they could easily pass as proper pens. They even have a ball point nib worked into them." Sarah took a deep breath. I was worried because she looked as if she was going to pass out. I had never seen her so pale.

"That's why he managed to bring it through security!" Razia said.

"Yes, they obviously thought it was a real pen. You know, as soon as we boarded the plane, I felt an aura of evil surround us. My anxiety levels increased by the minute... no, make that by the second. I know you were annoyed with my fidgeting, Tanya, but I just couldn't help it."

Slightly shamefaced, I put my arms around Sarah to reassure her that I wasn't upset with her. I resolved that I really needed to compartmentalize my negative emotions, especially where Sarah was concerned.

"Well, I stood up and started to walk down the aisle to see where the negativity was coming from, and when I passed him, at 9-C, the evil vibes I was feeling became much stronger." Sarah looked at me with such trust and intensity as she went on. "You have to do something, Tanya. The lives of everyone on board are at stake."

"Take a deep breath, sit back, and calm down. I will see what can be done." I tried to reassure her, but I knew that unless the threat was neutralized, she would be buzzing with anxiety.

"Razia, stay here for now. I'll go and talk to the captain. I will call you if I need your help."

Since a passenger walking into the cockpit was not allowed, I knew that I had to enlist the help of the senior air hostess. She was just starting to distribute meal trays to the passengers and gave me a mildly annoyed look as I walked up to her.

"Please go back to your seat; you are blocking the aisle. If you need anything, press the call button and someone will come to your seat to help you," she said firmly but politely.

"I need to talk to the captain immediately; can you help me please?" I said in a low voice. I didn't want to be heard by anyone nearby. She scoffed at me and gave me a strange look.

"For security reasons, we are not allowed to let passengers into the cockpit. Because of hijacking threats, the rules have become very stringent. It's for the safety of the crew as the well as the passengers."

"I understand," I said as I put my hand in my pocket to take out my Interpol ID. She flinched and turned to pick up the intercom. I held out my hand in a conciliatory manner and slowly withdrew my badge. She heaved a sigh of relief when she saw it and took it from my hand to examine it carefully.

"You can see that I am an Interpol agent, and one of my travelling companions is a senior police officer. I need to talk to the captain and the designated air marshal because I think there is a man with an unauthorized weapon on board."

The air hostess, whose name tag said her name was Marya, turned again to the intercom and spoke quietly into it while nodding as if the person on the other side could see her.

"The captain has agreed to allow you into the cockpit. Best of luck. I will send the air marshal in as well. Go ahead to the front and knock three times on the door. They will then know it's you."

She signaled to a man sitting near the back who was already looking at us with a curious expression on his face. He came over and, as if by an unspoken signal, nodded in greeting and we both walked towards the cockpit. I didn't want to stare at the man in 9-C, but I did look at him out of the corner of my eyes, and just like Sarah had noticed, he was acting quite strangely. To a regular person he looked like a country bumpkin who was trying to read the inflight magazine... upside down, but I saw him looking around furtively behind his "barricade".

Once we entered the cockpit, we were asked to sit in the vacant seats there. The captain was busy talking to air traffic control, so we had to wait until he was finished. I stood up and peeked out of the door while catching Razia's eye to beckon her to join us.

While we waited for the captain to finish, we introduced ourselves to one another.

"Salam, Sir, I am agent Tanya Kareem from Interpol, and this is my friend and colleague Inspector Razia Khan from the Pakistan police."

"My name is Yusuf Sanaullah, and I am the air marshal on this flight." He nodded deferentially while greeting us. It was rare for strangers to shake the hands of women in Pakistan, so we didn't expect him to do so.

"I am the co-pilot of this plane, and my name is Majeed Chaudhry." He looked at the captain to see whether he was finished with his transmission. "The captain has instructed me to talk to you, and he will join in when he is finished, since we have been told that it was a matter of urgency. Am I right?"

"Yes, unfortunately, you are." I took a deep breath and then told everyone present about the man with the pen pistol, leaving out Sarah's suspicions and 'feelings.' "Even though the weapon is just a small 25 bore pistol, it can cause mortal damage, especially at close range."

"How did you suspect that the weapon carried by the man was a pen pistol?" asked Majeed.

"The pen pistol looks uncannily like a pen. It even writes when needed. But the thing that gave it away was the large ring trigger, much like a grenade ring, on top of a seemingly harmless looking pen that is clearly made of heavy metal."

By then the captain had finished his transmission to air traffic control and had switched the plane to autopilot. Majeed quickly brought him up to speed. It was decided that we didn't want to alarm the passengers by accosting the perpetrator forcefully. Causing panic at ten thousand meters in the air was not something we wanted to deal with. Yusuf would approach the man cautiously, disarm him, and take him to the back of the plane, where he would handcuff him and make him sit with him until the flight landed in Peshawar. In the meantime, the captain would inform security and air traffic control about our situation. Razia and I were told to be on standby in case the passenger became violent and Yusuf needed help.

"Let's hope that he is the only one on board and he doesn't have any friends. We need to be careful," I said to Razia. Even though we had handed the situation over to the responsible authorities, I still had a bad feeling about it. Something didn't add up.

Yusuf stood up, straightened his jacket, and walked out of the cockpit. We waited with bated breath to hear anything out of the ordinary and were on high alert in case we were needed. When after about ten minutes nothing strange or untoward was heard, we stepped out of the cockpit and made our way to our seats. As we walked down the aisle, I noticed that 9-C was empty, but when we neared the back of the plane we heard loud and angry voices. The passengers were craning their necks trying to look towards the ruckus, obviously wanting to know what was going on. On my signal, Razia went to check on Sarah while I hurried over to one of the secluded areas in the back of the plane where the staff usually sat when they wanted to rest during the flight. It just had a privacy curtain around it, so whatever was going on was clearly heard by the people nearby.

Slipping in behind the curtain, I saw that Yusuf had the passenger from 9-C in handcuffs and he was putting the pen pistol into his pocket so that his hands were unencumbered. The man was agitated and was shouting in Pushto at the top of his voice. We tried to calm him down, but the more we tried the louder he got. We were so engrossed in trying to get him to shut up that we didn't notice that someone had quietly walked up to us. I felt rather than saw Yusuf crumple into a heap on the floor as he was hit with something heavy between his shoulder blades. Before I could turn around to help him, I felt something hard poke my ribs and a familiar voice speak into my ear.

"Release Bayram, Tanya. Unlock his handcuffs and let him go. There is a pen pistol pointed towards your ribs. It might be small, but when you are familiar with human anatomy like I am, a well-placed shot could be lethal. Now, you don't want to test that, do you?"

"Farooq! What in heaven's name are you doing on this flight?" I was infuriated because I had let my guard down and thought that we had an isolated perpetrator. Hijacking an airplane is always a team effort. We should have been more alert and not focused on just that one person. The fact that Farooq was one of the hijackers and had me captive was even more exasperating.

"In case you are wondering, your little friend Sarah and her companion, the steadfast Razia, are also having a visit from my friends." Farooq laughed as he saw the expression on my face. "You didn't think that you would see me ever again... but let me tell you this," he said lowering his voice, "I pop up like the proverbial bad penny when you least expect it."

"What do you want?" I spat out.

"Nothing much. We just want this plane to be diverted to a little airport outside Jalalabad, Afghanistan. It is conveniently near the border and my hometown, Parachinar."

"What on earth do you want to do in Afghanistan? What do you want with us?" I gestured towards the passengers, who had realized that something strange was going on and were craning their necks to try to hear us.

Farooq had a slimy smug look on his face. "This plane is a gold mine. There are a lot of medicines and relief materials on board. I especially love the tents; they would sell for a pretty penny on the black market. Actually, the whole cargo can be sold for millions... dollars, that is, not the poor little rupee."

I wanted to wipe away that smug evil expression off his face, but his men had Sarah and Razia, and one rushed movement on my part could get them hurt or be fatal for them. I had to see how this played out. Farooq was arrogant and tended to get careless, so I just had to bide my time and wait for him to slip up.

After I unlocked Bayram's handcuffs, Farooq snatched them from my hands and slapped them on my wrists, after which I was roughly shoved back to my seat next to Sarah and an unconscious Razia.

CHAPTER 6

"He who has a why to live can bear almost any how."
~ Friedrich Nietzsche

SARAH

What had happened? Where were we? I was groggy, as if I had been drugged. My mouth was dry and my tongue felt as if it had grown twice in size. I saw that we weren't on the plane anymore. Someone had tied our hands and feet and put us on what seemed to be a pile of dusty mattresses in the corner of a large warehouse that smelt strongly of cigarette smoke and goats. It was dark and I couldn't see much, but from the familiar groan I heard to my right, I was relieved to know that Tanya was next to me.

"Tanya!" I whispered urgently. "Where are we? What happened? Where is the plane?"

The only answer I received was an even louder groan. I was sure that Tanya was hurt. I needed to get rid of the plastic tie that bound my hands behind my back. I couldn't see anything in the murky gloom. It looked like it was around sunset, so there still was a modicum of light.

"Razia, are you there?" I tried again. I only heard someone snoring. If Razia was here she was out like a light. My heart started to thump loudly against my chest and I was getting more and more apprehensive as the seconds went by. Where in heaven's name were we?

Rattling sounds indicated that someone was unlocking the main door. A beam of light swept across the room as the door opened and provided a backlight for the silhouette of the man standing there.

"Wake up! I need you lot to wake up. Now!" That loud raucous voice! So familiar and so repulsive.

"What is your problem, Farooq? Why are you so loud? I am awake." I tried to sound dignified, but I ended my sentence with a groan as a wave of pain hit my temples.

"Ah, the princess awakes. Now see that your companions wake up too. There is work to be done," Farooq said roughly.

"Untie me so I can check on Tanya and Razia. What did you do to us?" I squinted at him trying to work through my pain as I spoke.

"Do you ever get out of your physician mode? Lighten up; you should enjoy your life."

"Turn on the light and let me see how they are!" I said while grinding my teeth in frustration.

With an evil smirk on his face, Farooq lit a lantern and hung it from a hook on the wall nearby. Then he bent down and cut the plastic ties around my wrists. They were so tight that they were chafing the skin and I had started to bleed. The rush of blood back into my hands and arms was excruciatingly painful, but very welcome. I rolled my shoulders and neck and heard my vertebrae pop into place, thus easing the tension of my abused muscles.

I looked around and saw that we were in a massive warehouse. Cargo containers bearing the logo of Pakistan International Airlines were stacked against the wall. Some of them had already been forced open while others were still sealed.

Tanya and Razia were lying next to me still in a deep sleep with their heads lying on dusty sacks of grain.

"What did you do to them? Where is the plane and all the other passengers?" I was anxious. What did this madman want from us?

"Your first and foremost task should be to see to your friends. Don't worry your little head about things that don't concern you." Farooq was trying to rile me up with his condescending tone, but I gritted my teeth and controlled myself. I turned towards the two slumbering women. Both of them had a strong pulse and were breathing normally. I heaved a sigh of relief because, after examining them, I concluded that they were just sleeping. I was certain that they had been given the same drugs as I had, which meant they would wake up any time soon. Sure enough, after about ten minutes, both of them started to stir and struggled to sit up while continuing to groan.

"What the hell happened?" Tanya was as confused and disoriented as I was when I woke up.

"Farooq drugged us and brought us here. How he did that is beyond me. One moment we were on a plane trying to stop it from being hijacked and the next minute we wake up here, wherever here is." I was annoyed and signed to Farooq that he should cut their restraints.

"That idiot hit me and knocked me out," said Tanya. She sounded annoyed at having been caught unawares.

"Now that you have reacquainted yourselves, ladies, I would suggest you have some food and then get up. There is work to be done." Farooq let out his raucous laugh, which I had always likened to that of a hyena.

We tried to stand up, but our legs were like wet noodles and all of us felt as weak as babies. No wonder Farooq had agreed to cut us free from our restraints so readily.

"What did you do to us?" I spat out again.

"Oh, nothing much." He laughed. "I for one think what I did is ingenious. Everyone was in such a lather when we insisted that the plane land at Jalalabad. No one cared for the cargo or in which country they were in. The captain was only concerned for the safety of his passengers." He paused and lit an obnoxiously smelling cigarette before he went on.

"When you were back in your seats, you were given water laced with a drug that knocked you all out. It was very satisfying to see you all sleep like babies." Once again, he started to laugh and ended up having a smoker's coughing fit.

"The air marshal and the captain negotiated the release of the plane and passengers by giving us the cargo and you three," he continued. "They were all let off quickly. We didn't want them with us anyway, and by the time they took off, the US air force had sent some planes to escort them back to Pakistan. Since it was a dark, moonless night, we could slip away easily and transport everything to our warehouse without anyone knowing where we were."

"But why did you want us? Didn't anyone negotiate our release as well?" I was confused. I didn't know what was happening and what this man had in mind.

"You were our security, our main negotiation points. We promised we wouldn't blow up the plane or harm the passengers as long as we had you. We promised the captain that we wouldn't hurt you and that if he would leave the cargo with us, we would in turn allow them to fly off unscathed. It was a win-win situation." He lit another cigarette and went on. "We were happy that we could send them away before the international authorities arrived. That was one of the reasons why we had to spirit you and the cargo here at night." Farooq looked very smug as he spoke.

"That seems too easy," Razia said. "Why do I feel there is more to this story?"

"Hmmm, I always thought you were quite clever, Razia, and yes, there is. We took the three of you hostage as well as the senior air hostess. When we landed at Jalalabad, we were met by my Afghan friends, who were quite well armed if I may say so myself." Once more he giggled maniacally. This man definitely needed to be locked up in a psychiatric facility. "My mistake was that I hadn't yet drugged the woman and she jerked herself out of my grasp and started to run. My trigger-happy friends unfortunately gunned her down. I am sure she will be hailed as a brave martyr, but that worked to our advantage..." He grinned as he looked at me.

"The captain flew off as soon as we unloaded the plane's cargo. He will also be hailed as a hero for bringing most of the passengers back in one piece, although I am not sure how pristine your reputation will be once the press gets to know your 'association' with me." Farooq was enjoying himself immensely and all I could do was control myself to not kick him where it would hurt him and his potential future offspring the most.

"What do you mean by that? You kidnapped us. We are NOT associated with you in any way!" I shouted.

"Oh, yes, regarding your reputation... I might have mentioned that you were my fiancé and that the three of you were family. That certainly cooled the captain's desire to have you back on board." He gave another one of his hyena-like laughs that were starting to grate on all of our nerves.

"You did what?!?" I shouted. But then, something so devious could only be expected from a low-life like Farooq. God only knew what stories the media would be spinning about us. Most likely, we would have also been implicated in the hijacking and the theft of the cargo. Seeing how agitated I was, Tanya put her arm around my shoulder to calm me, but my thoughts continued to spin around in my mind. How in heaven's name would we get out of this predicament where Farooq was the pivotal perpetrator?

"How long were we unconscious?" asked Tanya.

"About two days." Farooq laughed at our incredulous expressions.

"Two days!!" We were flabbergasted.

As if reading our minds, Farooq gave an evil chuckle. "Just to jog your memories... I do happen to be a doctor." He paused dramatically before he went on. "I inserted IV lines with dextrose and normal saline to keep you from being dehydrated and to give you some calories. I would inject the tranquilizers into the drips, but I decreased your doses at regular intervals and had some of the women from our camp take you to the bathroom for your bodily needs. Then I knocked you out once again." As he spoke, I vaguely remembered being led to a bathroom where there was just a place to squat. To my chagrin, I recalled that I had to be held steady to use it, but I was grateful that my memory was fuzzy.

"The last dose was laced with just a little bit of curare. That's why your limbs are wobbly, but you will be back to normal very soon. Maybe in another half an hour or so. It's such an ingenious way to ensure that you wouldn't run away, isn't it?" He was literally patting himself on his back.

"You are despicable!" Tanya shouted from where she sat on the floor while wearily leaning her back against a dusty crate. I could see that she was getting frustrated that she was so helpless.

"What do you want with us?" Razia spoke up again. The drugs had affected her the most and she was still trying to clear her mind.

"Weeeell... I promised the leader of the Taliban in this area that I would bring him a doctor for his village. He has promised me quite a tidy sum for that. Since Sarah is a foreign qualified doctor, I am sure I can get more money than what was agreed upon." He rubbed his hands together in glee. Now I knew for sure that he was demented. Did he actually say that he wanted to sell me to the Taliban?

"If you don't behave yourself, Sarah, I will personally see that Tanya and Razia get the signature Taliban execution of being stoned to death. I just have to accuse them of something lewd. No one will listen to them. After all, I am the man, and they are just...lowly women." More demented laughter followed him as he walked towards the warehouse door.

"What do you want with the cargo from the plane? Why did you hijack it in the first place?" Tanya asked. It was strange that Farooq, supposedly from a well-to-do family, was involved in all of this.

"Tanya, Tanya, Tanya, you aren't thinking properly, are you?" He giggled like a child. "The flight had millions of dollars' worth of medical equipment and medicines on it. There is a CT scanner, portable ultrasound machines, surgical instruments, medication, and operation theater paraphernalia. The Taliban is desperate for all of that and more. They are prepared to pay me in US dollars. I will make a very tidy sum when I sell the cargo. The added bonus is what I will get for you three." Then he walked out of the warehouse, his terrible laughter echoing from the high roof.

As he closed the door behind him, I got up on my still wobbly legs and walked slowly over to Tanya. She was so upset that I could feel her annoyance emanating in waves from her, but I needed to be reassured that she was all right. I gave her a perfunctory examination. She didn't have a concussion, but there was a nasty large bruise between her shoulder blades. She must have passed out because of the severe pain. Razia had a lump the size of a small egg at the base of her skull, but she was also more or less fine.

Having reassured myself that my partner and friend were as well as they could be given our situation, I sat down next to Tanya and snuggled into her side. There was nothing we could do until the effects of the drugs disappeared and we could move around more freely. In unison, our stomachs growled, which made us give each another watery smiles, but then our expressions revealed a disturbing thought that came simultaneously to our minds... would Farooq change his mind and decide to starve us?

Just then, the lock rattled again and two men wearing traditional Afghan clothes and signature gray striped turbans entered the warehouse. To our relief, one of them had a tray in his hand and the other carried a small portable water cooler with steel tumblers. They avoided eye contact and silently put everything in front of us and left.

The food was simple but enough for the three of us. There was mutton fried in tomatoes and green chilies and some eggs. This was accompanied by surprisingly hot naans. The water cooler had tepid water in it, but we were grateful to have something to drink as our tongues continued to remain dry and furry.

"Take only small bites and wash them down with lots of water because curare affects all of the muscles and the after-effects might make swallowing a bit difficult," I warned the others.

Since we didn't want to collapse due to lack of food and water, we slowly but painfully ate as much as we could. We didn't know what was going to happen and we definitely needed our strength.

Almost as soon as we finished, the same men came and cleared away the debris of our meal. They were followed by Farooq, who had a large cloth bundle in his hands. He threw the bundle at us and spoke.

"In the corner of this warehouse is a bathroom with a

shower. You can use it and then wear the clothes in this bundle. Just by wearing your western clothes you can be harassed here, and I want to give my clients their merchandise in one piece." He chuckled and walked out of the building, and we heard him lock the door once more. We were trapped and there was nothing we could do about it.

"He is right." Tanya looked down at her now grungy looking jeans and button-down shirt. "We would be quite conspicuous walking around like this."

"Let us get cleaned up and then we can plan what we should do. We need to know exactly where we are to plan an escape from here." Razia stood up and started to rummage in the bundle. She took out a woman's traditional Afghani dress that was about her size and a bar of soap. "I will go first."

Making her way shakily across the massive hall, she disappeared into the gloom. After a few minutes we heard her shout, "Found it!"

Tanya and I just sat there and held each other. We were shaken with this turn of events.

"Do you realize we are exactly where we are supposed to be?" Tanya suddenly said.

"How so?" I asked.

"We were supposed to get information about the slavers and child traffickers, and we have landed right in the middle of their den. Farooq even wants to sell you; what better proof than that?"

She was right. "We need to plan exactly what we need to do. Unfortunately, no one knows where we are, but once we have enough information about what seems to be a well-planned organization, we have to try to escape and contact Interpol."

"So you want me to play along when he sells me to the Taliban chief?" I asked her. I was worried; no, scrap that... I was scared!

"Since they want you for your medical skills, I think you will be relatively safe. It will give us time to plan. In the meantime, we need to find out what that man wants from Razia and me."

As soon as Razia came back we took turns to shower in the miniscule bathroom, and we felt much better, even though the clothes we were given had a distinct bovine pong to them.

There were also massive blue *burqas* in the bundle, and since it was getting chilly, we also put the heavy tent-like garments on. We were grateful that they provided us a modicum of warmth.

We weren't too anxious to go back to sleep, and anyway, Farooq came back just after an hour and herded us into a covered jeep. I tried to get my bearings, but it was difficult to see through the eye mesh in the burqa, especially since it was quite dark. We noticed that there were also trucks parked behind the jeep which were being loaded with some of the cartons and other contents of the airline cargo containers. As soon as everything was loaded into the trucks, we drove into the darkness. The convoy traveled most of the night over rough terrain. I held on to Tanya's hand and took solace in her familiar warmth as we were driven towards an uncertain fate. I sent a silent prayer upwards—Allah, have mercy on us and help us get out of this unprecedented mess unmaimed and unharmed.

. . .

Tanya

What on earth was happening to us? Waking up disoriented and semi-disabled was something out of a nightmare. I tried not to let Sarah know how worried I was, but I should have known better. She knew me so intimately that sometimes it was scary.

Razia and Sarah were right—we had to play along with Farooq and see what happened. We were in a very volatile area of the world and had to be careful. When we got the opportunity to escape, one of us would have to be disguised as a man. Three women traveling alone in Afghanistan would raise red flags immediately, but in our weakened states all we could do was wait and see.

"Farooq intended for us to be as weak as babies when he drugged us. He was actually right. It is an ingenious way to ensure prisoners don't escape." I was grumpy, Sarah was terrified, and Razia continued to look dazed.

Once we were bundled into the jeep we traveled for most of the night. There was no moon, so the almost impenetrable darkness was ideal for a covert journey. However, we couldn't see any landmark, which was disconcerting since we would need to know which direction to go when we were finally able to escape.

The noise of the diesel engine of the ancient jeep made conversing difficult, but I put my mouth near Sarah's ear and spoke to her. "Listen, from what Farooq was saying earlier, I think we might be separated when we reach wherever we are going." Sarah nodded as the fear in her expression intensified.

"Just do as they say. You are going there as a doctor and they need you, so I doubt they will harm you. Just start tending to the patients as you would usually do." She looked at me as if I had lost my mind. "You need to act just as they want you to," I added hastily. "It may take a couple of days, but Razia and I will come for you. If you act normally, they will be lulled into a sense of wellbeing and won't suspect us if we try to run away."

Sarah nodded to show me that she had understood.

I hugged her close and kissed her softly on her lips. I prayed that she would be safe. I would never forgive myself if anything happened to her.

"Where are our handbags, and more important, our passports?" Sarah asked. We didn't see any of our things in the warehouse or on the jeep. Farooq must have confiscated them. That made our situation difficult but not impossible. It would just take us a while longer to reach a safe place in case we took a roundabout way to avoid border patrols and officials. I had heard that most of the embassies had closed in Kabul, and the nearest British High Commission was either in Islamabad or in Ankara on the other side. For now, I wanted to see how things played out. I had a feeling that Farooq wasn't the kingpin in the smuggling ring, and it was imperative to find out who that was if we wanted to cripple the activities of the smugglers permanently.

The jeep was slowing down as I watched the sun peep over the mountains. The rays of sun were slowly painting the black and white vista into magnificent technicolor. From the direction of the sunrise and the mountains, I was certain that we were in the north of Afghanistan—I knew from what I had read and seen on the television that the land in the south was dry and dusty. We had entered a valley from a narrow river gorge. It was dry now, with just a few puddles and pools, but it looked as if it was a waterway in the summer months. The scenery before us was breathtaking. A crystal-clear lake twinkled in the morning sun and there were already a small fleet of fishing boats casting their nets into its depths. The rooftops of the village peeked through the trees and orchards giving the area an idyllic look, just like one would imagine the mythical Shangri-La to be.

"Wake up! We are here!" Farooq shouted in glee. His incessant good mood grated on my nerves.

With a flourish, he drove to a home built under a large walnut tree. There were many children playing in its shade, and one of the lower sturdy branches had a swing tied to it. As we stepped down from the jeep, we noticed that two children were squabbling to use it. The elder of the children pushed the younger one and somehow the wooden edge of the swing hit the young child on her head. She fell down unconscious and Sarah rushed towards her to see what she could do to help.

"What are you doing, Sarah? Are you crazy? Come here!" Farooq tried to pry Sarah away from the child, who was about four years old and was bleeding profusely from a cut on her head.

"Go and get me bandages and warm water. NOW, Farooq! I don't care what the protocol here is, but this child will die if we don't stop the bleeding. You know that. Bring me a suture kit as well."

The family came out of the house to see what the ruckus

was all about. The mother rushed to her child crying and wringing her hands helplessly.

Sarah knew a little bit of Pushto, so she told the mother, with the help of the few words she knew in that language and hand gestures, that she wanted to take the child inside, and that she was a doctor and would do what she could for the little girl.

A tall man, probably the patriarch, cleared the way as Sarah picked up the injured child and ducked into the house. She lay her gently down on the nearest bed and looked impatiently at Farooq, who still had not moved.

Sarah turned to the man of the house. "I am a doctor and I can help your daughter, but I need Farooq to get me something so that I can clean the wound and stitch it up."

"What are you waiting for? Help the *Doctora*! Can't you see that my child is hurt?" roared the man. Farooq sprang into action and Sarah then cleaned the wound and applied five stitches in record time. She had given the little girl a mild sedative and now she was sleeping peacefully in her mother's arms.

"Let us get down to business," said the girl's father. It turned out that he was the chief of the village and the person who had commissioned the cargo and the request for a doctor since he wanted to build a hospital in his village.

"You have brought me an excellent doctor. She is well worth the asking price. My men have also inspected the cargo and they have told me that every item on the list we gave you has been delivered. We have your money here, just as you asked—US dollars in small bills." He made it sound as if he was buying something from a supermarket instead of stolen merchandise and kidnapped human beings.

"I want the other two women as well. I will pay the same price as the doctor for the two of them."

"That is too little—they are strong and hardworking, and they will add value to the plans you have for your village. I would like to have the same amount for each of them," Farooq blustered.

"Take it or leave it," shrugged the chief and turned away.

Farooq seemed to consider the offer. "All right! They are yours. Just give me the money and I will leave." He didn't see the smile that the chief tried to hide, pleased that the deal was in his favor, but the price was satisfactory for Farooq since he hadn't considered the extra income before he boarded the flight. He would now make his way over the mountains back to Parachinar and wouldn't give another thought to the three women he had sold and stranded in Taliban country.

"What can you do? What is your skill?" the chief asked me after Farooq left.

"We assist Dr. Sarah," I said. "Razia helps her with the patients, and I help her with the surgeries and getting the instruments and other paraphernalia ready to treat her patients."

"All right then, I want you three to set up a hospital here. We have medicines and equipment, as you can see. We will be getting wounded and sick people from other areas. Since this is a little known and secluded area, many would be able to recuperate here and then go onwards to continue to fight for Afghan freedom."

He signaled to one of his men, who was armed with an AK47, and we were pushed into a hut that had three string cots and a pitcher full of water beside a basin to wash in on a wooden stand.

"Stay here," he said. "You will rest and the chief will summon you when he is ready." With that, he closed the door and locked it.

There was only a small window in the room, and once the door was closed the place looked quite gloomy. Sarah sat next to me. As she was usually wont to do, she held my hand against her chest and leaned against me, trying to draw strength from my presence.

"I am so grateful that we are still together," she whispered.

Razia sat on the other side of me. She looked as exhausted as I felt; actually, so did Sarah. It seemed that the aftereffects of the drugs hadn't yet worn off completely.

"We might as well get some rest while we can. Let's sleep for now and when we have clear heads, we will plan our escape." I tried to sound calm, but I was sure they heard the mild quaver that I had tried to hide in my voice.

CHAPTER 7

"It is impossible to escape the impression that people commonly use false standards of measurement — that they seek power, success and wealth for themselves and admire them in others, and that they underestimate what is of true value in life."
~ Sigmund Freud, Civilization and its Discontents

SARAH

We spent a fitful night, drifting in and out of sleep. We saw no one except a little girl, of about ten years old, who came in at dinner time and silently put a pitcher of warm milk and some buttered naan on the table. She left without making eye contact, as if she had been ordered not to interact with us and was afraid of any recrimination if she did. After she scurried out, we ate silently. The mountain air was becoming chilly as the sun set, but we found some thick quilts in an aluminum box at the foot of one of the cots. We took out three and wrapped ourselves in them, thankful for the warmth they provided. They were a bit dusty and had a similar pong to the clothes we wore, but we couldn't be finicky at this point in time.

Since the cots were very narrow, we shoved them together and all three of us lay down and tried to sleep, taking comfort that we were at least together. For now. Tanya and I held hands until the frigid air compelled us to put our hands under the warms covers.

The village was fairly quiet while everyone slept, but I still woke with a start at any unusual sound or movement. I consoled myself with the thought that no one would want to hurt me because the chief needed my skills as a physician, not as a courtesan or an additional wife. And, most importantly, I had Tanya with me.

The morning was crisp and very cold. The same little girl came in again with a similar meal to the one we had been served the previous night. A younger girl carried a jug of warm water, soap, and a towel that she placed near the wash basin.

"Eat and then wash. My father will be here to take you to the hospital in a little while," the elder of the two said before both turned around to scamper out of the room.

"I wish we could take the quilts with us; it's so cold," I said.

"It will get warmer during the day, love," Tanya replied. "The mountains do get chilly in the morning and at night, so we will have to move around to keep warm. We can't afford to get sick now."

The chief walked into the room just as we finished freshening up.

"Come!" he ordered. He turned around expecting us to follow right away.

Tanya winked at me and squeezed my hand to reassure me. Now was the litmus test of my courage. I didn't want to let anyone down, but I was quaking inwardly while trying to maintain a bold persona as we walked behind the chief.

The chief took us to a building that looked like an abandoned school.

"Most of our children have gone to fight in the war. The last teacher we had left when school attendance diminished, and we couldn't replace him. Therefore, the village council decided to turn this place into a hospital."

I looked around and liked what I saw. Six rooms surrounded a large ten-meter square quadrangle that had grass and wildflowers growing rampantly. There was a wraparound veranda in front of the rooms, which were littered with straw and empty cardboard boxes. There was a forlorn rusty basketball hoop attached to the side of the main building. Sad reminders of children were the occasional blackboards or crayons scattered amongst the debris. Next to the main quadrangle was a separate room that looked like an office.

I walked into the office and saw that it had some basic rickety furniture and some rusty filing cabinets. We examined them closely and concluded that they could be made usable with a little bit of elbow grease and a few nails.

"Where does this door lead to?" I asked, indicating a

locked door that was half hidden behind a tilted filing cabinet that was missing two of its drawers.

"That is just a storage area. You should not concern yourself with it. Mind your own business and see that this place becomes a workable hospital." The chief sounded impatient. "Take a table and a few chairs out onto the lawn and start seeing patients. If you need anything, your friends will help you." He then pointed to Tanya and Razia. "Come! We must decide where we will install the X-ray and the CT machine."

We were perplexed. How would he expect to use those machines? Where was the electricity going to come from? Tanya shrugged and followed Razia and the chief out of the room.

I pulled the table and a couple of passably stable chairs out onto the quadrangle. The sun was just warming up the area and felt good on my back.

If we hadn't been prisoners, this would have been such a beautiful place to stay for a short while. I would have loved to volunteer in a village like this, although it would have been in Pakistan. However, sitting in the sun surrounded by craggy snow-topped mountains, the orchards and fields in the valley, it seemed as if we were in a small patch of heaven on earth. Then the arrival of two men rudely brought my thoughts back to why we were there.

"We are here to help you set up the day clinic," one said in a rough mixture of Pushto and Urdu. "We were also told to help you with translations if you needed it," added the second man in a much more refined accent.

I nodded my thanks. I was wary and didn't want to trust them, but it was obvious that I needed them.

"Could you find a rag to clean the table and chairs?" I asked. "I would also need to have some medicines to dispense to the patients when I examine them."

One man left to do my bidding while the other beckoned me to follow him. He took me back to the office, drew a bunch of keys from the pocket of his jacket, and opened the storeroom door.

"You wait here," he said gruffly. "I will get the medicines, and if there is anything missing you just let me know and I will find it."

I heard his footsteps going down a staircase and then the scuffling sounds he made while rummaging around somewhere beyond the door. He came out with a cardboard box in his hands and set it in front of me.

"Have a look and see what you can use for now."

I was surprised. There were the usual medicines that one would need for an outpatient clinic. I looked at the man curiously and said, "You know how to read. And you also know something about medicines."

"Yes," he replied in English. "Let me introduce myself. My name is Gulab Khan. I was a medical student in Peshawar before I was forced by my family to come back here. My father, the chief, summoned me back home to run a clinic, but I have only studied for two years and I am not skilled enough."

I wasn't expecting that. This gentle, soft-spoken man in Taliban garb was an educated person who wanted to save lives instead of taking them.

"These people don't understand that two years of medical school are not enough for anyone to become a skilled doctor, so I was happy that you were brought here because the pressure will now be off me."

"Let's get things set up before we are reprimanded. Just tell me one thing. How does the chief want the Xray machine and CT scanner to work? We haven't noticed any electricity here or in the village."

Gulab gave a small laugh. He pointed towards the mountain behind the building. "There is a waterfall that runs quite swiftly most of the year, except in winter, when it slows down. My father had a small hydroelectric power plant built there. I believe the engineers working on it told us just last night that it will start to produce up to ten megawatts of electricity a day by next week. We have been told that is enough to provide electricity to the fifteen houses in the village as well as the machines in the hospital, but, since we don't want the village to be detected by air at night, we will be using the electricity only for the hospital and emergencies during the day."

"What will you do in the winter then?" I asked, fascinated by the way these people were self-sufficient even though they were ruthless in obtaining technology and the manpower needed to fulfil their needs.

"We have two heavy-duty Russian generators, and whoever comes for a visit or to trade, they are told to bring a couple of cans of diesel so that they can be stored for the winter months. We now have enough diesel to run the generators full time for nearly a year." He sounded quite proud of this achievement.

I was curious about Gulab. He sounded just like any young man who wanted to do something positive in the world, but circumstances had held him back. I noticed an undercurrent of frustration as he spoke to me—maybe we could use that to our advantage... I was still a bit wary and wasn't sure he could be trusted. He could have been sent to work with me only to ensure that I didn't try to escape.

"Don't you want to complete your medical education and then come back to help your village?" I asked while sorting the medical supplies into convenient piles so that they were easily accessible when I examined the patients later.

"Of course, I do. It has always been a dream of mine to be a doctor, a healer. I abhor war, murder, and mayhem, all of which my father is doing..." He stopped speaking and looked around to see if anyone was listening. The fear on his face was almost palpable.

"My girlfriend is still waiting for me," he shyly said. "She is probably a year ahead of me now since I have been gone that long. We were going to be married and migrate to Germany or England after we finished our studies."

"Does she know where you are?" I asked.

"We do correspond via email. I usually go on errands to Jalalabad or to get supplies for the village. They have one of these new-fangled internet cafés. If I can ditch my companions, I quickly duck in and check my mail and send one off to her. She knows I am alive and well, but she doesn't know where I am. As it is, I am not allowed to tell anyone my whereabouts for the sake of security." Gulab continued to look around to see whether anyone was eavesdropping on our conversation. Then, as if he realized who he was talking to, he cleared his throat and said gruffly, "I am going to round up the people who need medical attention. You wait here and don't go anywhere."

"Wait, Gulab. Help me get the other table from the room out here as well. We can spread a sheet on it, and I can use it as a makeshift examination table."

"That is a good idea. It seems sturdy and will hold the weight of anyone lying on it."

We were now ready for the patients, and as soon as Gulab signaled the men who were standing guard at the entrance, a steady stream of people walked in. I started to examine each one and was writing prescriptions so that Gulab dispensed the necessary medication. I was pleased to overhear that he took pains in explaining the doses and the way the medicine needed to be taken to each patient.

The work was tedious given the limited equipment we had, and the sun started to feel hot as the day went on. At midday, we pulled the furniture under the shady veranda that ran in front of the rooms. We had a short break when another little girl brought over a tray with salted buttermilk, naan, and boiled eggs for our lunch.

The more I interacted with Gulab, the better I liked him. However, I wanted to have Tanya's opinion before we recruited his help to escape.

One thing I found odd was that most of the patients I saw that day were little girls and young women. I occasionally saw a shadow pass over Gulab's eyes, as if it was painful for him to see them. I wondered what was bothering him...

During our lunch break, we discussed the common diseases we had treated that morning and what medicine or equipment would be needed.

"There are a lot of cases of scabies among the children. You need to tell the families that they must clean out their whole house, wash everything with hot water, including the bedding, and *everyone* should use the scabicide cream that we have prescribed them. This is highly contagious, and if proper precautions aren't taken, it will spread like wildfire throughout the village." I picked at my naan because I wasn't very hungry, but I forced myself to eat. I couldn't afford to skip a meal because I wasn't sure what Tanya had planned for us, and, knowing her, we could be on our way at the spur of the moment.

Gulab didn't say anything. He sat in front of me with his head bowed and I was surprised to see a glimmer of tears in his eyes.

"What is it? Have I said anything to offend you?" I wracked my brain and went over our conversations. I couldn't pinpoint anything that would cause such a look of anguish on Gulab's face.

"No, *Doctora* Sarah, you haven't said anything out of the ordinary." He discreetly wiped a tear from his eyes as he spoke. "I am just sad at the plight of those little girls that you examined today. They don't have any families and live together in rooms that are in fact makeshift prisons. What will become of them?"

"What do you mean?"

"How do you think my father can manage to pay people like Farooq in US dollars?" He spoke in a sarcastic tone. "Look around you. We aren't rich in any way. The crops that you see are barely enough to feed us. Yet, we have all this expensive equipment and medicines. Have you given any thought to how he earned the money?"

I was worried that the other men might notice Gulab's disquiet, so I held up a conciliatory hand to calm him down.

"We have just arrived here and have had neither the time nor the opportunity to think about the money the chief handed to Farooq. Why don't you tell me why you are getting upset? Maybe we can work something out together?"

I spoke softly to him, just like one would speak to an agitated child. Gulab responded to the positive vibes I was sending out to him and calmed down.

"Please, promise that what I am going to tell you is kept confidential. I don't want to be executed as a traitor, but I can't keep quiet anymore. Your kindness and compassion towards the little girls compel me to tell you the truth. Maybe you could help them..." He let out a shuddering breath. "Most of the girls you examined today are the property of my father."

"Property? What do you mean?" It was starting to dawn on me what he was trying to say, but I needed him to tell me the whole tale.

"These little girls are either orphans of war or have been sold by their parents to my father. The impoverished parents get paid for their children and they hope that he will ensure they will have a better life than the squalor they usually live in."

I knew that child smuggling was rampant, but to have parents sell their children to these men without even knowing or caring what would happen to them was despicable.

"The little children are sold for exorbitant fees to adoption agencies in the west, and the older girls are sold to brothels." He wiped away another tear. "My father says that these children are legitimate sacrifices for the freedom of our country. They should be considered the real martyrs of the cause...while he wallows in cash."

"What do you want to do about this situation?" I asked. "Can you free the girls? Can you get help?"

"I have gone over and over in my mind, trying to work out a solution, but I can't come to any logical conclusion. Where would these children go if I liberated them? There are no orphanages in this country. The little ones are well off because they get adopted into wealthy western families and they have a chance for a better life, but I shudder at the fate of the older girls."

"Your father comes across as a very pious man. Doesn't he realize that what he is doing is against the teachings of Islam? The Holy Quran emphasizes kindness and shelter for orphans. How can he trade in them?" I was appalled at the hypocrisy. The war that was supposedly based on patriotism, freedom, and Islamic values was a sham. Like all wars, it was a war of power, ego, and domination.

"As I said before, my father justifies this by saying that the women and children are martyrs of the cause and are doing their part in helping the war effort." Gulab sounded regretful.

"Would you like to resume your medical studies?" There was an idea brewing in my mind, but I needed Gulab's cooperation and I still had to consult Tanya about it.

"I would love to. It's my passion, but my father would never allow me to leave. Moreover, I would not be able to afford the fees and the living expenses, and I am certain he wouldn't give me any money if I left. Getting a job in Peshawar is difficult for Afghans unless one knows someone influential."

"Let me talk to my friends and I will get back to you. We can discuss this again tomorrow." I smiled at him and signaled to send the next patients over.

Tanya

This was a strange place. There were orchards and fertile fields all around us, and plenty of fish from the lake, but there was still a frisson of poverty that seemed to resonate within the village. The chief was enthusiastic about the hospital and, from what I gathered while he was talking with his men, it would be used as a covert hospital for the Taliban soldiers. Since the valley was well hidden and off the beaten track, they hoped it would not be found by the allied forces. It seemed that most of their money was being used for this project, but I wondered how they would be using the machinery with no power station nearby. Maybe Sarah knew something about it. As we passed her while she was seeing her patients, I saw her talking to a young man. I hoped she could get some information from him.

Most of our day was spent clearing out the rooms. The manual labor was tiring and we were grateful that some of the men helped with the heavier stuff because I wasn't yet completely fit after our interlude with Farooq.

"Are you all right?" I asked Razia at midday. She looked pale and was sweating profusely.

"I'm still a little weak from yesterday, but I think I shall be fine in a bit. I hope they don't forget to feed us."

We watched as the little girls from before brought a tray

of food for Sarah and the man who was helping her. We were about to join them when we heard a voice behind us.

"Leave the *Doctora* alone. She needs to eat and continue her work. Your food is in the room nearby. Eat and then we will keep working," ordered one of the men who were helping us.

We saw a covered tray on the floor in the room he indicated. Since there was no furniture, we sat down on the floor for our meal.

"Boiled eggs, buttermilk, and naan... These people live simply even though there seems to be money in the kitty." Razia looked at the contents of the tray speculatively, her investigator's brain kicking in.

"I think it is strange that the chief can trade in US dollars while the village looks to be on the verge of poverty." We spoke in Sindhi because we knew that our captors wouldn't understand us. They were not aware that we understood them very well because we were trained to learn the different colloquial languages in the area, so we were at an advantage.

"Let's keep our eyes and ears open and see what happens. I have this niggling feeling that we might find one of the links in the chain of child smugglers here."

We worked until the sun started to dip behind the mountains in the west. It became chilly, and before it was completely dark, we were escorted back and locked into our room once again.

Sarah was already there, but instead of looking tired as I had expected, she looked excited.

"Tanya! Razia! I found out that this village is one of the hubs for child trafficking!"

"Really? I thought you were with your patients all day.

How did you manage to do a bit of sleuthing as well?" I tried to inject a little humor, but it didn't seem to work—Sarah was too focused on what she wanted to share with us.

"Gulab Khan, the man who was working with me today, is the chief's son."

"And?" I was confused. What did that have to do with the smugglers?

"He used to be a medical student in Peshawar and was forced by his father to come back home so that he could run the hospital."

"Nice story, but I still don't get it..."

"Don't be impatient, love. I am getting there, but first I need to tell you his story."

"Yes, let her speak, Tanya. I am very curious to see where this is going," Razia jumped in.

"Well, he is not happy that he has been summoned here. He wants to finish his studies. He also told me that the source of income for the village, or at least for the hospital, is from selling little girls and orphan babies to people who would sell them again to international adoption agencies."

We were dumbstruck. Like I had said to Sarah on the way here, providence had placed us just where we needed to be.

"Gulab also said that there is a hydroelectric power station that will be providing electricity to the hospital once it's up and running. The amount of money spent is phenomenal, which means they must be paid very well for the children." Sarah looked troubled, and I understood why. She desperately wanted to help the children.

"We can't do much for the children just yet, but once we have given enough intel to Interpol, the masterminds of the smugglers could be caught, which will dry up the demand for children."

We were again served a simple meal, after which we sat down and brainstormed with the information we had.

"Gulab is ready to help us if we help him go back to medical college and to his girlfriend, who he intends to marry as soon as he can." Sarah sounded thrilled. "We would have to arrange paying for his tuition and expenses as well."

"That is no problem at all. If we can smash the smuggler's ring, any country involved would be only too happy to help him."

"I heard that some people are coming tomorrow to get a few children. According to Gulab, they are heavily armed and aggressive. Even his father is cautious when he speaks to them." Sarah looked worried, but I put my hand on her thigh to reassure her. If not tomorrow, then we would observe and try to escape another time.

"Does Gulab know what nationality these people are?" asked the ever-pragmatic Razia.

"He is not sure. He thinks they are a group of mixed nationalities: Iranian, Turkish, and Central Asian. There was a man who acted as the leader and he spoke Farsi with the chief, but Gulab says he looked distinctly Slavic."

"And so the network expands..." I said.

The next day, we were pulled out of our room as the day before. Sarah went off to her makeshift clinic while we were put to work once more in clearing out the rooms to make way for the hospital equipment. Now that we knew about the power station, we did not find it strange that a man arrived with a tool belt and started to lay in electricity lines and sockets. These people were prepared for every eventuality. We had to either plan very carefully or grasp any opportunity to escape by the seat of our pants.

By midday there was a sudden commotion in the village. The men who were working with us looked nervous and they hustled us along with Sarah into the room that was previously an office. Sarah had two little girls with her. One was a few months old and the other was a toddler. I wasn't surprised that they seemed to have recognized Sarah's kind aura and had latched on to her.

"Where did these little beauties come from?" I asked in a baby voice while tickling the toddler under her chin, making her giggle.

"I was just examining them when we were pushed in here. There was no time to send them back."

Suddenly, we heard loud noises and explosions coming from the village. The explosions seemed to be coming nearer and nearer.

Gulab opened the door to the storage basement and shoved Sarah and the babies into it. "Go down and hide; you will be safe there." He then turned to us. "Go down with the *Doctora*. I will close the door and no one will know that you are there."

Razia and I looked pointedly at each other and I said to Gulab, "We will go with you; maybe we can help. We are trained in using most weapons."

Sarah had now the responsibility of the two children with her, so she went down the stairs without arguing. "Please, Tanya, be careful and come and get us as soon as you can. I love you and I don't know what I would do if anything happened to you!"

I reciprocated by sending her a flying kiss and a

reassuring look. Once we closed the door and hid it behind the rusty filing cabinet, we loped towards the entrance of the building. What we saw was sheer mayhem—houses were on fire and people were running in panic. There were a few trucks on the outskirts of the village into which armed men were herding a large group of crying, bewildered children and young girls.

The chief was wounded, and his wife had propped him up against the wall of his house while trying to staunch the blood seeping out from a wound in his chest.

Gulab started to run over to help, but I caught him by the arm before he could leave.

"Wait, we don't know how they will react when you show yourself. You are the chief's son, and they might try to kill you." He nodded in agreement, and we crouched behind a low wall to see what was happening.

"Do you have any weapons?" I asked Gulab.

"Yes, I do. I have a pistol on me and there is a rifle and an Uzi machine gun in my room."

"Give me the pistol," I said. "Is your room nearby?"

"It's that one to your right. If I crawl behind this wall I can get there and bring out the other guns."

"Go then; we will wait here for you. If you have any extra ammunition, bring that as well." I hoped that he was safe. It was clear that he wasn't a fighter at all.

Suddenly, a missile landed and exploded near the building where Sarah and the babies were hiding. It collapsed, and the only hope that they were safe was that they were in the basement.

"Oh, crap!" Razia exclaimed. "Now what do we do?"

"Shh! I hear someone coming!" We ducked down. Two

men were rummaging amongst the debris, maybe looking for the supplies that had been stored there. Not many people were aware of the basement, so the men just had a perfunctory look at the debris.

"There is nothing of value. If the supplies were stored here, they were in all probability destroyed by that idiot Mahmud's missile. Who told him to fire in this direction?" one man said in Pushto.

"We were told there were more children in this building. They had a doctor examining them so that we were to be given the healthy ones..."

"Well, there is no one here now. Let's go!"

We heaved a sigh of relief when the men walked back to the trucks and signaled their men to climb in. Within just half an hour, the damaged village had a deathly pall over it. Not a sound was heard except for the scattering of rubble as it was disturbed by people looking for their belongings and valuables in the wreckage.

Gulab ran over to his father. His mother was crying hysterically and slapping herself just like the women of the region did when they wanted to express deep sorrow. The chief had died in the raid and Gulab's mother was so grief-stricken that she picked up an AK 47 and started to run after the departing trucks. A woman tried to take the gun away from her, and in the confusion of the skirmish, there was a loud gunshot followed by nearly pin-drop silence. We watched in horror as the matriarch slowly slipped to the ground and breathed her last. The woman who had tried to stop her threw the gun to the side and ran into her hut wailing loudly.

"We need to see where Sarah and the children are. I pray

that they are unhurt." The bloody scene in the village had affected us, and we just wanted to get Sarah and go as far away as we could from this carnage.

"I saw some spades and pickaxes in the hospital this morning; let's see if they are still there." Razia tried to speak normally, but I could hear her voice tremble. "We have to get Sarah out of that mess."

We started to remove the concrete and rubble where we estimated that the entrance to the basement would be. It was hard work and we soon had blisters on our hands, but we persevered. It was getting dark and there was no light in or near the village, so we wouldn't be able to see much as we worked. When we removed the bulk of the rubble, we started to call out to Sarah. After a few minutes we heard her faint answer.

"Tanya! Razia! We are here. We are not hurt; we are all right!"

Oh, thank God! I thought. "We are trying to get you out as soon as we can. Hold on!" I shouted back to her.

"Don't hurt yourself. The babies are asleep, but I really want to get out of here. I am slowly getting claustrophobic."

It took us a while, but we managed to make a hole large enough to allow Sarah hand the little girls out to us. We then made it slightly bigger so that Sarah could also wriggle out. It was such a relief to hold her close to me. For one frightening moment, when I saw the missile land near the building, I thought that I had lost her forever.

We were both trembling when we hugged and kissed each other. The embrace went on for a long time because neither wanted to let go of the other.

"You are safe! It's a miracle! Praise God!" I was so overwhelmed with the feelings of gratitude and love I had.

Razia tapped me on the shoulder. "Break it up," she laughed. "We need to make plans, and quick. I am sure these men will be back again. They know that there are valuable supplies stored here."

My stomach started to protest its neglect and Razia smirked at the sound. "To tell you the truth, I am famished too, but I doubt that we will be fed by the villagers tonight," she said.

"Why don't you make the hole a bit bigger and then we can go into the basement?" suggested Sarah. "There are a lot of supplies stored in cupboards down there—food, candles, torches, etc. I am sure if we look carefully, we might even find clothes and beddings."

Thinking of my blistered hands, I groaned inwardly, but I agreed it was a good idea.

Sarah saw me flinch when I picked up the pickaxe and silently took it from my hand.

"Let me try to enlarge the opening." I reluctantly handed it over to her, but then I became impressed with the strength and the diligence that she used to hack at the concrete. After about an hour, the opening was big enough for us to slip into the basement. We covered the entrance with a sheet of corrugated iron in such a way that it seemed it had fallen there in the explosion.

"I'll put the children onto the mattress and then we can have something to eat."

Razia and I looked at each other. "What could we possibly eat down here?" I asked.

"Well, canned baked beans for one, and if you are good,

I'll add some corned beef as well." Sarah laughed at our expressions. "I told you that there were different supplies down here. Razia, go over to that fallen cupboard and see what there is to eat. Can you also bring some bottles of water and a can of condensed milk? The baby might be waking up soon and will want to be fed."

"You are amazing!" I grabbed Sarah by the cheeks and kissed her soundly on her lips. "You are a life saver!"

Once we finished our banquet of corned beef, canned vegetables, and baked beans, we settled down for the night. We needed Gulab's help to leave this valley, but first we had to rally our strength and get a good night's sleep.

CHAPTER 8

"Times of great calamity and confusion have been productive for the greatest minds. The purest ore is produced from the hottest furnace. The brightest thunder-bolt is elicited from the darkest storm." ~ Charles Caleb Colton

SARAH

After a fitful night we woke up just before dawn. Tanya said she would go and look for Gulab after we made ourselves presentable and had something to eat. We wanted to take stock of what we had and then leave the valley. Gulab knew the area well, and we were sure that he also wanted to get out of there as soon as he could. His parents were both dead and he had heard from the villagers that the men had also taken his younger sisters along with the other children, so there seemed to be nothing holding him back. In all fairness, we were sure that he would want to help us find the smugglers so that his small family could be reunited again.

There was no doubt that we would take the children with us. I was pleasantly surprised when I saw Tanya holding the baby and looking down at her with a tender expression. I fell in love with her over again—maternal love was not something to be taken lightly.

"She has been fed and burped," said Tanya as she held the baby out to me. "I think she will be ready for her nap now." She smiled tenderly at the infant and gave her a kiss on her forehead.

"I am going to look for Gulab. I should be back very soon. In the meantime, eat your breakfast."

"I will have a look around and see what we can take along with us," said Razia. "We will need a few things besides food if we are to survive in the mountains."

Tanya nodded and looked cautiously out of the opening leading outside. Seeing that the coast was clear, she hauled herself out and carefully closed the gap once more and left.

We had decided the night before to call the baby Hana and the toddler Dania—simple and short names. I knew we shouldn't get too emotionally involved, but I fell in love with them the first time I saw them, and apparently, so did Tanya. Who could resist those big gray eyes and the unruly locks? Tanya noticed that the hair of both babies was the same color as mine, and she thought it was adorable.

"I have found some supplies that will help us when we trek over the mountains," came Razia's muffled voice from behind some cartons.

"Bring whatever you think we might need, and we can sort them out together."

Razia found military grade backpacks made of sturdy waterproof material with many zippers and pockets. "There is a whole carton full of these backpacks behind there," she said, pleased with her find.

She put five backpacks on the floor in front of the mattresses where we had slept the previous night.

"I am going back there." She indicated where the cartons were stacked. "There are aluminum blankets and heavy-duty sleeping bags in a box. We are lucky that we are just where we need to be right now. I wonder what they wanted to do with all this equipment."

Slowly, the pile in front of me grew. Razia had also chosen three light-weight tents, water canteens, and adjustable alpine walking sticks with a pick on top.

"Look at this piece de resistance!" Razia held out her hand to show me what she had. "Four Swiss army knives with every possible gadget needed for camping! What a find!" She was as thrilled as a child who had found a new toy. "Let me get the equipment ready, and you see what food you can put together for us to take," she said as she disappeared once again behind the stack of cartons.

We had to be sensible. We could only take as much as we could comfortably carry since we had the children with us as well. The fallen cupboard was my target and I looked beyond the canned goods. To my surprise, I found a lot of US military MREs as well as dried soup packets of various flavors. They would not be as heavy as carrying cans, and they had innovative flameless ration heaters in them that warmed the meals.

"Razia! See if there is a small butane stove or heater that we could take with us," I called out.

"Why do you want a stove? We must keep things to a minimum." She sounded grumpy.

"I know that! But we have two children with us, and we can't make them drink ice cold milk," I shouted back.

"Hmph! Okay, let me have a look." After a while, she found a small stove that ran on butane capsules. She put it and ten of the capsules onto the fast-growing pile.

"It looks like they were planning an expedition. These supplies are unusual for a village. There is every possible thing we would need here. There are even thermals as well as waterproof jackets and pants!" We were grateful for our treasure trove. The journey over the mountains would be hard, but we wouldn't be without relative comfort and resources.

"Breakfast is nearly finished. I hope Tanya comes soon. I am getting restless. I want to be as far away as possible when those men come back." I put a plate of food in front of Razia and indicated that she should eat. I couldn't make any tea, so we had to make do with the bottled water available.

"They must be after something else besides the children and the cargo hijacked from the plane. We need to look around. I feel that we are missing something." I closed my eyes and visualized the basement. With my mind's eye, I explored every nook and cranny. At first, I couldn't sense anything, but on my third virtual sweep around the room, I noticed an unusual shadow near one of the walls near us. It was mostly covered with rubble, but I was suddenly compelled to move everything away and uncover what was silently calling out to me.

Without saying anything to Razia, I got up and started to remove the loose rubble with a spade. Seeing what I was doing, Razia got up and started to help me. After a few minutes, we unearthed a large steel safe. The door had buckled with the weight of the concrete and rubble falling on it, so trying to open it was not very difficult.

"We will need a crowbar to pry it completely open," said Razia.

"How about using that steel bar lying in the corner? Maybe that would work?"

"Let me try. It might slip because it's round, but beggars can't be choosers." She grinned. She was as excited as I was with our find.

After a few tries and a few scraped knuckles later, we finally got the safe open. We just stood there with our mouths open in shocked wonder at what we found inside it.

The safe was about 170 cm x 100 cm and had various compartments and drawers in it. Each drawer contained something different. A few had currencies of various countries, predominantly US dollars and euros. There were also Turkish and Iranian banknotes and some others that we couldn't identify. Another drawer had rolls of gold coins and ingots while the rest of the safe was full of an Aladdin's cave of jewels. All that was missing was the lamp.

"What in the name of heaven is this?" Razia let out a whistle of surprise. No wonder the men wanted to come back. "The contents of this safe must be worth a few million dollars!"

"Do you realize that if the men knew about this safe, the cargo and the other equipment in the basement, it's because someone within the village was giving them information? We need to leave as soon as possible!" I started towards the door as I wanted to go and look for Tanya.

"Stay here." Razia pulled me back. "She told us to wait for her and I'm sure she will be here soon. I am getting the backpacks ready, so that as soon as she comes, we can pick them up and leave."

"What do we do about the safe?" I was worried because I realized that all that money could buy weapons. "We need to hide it properly. We can't let those people have access to its contents."

"Let's see what Tanya says when she gets back. For now, let us just focus on getting ready to leave. I have found some rolls of cotton cloth in a carton. I think they are supposed to be used as turbans, but we can use them to tie the babies to us when we get out of here. You can carry Hana while Tanya and I take turns in carrying Dania. I have also packed a box of disposable gloves and the condensed milk." Razia was pleased with how things were coming together. "There is also a large tin of powdered milk. We will add it to our packs if we have enough space or if we can carry a bit more weight."

It was important that we thought of the children. Dania would be able to share our food, but Hana was still too small to eat solids.

Razia packed the bags with military precision. I was impressed, but then she had been trained by the police.

"Have a look at the clothes back there and wear something under the *burqa* that you will be wearing. Remember that it will be very cold in the mountains. "

I sighed and went to rummage in the boxes while wondering what dangers and adventures awaited us.

. . .

Tanya

The village was in shambles and hardly anyone stirred at this early hour. I loped from shadow to shadow trying to avoid everyone. I didn't know what the emotional mood was among the people in the village, and I didn't want to trigger anything by blatantly moving around. I was an outsider, and for all they knew, we could have been in cahoots with their attackers. I didn't want to deal with mass hysteria. I reached the chief's house, peeked inside the window, and saw Gulab sitting on the bed in the room.

"Psst! Gulab!" I whispered.

"Yes, what are you doing here?" he looked surprised to see me.

"We wanted to know whether you were all right. We also want you to come to the hospital building. We need to talk to you." I kept my voice very low so that I didn't attract attention. Gulab nodded and came out of the house by the back door.

Flitting from shadow to shadow, we reached the basement where the others were hiding. We didn't speak to each other until we were inside our hiding place.

"Gulab! We are so sorry about your parents and your sisters. Please, accept our heartfelt condolences." Sarah was the first to greet him, and we added our commiserations along with hers.

Gulab stood there for a while, his head lowered in grief as he tried to hide his tears.

"We buried my parents at dawn today," he said in a quiet

voice. "However, I must find my sisters and take them away from all of this madness."

"Razia is a policewoman, and I am an agent from Interpol. We were on a fact-finding mission regarding the child smugglers and slave traders when Farooq hijacked the plane and brought us here. Now that we have a few clues, we will pursue them, and I promise we will bring your sisters back to you."

Gulab opened his mouth to protest, but Razia interrupted him.

"Let the professionals handle this. You can help by going back to college in Peshawar, and then when you have graduated, you can take your sisters and go to England or Germany just as you had planned before."

"If you think that Peshawar is too dangerous for you, we will arrange that you finish college in England. Would you like that?" I asked him.

"These people have violated my family honor by killing my parents and taking my sisters. Even though your offer is tempting, I still would like to go with you and bring the smugglers to justice." Gulab was bristling.

"We empathize with you and your situation, but we believe that these men are not the actual masterminds. The network is much larger than anyone thought it was, and we would need every bit of our special training to be a step ahead of them and finally bring them to justice." I tried to persuade him to change his mind.

"Why don't Gulab and I take the children to Parachinar, and from there to Peshawar? We need to tell the authorities what happened, especially about the hijacking. Farooq must have really maligned us if the captain left us behind so easily. There might be a lot of damage control required in that regard, and I can file a report on what we know so far about the smugglers," Razia suggested.

"That would certainly give us the freedom to follow them. Taking two children along with us would be dangerous and distracting." Sarah liked the idea of sending the children to safety with Razia and Gulab. "You won't be conspicuous because you would just look like any young family traveling between villages."

"You are right," said Gulab, who had calmed down and was listening carefully to our plans. "There is just one flaw in your plan, Tanya," he said. "Women are not allowed to travel alone in this country, and you will be interrogated or even arrested if you are caught."

"What do you suggest we do then?" An idea was forming in my mind, but I wanted to see whether he was on the same page as I was.

"When I was in college, I used to act in plays. I didn't have a beard at the time, so my drama teacher showed me how to use my own hair and some glue to make a natural looking beard for my stage character. It was so realistic that I wore it for a short while just for fun. I can show you how to do that and you can then travel disguised as a man." Gulab smiled.

"That is exactly what I was thinking," I said. "We had classes on how to disguise ourselves. I also walked around dressed like a man for one day and fooled my colleagues." I started to laugh as I remembered the look on Razia's face when I removed the beard.

"Yes, I do remember that," said Razia. "I also remember

how furious I was with you because you had convinced me that you were your brother."

"Before we do anything, there is something we need to discuss, especially with Gulab," said Sarah in a serious voice. "We have found something that we don't want to fall into the hands of the smugglers if they were to come back again."

"What is it?" asked Gulab curiously.

"It is better that we show you."

Sarah took us to the back of the room, where there was a mangled safe. As she opened the dented door an involuntary whistle escaped my lips. "What is that?" I asked.

"We don't know, but I think Gulab's father collected all this from various sources to pay for the hospital equipment and weapons. Now we need to know what we should do with all this. Do we hide it, or do we take it along with us?" Sarah looked at Gulab as she spoke. "Since it is on your property, that makes you the owner of the contents in the safe. Therefore, it's up to you to decide what you want to do with it."

Gulab looked at the contents of the safe with a mixture of surprise and horror. "This is tainted money!" he exclaimed. "This is what my father was paid when he would sell the children to the smugglers. It seems they realized how much wealth he had collected and most probably wanted to steal it back from him."

"What should we do with it? We can't just leave these valuables here. Even if we hide everything away it might still be found later if they are thorough in their search for the 'treasure' since there is more than a couple of millions of dollars' worth of cash, gold, and jewelry here."

Gulab was silent for a while and then said, "Our prime

goal is to find these men and bring them to justice. We will need funds for travel and other incidentals. Therefore, I suggest we take as much as we can with us and use it to get justice for the children and the girls who were sold to get my father's ill-gotten stash."

We stuffed most of the money into the pockets of our waterproof cargo pants. We then divided the gold and jewelry into four portions and each of us packed it on the bottom of our backpacks and covered them with the provisions we were taking along with us.

"We will give you whatever we have left over afterwards so that when you and your sisters reunite, you can start a new life." Sarah squeezed Gulab's arm in encouragement.

"I just want justice for all the children that were sold or kidnapped." Gulab was resolute in his decision about how we should use the money.

While we were discussing routes and weather conditions, Razia cut off about seven centimeters of my hair. She found some glue in one of the boxes and started to painstakingly stick it onto my face until a short scraggly beard emerged through her efforts. She didn't put anything on my upper lip to conform with the local style, and in any case, it would be easier to eat and drink that way. Gulab showed me how to wind a turban on my head. That took some time and some giggles, but I finally managed to have a passable turban on that didn't unravel when I moved.

"Let us all wear the waterproof clothes and thermals that I found," Razia said as she disappeared behind the wall of boxes to change her clothes. "Sarah and I will wear *burqas* over our clothes. We can discard them if we get to places where we must climb or walk on narrow ledges and they become unwieldy." She looked at me and Gulab. "Both of you need to wear traditional clothes over the warm clothes. How is your Pushto, Tanya?"

"I did very well in class and my instructor said I had a good grasp on the language."

"Good. If anyone finds your accent suspicious, you could always say you were here for a visit from the Pakistani tribal area." Razia turned to Sarah. "Sarah, you won't need to talk... much. The Afghans don't expect the women to talk, so your Pushto won't be put to the test."

We got ready and said our farewells. Sarah had tears in her eyes when she kissed the babies goodbye. It was for the best that they went to Pakistan since we didn't know who or what we would encounter. Gulab and Razia would be travelling with them east to Parachinar while we were going to track the smugglers. They'd probably be heading west since they had a lot of "cargo" with them. I prayed that God bless the children and keep them safe.

CHAPTER 9

"To get through the hardest journey we need take only one step at a time, but we must keep on stepping." ~ Chinese Proverb

SARAH

As soon as Razia and Gulab left with the children, Tanya and I sat down to plan our route. We had found a map of Afghanistan with the supplies and had already gone over suggested routes *ad nauseam*. Gulab believed the smugglers were most likely heading west. From what he knew, they usually travelled by lesser-known back roads to Iran and entered Europe through Turkey. After rummaging in the debris of his destroyed house, Gulab had found his father's diary the night before, and even though it was in Pushto, we managed to decipher the addresses written there. Tanya agreed that our best bet would be to make our way to Herat, which was the main conduit to the Iranian border, and catch up with the smugglers there. Usually, trucks had to use the main highway, which, though destroyed in quite a few places, was still used as a major trade route. This highway passed through Kandahar in the south and then made a hairpin turn northwest to Herat. The direct roads to Herat were just small two-lane roads used by the locals and were not big enough for the trucks.

"The road to Herat will be difficult to travel, love, and we might have to walk sometimes, but I hope that we can reach the city before the smugglers do," said Tanya as she charted a route on the map with a piece of charcoal.

"Let us hope so," I said.

"The best option for us would be to catch a bus in Jalalabad. If we are lucky, we can get one that travels directly to Herat. Then the driving distance from there to Herat would be about nine hundred and thirty-two kilometers, which could take approximately ten more hours or so. That is if all goes well." Tanya was in her agent mode once more, and I marveled at her meticulous preparations.

"I am going to get a first aid kit together while you finish up here." I didn't want to just cobble together the usual lay person's kit—I needed to anticipate medical emergencies, just like Tanya was anticipating unusual risks in our journey. Searching amongst the stores, I found a smaller tote bag which had many zippers and pockets. It was ideal for a medical kit. I filled it up with whatever I thought would be needed in the eventuality of a serious medical emergency: Suture kits, basic surgical instruments, local anesthesia, antihistamines, bandages, pain killers, anti-pyretics, and antibiotics were compactly packed into the bag. I hefted it to assess its weight and was pleased that it wasn't as heavy as I thought it would be. Of course, if we got tired, even feather weights would seem as heavy as lead. However, I ignored the feeling that I might have gone a tad overboard since we needed the comfort of having the means to take care of ourselves in case we got ill or hurt.

"Let me look around to see whether the coast is clear, and then we should leave," said Tanya.

"Do you know the way out of the village?" I asked. It was a reasonable question since it had been dark when we first arrived.

"Yes, Gulab showed me the way out, and he has drawn me a map that shows the location of the main road to Jalalabad. We aren't very far away—just a couple of kilometers. Farooq brought us here in a roundabout way to confuse us and make us think that we were far away from civilization... the city... people... Oh, well, you know what I mean," Tanya said with a laugh."

"Lead on then, oh, fearless chief. My life is in your hands!" I mock saluted Tanya, lifted my backpack onto my back and picked up the duffle bag with the medical supplies.

"Are you sure you can carry that? It's not too heavy for you, sweetheart?" She looked at me with concern in her eyes. I frowned, mildly annoyed that she doubted I was strong enough.

"Hey! I didn't mean that you can't do it!" Tanya held her hands out in a conciliatory manner. "I am just worried that you might get tired, but if you think you can manage, then that is great." She bent down and picked up her backpack as well. "Let's get out of here. And please, Sarah, no medical sidebars this time." She smirked at me, knowing that I would never be able to leave a person in need of medical attention. But she had to try, didn't she? I grinned back cheekily but didn't respond.

The coast was clear when we left our hideout. Most of the villagers were busy clearing away the debris or trying to rebuild their houses with whatever material they had on hand. A few newly dug mounds in the graveyard were grisly evidence of the devastating effects of the raid. Gulab had said that the villagers were angry because they were attacked by who they thought were their own people, and that made their losses even more poignant.

We left the village behind us and were glad that everyone was too busy to notice our departure. We had decided not to walk on the main track that led to the village since it wasn't that well-travelled and we didn't know who we would encounter on the way, so we walked parallel to it instead and took care to stay hidden by the trees. Even though we tried to hurry along, the uneven ground slowed us down in a few places, and it took us more than an hour to reach the main road that led to Jalalabad.

"I am tired!" I whined like a small child. The effort of jumping over pools of water and climbing over little hills was taking its toll on me.

"I already hear the traffic on the main road. We are not very far. Once we reach there, we can hitch a ride to the city," Tanya placated me gently.

She was right. I also cocked my ears to listen and heard the rumbling of trucks and cars as they went on their way. She was confident that someone would stop for us because we looked like a typical young Afghan couple—Tanya with her turban and bristly beard, and me with my billowing blue *burqa*. Now we needed to see whether Tanya's disguise was believable. In my opinion, she looked like a cute young man even though her beard tickled me when I kissed her. But then, I was biased.

Tanya

Getting out of the village was a relief. Once we were on our way, I kept a vigilant look out for any unusual movement or sounds. I didn't want to put our disguises to the test so close to the destroyed village. Since we were travelling away from there, we could have been arrested and falsely implicated in the raid if we were caught.

Walking over the rough ground was tedious, and I admired the way Sarah stoically plodded on. She only complained a couple of times, but she was doing so well for someone who wasn't as physically trained as I was.

Finally, I heard the sounds of traffic ahead. We had reached the road to Jalalabad. The area was renowned for the export of fruits and vegetables, and there was always a convoy of trucks moving between this area, Iran, and Pakistan.

We stepped onto the shoulder of the road and waited a short while until we saw a small pick-up truck head our way. I flagged it down and it stopped.

"*Asalam alaikum*, brother! Where do you want to go?" said the cheerful driver.

"My wife and I want to go to Jalalabad. Can you give us a lift?" I asked gruffly, consciously deepening my voice.

"Sure; tell your wife to hop on in the back and you can sit here with me in the cabin."

Acting like the young husband I was supposed to be, I hoisted our bags onto the bed of the truck and helped Sarah climb up. Fortunately, it was only half full with bags of wheat, so Sarah would travel comfortably. I closed the tailgate, winked at Sarah, and then went to sit next to the driver, who immediately started the truck with a lurch and an ominous grinding of the gears. He was a chatty young man and kept me entertained until we reached the outskirts of the town. I was glad that I didn't need to say much because I wasn't sure I could keep the lower male cadence my voice needed for a long time.

"Where would you like to be dropped off?" the driver asked.

"Anywhere convenient for you. We are looking for the main bus terminal as we would like to travel onwards to Kabul." I didn't want to tell him exactly where we were going in case someone came looking for us, even if I was confident that they would be looking for two women and not a young couple.

"I am going to pass by the bus terminal, so I can take you there," said the driver.

"That is very kind of you. If we ever meet again in this area, I hope I will be able to return the favor." I felt like a hypocrite as I shook hands with him when he stopped the truck. I quickly went to help Sarah down from the vehicle and waved as he drove off.

"Let me go and see when we can get a bus to Herat. Why

don't you sit on the bench over there and wait for me?" I said to Sarah. She looked anxiously at me and held onto my jacket almost convulsively.

"I don't want us to be separated. Please take me with you."

I nodded. I should have thought of that myself; it was better that we stayed together.

"Just remember to stand behind me, keep yourself covered, and don't talk to anyone," I reminded her. Sarah nodded to show that she had heard me, but she covertly pinched my arm to show that she didn't like to be dictated to. She knew that we needed to keep a low profile to stay safe, so she prudently didn't say anything. I had a feeling that I would have multiple bruises on my arms by the time our assignment was over. I chuckled quietly at the thought.

Because it was already nearly noon, there was just a short queue at the ticket office. "Two tickets to Herat via the direct route," I told the man sitting behind the window that was reinforced with iron bars.

"The last bus that travels directly to Herat has already left. You could catch the next bus to Kabul and get another bus to Herat from there if you are in a hurry," said the ticket collector.

"All right then, give me two tickets on the next bus to Kabul," I said decisively.

"It will be leaving in the next ten minutes." He pointed to a bus that had just started its loud diesel engine. "Fifty Afghanis for two tickets. Hurry up so you don't miss it!" He shoved two pasteboard tickets towards me. I was grateful for the money we had taken from the village and promptly pushed the exact amount towards the ticket seller.

"Let's go!" I said gruffly in Pushto to Sarah. I took her firmly by her upper arm and hustled her towards the bus. We were just in time because the driver was already revving his engine, indicating that he was about to leave. We were lucky that we found two seats right in the back where we would be away from prying eyes.

"Did you have to choose the back?" Sarah whispered. "It's going to be rough when we are on the road, especially if it gets bumpy."

"I know, love, but it was a toss-up between comfort and privacy, and I chose privacy." I grinned. Maybe she smiled back, but I didn't know because I couldn't see her face behind the burqa. She squeezed my arm reassuringly though.

The journey was indeed bumpy, but it only lasted two and a half hours. The bus stopped two times on the way at makeshift mosques for prayers, and all the men travelling in the bus were told that it was mandatory to join the prayer congregations, so I had to go with them to avoid being questioned or even arrested. Sarah stayed on the bus because women were exempt of entering a mosque when they had their menstruation since they were considered impure at that time.

"Remember to pray like a man..." Sarah whispered in my ear when we stopped the first time. It was good advice, although there wasn't much difference in the way men and women prayed—men folded their hands over their abdomens while women folded their hands across their chests. I did the required supplications without causing any suspicion, and I took advantage of the position I was in to pray to Allah to keep us safe, that we were not found out and succeeded in our mission.

For the rest of the journey we leaned against each other and fitfully napped, but even in my sleep I was alert to any unusual movement. It was already late afternoon when we saw the outskirts of Kabul.

The bus stopped and let us off at the main bus terminal of the city, and we immediately went to the ticket office to ask about a bus to Herat.

"The next bus is after the morning prayers tomorrow," said the ticket seller, who looked like a clone of the one we had encountered in Jalalabad.

"May I buy the tickets now?" I asked.

"Yes, you can. One hundred Afghanis for two tickets directly to Herat via Sharak." He pushed the pasteboard tickets towards me.

"Can you recommend a reasonable place where I can spend the night with my wife?"

"Yes, there is a traveler's inn just three hundred meters from here. It is called *Afghan Serai*. It's nothing much, but it's clean. Tell them that Anar Khan sent you. The proprietor is my cousin. He will give you a room for the night."

"Thank you for your help," I said gratefully, and walked with Sarah in the direction where he pointed. We soon reached a ramshackle inn with a half-fused neon sign proclaiming it was the *Afghan Serai* we were looking for. There were small groups of unsavory characters standing or squatting nearby, and there was a distinct aura of danger emanating from the men staring at us. One of them looked vaguely familiar, but then the clothes the men wore were so similar that I wasn't entirely sure. He was staring at us and that made me uncomfortable. If they had an inkling that we were both women, we would have been in unspeakable danger.

"We can't spend the night here," whispered Sarah as she tugged on my sleeve. Since I was also uncomfortable with the surroundings and the people there, I agreed, so we turned around and walked for another ten minutes through the city. It was sad to see what destruction the war had rendered. What was once a proud metropolis with historical beauty lay in shambles. Bullet holes on the walls were the norm rather than the exception. We noticed there weren't many people on the road, and those that we saw scurried along while looking furtively around. We hastened to find accommodation for the night. There was an ominous quiet in the air which was occasionally punctuated by explosions and the rat-a-tat of machine gunfire somewhere far away, which meant there was a battle going on at the outskirts of the city.

After a while, we came upon a presentable looking inn. It must have been a three-star hotel in its heyday, so with a nod of consent from Sarah, I walked inside and rang the bell for service. A young, fresh faced Afghan boy whose whiskers were just starting to sprout came to the ornate marble counter and spoke with a voice that cracked, belying his age.

"*Asalam alaikum*, my name is Jan Ali. How can I help you?"

"May we have a room for the night?" I asked. "I mean... do you have any vacancies?"

"Yes, we do. Two hundred and fifty Afghanis for the night," he said warily, as if he thought we might not be able to pay him. "We get paid beforehand, but we will also provide you dinner this evening and breakfast in the morning."

"Perfect. We need to leave early, that is, as soon as the morning prayers are over, so by settling our accounts now, we won't disturb you in the morning."

Jan Ali nodded as he took the money and wrote out a receipt for me. "I will have dinner sent to your room in a little while, and I will instruct our kitchen to send you your breakfast before the morning prayer."

"Thank you." I took the room key and followed him with Sarah trailing demurely behind us.

The small room we were ushered into was simple. The space was mostly taken up by a double bed and one chair. There was also a small table near the window. The room was clean and thankfully, there was an en-suite bathroom. After the stresses of the last few days, this looked like sheer luxury to us.

As soon as Jan Ali left, Sarah stripped and went to have a shower. Her relief at getting out of the bulky clothes was almost palpable. I was also looking forward to having a shower. If we had been at home, I would have joined her, but the shower stall was miniscule, and as someone would be bringing the food anytime, I didn't want to be caught literally with my pants down.

I rummaged in my backpack and found the spare glue that Gulab had given me. The stresses of the day had loosened my beard a bit, but I was grateful that it had held up quite well. I would need to get up a bit earlier in the morning to repair it and make it presentable again.

Sarah came out of the bathroom rubbing her hair dry. She smelled of soap and looked squeaky clean. "We need to discuss what we should do next," she said as if she was reading my mind.

"I was just about to say the same thing." I smiled. "Do we confront the smugglers when we find them? We were told that our mission was strictly to collect facts and proof of the people involved in this heinous trade, so do we stick to that?" I mused. "We are stranded without passports or IDs in one of the most volatile places in the world. We need to be exceptionally careful because just one false step and we could be imprisoned, and no one would know where we are, or worse, I could be exposed as a woman in disguise and they could stone us to death since our sexuality and wearing men's clothes are strictly against the law here. Therefore, the point of the matter is... do we follow the smugglers to find out more about the central linchpin of the organization? Or do we try to get back home again?"

"Where I am concerned, I just want to get Gulab's sisters and the other little girls away from the men, but if we kept an eye on them and followed the truck to wherever they are going, we could gather as much intel as possible and then let the local law enforcement agencies and Interpol arrest the suspects," Sarah said. I was amazed at her strength and bravery. A lesser person would have given up by now. I was proud that she was my partner, my wife.

"Let us reach Herat and see where the clues lead us," I said.

Since the lock on the door was quite sturdy, I allowed myself and Sarah to sleep deeply after a substantial dinner of kababs and naan. We needed the rest, and we didn't know what was waiting for us in Herat, so we needed our wits to be as sharp as possible.

The next morning, we were rudely awoken before dawn by a loud knocking on the door. I signaled to Sarah to go into the bathroom while I looked out to see who it was. Jan Ali looked upset and kept knocking until I opened the door, and then he pushed his way into the room.

"I know you aren't Afghani; that is why I didn't ask for your identification yesterday. Unfortunately, someone saw you come to this hotel last night and they have alerted the authorities. They are coming to arrest you. Please get ready. I will show you a back way from where you can escape. Hurry up!"

"Why are you helping us?" I asked curiously.

"Not all Afghans agree with the present regime, and we know how cruel they can be. Once you and your wife are locked up, you will be lost to the world. No one will know whether you are dead or alive. Hurry up; they will be here soon!"

"Please wait outside. My wife needs to get ready as well. Just give us a few minutes," I told him. He nodded and went to wait for us in the corridor.

"Sarah! I think those men who were outside that seedy inn must have followed us yesterday. We need to hurry up and get to the bus station as soon as we can."

Sarah emerged from the bathroom already fully dressed. She had heard what Jan Ali was saying and was galvanized into action. I dressed while she packed our bags. I checked my beard in the mirror and saw that I just had to touch it up with a bit of glue, so we were both ready in record time.

We picked up our bags and looked out cautiously. Jan Ali was still waiting for us and was fidgeting restlessly.

"Come quick, follow me! There is a secret panel in the

room next door. It leads into a tunnel that opens in the market near the bus station. My father had it built at the beginning of the war because we had many foreign patrons in our inn who were stranded and the authorities tried to arrest them on false charges, just like they want to arrest you."

As we hurried along, we heard loud voices proclaiming that the people banging on the main door downstairs wanted to search the inn for "insurgents and spies." Jan Ali beckoned to us and literally shoved us into the room next door and locked the door behind us. The walls of this room were covered with beautifully polished walnut wood panels. He went to one in the right-hand corner and pushed a knot in the wood. The panel opened soundlessly, exposing a narrow corridor whose walls and floors were made of packed clay. It smelled musty, but we felt a breeze coming from somewhere so we were relieved that we wouldn't suffocate when we stepped in.

"Please hurry! If they catch me with you, I will also be arrested. Be careful and look through the little peep hole before you emerge at the end of the tunnel. The bus station will be just a few meters away. Allah be with you!" With that, he shoved us into the tunnel and quietly closed the panel with a firm click.

"There are torches on a shelf above you. Use them but leave them in the little alcove at the end of the tunnel," we heard him whisper before we heard the sound of his footsteps as he walked away.

"One of the men who were staring at us last night did look familiar, and I was wracking my brain thinking where I knew him from. It just occurred to me that he was one of

Farooq's men!" Sarah whispered. I groaned inwardly. When would we ever be free of this man? He was like a fungus that refused to go away.

There was no sound coming from the room we had just vacated. Jan Ali must have diverted the men from where we were. I reached up and fumbled around until I found a little shelf on which two powerful torches lay. I switched one of them on and looked around at where we were hidden. The tunnel sloped gently downwards. The packed earth was clever because it muffled our footsteps.

"Here, Sarah, take the other torch and let's go. Just try to be as quiet as you can. We don't know whether sounds travel from here."

We slowly made our way down the tunnel until we came to a sturdy locked door. Just at eye level was a small peephole covered by a black cloth. I drew the cloth aside and looked out. I could see most of the empty street. It wasn't yet completely light, so there were still shadows in the early morning light.

"What can you see?" asked Sarah. "Is the coast clear?"

"From what I can see, the door opens into a cul-de-sac. We can stay in the shadows till we reach the main road."

We waited a few more minutes to be sure that no one was there and then cautiously opened the door. The alley was deserted, but we heard the sounds of the city waking up in the next street.

"Let's go but be careful. Keep a look out for any strange people who look unusually interested in us." I grasped Sarah's hand and we flitted from shadow to shadow until we emerged onto a busy street.

"We are at the bus station!" Sarah sounded pleasantly surprised.

We looked around to make sure it was safe and then ran towards a bus that had Herat written on it. I gave our tickets to the driver and found the back seats vacant, so we sat there once more. By my calculations, we would see the mountains of Herat in the evening.

CHAPTER 10

"Courage: a perfect sensibility of the measure of danger, and a mental willingness to endure it." ~ William Tecumseh Sherman

SARAH

The swaying of the bus tried to lull me to sleep, but the occasional bumps over potholes and damaged, untarred roads would rudely wake me up. The landscape we passed by was nondescript and dry—we were passing hills and mountains that didn't have much vegetation, and the scenery remained relatively the same. The only thing that jarred on my empathic sensibilities was the sight of the occasional destroyed villages that were either abandoned or ransacked by a few people trying to salvage what they could from the smoldering wreckage. I was sitting near the window and I could lean on the wall to make myself comfortable. I didn't let go of Tanya's hand because I wanted to be reassured that I was safe. She didn't say anything, but, from the occasional squeeze of my hand, I knew she felt the same way.

The bus was too loud to have a conversation, and I wasn't allowed to talk anyway, so I ruminated inwards with my thoughts. What were we doing in this desolate and dangerous country? There was a war going on, for God's sake! When would we go back home? My feelings of disquiet were disturbing, but I knew that we had a task to fulfill before we could go home again. I thought of the babies, Dania and Hana, and my heart filled with a loving light. They should have reached the Pakistani border by then. Tanya and I looked forward to seeing them again and it was clear that they had finagled their way right into our hearts.

Just before I tried to hunker down and close my eyes again, I heard an anguished cry over the noise of the diesel engine from the woman sitting across from us. She had a baby in her arms and was shaking it and crying out loud, pleading it to wake up. Reacting to her plight, I hurriedly climbed over Tanya and went over to see what was wrong. The baby, a little boy of about fourteen months, was burning with high grade fever and his eyes were closed. He seemed unconscious, but his facial muscles and little fists were twitching gently. I came to the conclusion that he was on the verge of a full-fledged bout of febrile convulsions.

For the sake of our safety, Tanya had told me to act mute since I wasn't proficient in Pushto, so, keeping that in mind, I signed to her to tell the husband that I had medicine for the baby. Tanya had to talk to the husband because she was disguised as a man, and it wasn't culturally acceptable that she addressed the woman directly.

My medical bag held mostly medicines for adults. I

hadn't thought that we would need any pediatric medicine on our travels, but I rooted in the bag and found some paracetamol and valium tablets. Looking around to see what I could crush the tablets with, I saw that the woman had some cutlery sticking out of the front pocket of her bag, therefore I signaled to her to give me two of the spoons. I crushed the tablets between them and mixed the powder in a small quantity of water. Then I signed to the woman to feed the mixture to the baby in small sips.

"Strip the heavy clothes off the baby," Tanya told the father. She instinctively knew what I would have done and acted accordingly.

"Here, take this cloth, wet it, then wipe down the face, arms and legs of your baby," she instructed the parents while tearing a scarf into strips.

We monitored the little boy for about fifteen minutes, and I was happy to see that his fever was coming down and he was now sleeping peacefully, the valium having done its work to stop the impending convulsions while the paracetamol brought the fever down. I still needed to examine him, though, which I did without waking him up. Unfortunately, I discovered that he had an infected boil on the calf of his left leg. The skin around it was swollen, tender, and was an angry red in color due to the infection. No wonder the poor boy was restless and feverish. I signaled Tanya once more to show her that I wanted to put a dressing on the boil to keep it sterile and covered in case it burst during the journey.

"My wife would like to put some medicine and bandage the leg of your son. She thinks that the boil might burst soon and it's better that it is bandaged when that happens until you can show it to your doctor. The bus is not sterile, and his leg can get even more infected than it presently is if it is left open," Tanya explained.

After applying an ointment and a sterile bandage to the leg, I rummaged a bit more in my bag and found a vial of an antibiotic injection. Gauging the child's weight at ten kilos, I pulled the right dose from the vial into a disposable syringe and signed to the mother that I wanted to give the injection to the boy. She looked worried and glanced at her husband, presumably for permission.

Tanya realized her unease and spoke up. "This injection is an antibiotic. We will give the used vial to you so that you can show it to your doctor when you reach your destination," she told the father. "My wife cannot speak, but she is a good doctor and she has just saved your son's life."

The man thought for a moment and then nodded and told his wife to let me do whatever I needed to. The baby whimpered when I gave him the injection, but I was satisfied that the medicines we had given him were doing their work.

"Please take these tablets for your baby. You are to crush half of one of the white tablets, mix it with water, and give it to your son every four to six hours. It is to keep the fever down. If you feel that he is starting to twitch again like he did before, then crush this yellow tablet and give that to him. But remember; this tablet is to be given only if it is needed."

The father listened to Tanya attentively, then gave the tablets to his wife and explained to her very carefully what Tanya had said to him. He nodded in my direction, shook hands with Tanya, and thanked us both profusely, then settled down next to his wife. We were surprised that most of the other passengers had remained asleep and no one had bothered to know what was happening while we had this drama going on, which suited us fine because we didn't want to get unnecessarily noticed.

I was tired and tried to have a nap again while holding Tanya's hand for dear life. "I told you no medical side-bars." She laughed in my ear.

I just punched her arm and went to sleep while listening to her quiet chuckles.

Tanya

Sarah didn't go looking for trouble, but trouble seemed to find her in the strangest of places. We were relieved that the baby boy was stable and we were assured that he would be taken care of when the parents reached their destination.

Just like on our journey from Jalalabad to Kabul, we stopped at little roadside mosques when it was time for the mandatory midday and afternoon prayers.

It was already sunset when we stopped at a small hamlet just an hour away from Herat. As I prepared to go with the men into the mosque to pray, Sarah got off the bus as well.

"I would like to stretch my legs. My lower back and calves are starting to get a cramp." She picked up her medical bag with both of our backpacks and walked over to a grove of juniper trees that were about twenty meters away from the road. I watched as she set down our bags and started to wash her face in the little mountain stream that bubbled over the rocks there.

After assuring myself that she was safe, I went to play the drama of being a man again.

We were halfway through our prayers when we heard a high-pitched whistling sound and then a loud explosion. Then there was what could only be called the "sound of silence."

All of the men left the rituals of their prayers and ran out to see what had happened. We all stood in shock at what we saw. Our bus had been hit by a rocket missile and was now lying on its side. Most of the women and children who had been sitting in the bus were trapped in the smoldering inferno. Before we could do anything, we heard their desperate cries slowly fading away.

I looked around for Sarah and breathed a sigh of relief when I saw her and the sick boy's mother in the grove. They were sponging the little one, presumably to bring his fever down once more.

"Gulsanga! Gulsanga! Allah be praised!" the boy's father raced by me to reach his small family.

"Just a few minutes before the explosion, *Doctora* signaled to me to come and sit with her. She has saved our lives!" Gulsanga said tearfully as she hugged her son. "Allah bless you!" she said to Sarah.

After confirming that our families were safe, the baby's father and I ran back to the mosque and joined in with the other men, who had already formed a makeshift bucket parade where a motley collection of utensils were being used to fling either water or sand onto the burning bus. Even though we were certain that there were no survivors, we still wanted to lay the poor souls to rest. Some other people from a nearby village had also arrived just then and started to help out as well.

"I would suggest you let the bodies cool down before you bury them," said the man who had introduced himself as the chief of the nearby village. "Till then, come to our village and we will give you food and a place to stay. If you don't mind travelling at the back of a truck, anyone in a hurry to reach Herat can do so early in the morning after the collective funeral prayers of the deceased."

I went back to where Sarah was sitting. "Thank goodness we have our bags. If it weren't for the valuables we hid in them I might have left them on the bus," she said, visibly distressed. "Who did this? Why are they targeting innocent travelers, their own people?"

"You have to understand their history, Sarah. The Afghan war started when internal factions and tribes started to fight each other. The reasons why they began fighting are no longer important, and I am sure no one remembers what it was all about. It has become a pointedly useless fight with foreign governments coming in and 'helping' them whether they like it or not."

"I saw that on the news, but what did actually happen?" Saran wanted to know.

"The chaos historically started when the last Afghan king, Mohammed Zahir Shah, was exiled after his cousin, Mohammed Daoud Khan, took over after a coup to establish a republic. The USSR welcomed this shift to the left, but their delight soon faded as the authoritarian Daoud Khan refused to be a Soviet puppet. The communist People's Democratic Party of Afghanistan (PDPA) then overthrew Daoud Khan in what became known as the Saur Revolution." I took a deep breath and looked over at the burning bus while a strange feeling of melancholy spread over me. "Unfortunately, he and eighteen of his family members died in that coup. The Soviets found their foothold into Afghanistan and thought it would be like taking candy from a baby, but it snowballed from there with different factions or nationalities claiming sporadic victory while there was a mass exodus of refugees from the country which prevented any proper resistance or development from happening. That is when the Taliban reared its head and started to resist the 'foreigners' and influence the people by imposing a firm 'Islamic' dogma while forcing them to comply by their rules. That only increased the numbers of refugees worldwide, Pakistan taking the brunt of it all."

As we spoke, we noticed some unusual movement near the mosque and saw that a group of men were making their way towards us. They did not look friendly. Sarah suddenly clutched my arm and said, "One of those men is the one who was staring at us in Kabul! He is Farooq's man!"

They were still a short distance away, so we quietly picked up our bags and walked into the grove. We were just out of sight of the men when we heard an angry shout. "They are getting away!"

I tried not to push Sarah, but I did put a bit of pressure on the small of her back to indicate the urgency of getting away. We were stranded in an unknown place and I was now certain that it was Farooq's men who had attacked the bus.

As we crested a small hill, I crouched down so that I wouldn't be detected and looked towards the sun to get my bearings.

"The sun is nearly setting, so that's the west," I said. We

continued to hurry towards the sun since that was the approximate direction that would take us to Herat.

We found a cave by accident. Actually, Sarah did. She was adjusting her backpack and wanted to steady herself on an outcropping that was covered with vines.

"Oops! Help...Tanya!!" she yelled before she disappeared.

"Sarah! Where are you? Are you alright?"

"This place is amazing!" I heard her exclaim after a few seconds. "It's a hidden cave. Come on in; it's a perfect hideout until the men give up looking for us."

I lifted the vines and found that they covered the entrance to the cave. I tried to put the vines back just like they were before so that no one could find us.

As soon as I stepped into the cave I looked around and was amazed. It wasn't dark because light filtered through the vines in a greenish hue, giving it the appearance of being underwater. I estimated that it was about fifty meters in diameter, and there seemed to be a tunnel leading away from where we stood at the other end.

"Look at the walls! They are shining!" Sarah whispered excitedly.

The light from the entrance was reflecting off crystals that were embedded in the walls. It made our new temporary home look just like Aladdin's cave, but the best part was the pool of fresh water that was fed by a small mountain spring right in the middle of the cave.

"Let us wait before we get too comfortable," I said. "I want to be certain that the men don't find us before we set up our camp."

It made sense to spend the night in the cave because we weren't familiar with the area and could easily fall into a ravine or down a mountain in the dark. The other factor was that there was now a moon, which meant we could be easily detected no matter how careful we were. And yet, I had this feeling that we should move on. I took my revolver out from where I had hidden it in my clothes and sat near the entrance. By unspoken mutual agreement, neither of us spoke a word. After half an hour, we heard the men pass by.

"Let us go back; it is getting dark," said one of the men.

"Yes, we won't find them now, and if by any chance they don't fall in a ravine and make it to Herat, let Farooq deal with them."

Sarah and I looked at each other in shock. We thought that Farooq had taken his payment from the chief and had gone to Parachinar. Now I had a deep suspicion that the raid on the village could have been Farooq's doing as well. He was becoming more and more ruthless by the day.

As soon as we heard the men walk away, I signaled to Sarah to follow me. I didn't want to light a fire or speak in case the men were bluffing and hadn't left.

"Pick up your bags. I would like to check out that tunnel there. The bus driver said that we were about an hour away from Herat. If that is the case and the tunnel takes us towards the west, we might just be in the city sooner than we thought we would." I picked up my backpack and started to walk towards the dark tunnel.

Sarah looked worried. She hated dark places. "If the tunnel is a dead end, we will just come back and camp here," I tried to reassure her.

Once we were a few meters into the tunnel, I took out the torch from my bag and shone it on the ceiling and the walls. There were the same crystals embedded in the walls as there were in the main cave. Water dripped in a few places and there was a small stream that flowed along the direction of the tunnel.

"It seems to be going on. There is no dead end," whispered Sarah. She was right. Although the tunnel curved at a few places, the direction was more or less consistently west. That was confirmed by the small compass I had on my Swiss army knife.

We walked for a while, only stopping for a drink of water and a light meal of cheese and naan that Sarah had packed the night before into her bag. We were grateful that she had the foresight to do so since we had to leave so abruptly in the morning.

"When will we get out of this tunnel?" Sarah was getting frustrated, and to be honest, so was I. However, the air in the tunnel remained fresh, so I knew that we would come upon an exit soon. After a short while, I struck a match and saw that the flame flickered, indicating that there was a breeze. I lit another match to check where the breeze was coming from. We had come upon a fork in the tunnel and the flame indicated that the breeze was coming from the right-hand tunnel.

"I think we will be out of here very soon," I said to Sarah as I held her hand and pulled her along. "Come on, sweetheart, you are doing so well."

I didn't want to give her false hope by saying this adventure would soon be over, because I didn't know myself, but I could assure her that we were there for each other... no matter what. Always and forever.

CHAPTER 11

"Hope is like the sun, which, as we journey toward it, casts the shadow of our burden behind us." ~ Samuel Smiles

SARAH

I hate the dark. My fear probably goes back to the time when my kindergarten teacher locked me in the cupboard under the stairs. I just remember being terrified because there wasn't even a sliver of light as the blackness enveloped me, but I also remember what a stubborn little thing I was and refused to shed even one tear. I didn't want the cruel teacher to know how much the punishment had affected me. I drew upon that same stubbornness as I followed Tanya down that dark, dank tunnel. The only relief I had was my firm hold on the back of Tanya's jacket and the weak beams of light from our torches.

"From that pile of rocks there, I believe we have reached the end of the tunnel," Tanya finally said after what felt like an eternity in the dark. "We can feel the breeze coming from somewhere, so I am sure that we just have to dig a little bit and then we are out of here," she went on.

"Do you think we could see better if we waited for daylight? I mean, we could then investigate where the breeze is coming from." I was tired and grumpy, and I wasn't in the mood to dig our way out of the tunnel even though the darkness still taunted me.

"We would make quite a spectacle if we emerged from the mountainside in the morning and in the middle of a market." Tanya laughed. I could imagine a cartoon video clip where the characters emerged from a tunnel in front of strangers, and everyone stared at them in surprise. While people decided how to accost them, the characters calmly dusted themselves off, took a couple of self-conscious steps and hops, looked around, and then ran off Charlie Chaplin style. The picture was so vivid in my mind that I started to giggle.

Tanya gave me a strange look and picked up a flat stone to start digging at the pile of earth and stones that blocked the exit. I shone my torch around until I found another similar stone and started to help her.

"The earth is soft and easy to dig," I observed as we used our makeshift spades.

"The block could be recent, maybe because of an earthquake or an explosion," Tanya said, getting breathless with the effort.

It didn't take us long to dig through. We cautiously looked out and saw that the coast was clear, so we hauled ourselves out of the opening we had made and dusted ourselves off. Tanya then covered it with a rusty discarded billboard that was conveniently lying there.

Finally, we looked around and saw that we were in a secluded area of what we considered to be the outskirts of a town.

"How do we know that this is Herat?" I asked.

"It is the only large town in the area, and look over there! You can see the historical Musalla Minarets of Herat."

"Musalla Minarets? I just see some ruined towers," I said as I peered upwards to try to focus on the ruins.

"It seems you need a little history lesson," said Tanya with a smile. "The Musalla Minarets are five ruined minarets which are what remains of the twenty original minarets of the Musalla Complex built by Queen Gawhar Shad in 1417. Actually, history books say that they resemble crooked chimneys of an old factory."

"From their height and size, I would imagine that the complex must have been grand," I said while feeling that familiar twinge of melancholy when I thought of people and eras of the past.

"Well, we know now that we are in Herat, and we must plan our next move. It's nearly dawn, so we won't look strange if we have our breakfast in one of the roadside cafés. Afterwards, we might find some information about the addresses in Gulab's father's notebook."

My growling tummy agreed with the plan. Tanya couldn't see my smile since I had once again covered myself with the *burqa*, but I saw her amused look and I lightly pinched her arm.

The town was waking up while we walked in the streets looking for a place where we could sit and have a proper breakfast. The cheese and naan that we had eaten the night before were not enough considering the physical activity we had since undergone.

"Have you noticed that the people here speak predominantly Farsi?" I asked.

"Yes. We are near the Iranian border, and the people tend to favor Farsi instead of Pushto," Tanya replied.

"Will you be able to manage?" I was worried for her. Her Pushto was good, but I didn't know the extent of her Farsi vocabulary.

"I also studied Farsi at the academy, and if they think my accent is weird, I will just say we are from the mountains near Jalalabad and speak Pushto most of the time."

Clever. But then Tanya was very clever. I learned more of her capabilities every day, and I was always very impressed with my partner, especially as I could now see her working as an Interpol agent. She was amazing.

We found a small café where a young boy had just swept the shoulder of the road in front and was setting out scuffed wooden tables and chairs. Tanya pointed to a table inside and in the back of the café and raised her eyebrows in an unspoken question which the boy answered by waving us towards it. He came over with an aluminum jug filled with water and two tumblers and put them down in front to us.

"What can you give us for breakfast?" Tanya asked him in Farsi.

"We have omelets, vegetables, and naan. You can have tea or milk with that," he said quickly as if by rote.

Tanya smiled and told him to bring two omelets, one with and one without chilis, as well as one naan. She also asked him to bring us some tea after we had finished eating.

"Only one naan?" I pouted. I was hungry and she ordered just ONE blinking naan?

"Calm down, Sarah." Tanya couldn't stop laughing. "You won't go hungry; I promise you that." I was sure I would be deprived and hungry. Tanya kept snickering and shaking her head while I sulked, and she laughed outright when the boy put an immense naan in front of us. It must have been nearly a meter long!

"Now, do you believe me? I would never starve you," exclaimed Tanya while wiping the tears of mirth from her eyes.

"Hmph!" I said and started the tedious task of eating with a *burqa* on while trying not reveal my face—it was a formidable task.

We were halfway through our surprisingly tasty meal when there was an explosion nearby. Tanya pulled me under the table and signaled that I should stay down. She also hunkered down with me but looked occasionally over the top to see what was happening. I heard the sounds of chaos —people running around and the frightened, heartrending cries of women and children.

After a short while, I peeped over the table and looked towards the entrance, where, to my horror, I saw the inert body of the boy who just moment ago had served us our breakfast. I stared at him, willing him to get up, thinking it was too late, when he suddenly took a deep shuddering breath. Before Tanya could stop me, I shed the constricting burqa and crawled over to the boy. He was conscious but had a large piece of shrapnel lodged in his upper thigh. From the bright red color of the blood, I was certain that it had hit an artery, but it was fortunate that the boy wasn't hemorrhaging that much, since the fragment was applying pressure to the wound. The situation would become critical when we tried to remove the shrapnel. He could bleed out rapidly and die from this injury. I just couldn't leave him there; I had to do something, and fast.

Tanya heaved a long-suffering sigh, crawled over, and helped me pull the boy to the shelter of two overturned tables. I tied a tourniquet around his leg with a kitchen towel I found nearby and opened my trusty medical bag. I was glad that I had packed surgical instruments and sutures. I cut off the boy's pants and started to clean the wound with disinfectant. Now that the blood had stopped due to the tourniquet, I needed to work quickly. If I stop the blood flow to the lower limb for a longer while, I was concerned that he might get gangrene. After I sedated the boy, Tanya held him as I gently removed the shrapnel and sutured the ruptured arteries and damaged muscles. Every few minutes we loosened the tourniquet, but even though it was messy without a proper suction machine and other instruments, I managed to stop the bleeding, and his pink toes confirmed that there was adequate blood circulating to them.

We made the boy as comfortable as we could and repacked our bags. Tanya went to the entrance of the café and peered around the corner. The streets were empty now, but she saw some men run and climb into a battered car just a few meters away.

"The man driving the car looked eerily like Farooq!" she exclaimed. "Are you finished here? Can we leave? I have a bad feeling about all this, and I think that Farooq knew that we were here in this café all along, and that is why it was attacked. We need to find a safe place to stay and then we will have to stake out the addresses in Gulab's father's notebook." Tanya pulled me up and helped me wear the *burqa* once more.

By now, the owners of the café had returned from where they had been hiding and a distraught woman was kneeling near the injured boy, stroking his head while talking softly to him. When she lifted her tear-streaked face and saw me, she came over and hugged me while thanking me profusely in Farsi and Pushto. When we tried to pay for our meal, they waved our money away and said that anytime we wanted to eat at their café it would be on the house.

Tanya had to pull me away because the woman was still talking and trying to feed us some more. I politely extricated myself from her grasp, thanked her, and ran after Tanya as she resolutely strode out of the café.

Tanya

Of all the horrible, inconsiderate, callous... horrible... did I already say horrible? Well, this warranted saying it twice. Farooq was the dregs of humanity. He had taken the mantle of a terrorist for his own personal gain, and he could do it with ease because he was in a war-torn country, so anything out of the ordinary could and would be blamed on the enemy. His hands were covered in blood and he didn't care.

"What is that sociopath up to?" Sarah was upset. "He has killed so many people, and that too in front of us... God help the poor babies he has kidnapped. They aren't human beings, but just 'cargo' for him."

I grunted and kept my eyes open as we flitted from shadow to shadow in the streets. Some road signs were still intact and could be easily followed, while others were either missing or damaged. My frustration was growing, and we were nowhere near finding where the children were hidden.

I was tired and was nearly at the end of my tether, and then a man with a scruffy face and Afghan clothes approached us from one of the side-streets. My hair stood on end and I went into protective mode as I pushed Sarah behind me and put my hand on the hilt of my gun in case this man tried to attack us. However, before I could say or do anything, he held up his hands with his palms out towards me in the universal gesture of surrender or peace.

"Agent Kareem! Tanya! Relax. It's me, Andy!"

It was such a relief to hear his voice! "Andy! What are you doing here? I didn't recognize you! How did you get here and how did you find us?"

"So many questions," laughed Andy. "Let me get you both to our safe house and then I will tell you everything, but we need to get off the streets as soon as we can. It's not safe for any of us." He smiled ruefully and motioned for us to follow him.

Sarah leaned against me in relief. "Oh, thank God, a friendly person!"

Andy led us to a nondescript house in a narrow street. I

wouldn't have thought that there was a safe house there, but that was the whole idea, wasn't it? To keep a low profile.

Inside the house was a different story. It was fitted out with all possible modern equipment, from surveillance tools to computers. There was a well-appointed kitchen and the bedrooms had comfortable beds and en-suite showers with running hot and cold water. To our tired eyes, it looked like a luxurious spa.

As we entered the house, we met a man with distinctive Mediterranean looks who was wearing headphones and looking intently at one of the computers. When he saw us, he immediately got up and introduced himself. "My name is Yiannis. I am glad Andy finally got hold of you. We've been tracking you from Kabul, but you've cleverly eluded us. I must say you ladies are quite good at what you do." He laughed heartily and extended his hand to shake mine.

"Before we say or do anything, I would like you to have a look at the addresses in this notebook. I believe they are the key to finding out who the puppet master is in this whole smuggling ring." I handed the notebook to Andy, who started leafing through it.

"This is amazing, Tanya! Yiannis is the expert on Urdu, Pushto, and Arabic script, and he will have a look at the notebook. I am sure this is a font of information. Well done!" Andy sounded pleasantly surprised. "We have a change of clothes for both of you in one of the bedrooms. I took the liberty of buying a few things in your sizes. I hope you like them, because this is the first time I have ever shopped for women," he said. "I would suggest that you clean up; I bought some toiletries as well. You do smell oddly like cows..." He laughed at his own joke.

"It's not even funny, Andy! We do smell, and we agree that we need to clean up before we can even think of sitting in polite company." I winked and grinned at Sarah's outraged face.

We were relieved to finally close the door of the bedroom we were ushered into since we certainly were scruffy and exhausted after our night in the tunnel.

"You go and have a shower first and then I will have mine," I told Sarah.

"This shower is big enough for both of us," she said in a sultry voice and with a seductive smile.

"Believe me, my love, there is nothing I would like better than to join you, but we have two people in the house who might hear us, and I want to learn from them what is happening with Farooq and the smugglers without being embarrassed." I smiled. "When we have the luxury of time and privacy, I will be all yours. I promise you that."

Sarah pouted, but then she smiled and went into the bathroom for her solitary shower. I looked longingly at the closed door and wished we could have shared the shower, but now wasn't the time.

Once we were clean and wearing the jeans and t-shirts that surprisingly fitted us well, we found Andy and Yiannis in the kitchen.

Andy was peeling potatoes and Yiannis was using a wooden spoon to stir something in a pot from which the most heavenly of smells wafted out. He seemed very comfortable in the kitchen as he skillfully layered meat, potatoes, and eggplants with a fragrant sauce in a tempered glass dish and put it in the oven to bake. "I am making moussaka just like my mother taught me," he said as he proudly puffed his chest out. "Andy, give the ladies something to drink... I was told that you are teetotalers, so I have made a jug of iced tea for you."

"That was very thoughtful. Thank you," said Sarah as she sat down at the table.

Andy poured us two large glasses of iced tea, and also one for himself and Yiannis. He pulled up a chair and sat down with us.

"So far, the intel we have is not much different than what you have. Farooq seems to be the main smuggler for this area, and I believe his reach covers the Middle East. It would seem that he swoops in where there is a disaster and 'harvests' the children from there. More often than not, the parents are either dead or so injured that they are not aware of what is happening, but from the notebook that you gave us earlier, we have deciphered a few addresses here in Afghanistan, Iran, Turkey, and Eastern Europe. We think that the people we are looking for might be in one of these countries."

"That is exactly what I thought when I saw the addresses. I couldn't read them very well, but that was what I garnered from them." I was excited that the notebook was just as valuable as I thought it would be.

"Let us eat, then you ladies go to sleep. You look exhausted. In the meantime, we will look more closely at the notebook and plan our next move."

The moussaka was delicious, and we ate until we couldn't eat anymore. Finally, with a polite burp and a yawn, we stood up and went back into our room.

The bed was immense and had a duvet, crisp sheets, and fluffy pillows... heavenly! We undressed and fell asleep as soon as our heads touched the pillows, and didn't wake up until we saw the morning sunlight filter into the room heralding the new day. We had slept the whole day and night away. We were exhausted, and our deep sleep, while we were closely intertwined, was precious since we were in a safe place. Now we were ready for the next phase of our investigations.

CHAPTER 12

"This journey of Life is for those who are guided by their inner consciousness." ~ Malika E. Nura

SARAH

I was feeling so comfortable. The bed I was sleeping in was a haven from the cruel outside world and I didn't feel like emerging from my temporary cocoon. I was surprised that Tanya was still fast asleep. She must have been exhausted, even though she rarely complained. I tried to snuggle down into the comforter and go back to sleep, but my traitorous tummy started to growl in indignation.

"The beast awakens," laughed Tanya sleepily, her eyes still closed.

"I wonder what the time is, but I must confess I feel hungry," I said, mildly embarrassed at my bodily protests.

"Haha, you think?" Tanya gave me a playful poke. We were just starting to wrestle each other when we heard a knock on the door.

"Breakfast will be ready in fifteen minutes. Get ready and come; there is a lot to do today!" Andy called out.

We jumped out of the bed and while I straightened it, Tanya went first to use the bathroom.

As soon as we were ready, we went to the kitchen. Yiannis had cooked once more, and what a spread! There were three types of bread as well as eggs and fried potatoes. Just looking at the food caused my tummy to sing its growly hungry song again.

"Here, Sarah, I think you should start before your stomach jumps out and bites me." Yiannis laughed. Tanya giggled in the corner and Yiannis rolled his eyes as he broke some more eggs into the frying pan.

Just as Yiannis abruptly turned, the spout of the kettle that was boiling on the stove caught his sleeve. We looked on in morbid fascination as the kettle flipped over in the air and splashed the boiling water over his right hand and arm.

"Yiannis!" I shouted in alarm. "Put your hand and arm under the cold-water tap."

He stood there with pain contorting his face and didn't move. He was clearly in shock. I hurried across the room and pulled him by his uninjured arm towards the sink and ran the cold water over the burn blisters that were already forming.

"Do we have to pop the blisters before we apply any dressing?" asked Andy.

"Oh, no! Never do that!" I exclaimed. "You should never try to pop a burn blister, because they are the body's way of protecting the underlying skin while it heals, so popping them can cause infection and slow down the healing process. However, if a blister pops on its own, we shouldn't peel off the skin, but just keep the area clean and covered." I sounded like a teacher lecturing her students, so with a laugh, I turned back to tend to Yiannis.

"Do you have any antibiotic cream?" asked Tanya.

"Yes, I do, but I will have to look for it. For now, let us put some honey on the blisters once the pain subsides. Applying honey over the burn can help sterilize the area and prevent infection. It may also soothe Yiannis's burned skin."

"I heard somewhere if you cover the burns with cling-film it also helps," Andy said, desperately wanting to be helpful.

"Good idea." I smiled. Andy turned to rummage in one of the kitchen cupboards and brought out a new roll of cling film. I cut off a few squares and gently applied them over the honey covered blisters.

"We have some ibuprofen; would that help for the pain?" asked Tanya.

"Yes, please, give me some," said Yiannis, who finally spoke after being quiet for a while.

Tanya brought my medic bag to the kitchen and found the ibuprofen. She shook out two tablets from the bottle and gave them to Yiannis with a glass of orange juice.

I also found a tube of antibiotic cream in the bag. "You can apply this on your burns tomorrow. For now, just take the painkillers and drink lots of fluids," I instructed.

"Sit down, Yiannis; you are looking pale. Sarah and I will

finish getting breakfast ready and we will clean up afterwards."

"I am all right," he said gruffly. "I need to brief you all what I did this morning. I don't have time to rest."

"Don't argue. Just rest a while; you have had a shock. We will all talk after we have eaten." I tried to speak in a strict schoolteacher voice, but I spoiled the effect by giggling at the end.

Breakfast was delicious and we cleaned up afterwards in record time to finally sit down and hear what Yiannis had to say that would affect our plans for our next move.

Tanya

After the dramatic medical sidebar, which Sarah handled with her usual aplomb, we sat down at the kitchen table to brainstorm.

"Unfortunately, there is no one at the addresses you have given me," Yiannis said. "I went there early in the morning to see whether anything was happening. The surrounding area had fresh tire marks made by heavy vehicles, probably trucks. I stayed a while looking around for some more clues but didn't find any. The windows of the building were shuttered, and the doors were locked. After a while, a young boy came up to me and asked what I was doing. So, on a hunch, I bluffed... I told him that I came from Kabul and wanted to speak to Dr. Farooq. I also emphasized that he had given me that address and had told me to meet him there."

"That was clever of you," said Sarah. "What did he say then?"

"Well, he told me that I had just missed him since he had left two hours before for Mashhad, and he wouldn't be back for another two weeks. He also asked me if I wanted to leave a message for him." Yiannis smiled. "I told him that it wasn't urgent and that I would be back again next month."

"Well, that is unfortunate. I think Farooq sensed that we are getting closer, so he left earlier than planned," I said. "Do we have an address for him in Mashhad, Andy?"

Andy handed the notebook to Yiannis, who leafed through it. He let out a triumphant whoop and showed an address to us.

"This is near the shrine of Imam Reza in Mashhad, where many acolytes come from far and wide to pray and to pay homage to the eighth Shiite Imam buried there. It's a very prominent landmark and not difficult to find, so if we leave soon, we might catch Farooq red-handed," I said. We were so close and yet so far away. Farooq had to be taken into custody as soon as we could catch him. The havoc he was creating had to be stopped and the poor children needed to be rescued. They had to be feeling wretched while they were being carted around in rough conditions in the uncomfortable trucks. Who was looking after them? Did Farooq employ any women to help them? Or were they left at the mercy of the rough men? I fervently hoped it was the former rather than the latter.

"Well, Iran, here we come," sang out Sarah, trying to lighten the atmosphere.

"I wanted Yiannis to go with you since he looks like a local with his dark hair and olive skin, but now that he is temporarily out of commission with his burns, you will have to go to Mashhad with Sarah." Andy sounded upset. "I really would prefer to go along with you, but we are monitoring two other terrorist groups and we would have to dismantle the safe house and all of its expensive equipment if one of us left. Even though Yiannis is injured, I am grateful to have his help. Unfortunately, our mission here is a two-man job, and we have gone too far ahead to abandon everything now."

"We can manage," I said dismissively.

"I don't want you to just 'manage'!" he said vehemently. "You do realize that Sarah is not an agent like us, and we are repeatedly putting her, a civilian, in danger. She has to leave for England as soon as it is safe and possible."

I was stunned. I had enjoyed working with Sarah and she was holding up so well in the various situations and scenarios thrown at her that I hadn't given her official status much thought, which I agreed with Andy, was quite reckless.

"I don't mind being here with you," said Sarah in a small voice.

"That is true, but..." Andy was starting to get annoyed. "Sarah, you were recruited by Interpol to gather information while working in a more or less safe environment. You weren't supposed to leave Pakistan at all or to be thrown into the experiences you've had these past few days."

Sarah looked dazed. "I was just grateful that I was with Tanya and that we could support each other in times of danger."

Andy looked at her with a mixture of exasperation and admiration, and then turned to me.

"The British High Commission is unfortunately still

closed in Tehran, so Sarah will be your responsibility until you reach Turkey. She can't travel with an Iranian passport to England, which is the only one we can get for both of you just now, because she would need visas for the UK and any other countries visited."

"You foresee that we will travel to Turkey?" I asked.

"You never know with Farooq. Even if you manage to pinpoint his whereabouts in Iran, you might still have to follow him to Turkey and even so far as to Europe. You have to keep all of your options open."

We were all quiet for a while, each one of us lost in our own thoughts trying to find a solution to the situation we were all in.

"You need to use a disguise again, Tanya, because, even though they aren't as bad as the Taliban here, the government of Iran does strictly adhere to Islamic rules, one of which is that they still frown upon women travelling alone." Andy stood up to examine my roughened skin where I had previously glued on my beard. "Iranian men have a shorter beards, or just a stubble, and they wear European suits without ties. Your skin has had a slight reaction to the glue you have used, so we will have to work on creating a believable five o'clock shadow for you." Andy's eyes twinkled as he tried to suppress his laughter.

"Why don't they wear neckties if they are wearing European clothes?" asked Sarah. I knew she wanted to distract Andy because she realized that his giggling was getting on my nerves.

"After Iran's Islamic Revolution in 1979, which was spearheaded by Ayatollah Khomeini, the government banned the wearing and sale of neckties as they were considered decadent and un-Islamic. Some even thought they were 'symbols of the cross' or a sartorial marker of Western subjugation under the rule of the secular Pahlavi monarchy," Andy explained. "Anyone who wants to do business or visit Iran nowadays are advised to leave their neckties at home."

"It is strange that even in these modern times people hang on to symbolism and superstitions," Sarah said absently while doodling on a paper napkin.

"At least you won't have to wear that heavy, smelly *burqa* anymore," Andy said.

"What will I wear then?" asked Sarah curiously.

"You have a choice," said Andy. "The women in Eastern Iran usually wear jeans or tailored slacks with long tops, but they cover themselves with a solid black or printed *chador*, which is a full-body-length semicircle of fabric that is open down the front. It can be pulled over the head and is held closed at the front by the wearer."

"The closer you get to the West you will notice that the women wear cotton coats and cover their heads with colorful silk or cotton scarves," I finished for him.

"Since we need to be disguised, I would choose to wear the *chador*," said Sarah.

"That is exactly what I thought, and I have bought two of them for you," said Andy. The jeans and t-shirts he had also bought for us would be suitable as well as comfortable for Sarah to travel in, but he was going to buy a man's suit for me as soon as we finished our brainstorming.

"Both of you go to the shrine in Mashhad. We have a man there who will contact you and help you move around the city," said Andy. "I know your Farsi is good, Tanya, but you might be caught because of your accent, so it is better that you have someone local helping you out."

"That is a good idea. Since Yiannis can't come with us, I guess that's the next best option."

Andy left soon after breakfast to go shopping for me. Yiannis started to translate the addresses and enter them into a small black notebook for us. In the meantime, Sarah and I cleaned up the kitchen after which we found the *chadors* and I made Sarah try them on so that she would be comfortable in them when we traveled. It was a bit awkward for her initially, but since she had worn a variation of the *chador* in Pakistan a few times, she caught on quickly on how to drape and keep it secure without it flopping over the place.

Andy came back within an hour. He had one polyester and one woolen suit with him. They were not very well made, but then we had decided to present ourselves as middle-class people, so they were appropriate. I tried the polyester suit and one of the collarless shirts that came along with it, and I was pleased to see that it fitted quite well. The only thing that looked odd was that, even though I wasn't that well-endowed, I still looked distinctly womanly.

Andy saw my predicament and started to laugh. He reached into his shopping bag and pulled out two broad crepe bandages. He lobbed them over to me, and I looked at him with a raised questioning eyebrow.

"You know what to do!" he exclaimed, trying unsuccessfully to keep the mirth out of his voice. "Go into the bedroom and ask Sarah to help you bind your 'attributes.' Then come back out so I can experiment with a few make up techniques to turn you into a pretty boy."

Grumbling under my breath and cursing seven

generations of Andy's family, I grabbed Sarah's hand and stalked into the bedroom.

Sarah took the bandages out of their wrapping and indicated that I had to put off my jacket and shirt.

"Take off your bra, love, or the straps might show and the buckles could press into you, making you uncomfortable." Sarah could not hide her smile as I became grumpier and grumpier. "You look like a two-year-old who wants candy and didn't get it." She laughed and promptly kissed me on my lips just as they were curling into a sulky pout.

"I know that I have to do this, but that doesn't mean that I have to like it." I continued to act like a sulky child and Sarah couldn't stop laughing. "Well, I am glad at least one of us is amused," I said as I shed my clothes and held my arms out to let Sarah wind the crepe bandage firmly over my torso.

"Are you comfortable? I hope it's not too tight." Sarah looked worried. I smiled at her, mildly ashamed of my small tantrum. She had done a good job, especially avoiding unnecessary pressure under my armpits, where the bandage would have chaffed if it hadn't been applied properly.

"I am quite comfortable. Did you learn this in medical college as well?" I laughed.

"As a matter of fact, I did," she said, to my surprise. I was just trying to act smart, and it turned out that she knew what she was doing. "We use crepe bandages not only to bind ribs but also as pressure bandages after surgeries, especially breast surgery." Wow, one lives and learns. I was becoming smarter by osmosis just by being with Sarah.

"Thank you, sweetheart. Now let me put on the rest of

my 'man' clothes and let's get on with the rest of the transformation." When I looked in the mirror, if not my face, at least my body now looked male.

"Ah, there you are! It's about time. We need to get your make up done."

"Where is Yiannis?" asked Sarah.

"We have paid someone to make fake passports for you. He has gone to fetch them since he was the only one who knew where the forgers lived." Andy looked a little shamefaced because he was aware that Yiannis was in pain. "We have arranged for two passports each, one Iranian and one Turkish. Unfortunately, like I mentioned before, since the British High Commission in Tehran hasn't reopened, we can't get you copies of your original ones. However, I won't give you any papers in case you are discovered, but if it comes to the point that you have to travel to Turkey, there will be other Interpol colleagues contacting you in Ankara and they will help you get new British passports."

"Will you and Yiannis be safe while we are gone?" I was concerned for their safety.

"We will stay here and keep an eye on Farooq's addresses, as well as monitor our other projects to see if there is any unusual activity within the two groups we have been assigned to gather data from. Only if it becomes absolutely necessary, will we come to meet you in either Mashhad or Tehran, wherever you are by then," he said with regret. "If we dismantle all the equipment and close down this safe house, we will lose months of data, and we wouldn't know where to store the everything. It is convenient that you two go ahead as planned even though Sarah isn't an official agent. We will be informed of your whereabouts by our Interpol liaisons."

I nodded, completely understanding his reasoning and agreeing with the plan.

"Okay then, let's turn you into a handsome, young man," Andy said with a smile as he made me sit down on a chair in the kitchen. To my surprise, there was a palette of strange cosmetics and a couple of wigs on the table.

"Sarah, can you brush and pin Tanya's hair back and then put this stocking cap firmly on her head, please?" Andy was all business now and proceeded to work on my face as soon as Sarah completed the requested task.

He left most of my skin make up free, but I felt he was brushing my eyebrows and he used a strange sponge on my chin and the side of my face.

"What are you doing?" I was curious because I wanted to learn how to touch up my face if I needed to do it later on.

"Don't worry, I will show you what I am doing when I am finished, *and* I will also instruct you how to do it," he said when he saw me open my mouth to speak.

After about ten minutes, he showed me what he had done in a handheld mirror.

"That's amazing! I didn't know you were an artist, Andy!" I was surprised at the transformation. I had a five o'clock shadow and bushy eyebrows—not too bushy, but they looked as if I had never shaped them. That gave a distinctively masculine look to my face. I was shocked to see the image of my brother looking out at me from the mirror!

"Sarah, hand me that short wig, please." Andy held out his hand as she gave it to him. He tugged it onto the stocking cap that I wore and then fussed about the edges until he was satisfied at what he saw. Once more he showed me the mirror. This time the transformation was complete. I had a very short hairstyle that was stereotypically what Iranian men sported. If I didn't know better, I would have believed that my reflection was that of a man from that country!

"Here, take this." Andy handed me a pouch with a stippling sponge and a small makeup pot containing a dark brown cream. "I have also added some extra eyebrows and glue in case the ones you have are damaged or fall off."

Just then Yiannis walked in and did a double take. "For a moment I thought you were someone else." He smiled. "Well done, Andy!"

Andy gave a mock bow and we all started to laugh, though I think it was more because we were nervous than amused by his antics.

"I just need to take your photos for the passports and then I will affix them. I have brought the embossing stamp from our local 'artiste' who made these passports for us. I have promised to bring it back as soon as I am done." Yiannis bustled about and brought a camera from the living room and made us stand in front of a white background, which in this case was the kitchen wall, and took a few photos of us, all the while reminding Sarah to look serious because whenever she looked at me, she would start to giggle. Once he was satisfied, he went to his room, where he had converted the bathroom into a dark room to develop the photos.

We looked strange in the photos, not like ourselves at all, but now that the passports were ready, we were raring to go.

"How will we travel to Mashhad?" asked Sarah.

"We have created an identity for Tanya as an Iranian archeologist, Cyrus Kareem, who came to examine the Musalla minarets with the future intent of restoring them.

You are on record as his wife, Fariba Kareem. We have a Pars Khodro car registered in your name, and you will be driving it across the border and while you are in Iran."

"Pars Khodro? Do they still manufacture these cars in Iran?" I was intrigued. How did the Khomeini government allow 'infidels' to still manufacture anything in their country? From what I understood, they were prototypes from a popular Japanese car manufacturing company. Apparently, they were also licensed by General Motors (GM) for some of their products.

"Not anymore," said Yiannis. "The last car manufactured by them was nearly two years ago, but a local company took up the brand and the cars are still called by the same name, though I heard that they were going to change that soon. The one we have for you is about two years old and drives well. We have equipped it with canned and dry goods, and we have also put a tent and sleeping bags in the trunk in the eventuality that you have to sleep outdoors. It's always better to be prepared." He grinned. "There is also a cooler with fruit, sandwiches, water and cold drinks for your journey."

"You have thought of everything, except how I will transport my gun over the border..."

"Our man in Mashhad will give it to you. It would be dangerous if you carried it yourself over the border. We have placed a knife in the cooler with the fruit, and once you have crossed the border, you can keep that close to you."

They really had thought of everything!

"Oh, yes, one more thing..." Yiannis handed me a packet of papers that seemed to have been folded and unfolded many times so that they looked a bit frayed. "This is the carnet de passages for your car. You will need it at the border."

"Carnet de passages? What is that?" I hadn't heard of such a strange sounding document before.

"The Carnet de Passages en Douane is a customs document that identifies a traveler's motor vehicle or other valuable equipment. It is like your car's passport and is required in order to take a motor vehicle into a significant number of countries around the world," explained Andy.

Well, it seemed we were ready for the next stage of our adventure. Sarah quickly went to change into her "Iranian clothes" and presented herself for inspection in front of us. We all gave her a thumbs up and finally left the house. At the back of the house, there was a dark blue SUV which was slightly scratched and had a few dents, but when I started it I realized that the engine had been souped up and I was confident that it was reliable.

"See you on the other side." I said to the men as we shook hands. We were on our way.

CHAPTER 13

"If it were easy, it would not be any fun." ~ T. Jay Taylor

SARAH

We were off to Iran. We had this false sense of security because of our disguises and the car we were driving, but the litmus test would be when we got through the passport control at the border.

"There is a map in the glove compartment; can you check our route? I don't want to miss any turnings. Believe me when I say that I have had enough of this country." Tanya spoke while concentrating on the road. Unlike England and Pakistan, everyone here drove on the right-hand side instead of the left; therefore, until she was used to it, she wanted to be careful and not unconsciously drift to the other side.

"We have to follow the road we are on to a border town called Islam Qala, where they have the overland passport control, and then from there we will travel to Taybad, which is the closest town on the other side near the border in Iran."

Tanya nodded indicating that she had heard me, all the while keeping her eyes on the road.

"Oh, listen to this!" I said excitedly as I read a footnote on the map. "Did you know that the road we are on is part of the Asian Highway Network? Apparently, it starts in Tokyo and then winds via Istanbul until it connects with a major highway that ends in Lisbon! How cool is that?" Since we were travelling on relatively unknown roads for the next couple of days, I wanted to learn as much as I could about the places we were going to visit. Maybe I would write everything down in my journal... No, not then, but I would write down everything once we got home. For now, it could be a security risk if my journal landed in enemy hands.

"Andy said it was a ninety-minute drive to the border, so why don't you lower the back of your seat and have a nap?" said Tanya. "When we reach Iran, if I am tired, I will ask you to drive for a little while."

"Are women allowed to drive in Iran?" I was intrigued. After seeing how women were suppressed in Afghanistan, I wondered how they were treated in Iran after the revolution.

"Yes, they are. Even though Islamic laws are strict in Iran, women have some sort of freedom and are allowed to drive, though many with chaperones. And I heard they are slowly softening their stance on that as well." Tanya gave me a quick look and a smile. "Especially for professional women like doctors."

"Hmmm..." I murmured. I was already lulled to sleep by the movement of the car. I had chosen a black chador with very small white daisies printed on it. It was big enough for me to cover my face to block out the sunlight as I slept. When I drew the chador over my head, I heard Tanya chuckle. "No need to laugh at me; I am just being the good little Iranian wifey," I said in a whimsical voice. The last I heard before I fell asleep was Tanya's belly laugh.

It seemed I had just closed my eyes when I felt the car slow down and then stop with a jerk. I opened my eyes and asked Tanya why we were stopping. "Have we already reached the border?"

"No, my love. Stay in the car and don't say anything, and I will go and find out what is wrong," she said before she stepped out of the car.

I kept my face covered by the chador, but I peeked out to see what was happening.

There was an overturned donkey cart in the middle of the road. A burqa-clad woman was sitting a small distance away on a little mound on the roadside with a baby in her arms. Tanya was talking to the man, who was gesticulating wildly as he told his tale.

Tanya came back to the car and gestured to roll down the window so that she could talk to me.

"The man says that a couple of trucks passed by at high speed and when he tried to avoid them, his cart tipped over and spilled his sacks of wheat. His wife also fell down. He says she wasn't injured, but they were on their way to the hospital because it seems that the baby is not well," she explained.

"And you want me to have a look at the baby while you help the man reload his cart?" I said with a laugh.

Tanya winked at me, smiled, and then went to help the man. I got out of the car and took my medic bag from the trunk. I walked to the young mother, who sat silently on her knoll while trying to rock her baby.

"*Asalam alaikum!*" I greeted her. "May I have a look at your baby? I hear that it's not feeling well," I said in Pushto. Since the Afghans here spoke Farsi with only a slight understanding of Pushto, my broken grasp of the language wasn't very significant.

The woman nodded and drew aside the shawl in which she had wrapped her baby. It turned out that she was a little girl about a week old...and she was as yellow as a sunflower.

"Since when has your baby been this color?" I asked.

"Ever since she was about three days old...she is a week old now, and my mother said that the yellow color goes away, but it's not!" She sounded agitated. "Now she is sleeping most of the time and her feeding is sluggish." She looked very worried, and continued to rock her baby drawing more solace from the motion herself than her baby.

"Was that why you were going to the hospital?" I asked her, and she nodded in agreement. "Your baby has what doctors call neonatal jaundice."

"What is that? I only know that the skin of some babies gets yellow. Most of the children in our village get better, but some need treatment in a hospital," she said mournfully.

"You are right. Sometimes the babies need to go for proper care to the hospital, but most of the times they do get better on their own, but since your baby is not feeding well, you need to get medical care as soon as possible."

"What should I do? It will be some time until my husband finishes loading the cart again."

I knew that we had to be on our way because we were just a few hours behind the smugglers' trucks. There was a distinct possibility that those very trucks were the ones who had driven the poor family off the road. Tanya would be very annoyed with me if I volunteered to take the mother and baby to the hospital. I was happy that it wasn't a life and death situation, but it could be if treatment were delayed.

"Most of the time the treatment for neonatal jaundice is to put the baby under a special light that alters the bilirubin, the pigment that causes the yellow color of the skin, into a form that can be easily broken down by the baby's liver."

"Huh?" The woman looked puzzled.

"Doesn't matter," I said. "Have you heard that babies with jaundice need to be put under a light?"

"Yes...yes! My sister-in-law told me about that. That's why I have been sitting in the sun with her for a while now."

"If you keep her covered it's not going to work. Sunlight can help to some extent, but she will still need to go under the special 'phototherapy' light at the hospital. Till then, take off all her clothes. She needs to be naked so that the sun can work its miracle." I smiled. The weather was pleasant, not too hot and not too chilly, so I was certain that the baby wouldn't catch a cold. I just hoped they could get to the hospital in time to continue the proper treatment.

Tanya

. . .

My hands developed new callouses upon the old ones as I helped the farmer load his sacks onto the donkey cart. He was grateful and wanted to give me a small sack of wheat as payment. I refused and explained to him that we were traveling and we wouldn't be able to take it to a mill to get it ground into flour, but he still pressed a bag of walnuts and dried apricots in my hand.

"Please, thank your wife for having a look at my baby and advising my wife. Allah bless you both." With that, we climbed into our car, waved to the small family, and drove onwards to the border.

The town of Islam Qala, though small, was bustling with activity. There were trucks queuing right into the town from the border check-post, waiting to have their cargo inspected and their passports stamped. There was another smaller queue for private cars, so, even though we had to wait a short while, it wasn't that long until we drove up to the booth where the Afghan customs' officers sat.

"Anything to declare?" asked the bored man behind the glass. "Why did you visit Afghanistan?"

"I am a professor of archeology and I came to study the Musalla minarets, and this is my wife," I said, trying to make my Farsi as impeccable as possible.

"Hmm...." he said, "Ok, drive on." He stamped our passports and waved us onwards to the Iranian check post.

The Iranian officials were just as bored as their Afghani counterparts and soon we were on Iranian soil. I drove the car a short distance away and parked on the curb. We were sufficiently far away not to look suspicious, but near enough to be able to look at the trucks as they drove through the inter country barrier. We stayed there for about an hour, drinking water and eating fruit like any normal travelers would do at midday, but none of the gargantuan vehicles passing us looked familiar.

"Why don't we go to Taybad and see what we can find there?" suggested Sarah. She was right. Instead of suspiciously loitering on the roadside, we could observe from a restaurant or a cafeteria in the Iranian border town, since most of the cross-border traffic ran through it. "Good idea. Let's go!"

Taybad was just as busy as Islam Qala, but we found a passably good restaurant which had a very large picture window. We sat there comfortably and looked at the traffic as it passed by.

"Did you know that this is where the Persians had a victory against the Afghans in 1729, and as a result the Persians advanced and captured the city of Herat? That is probably why the western part of Afghanistan speaks more Farsi than Pushto." Sarah was excited. She always liked to know the history and culture of places she had either visited or read about, and even though this was a different sort of journey, she was still looking for things to learn and see. It was quite an admirable habit of hers, if I may say so.

We stayed in the restaurant for over two hours and ate the local version of *chalo kebab*, which was rice with barbequed meat. The food was served with immense naans, not as big as their Afghani counterparts, but big enough to tame the beast in Sarah's tummy.

"What are you smirking about?" asked Sarah.

"I was remembering your reaction when I ordered only one naan in Kabul."

She threw a slice of cucumber at me and said, "Well, I have to eat; I am a growing girl." She winked and got up to go and wash her hands at the sink that was set in an alcove just outside the restrooms.

After we left Taybad, Sarah and I switched seats and she drove most of the two hundred kilometers to Mashhad. Compared to Afghanistan, the roads were much better, except for an occasional pothole that Sarah deftly avoided, so we made it in good time to the holy city. We only stopped once to fill up our tank, but that happened without any untoward incident.

Before we reached the outskirts of the city, we changed places again. The roads were crowded, and I wanted to find an inn or a motel near the shrine as planned.

"Look, there is a hotel!" exclaimed Sarah. "It doesn't look that good... Maybe it just has a two-star rating, but as long as the sheets are clean, I don't mind where we stay."

"Edris Hotel," I read the Farsi script on the board. It looked clean, and I concurred with Sarah—we just needed a clean place to lay our heads for a couple of days, until we either had information about Farooq or had to move on.

"Wait here in the car. I will go and find out if they have any rooms available," I instructed Sarah. But I didn't need to, because she had understood the role she had to play as the obedient wife, and she covered her face and sat back while I entered the cool foyer of the hotel.

The place looked shabby, but it was spotlessly clean. One could see that once upon a time this had been a place of luxury and opulence, but due to economic fluctuations, the owners couldn't renovate the premises. In spite of the crowds in the city, there was a room available, and I paid the exorbitant rates in cash and went to get Sarah and our bags from the car.

"Does the hotel have a parking place for my car?" I asked the concierge.

"Yes, you can drive the car behind the hotel. There is a parking place and your car will be safe there," he informed me.

I drove the car where I was instructed to, but to call it a parking lot was a joke. It was an undeveloped field, but at least the car would be away from the traffic on the main road. We left most of our luggage in the car, and Sarah and I hefted just our backpacks and entered the lobby of the hotel where a bellboy immediately leaped forward and took them as he ushered us to our room on the second floor.

Just like the lobby, the room was shabby, but the sheets and towels were meticulously clean.

"There is nothing I would like better than to have a nap," said Sarah.

"Wasn't the nap you had in the car enough?" I asked with a laugh.

"Maybe, but the stress of the journey, hoping and praying that no one would see through our disguise, especially at the border, and then finally reaching here has given me a strange feeling of fatigue." Sarah pulled her flowered *chador* off while she spoke. "Moreover, I need a bath—I am sticky." She laughed.

"Let us have a bath and change, and then go look for something to eat. It will be evening soon, and the pilgrims will be praying at the shrine before they go home. We can go to the shrine after dinner when it's not so crowded and have a look around."

We found a restaurant nearby, and although it was crowded, we managed to get a table near the window overlooking the pedestrian zone.

We looked like a young couple having a leisurely meal, but our eyes kept wandering to the road to see if we would recognize anyone. I was surprised at our acting abilities because I was sure Sarah was as tense as I was, and yet we both came across as relaxed and enjoying each other's company. Which we actually were and, in another time or place we would have relished the adventure and the thrills. We would definitely have amazing stories to tell our children and grandchildren one day.

"Look! Isn't that one of Farooq's men?" whispered Sarah as she pulled on the sleeve of my coat to get my attention.

"Yes! I do believe he is." I signaled to the waiter to bring our bill, which I promptly paid. We had Farooq's man still within our sight when we stepped out of the restaurant.

"There he is!" said Sarah as she looked in the direction he went. She was clever not to point at him so as not to attract unwanted attention.

It wasn't unusual for couples to hold hands in the crowd, especially if they didn't want to lose each other, so we held hands while we hurried in the direction we saw the man going. We would hide within the crowd whenever he looked back, but he seemed uncomfortable, as if he was aware that he was being followed. He still walked on and finally stopped outside the iron sliding door of a warehouse. He knocked a few times and the door opened just a slit and someone spoke to him. He looked around to see if there was anyone in the street behind him. We had ducked behind a barrel that was used for garbage, so I hoped that he wasn't aware of our presence. Once the person inside the warehouse was assured that the man was a friend, the door was opened and he was let inside. It was no surprise at all when we saw who was at the door...Farooq!

"Let us go back to the hotel," I told Sarah.

"But that was Farooq! We have to do something! What if he gets away again?"

"We have been categorically told not to engage with them. We are here only to gather information. According to Andy, our Interpol agent will be contacting us soon. Let's hope he comes quickly so that we can hand Farooq over to him."

Sarah was disappointed, and actually, so was I. It would have been interesting to see the expression in Farooq's face when he saw us standing there, but I still hadn't received my weapon, and Andy's admonishment made me aware that Sarah was not trained as we were. If anything happened to her... that was something I wasn't willing to think of. I needed to keep her as safe as circumstances allowed.

"You know that I signed a consent form before we came on this adventure, right?" said Sarah. Once again, she knew what I had been thinking. "I promise not to take any risks, but you have to trust me as well. I am not a child."

"I know that, sweetheart, but you mean a lot to me. You are my life—"

"I know," she interrupted me. "Just like you are mine, so we will take care of each other as we go along. Don't worry; all will be fine in the end."

By the time we reached our hotel it was already quite

late. I was getting nervous. I wanted our local Interpol liaison to contact me so that Farooq was arrested. Just the thought that he could slip away because of this unprecedented delay was gnawing at my innards. I felt as if something was going to happen soon, and it wasn't going to be nice.

Once we were in our room, Sarah took off her confining *chador* with a sigh of relief and went into the bathroom to freshen up. As usual, she didn't close the door completely. Just as I was about to change out of my clothes, I heard a knock on the door. I went over and told Sarah to stay in the bathroom until I said it was safe to come out and then I closed the bathroom door.

"Who is it?" I called out gruffly in Farsi.

"Agent Tanya! I am your Interpol liaison. Open the door," said the man on the other side in English. I was relieved that we had been contacted, but I knew that voice. I was all of a sudden wary to open the door.

"One moment, please!" I called out as I slipped our fruit knife into my boot and opened the door a fraction to look out.

Farooq stood there with the man we had followed that evening. Both of them had grins on their faces as they shoved the door and forced themselves into our room.

"Do you think you can fool us with that weird disguise? No matter what you do to yourself, Tanya, you will never be the man that I am!" Farooq laughed raucously and touched himself in a lewd manner. "Would you like to find out just how manly I am?" He laughed even harder. "Where is that idiotic sidekick of yours? I would like to have a taste of her as well."

I had to steel myself not to lose my temper. I knew that once I lost it, he would have control over me.

"Well, Farooq, you have found us. Now, what do you want?"

"Do you think that the pathetic way you trailed my man today wasn't noticed? He was instructed to lead you to me." He patted his companion on the shoulder. "I will not let you interfere in my lucrative business. I will give you a choice because you are old 'friends'... go home and forget what you saw or you will end up in an unknown ravine just like your friend from Interpol."

I was shocked! He had the audacity to murder an international law maker! An agent from Interpol! And then he bragged about it? I was certain that he would never let us go easily. If at all.

"So, you will just let us leave?" I was stalling for time. I prayed that Sarah wouldn't come out. The walls were quite thin and I knew she heard everything that was being said.

"I give you my word, but there is one small condition," he said.

"Ah, I knew there were strings attached. That is what I would always expect from you. Thank you for not disappointing me," I said sarcastically.

"Oh, no, no, no, no! It's nothing sinister and it hasn't got anything to do with you and Sarah. Well... not directly. I just want the two babies that you stole from my 'stable' back." He smirked while he cleaned his nails with a lethal looking knife.

"Those babies are now in Pakistan. Do you think we would be hauling them around the country in our backpacks?" I retaliated.

"You can call your freaky police friend Razia and tell her to hand over the girls to my men. Once I get the green light that they are in my men's custody, you and Sarah will be released to go wherever you want to and in any disguise that you like," he said while he looked up and down in disdain at my clothes and hairstyle.

"How dare you?" I heard Sarah shout and then there was a clanging sound as Farooq silently slid unconscious to the floor. The other man was distracted, and I wrestled him to the ground and then tied him up with some scarves that we had in our luggage. I looked open-mouthed at Sarah, who had a pipe in her hand and was triumphantly holding it up.

"Well, what are you waiting for? Tie Farooq up as well. He won't be unconscious for long," she said.

I didn't know what we'd do with Farooq and his henchman. If he was to be believed, our Interpol liaison was dead, and we had no way to contact Andy unless he sought us out.

CHAPTER 14

"I save myself in the act of saving others."
~ Craig D. Lounsbrough

SARAH

We were facing a strange conundrum—two unconscious criminals in our room in a strange land where we knew no one and had no legal or any other support whatsoever. We knew that we had to get out of there as soon as we could, but we agreed that it would look suspicious if we checked out of the hotel in the middle of the night.

"Thank goodness we didn't bring all of our luggage inside. I think we can sneak out the back exit. I will leave some money on the nightstand to cover the expenses so that it doesn't look like we are cheating them with the room charges," said Tanya. "Let me quickly go into the bathroom to check my makeup and then we can go."

While she checked her appearance, I rushed around the room haphazardly stuffing our belongings into our backpacks. Then just before we left, I went to see how our 'guests' were faring. Farooq was still unconscious but relatively unharmed, except for a lump the size of an egg where I had hit him with the pipe. The other man was sullenly following me with his eyes since he couldn't speak because of the firmly tied gag in his mouth.

Tanya emerged from the bathroom with her make up refreshed and started to drag Farooq into the bathroom by pulling him under his arms. He was heavy, and she grunted while she pushed and pulled his bulk. The other man seemed even heavier, so I helped her by picking up his legs while she hauled his upper body. Even though there were two of us, we were out of breath and sweating once we stuffed both men in the bathroom.

"I will inject a low dose sedative into both of them; that will give us a bit more time while they sleep it off." I went to get the injections from my bag. Farooq was easy since he didn't even flinch when I administered the drug, but his crony tried to wriggle about. I was quick as I held him down and injected the drug through his clothes into his right buttock. His expression of surprise and rage was so comical that I started to laugh.

"Are you ready to go?" asked Tanya as she picked up her bag.

Silently nodding, I also picked up my bag while I looked around to see whether we had forgotten anything, but the only thing different in the room was the pile of banknotes that Tanya had placed on the nightstand. We peeked out of our room and were relieved that the corridor was deserted. Lady Luck was on our side because we reached our car without seeing anyone, and we quickly drove away.

"Where are we going now?" I asked. Tanya's face looked grim in the dim light from the dashboard. It was her 'Agent's' face, and at that point I was so glad that I was on her side.

"We are going back to the warehouse to see what information we can gather there," she said, simmering with anger. "I am worried about the children, and yes, we were told not to engage or be reckless, but how can we leave them here, especially with Farooq tied up?" She spoke desperately, as if she wanted to convince herself that she was doing the right thing. "Moreover, I am sure that there is an international phone connection there. Otherwise, it would have been difficult for Farooq to contact his prospective buyers or his alleged boss."

"Oh, I understand!" I exclaimed. "We can call for help and tell the authorities where we tied the men up. Then they can come and arrest them."

"No, that is too dangerous. I will call my boss, Mr. Humphrey, and he will contact the authorities through the proper channels, but we have to be as far away as possible from here when the local police arrive. We are illegally in their country, and what little I know from the Iranian legal system, they might find all sort of excuses to arrest us, even though we are working on their side of the law." Tanya shivered in dread as she spoke.

Since it was nighttime and there was nearly no traffic on the roads, we arrived quickly at the street where we had followed Farooq's man the day before. There was a large padlock on the door of the warehouse, but that did not bother Tanya. She unscrewed the handle of her knife and took out a lockpick from a hidden compartment. Then she rummaged in her backpack and gave me the torch she found there.

"Shine the torch on the lock while I try to open it with the lockpick," she said with a mischievous wink.

She was obviously skilled because the lock was opened within seconds.

"Don't make a noise now. Just because we temporarily eliminated two people doesn't mean that there aren't more guarding the children, and they might be armed." Tanya put her fingers to her lips and slowly slid the well-oiled bolt to the side. She opened the door and we entered into a large, empty hall. I swept the torch around and into the dark corners. This was strange. Why would they lock an empty warehouse? Then, as I continued to sweep the torch into all of the shadows and crannies, I saw a smaller door at the far side of the hall from where I suddenly heard the sound of a soft whimper.

"They are in there!" I told Tanya excitedly. We had found the children! Opening the door cautiously, I looked inside and saw that it was dark, but there was a small lamp shining in one of the corners, casting a soft glow on the inhabitants of the room. There they were... all of the kidnapped children spread out and sleeping on mattresses or pallets on the floor.

At a glance, it seemed there were about fifty little boys, girls, and babies sleeping on the makeshift beds, but everyone seemed to be in a deep sleep. Apart from the occasional whimper, no one stirred. I shone the torch in the nearest child's eyes and my suspicions were confirmed. They had been drugged with an opiate, most probably morphine, and that was proven by the pin-point pupils of the child I examined. What was also strange was that there didn't seem to be any adult or supervisor with the children.

"I think Farooq has been using morphine as a babysitter," I said in disgust. Didn't he realize that he was creating future drug addicts if he kept this up much longer?

I went from child to child, trying to arouse them, but they wouldn't wake up. I turned the ones sleeping on their backs to their sides in case they vomited and aspirated, which can happen when children are drugged. Treating aspiration pneumonia of a small child while traveling would not be effective or pleasant for anyone taking care of them.

Tanya had in the meantime found the office and was looking through papers and ledgers for evidence that we could use against this heinous gang.

"I'm going to look around to see if there are any medicines for the children. If they keep them drugged with opium, they must be having antidotes somewhere," I called out to Tanya. There was no need to be quiet since we could have brought a loud brass band to play and it still wouldn't have woken up the slumbering children.

"Okay, love, just don't go too far," Tanya said absently as she shuffled through the papers.

I wandered into the next room, and I was amazed at the things, from dried milk and baby food to medicines, that were stored there. I found naloxone vials (the antidote of morphine) that confirmed my suspicion that the children were drugged and then periodically brought out of their fugue, probably to eat or use the bathroom. That in itself was child abuse of the highest nature. As I looked through the shelves, I decided that we would let the children sleep until we knew for sure what we were going to do. I grabbed a few vials of naloxone and put them into my medical bag in case they were needed later. I turned to go back out, but then went back to the medicine shelf and picked up a few vials of morphine as well. They would be useful in case I had to sedate a patient or perform a minor surgery while we were on the road. I shivered as I closed the door. This place had a feeling of death and evil, and I wanted to leave right away.

Tanya

We had to work fast, so I gathered as many documents and ledgers as I could and stuffed them into a clean garbage bag. Amongst the chaos, I found Sarah's and my British passports in a manila envelope. I had nearly tossed it aside when I realized that the envelope was quite bulky. To my surprise and relief, our travel documents as well as our wallets with our money, credit cards, and IDs were also in it.

"Sarah, take this envelope and keep it safe," I told her as I flipped it over to her as she walked back into the room. She caught it deftly, looked inside, and gave a whoop of delight and then stuffed it into her medical bag.

"There is a landline telephone here," she said as she swept away a few papers covering the instrument. "I would suggest that you call headquarters so that we can get out of here."

I passed the garbage bag with the documents to Sarah. "Put any paper or file that you think might be helpful in here. I will try to get Mr. Humphrey on the phone." Sarah nodded and hastily started to do as I asked.

Mr. Humphrey's number was one of the many numbers that I had memorized, and I was pleased that the connection to his office went through immediately. It was just afternoon in London, and I knew that he usually worked late, so I was confident that I would get through to him.

"Tanya! Is that you? We were worried since we hadn't heard anything from you since you entered Iran. Fortunately, Andy sent us a message that he had seen you in Herat two days ago!"

"Sir, I need to give you an update and I would like you to send someone to rescue the kidnapped children that we've found in a warehouse here, and to arrest the smugglers who we have tied up and drugged in the hotel where we were staying."

"Proceed, Agent," he said, all business. I updated him on Farooq, the children, and how to find the hotel and the warehouse.

"I am taking documents and ledgers with me and will try to send them to you soon," I went on.

"Leave the warehouse and take Sarah with you. Take care of her; we can't afford anything to happen to a civilian," said Mr. Humphrey urgently. Little did he know that I would rather die than have anything happen to Sarah...

"You need to go now. The authorities monitor all international phone calls. Leave! You have a very narrow window to escape. We will take care of everything."

"Yes, sir," I said quickly. "We will contact you again from Ankara or Istanbul."

"God speed," he said and hung up.

"Sarah! We need to go. Now! Just take what you have gathered and leave the rest." I was getting anxious because I could hear the faint sound of a police siren that was getting louder as it neared our location. I grabbed Sarah by the sleeve and pulled her along until we reached the car. I took the bag with the documents from her and flung it in the back while she sat on the passenger side and fastened her seat belt. I ran around to the driver's side, jumped in, started the car, and sped off down the lane hoping that I would reach the main road before the police got there and stopped us. Fortunately, my imitation of an Indy 500 racer ensured that we just made it out of the street in time. I saw the police cars careening around the corner from my rear-view mirror, but since we didn't want to attract any unwanted attention, I slowed the car to the required speed limit when we reached the main highway and continued to drive on. If anyone noticed us, they would think we were just a young couple out for a drive.

"What did Mr. Humphrey say that galvanized you into action?" asked Sarah. I could see that this frantic dash had made her anxious and scared. If I was honest with myself, I would agree that the adrenaline pumping through my body was also giving me the jitters.

"He said something that I should have thought of myself." I was mentally kicking myself for being so careless, especially since Sarah was with me. "All international calls are monitored here, and our call triggered the police to come to our location. In a way, that is good. They will find the children sooner rather than later, but if we had been caught, we would definitely have been arrested for a multitude of crimes against the country." I carefully looked at the Farsi road-signs and turned onto the highway where the road sign indicated the way to Tehran. We needed to be as far away as possible when Farooq was arrested at our hotel since the management could easily describe our appearance to the police. Getting arrested was not on our agenda in any way.

"We would still be there if Mr. Humphrey hadn't warned me! I am really upset with myself for being so careless."

"We got away in time, so don't mull on it; let it go," said Sarah gently as she stroked my arm trying to soothe my irritation and anger. "But tell me, if they could track our phone call so quickly, why didn't they catch Farooq as well?"

"Since he arrived here in Mashhad just a few hours before us, it is possible that he hadn't yet called anyone internationally. That means his contact could be in Iran. I think what alerted the police was that I called Interpol. That must have been a trigger for them."

Sarah nodded and then took out the road map from the glove compartment to study it carefully.

"By car, the driving distance between Mashhad and Tehran is eight hundred and ninety kilometers. I think if we drive at an average speed of one hundred kilometers per hour, our travel time there would be about eight hours."

"Let us drive as far as we can for now and see whether we can find a place to spend the night and then travel the rest of the way when we are properly rested," I said, as my voice slurred with fatigue.

Sarah laughed. "You do realize that it's already morning, my love?"

She was right. As I looked out of the window, I saw the faint rays of the sun trying to peep over the horizon in the east. The sky was already painted a pale pink. I also realized that we were exhausted and needed to rest for a short while, but I wanted to be far from Mashhad before we relaxed. "I wish they still had *caravanserais*," I said wistfully, thinking about my history lessons in school.

"What is that?" asked Sarah curiously.

"A *caravanserai* was a roadside inn where travelers or caravanners could rest and recover from the days' journey. They usually supported the flow of commerce, information, and people across the network of trade routes, especially the Silk Road. You can still see them on the main roads here in Iran, but they are now mostly ruins or historical monuments," I explained. "There was always food, water, and a bed for caravan travelers, and they were very popular places to get information and to socialize."

"According to the map, there are some places to stay along the highway. They are indicated with a little bed icon, so I think we can safely say that they are inns or motels rather than hotels, maybe even modern versions of *caravanserais*," said Sarah pointing at the map. "There is one about a hundred kilometers away from here. Let's drive there and we can rest for a while. Both of us are exhausted and it's dangerous to drive when we are so tired." I agreed with her wholeheartedly, because even though I wanted to remain stoic, I was on the verge of exhaustion.

CHAPTER 15

"He who learns but does not think is lost! He who thinks but does not learn is in great danger." ~ Confucius

SARAH

After a twenty-four-hour rest in one of the roadside inns that we saw marked on our map, we reached Tehran without any untoward incident. Actually, driving down the broad highway and stopping at tea houses or *chalo kabab* restaurants was quite pleasant. I had almost forgotten why we were in Iran because it felt like we were on a holiday. Even Tanya was more relaxed once she was rested. We shared driving to the capital so that one of us could nap while the other drove.

On one occasion, when it was my turn to drive, I stopped at a tea house and we were served tea while we sat in the car. The unsweetened black tea was accompanied with a plate of delicious looking white sweets that were stuffed with different nuts. I could identify almonds and pistachios, but unfortunately not the others.

"What are these delicious, gooey sweets?" I asked Tanya, who was just stirring from her nap.

"Oh! Those are *gaz*." She snatched one from me and unwrapped it. Instead of eating it herself, she put it near my lips and urged me to take a bite.

They had a strange but pleasant taste. I opened my mouth for more and just as I was about to bite down on the delicious morsel, Tanya pulled it away and stuffed it into her mouth and laughed at my disappointed pout.

"There is more from where that came from." She laughed even harder when I scowled at her. "Here, take the other one." She unwrapped the other sweet for me and held it to my lips. "If you like them so much, we can buy a few from the shop." My mouth was full, and I couldn't say much because the sticky morsel had jammed my teeth together, but I nodded my head in delight.

"*Gaz* is prepared following an over 450 years old recipe from Isfahan. It is made from pistachios, almond kernels, rose-water, egg whites, and sap from the tamarisk tree," said Tanya. I knew I had identified the nuts right, and I couldn't get enough of the tangy sweetness. She stepped out of the car and stretched.

"I'll be back in a little while," she said and sauntered over to the general store next to the tea shop. She came back within twenty minutes and was laden with grocery bags. I took the bags happily from her and started to rummage through them. I was curious to know what Tanya had bought, since she was not a person who likes shopping.

"Those are just snacks for the way," said Tanya off handedly. "By that I mean the usual Iranian snacks." She grinned as she sat down in the car. "*Gaz*, pistachios, almonds, and another sweet that I thought you might enjoy, *sohan asli*, which is made of honey, sugar, saffron, almonds, and pistachios. It's like a hard toffee, quite brittle and breaks into shards." She looked at me with an amused expression on her face. "My dear darling, you are drooling!" She laughed. "I think it's better that I drive now—you might faint if you don't dive into that bag of sweets."

I stuck out my tongue at her, made a funny face, and got out of the car to sit on the passenger side. Tanya slid over the seats and made herself comfortable in the driver's seat. She honked to signal to the tea boy to fetch our empty cups and to pay our bill, and then we were off.

The outskirts of Tehran were impressive. This was an ancient metropolis that had seen many dynasties and political changes, and yet it retained its unique character. "How old do you think Tehran is?" I asked, my inherent curiosity coming to the fore once more.

"I heard that archeologists have unearthed evidence that Tehran could be up to eight thousand years old, but it was only established as the capital by Agha Mohammad Khan about two hundred years ago."

"Only two hundred years ago!" I was surprised. "Where was the capital before that?"

"I am not exactly sure, but the earliest capital was Persepolis, so named by Alexander the Great. Thereafter the capital kept changing. Iran then had numerous capitals, including Isfahan, Qazvin, Shiraz, and even Mashhad."

"I am impressed with your information, but I find it hilarious that the Iranians can't make up their minds where they want their capital city to be. Maybe they'll change it again in the future. It would be interesting to keep an eye on the geopolitical scenarios here," I said with a grin.

After studying our map once more, we found a small boutique hotel in a quiet street and were checked in quite easily. Tanya was relieved that she could take off her wig and makeup for a short while. "I am sick and tired of this itchy wig, but I will wait until we have had something to eat before I take it off," she said wearily.

We stretched out on the bed, physically and mentally exhausted, and decided not to go out to eat that day. Instead, we ordered something from the room service menu. And for dessert we had my latest passion... *gaz*!

Our food came quickly and the aromas wafting from the covered tray were divine manna from heaven for my food-sensitive olfactory nerves and rumbling stomach. Tanya turned to pay the waiter with a knowing smirk, and as he extended his hand over to take the bill from her, she gasped in surprise. His hand was red and quite swollen.

"Sarah! Come here! Have a look at this man's hand!" The man had started to back out towards the door. He looked confused and frightened.

"What...?" was all he could say.

"Don't worry, my wife is a doctor and clearly you need medical attention. What happened to your hand? Let her have a look." Tanya was visibly upset because she had never seen such a severe inflammation before.

I reached out and grasped his hand, and I tried to reassure him while showing my concern for him.

"I am so sorry *Agha, Khanum...* It is nothing. We are not supposed to bother the hotel guests, so if you just pay the bill, I will be on my way." The man was flustered and tried to pull his hand away.

"It is no bother," I reassured him. "Sit down and let me have a look."

"Please, your food is getting cold. It's nothing. I was just stung by a bee on my way to your room. I am lucky that I didn't drop the tray," he said trying to make light of his swollen hand. I could see that the swelling was getting worse and, even though he tried to hide it, he was clearly in a lot of pain.

"What is your name?" asked Tanya.

"My name is Ali," he said after a reluctant pause.

I pulled Tanya aside. "He is having an allergic reaction to the bee sting. If he is not treated immediately, it can be dangerous for him. I am just happy that the reaction is fairly slow at the moment."

Tanya nodded and went back to Ali. "Let my wife give you some medicine. It will help you. The swelling on your hand is increasing and if I am not mistaken, your breathing is getting erratic as well." She looked at me for confirmation.

Ali was definitely on the verge of respiratory distress and realized that he did need medicine to reverse the uncomfortable feeling he had started to get in his chest, so he nodded in my direction, leaned back in the chair, and closed his eyes.

"We have to hurry or he could go into *anaphylactic* shock!" I knew I had an EpiPen with me and I looked through my bag for it. I had a small frisson of panic when I initially couldn't find it, but then I felt the edge of the pen right at the bottom of the bag. I took it out, administered the required dose, and was rewarded by Ali's respiration slowly but gradually coming back to normal.

"How are you feeling now, Ali?" I asked.

"Much better, thank you so much," he replied in a voice that was mixed with gratitude and awe. He looked at his hand closely. "I thought it was just a bee sting, and though it hurt a lot, I didn't realize what a strange reaction I would have. Thank you so much! You have saved my life!"

I swept aside his thanks and went on to give him a couple of injections, including a steroid. I found some antihistamine tablets and a soothing gel and instructed him how to use them for at least three more days.

Ali left the room soon after and, to my consternation, he took the tray along with him. He didn't say anything, but I guessed he was getting our food warmed up since it had congealed to an unappetizing mess.

After about half an hour, Ali returned with a tray that was even more laden than before. Besides our original order, there were a few Iranian dishes that Ali said we just had to try. As far as my *gaz* was concerned, instead of just a few, Ali had brought a whole one kilo box! The cherry on top was that he didn't let us pay for the meal.

"That is the least I can do for you, *Khanum* and *Agha*. Bless you," he said before he left the room to let us enjoy our dinner together.

Tanya

. . .

I had been to Tehran once before and was impressed by its cosmopolitan atmosphere. However, this time there seemed to be a poignantly sad vibe hanging over the city. Was it the destruction of the city monuments due to the revolution? Or was it the significantly visible *Gasht-Ershad*, the main religious police of the country seen on nearly every street corner? I didn't want to alarm Sarah, but I saw this faction of the morality police harshly correcting women about their *hijabs*, and on one occasion, I saw a woman being arrested... her crime: she wasn't wearing a 'proper' head scarf. And that was only while we drove down the main boulevard... I felt an involuntary shiver of fear run its icy fingers along my spine and looked over to see whether Sarah was properly covered. Moreover, if they found out that I was a woman in disguise... I shuddered once more when I thought what they would do to me. I shook my head and concentrated on the road while thinking that we had to be even more careful in this country. We were more exposed than we were in Afghanistan.

"Please, cover your head properly while we are in Iran. They don't allow visitors in the jails here." I joked about it to create some levity, but I knew Sarah was a clever woman and wouldn't try to invite danger by being contrary about her head covering.

When Sarah treated Ali for his allergic reaction to the bee sting, I was worried that he might take offence that a 'lowly' woman was trying to touch him, but he realized the gravity of his situation and readily accepted her ministrations. It was a lucky break when everything turned out well. I certainly heaved a sigh of relief.

"How will your Interpol colleagues contact you here?" asked Sarah after Ali left us.

"I am sure they know by now that we are in Tehran, and they will contact us. I don't want to risk using a telephone again, but if we aren't contacted within two days, we should move on to Turkey. I know that Farooq's contacts might be here because he didn't trigger the police response with an international call. Unless he didn't have the time to do it before he accosted us."

Sarah looked pensive.

"What are you thinking?" I asked.

"How about we check out the addresses that we have from Farooq's notebook?"

"That was just what I was about to suggest. You are becoming quite a good agent." I poked her in the ribs and laughed. "Andy must have passed on the addresses to Mr. Humphrey by now, so it is possible that my colleagues contact me at one of them."

Sarah was busy making inroads with the food on the tray, and just grunted to show that she heard me. Waving me over, she prepared a plate for me and pressed it into my hand, indicating that I should eat.

"You need to get something in you. I know that you are tense and worried, but you can't faint with hunger when you go to check out the addresses," she said with a smile as she also handed me a glass full of salty buttermilk, which is a staple drink with Iranian fare.

We ate our meal in comfortable silence, each of us lost in our thoughts. I am sure Sarah was also thinking of ways to address our predicament. We needed to find out who the ringleaders of Farooq's smuggler's gang were. While we were aware that there would always be people who would try to sell or prey on children, whether for adoption or any other heinous reasons, I knew that we could make a significant difference if this gang was caught. Many lives would be saved, and many children would be back in the arms of their loved ones.

"Let us go to bed early and start looking for the addresses early tomorrow morning," I said after we finished our food and put the tray in the corridor for Ali to collect later. I stretched and yawned.

I was just on the verge of falling asleep when I heard someone softly but frantically knocking on the door.

"Agent Kareem! Open up," I heard someone whisper. "It's me, David Barstow, from the Interpol London office."

"David!" I exclaimed. I had worked with him on many cases in the past. He was one of our steadfast and trustworthy agents. I liked him because he was one of those people you could blindly rely on. "Hold on a minute!" I had to make myself presentable since I had removed my man-makeup before I went to sleep. I didn't want to bother Sarah, but it was already too late—she had also woken up.

"Let me get tidy as well and then let him in," she said calmly as she walked to the bathroom.

After we were dressed, I opened the door for David. He looked anxious, but I shrugged apologetically and ushered him into the room. "I am sorry, but we were in our night clothes." I laughed as I shook hands with him.

David nodded a greeting to Sarah and sat down.

"Would you like to have a cup of tea? We have an electric kettle and teabags here." Without waiting for his answer, I got up to fill the kettle and switched it on. In any case, I needed a cup of tea to get through what I foresaw would be a long night.

"Yes, please, Agent Kareem... Tanya, I would appreciate a cup of tea. It is getting quite cold this evening," replied David.

Once I gave him his tea, he wrapped his hands around the cup to warm his hands. I came directly to the point as there was no time for niceties or for us to be politely skipping around issues.

"Have you been to the addresses that I presume Mr. Humphrey has sent you?"

"Yes, I have. That is why I needed to talk to you," David said.

"How did you find us?" asked Sarah. "We haven't yet told anyone where we are."

"That is not difficult at all." David laughed. "I just called a few hotels and asked whether Ali and Fariba Kareem had already checked in. After speaking to four hotels, I was finally told that you had checked in here a couple of hours ago." David smiled at us triumphantly.

"So much for customer confidentiality," I grumbled under my breath. But I was pleased that we had finally been contacted.

"Farooq and his accomplice were arrested from your hotel room in Mashhad. An 'anonymous' tip had alerted the police that he was a wanted man in Pakistan and that he had attempted to murder a respectable Iranian couple who had managed to overpower him and flee for their life." He sipped his tea while he grinned at us. "I doubt he will see the outside of the Iranian prison system for a while. Once he has served his sentence here, he will be extradited to Pakistan." He took a gulp from his cup and continued. "Even though we know that he had killed our Interpol liaison officer, we still don't have proof and that investigation is still going on. Once it is proven that he is the murderer then God help him. No one messes with one of our own!"

"What about the 'respectable Iranian couple'? Are the police looking for them?"

"No, they are not. Somehow, they have been persuaded... don't ask me how, that the couple were unfortunate victims of the two and they were justified to escape. You both are clear."

"That is a relief," said Sarah as she looked at me.

"The addresses David... did you go there?" I said a bit impatiently.

"Oh, yes, the addresses." David cleared his throat and took another sip of tea. He was always so slow and deliberate; I nearly strangled him in my impatience. "I went to both of the addresses. It seems they were tipped off because even though there were signs of recent occupation, the places were empty. I tried to look for clues, but the only significant thing I found was this address scribbled on a note. It was crumpled and thrown into a wastepaper basket."

I smoothed out the paper and looked at the address written there. It was for an upper-class neighborhood in Ankara. "If I am not mistaken, this address is near the diplomatic enclave in the Turkish capital," I remarked to David.

"You are not far wrong. It is an address *within* the diplomatic enclave. I would suggest you memorize it because I will be taking back this paper for evidence to London."

"Do you think that we should go and look for more clues

tomorrow?" I asked David. "I know you must have been thorough, but sometimes looking at something with fresh eyes does help."

"I was going to suggest that myself. It's a good idea." David coughed politely and then tipped his head back to finish the last sip of tea. "I would go along with you, but I have to go back to London in a couple of hours. Headquarters are waiting for information regarding two other projects that I was monitoring for Interpol in Tehran. Since the data I have collected is sensitive (I would in all fairness consider it even a matter of life and death), I need to talk to the boss in person." I understood that. Sometimes one had to pass on sensitive information verbally when one wasn't sure if the other channels were secure.

"Well, I need to go now. Good luck to both of you. If you don't find anything here, I suggest that you go straight on to Ankara. This country is not safe for you even if you are in disguise." David stood up and shook hands with us once more. "You will be safer in Turkey, and you can use your own passports and identities there. Just remember to go to the British High Commission so that they can help you with the required travel documents and visas to legitimize your stay in the country."

"That is exactly what we discussed before your visit," said Sarah. "I am relieved that we will be more or less back to normal when we cross the Turkish border."

Once David left, I double locked the door and drew the security chain across it. I wasn't sure whether he had been followed and I wanted to keep us safe. I wasn't worried for David; he was a seasoned agent and knew how to take care of himself. My prime concern was Sarah. However, the way she took everything in her stride and met each challenge with courage impressed me every time. I had to learn to stop treating her like a child and embrace the amazing adult she had evolved into since we first met over fifteen years before when she was still a medical student.

"We will pack all of our things and put our bags in the car when we go sleuthing in the morning," I said. "I am not sure what we will find, but if we have to leave suddenly, we won't be able to come back to the hotel to get our stuff."

"That is sensible," said Sarah yawning. "We can also check out from the hotel in the morning. If we still have to stay another day in Tehran, we can always find another hotel. But now we need to catch up on our beauty sleep." She chuckled as she lay down on the bed and held her arms out to me. Once we were in each other's comforting embrace, we slept deeply until we heard Ali knock on the door when he brought our breakfast early the next morning.

CHAPTER 16

"Supposing is good, but finding out is better."
~ Mark Twain

SARAH

The morning sunlight shone through the window blinds waking me up as it caressed my eyelids. It was strange that Tanya and I had slept so deeply knowing we could have been in danger. It was as if someone had sprinkled magic dust on us and we were lulled to sleep. Whatever the reason, we were both refreshed and rejuvenated. As I heard the knock on the door, I looked at my watch and was shocked that it was already eight a.m.!

Tanya lazily opened her eyes, looked at the sunshine streaming in with an astonished expression on her face, and immediately jumped out of bed. She stood at the bedside in all her beautiful glory and stretched with a smile. Seeing her so relaxed warmed my heart since she had been so stressed the past few days.

"I am going to have a shower. I hope that is Ali with our breakfast." Tanya picked up her clothes and went into the bathroom.

Just as I heard her start the shower, Ali knocked once more and called out, "*Agha! Khanum!* Breakfast!"

I went to open the door and let Ali in. Like the night before, he had a massive laden tray in his hands.

"*Khanum*, did you sleep well?" asked Ali with a smile.

"We certainly did. It was amazing; we haven't slept that well in days. It is as if our batteries have been recharged," I said with a chuckle.

"That is good; I am glad." Ali had an enigmatic smile on his face as he arranged our breakfast on the table. "May I say something to you?" he asked shyly.

"Of course you may," I replied.

"Well, it's more like a question... something I would like to verify."

"Go ahead, don't be shy." I smiled.

"You have the 'inner-eye,' don't you? I mean, I felt it last night when you were tending to me. That's why I calmed down the moment you put your healing hands on me." His voice was tentative, as if he wasn't sure of my reaction and didn't want to offend me.

I looked at him for a while, wondering where this conversation was going, and then I slowly nodded. "Yes, I do 'feel' and 'see' things at times, but why do you ask?"

"There is an atmosphere of mystique and supernatural in

Iran, and I believe you might have felt it as well. I wanted to be sure that you were a 'believer' because I wanted to—"

"Salam, Ali, how are you?" Just when the conversation was getting interesting, Tanya emerged from the bathroom with her disguise impeccably in place.

"Salam, *Agha*. I have brought your breakfast as you requested last night." Ali turned away to leave, but I called him back.

"Whatever you wanted to say, you can in front of *Agha*. He knows and understands." Ali looked at both of us, took a deep breath, and started to talk.

"*Agha*, I know that you aren't a man." We looked at him with shocked expressions on our faces. He smiled but went on. "You are in disguise because you are on a noble quest. *Khanum* is a great healer; she will always be by your side whenever you need her, as will you when she needs you."

Tanya jumped up from her chair in surprise. "How did you know? Who told you?" She was getting agitated. If a waiter could see through her disguise, that meant it wasn't very good and anyone could find out her secret. She started pacing, her disquiet very apparent on her face.

"No, no, *Agha*, it is not what you are thinking... I am a jinn. It is my nature to see the truth. My human form indicates that I have been banished to your world by my father because I displeased him in our realm. To go back I have to find two people who are pure of heart and help them, and then my father *might* consider letting me come home." Ali looked desperate. One could see that he was trying his best to convince us of his reality and predicament even though it sounded like a tale Scheherazade of Arabian Nights would have spun.

I closed my eyes and willed myself to feel Ali's energy. As soon as I tuned in, I felt warm and slightly off balance. There was something pushing my senses that was new to me, and though it was disturbing, it didn't feel dangerous. I opened my eyes and caught Tanya and Ali watching me intently, as if they were waiting for my verdict. I was still overwhelmed, so I just nodded and took a deep cleansing breath.

"Why were you banished from your realm?" asked Tanya.

"I fell in love with my beautiful Sharmeen. She was human and lived a long and happy life with me. Now she has left me to go to her Maker and I am alone again." Ali bowed his head to hide the tears that were threatening to fall, but he soon recovered and held his head up again. "Whatever reason you have for your disguise, I sense that both of you are in grave danger—from the Iranian government if they catch you, and from the people you are pursuing. You have been very kind to me and have shown me that you are pure of heart. I want to help you and then send you off on your journey before I go back home." Ali gestured with his hand towards the food on the table. "Please eat; the food is getting cold, and then we need to go."

Once we had eaten our fill, Ali left with the remnants of our breakfast while we packed our bags.

"What do you think of Ali? How do you think he can help us?" I asked Tanya.

She smiled. "Sweetheart, I leave the occult things to you. You need to be sure that we can trust him. That is enough for me." Tanya walked over to where I sat and hugged me. Her hug and the subsequent kiss were enough to assure me of her love and her trust, but I knew that she was worried. This whole mission was developing so many twists that every time we tried to plan ahead we just walked into a fog and couldn't figure out our next move.

Ali came back almost immediately. Did he dump the tray nearby? Or did he fly back? Now I was thinking of all sorts of outlandish things, and I smiled inwardly at the absurdity... and yet, were they absurd? He had a crimson velvet pouch in his hand that he handed over to me as soon as he entered our room.

"*Khanum*, please accept this ruby pendant. It has mystical powers and will always help you diagnose difficult conditions in your patients. And *Agha*..." He turned to Tanya.

"Why do you address me as *Agha* when you know that I am not a man?" asked Tanya.

"Because when you are disguised as a man, you need to think and feel like a man to come across as authentic. Therefore, I'll keep addressing you as *Agha*." Ali pulled out a small black velvet pouch from his coat pocket as he spoke and handed it to Tanya. "Please accept this medallion. It has been blessed by the angels of Solomon. Just fasten it around your wrist whenever you want to disguise yourself and say out loud what you want to be seen as. It will create a glamour around your real persona and people will see you as you want them to. You won't have to change your clothes or use make up when you wear the medallion."

Tanya opened her mouth to say something, but then closed it again when he held up his hand indicating that he was not finished.

"I will go with you on your quest today and try to help you, and then I will leave for my realm. In case there is no time to say so, I would like to thank you both for your kindness to me and for the opportunity you gave me to go back home."

Tanya

It was a relief to wear my normal clothes. The medallion that Ali gave me actually created an extraordinary glamor around me. I activated the medallion and looked in the mirror. There I was in men's clothes with a very real, short and fashionably trimmed beard.

"This is fantastic!" I said. "Now I can move about without worrying that my beard will either slip off or fade away in case I am applying one with makeup. It's such a relief not to have all that itchy hair on my face. I wonder how men handle it."

"I need to caution you, *Agha*. The effect of the medallion stays only for six hours. Then you will be seen as your true self. When that happens you need to recharge it in the sunlight."

"Well, then we need to hurry," said Sarah. "You have already been admiring yourself in the mirror for a while..." She broke of giggling.

Once we checked out of the hotel, we gathered our bags and piled into the car. Ali sat with me in the front while Sarah sat at the back. I handed the paper on which the addresses were written to Ali. "Do you know where these addresses are?" I asked.

"Yes, I know where the first one is. It's near *Shahrah-e-Takht-e-Taos*."

"While I understand that is the name of a road, what does it mean?" asked Sarah.

"It means the road of the Peacock Throne," answered Ali.

"The Peacock Throne... hmmmm... Wasn't that stolen by Nadir Shah from the Mughal Emperors of India?"

Ali sniggered. "Yes, that is true, but the Shahs of Persia always laid claim to it saying it was a legitimate spoil of war. Though if you ask the Indians, they will say it was stolen."

"I read somewhere that the Peacock Throne initially had the Koh-i-Noor diamond embedded in it, but now that famous diamond is one of the main jewels in Queen Elizabeth's crown." It seemed Sarah had been reading up again.

"Not many know that the Peacock Throne was built with the help of jinns. While the opulence of the throne is admired, no one knows that the actual mystique and power was in the pedestal on which the throne rested that Nadir Shah left behind in India because it was too heavy to carry. Persia would have conquered the world if he had realized what he had left behind," said Ali regretfully.

We found *Shahrah-e-Takht-e-Taos*. It was difficult to miss because it was decorated with peacocks that formed an arch over the road. They were massive and quite decorative. We gawked at them as if we were children out on a day trip, but I snapped out of it when I heard Ali chuckle.

"Those peacocks were neon signs and used to light up at night, but the present regime is dismantling them now, which is sad because the road used to look very pretty at night."

Turning away from the main road, Ali directed me into

a side street where we found a convenient parking place. "The address you seek is just around the corner. Let us go on foot from here." Ali hopped out of the car and looked back, expecting us to follow.

We scrambled out of the car and followed him. Sarah had a plastic bag in her hand with something soft inside it. "What is that? Leave it in the car." She just shook her head and hurried after Ali.

As we neared the address that we were looking for, we noticed it was a large building, more like an office block than a warehouse. I guessed that there might be some storage spaces in the back. The parking place was empty, which was strange since it was nearly noon on a working day. Ali walked up to the glass entrance and tried the doors. They were locked and there was no sign of life from within the building.

"Let us go round the back to see whether we can get in," I suggested. Ali nodded and Sarah started to walk ahead of us to a small gate that was embedded to the side in the wall that surrounded the building. She pushed it and it didn't budge. Then I saw her reach across and pull; there was a click and the door swung open.

"How did you do that?" I asked her. That was such a remarkable trick!

"We had a similar gate that led to the garden at our house in Karachi. I just tried that on a hunch, and it worked." She smiled as she leaned over and kissed me gently on the lips and then walked through the gate. It led to a beautiful garden with green lawns and seasonal flowers. There were fruit trees and splashes of color that were accentuated by the different shades of bougainvillea that climbed up the side of the building. The jungle gym, slides, and swings that were in a sandy corner of the garden looked out of place. These were not usually seen in an office, but they proved that there were or had been children there.

We looked furtively around and still didn't see anyone. The back door was conveniently unlocked, so we snuck inside, although we soon realized that we didn't have to be quiet because the place was deserted. That was very strange.

"Let us look around and see if we can find any clues, and then we can either go to the other addresses or we can leave town," I said while rolling up my sleeves and picking up a clean garbage bag from the kitchen.

"I have a feeling the other addresses will also be abandoned," said Sarah.

"Unfortunately, I have to agree with you, but let us see what we can find here before we jump to conclusions." I started opening drawers and cupboards to look for anything that we could use as clues to incriminate the smugglers.

Sarah walked up the stairs to the offices on the first floor. I listened to her footsteps and her slamming doors as she looked into the rooms upstairs. "Tanya! You have to come and see this!" she suddenly called.

I ran up the stairs and followed the sound of her voice as she talked to Ali. They were in a room that had large double doors that stood open. I stepped in and was dumbstruck. One wall of the room was made out of glass and overlooked a large hall.

"Look! We have found where they kept the children!" The hall below had rows upon rows of small cots that were empty now, but there were a few scattered toys that were evidence that this massive room had at one time housed children.

"These electronic consoles are to communicate with whoever was looking after the children below." Ali was just as stunned as we were.

All three of us started to look into the cabinets and drawers in the 'control room' until we found a small safe hidden in one of the cupboards. It was a simple enough safe and easily opened. I was just going to try my luck with my trusty picks when Ali stepped forward and pointed at the lock. A bolt of lightning came out of his fingertip and entered the keyhole. After a mere second, the lock frizzled and the door swung open.

"Nice trick!" said Sarah with a laugh.

Ali smiled cheekily and blew on his fingertips.

I was surprised that there were ledgers in the safe. The smugglers must have thought that no one would find them there. I stuffed them all in the garbage bag, but I left the valuables behind and closed the safe again.

Sarah looked at her watch. "You have been under the medallion's glamor for five and a half hours now. We need to be careful." She handed me the plastic bag that she had brought with her. I was surprised to see that it had a *chador* inside. She had been prepared in case the magic wore off. Ali also checked his watch and smiled at Sarah.

"She is right, *Agha*. We need to go, but I would suggest that you wear the chador in case we are discovered by the police and they start to harass you for not covering your head."

We reached our car without running into anyone. We loaded the ledgers into the trunk and drove off without any untoward incident. I was disappointed. I really wanted to catch the smugglers red handed.

"Seeing how they abandoned this large operation, I doubt there's anyone at the other addresses," I said. "It would be a better idea to travel on to Turkey to see what we can find in Ankara or Istanbul. My only concern is that the longer we take the more elusive they will be, and we need to rescue the other children and get enough proof so that the smugglers can be incarcerated once and for all." I was wondering if we would ever catch up with them. Then I reassured myself that we had the ledgers and papers from Farooq's offices as well as the ones we just 'liberated' in Tehran. I hoped we would be able to make a case against them with the information we had. However, witnessing and identifying the men personally would strengthen our case against them. We had to pursue them.

"Our target is to reach Tabriz today and then drive the three hundred kilometers to the Turkish border and cross over tomorrow," I said.

"I look forward to seeing Mount Ararat. It will be like seeing biblical history in real time. What a privilege!" Sarah was excited that she would be witnessing a piece of the past. Her enthusiasm was endearing, and if we hadn't been on a dangerous mission, I would have shown her so much more.

"Please drive ten kilometers out of Tehran and stop at the nearest rest area," Ali suddenly said. He had been a good navigator and showed me the shortest way to the main highway that would take us to Tabriz, and I had hoped that he would come along with us.

I nodded that I understood and we reached the designated area within ten minutes. The rest area was heavily wooded and had a WC that was constructed of material that made it blend into the surroundings. Ali hopped out of the car and bowed. "*Agha, Khanum*, I'll leave you here. I was told last night by jinn emissaries that my father has granted me permission to come back home. Thank you so much for trusting and helping me. I would like to do something for you as a farewell gift if you allow it."

I nodded and waited to see what he would do this time.

Without much ado, he disappeared in a puff of smoke. Sarah and I looked at each other wondering what that was all about, but then we shrugged and walked towards our car. But...where was our car? In its place stood a silver Mercedes with Turkish number plates. The interior was a soft leather, and the seats were as comfortable as those of a car of that caliber could be. The only indication we had that it was our car was the presence of our luggage in the trunk and the fact that the carne du passage was in my name...—in my own name! I checked my Iranian passport, and it still had my male name on it, but the Turkish passport had my real name citing me as female.

"Look! the ledgers and papers that we had with us have been neatly compiled and put in a hidden compartment under the footrests in the back." I heard Sarah's muffled voice as she bent over to explore the interior of the car. On the back seat there was also a large cooler with ample food and drink. There was a note taped on it that said, "Thank you, dear friends. I wish you luck in your noble quest. Have a safe journey."

Ali knew that if we drove in Turkey with Iranian number plates, we would be conspicuous, especially being two women. We were grateful that Turkey was more liberal towards women than the other two countries we had just passed through, but until we could update our travel documents at the British High Commission, we still had to pose as Turkish nationals. Ali's gift was much appreciated. Now the only thing we had to do was drive towards Turkey and try to find the smugglers.

CHAPTER 17

"Maybe I'll obey the rules. Some of them, anyway, who knows? What are you going to do if I don't, by the way, and haven't I asked you this before?" ~ Anne Rice

SARAH

We spent most of the day driving towards Tabriz. Tanya alternated using the glamor medallion with wearing the *chador* while it recharged on the dashboard in the sun. Whenever that was the case, I drove to let her cover herself completely and have a nap. We were lucky that no one stopped or questioned us. The only times we stopped were for restroom breaks and to eat something. Thanks to Ali's generosity, we didn't need to stop at restaurants—we just pulled onto the picnic areas at the rest stops and ate the delicious food that he had chosen for us.

I continued to study the road map and navigate our journey, and it was just nearing sunset when we drove into Tabriz.

"Since it's getting late and we don't want to brave unknown roads in the dark, let us look for a hotel or an inn to spend the night," said Tanya. "Are there any inns marked on the map?"

"There is one hotel indicated here with three stars. It is called the Elgoli Park Hotel, and it is supposed to be near a park with the same name. We must drive to the southeast of the city center to get there." I indicated that she should turn left at the next intersection. "Oh, look! There is a footnote in the map where it says that the hotel is near a small artificial lake and palace that dates back to the beginning of the Qajar Dynasty about 400 years ago." I looked out of the window wistfully.

"Once our mission is over, and if we are still allowed into the country..." Tanya paused and chuckled, "I promise I will take you on a 'historical safari' and you can indulge in your obsession of looking around old dead people's ruins." She laughed at her own joke so hard that I stopped pouting and joined in her hilarity.

We found the hotel quite easily and were charmed by its old-world ambience. Tanya persuaded the receptionist to give us a room overlooking the lake. We couldn't see much because it was already dark, but the path around the lake was well lit with golden lights which gave it an almost fairy tale atmosphere. We could see people there taking advantage of the balmy evening.

Although it had become cooler and there was a slight chill in the air, it was still pleasant enough for people to spend the evening walking in the park and the path around the lake.

"Would you like to go out? Or shall we order in?" asked Tanya. "But please, let's not have any more jinns on the menu." She looked at me with twinkling eyes. She found my supernatural encounters amusing and that didn't stop her from pulling my leg occasionally.

"We drove the whole day and I am very tired. You also look exhausted. Let us order something from room service and sit here on the balcony and enjoy the view of the lake," I said wearily.

"All right, have a look at the menu while I try to make sense of some of these files I have brought up from the car. I might as well have a look and see whether we are heading in the right direction with our investigation."

The room service menu boasted simple but traditional Iranian food. I was famished and my mouth watered as I read what the kitchen had on offer.

"Everything on the menu has a little photo of the dish next to it so that you can see what it will look like when we get it. Well, at least I hope so!"

"I think they do that for people who are not able to read or understand Farsi. It's an innovative idea, isn't it?" Tanya was just as amused as I was to see the little photographs on the menu.

I chose *Ash reshteh*, a traditional soup made of greens, beans, and noodles topped with a dab of Greek yogurt or sour cream. According to the little note on the menu, it was supposed to be quite popular. Tanya decided not to be adventurous and chose the usual *chelo kabab* she had been eating since we started our travels in Iran.

"I will take a few bites of your concoction, and I will share my kebabs with you if you want," she said distractedly. I knew that she wouldn't be coherent as long as her nose was stuck in that musty file, but I needed her to order the food since I hadn't yet mastered the nuances and accents of a good Iranian citizen who spoke fluent Farsi.

"Okay, love, just a minute," Tanya said in a voice I knew could mean a minute or an hour.

"Tanya!!" I said a bit louder.

"Hmm? Yes?" She looked at me as if she had just realized where she was.

"Please, order the food. I am starving." I pouted and plonked myself quite unladylike onto the bed.

"Of course, dear." I had to grin because she sounded distinctly hen-pecked. "I will do that right now." After she ordered our food, she buried herself in her files again. I knew she would be in her own world until the food came, so I decided to take advantage of the large tub in the bathroom.

The complimentary bubble bath smelled like a bouquet of summer flowers, and I leaned back into the bubbles with a satisfied sigh. I closed my eyes and drifted off for a while. As I was in that undefined zone between being awake and asleep, I felt that I was not alone. That had happened many times before when I used to float between two worlds, but this time, I saw some children who were desperately reaching out to me. They looked just like some of the older children we had seen in the village in Afghanistan, and I could clearly hear their voices calling.

"Doccy! Please find us! We need you! Come quick!"

"Where are you?" I asked them, fascinated that the children were communicating with me this way, but then, people have said that children are more intuitive than adults.

"We are in a large, locked room with just a small window, but Sadia climbed on my shoulders and said that she saw a big mosque with a blue dome. Oh, please, hurry!"

Overwhelmed by the feelings of despair that I felt radiating from the children, my body jerked involuntarily and I was snapped back into my reality. I quickly got dressed and went to tell Tanya what had happened. Our food had arrived by then and the waiter was setting the tray on the little table in the balcony. He was fussing with the cutlery and the napkins, and I wanted to scream at him to hurry up and go, but finally he arranged our meal to his satisfaction and left with a substantial tip in his pocket.

"We need to leave as early as possible in the morning," I said.

"What is wrong, love? Why are you upset?" Tanya looked at me with concern and love in her eyes. "Are you unhappy because I ignored you while looking through the files?" she said with a little rueful grin.

"Of course not!" I scoffed. "I know how important your work is."

"Then why do you want to leave your nice and warm bed early in the morning to drive all the way to the border?" she teased.

"I know where the children are!"

Tanya suddenly sat up straight. "Did you get a vision or a message?"

"Yes, I did... from the children. They said they could see

259

a mosque with a blue dome from the window of the room where they are being held."

"Hmmm, that could be the Blue Mosque in Istanbul." Tanya looked pensive as if she was deciding what we should do. The question now was whether we would be able to reach the children in time.

"All right," she said with a firm nod. "We won't waste much time in Ankara. You know that it is mandatory that we go and legitimize our travel documents at the embassy, but from there we will travel to Istanbul. I have to check my notes, but if I remember right, one of the addresses we have is for *Taksim*, which is a very busy tourist area close to the four-hundred-year-old Blue Mosque, which was built by Sultan Ahmed during the Ottoman-era."

I laughed at her attempt to give me a mini history lesson. She called down to the reception for an early wake-up call and to arrange a light breakfast to be sent to us in the morning. We didn't dawdle like we wanted to after our meal, and after pushing the tray with the remnants of our meal into the corridor, we quickly got ready for bed. There were places to go and children to rescue. We slept deeply, confident that we were safe in each other's embrace while drawing comfort in the fact that the person we held dearest in this world was sleeping peacefully in our arms.

Tanya

We slept well, probably because the thought of Farooq behind bars and the fact that we would be soon far away from Iran gave us a strange sense of comfort. Our work was not yet completed, but in spite of contrary opinions from others and my occasional misgivings, I was grateful that Sarah was with me. Her courage and intelligence were an asset on this mission.

As Sarah suggested, we woke up early and, after a light breakfast, started driving to the Turkish border.

"May we stop for ice cream before we cross over to Turkey?" asked Sarah in a little girl's voice as she grinned at me.

"What is so special about the ice cream here? You can eat all you want once we cross the border."

"I overheard someone in the lobby say that the *gaz* flavored ice cream is delicious and I just wanted to try it."

I gave in to her request and we stopped for ice cream in one of the small towns, but we didn't linger there and ate our cones as we drove along. I wasn't too enthusiastic about the taste, but Sarah was savoring hers as if it was manna from heaven—the look on her face as she ate the cold dessert was almost erotic.

It was midday by the time we reached the border at Bazargan and saw that the usual long queue of transport trucks was already in place to cross over to Turkey.

Sarah excitedly pulled on my sleeve. "We can see Mount Ararat from here! Isn't it magnificent?"

I hadn't noticed the view as I was concentrating on the road, but now I saw the mountain and I agreed that it was impressive. It was mind-blowing to know that Mount Ararat lay on the borders of three countries—Turkey, Iran, and Armenia, and we could see all three from where we were waiting to cross over into Turkey.

"Those are the two dormant volcanic cones that make up the Mount!" said Sarah as she pointed to them. She was so excited that if we had had the time she would have tried to go a little closer for a better look, and maybe even to look for the Ark?

"They don't look too steep. I could climb them... as a matter of fact, so could you," I said, finding her enthusiasm amusing as well as endearing.

"Well, Noah's Ark had to land somewhere that was easy to descend from. All those animals couldn't have used ropes and climbing equipment to come down." Sarah giggled.

I eased our car into the queue and was pleased that we didn't have to wait long before it was our turn with the immigration and customs officials. Thankfully, this was the last time that I was travelling as Ali Kareem. From the Turkish border onwards until we had our proper visas and other travel documents legitimized, we were Mehmet and Aiyla Demirci going back home from our honeymoon in Tehran.

The Iranian officials were suspicious of us and looked carefully through our luggage for any contraband. It was irritating since we had to park on the side of the road after we crossed the border to tidy up what they had disturbed. Toiletries were smashed in between clothes, and food was dumped on the seat and not put back into the cooler. It was chaos, but we were glad to finally be out of there.

"Thank goodness they didn't find the files hidden under the footrests in the back," said Sarah as she folded our clothes and put them neatly back into our bags. "I am also happy that you had the good idea to hide our money and the other valuables that we took from the Chief's camp along with the files."

"Well, it's a two-door car and it would have been a tight fit for that fat guy to squeeze inside to see whether we had anything hidden there, so I am grateful that he likes his kababs a bit too much." I laughed as I started the car and slowly crossed the border to be questioned again, this time by the other customs officials as we entered Turkey.

"Why is your *carne-du-passage* in the name of Tanya Kareem?" asked the official sternly. Apparently, the Iranians had been so focused on our luggage that this point had slipped by them.

"We borrowed this car from our friend, Ms. Kareem. Here is a letter of authority from her that says we can use her car and take it out of the country." I silently blessed our friendly jinn for slipping that note into the *carne*. I hadn't even though about that!

Heaving a sigh of relief as soon as our passports were stamped, we took the mountain highway that led to Erzurum.

"We have another three hundred kilometers to drive before we reach the city. Let's drive as far as we can, and if we get tired, we can stop and look for a motel or a campground to spend the night." I was looking forward to driving through Turkey. It was a beautiful country, especially the drive along the Black Sea.

"I will keep looking at that magnificent edifice of nature as long as it is visible. It is so humbling to be in the presence of history. All three major religions have talked about Mount Ararat and Noah. It's amazing just to be in its presence!"

I chuckled at Sarah's enthusiasm as I drove along.

Honestly, I was also overawed by the sight and would covertly look at the mountain as it became smaller and smaller in my rear-view mirror.

Suddenly, Sarah cried out and clutched my arm. "Tanya!" she said with a distinct note of panic in her voice. "Stop the car!" I wondered what had happened. Was she in pain, or was she feeling ill? I slowed down and parked the car on the side of the road.

"Did you see the truck that just passed us?" she asked anxiously.

"Yes, what about it?" I didn't know what that was all about.

"It had Afghan number plates! The same ones Farooq's truck had!" she literally shouted.

"Are you sure?" I asked as I looked towards the vehicle that was rapidly moving away.

"Yes, I certainly am! I made you stop the car so that we could put a bit of distance between us in case they recognized us." She anxiously peered out of the window.

I started the car and gunned the engine, but even though I wanted to go after them, I didn't want to alert them to the fact that they were being followed.

"We will follow them as long as we can and maybe we'll learn something about their movements on the way, but in case we lose them, we know that they will be going to Istanbul. We have the address with us," I said calmly.

"Do you want to bet that the trucks are carrying the children who were in that warehouse in Tehran? The ones we saw evidence of but had already left the premises," she said as she nervously started to bite the cuticle of her little finger.

"I am just as sure as you are that they are transporting the children in that truck. I hope they have dressed them in something warm, or that the truck is heated, because most of this highway is through the mountains at a high altitude, and it gets very cold at night."

We stayed at a respectable distance but didn't leave the truck out of our sight. They didn't stop at all until they reached the outskirts of Erzurum and stopped outside a shabby trucker's inn.

We parked a short distance away and watched as one of the men, who we recognized as one of Farooq's cronies, jumped out of the truck and opened the back. No one came out, but we saw him haul inside a lot of full grocery bags and bottles of water. He then jumped out and slammed the door shut. Now we were certain that there were people in the back of that truck, although we didn't know whether they were adults or children. I couldn't understand how they had managed to cross the border and go past the immigration officials.

"It looks like they didn't come the same way we did," said Sarah almost as if she had read my mind.

"You are right. Look at the wheels and the undercarriage of the truck. It is caked in layers of clay and mud," I said as I peered out through the windshield. I couldn't see much because it was dusk now and it was fast getting dark. Also, the truck was parked in the shadow of a large billboard a short distance away from the inn, probably to prevent anyone from hearing any cries or whimpers from inside.

"They must have drugged the children; otherwise, they would be very restless back there." Sarah looked upset, and rightly so. Drugging children was something she hated with a vengeance.

"They seem to be settling down for the night. Let us check into the hotel across the road. It's a much better place than this rough trucker's inn. I am certain they are traveling to Istanbul. We will catch up with them, but only after our detour to Ankara." Sarah was right. We had all the information to catch them once we were on the road again.

"Thank God, they didn't spot us. If they had recognized us, we would have been in danger. These people seem to be desperate." Sarah continued to look worried and I could only agree with her, but I didn't say anything because I didn't want to make her any more anxious.

"Well, we are trying to take away a lucrative livelihood from them," was all I said.

"Come on, let's check in. I am ready for a hot bath and a warm meal." Sarah indicated that I should start the car and drive towards the hotel parking place that was just a few meters away.

CHAPTER 18

"I may not have gone where I intended to go, but I think I have ended up where I intended to be." ~ *Douglas Adams*

SARAH

When we woke up just before dawn, I looked out of the window of our hotel room and saw that the truck had already left. We could have followed them if we had heard them drive away, but we were tired and we hadn't heard a thing.

"Tanya! They have gone!" I woke up my sleepy partner.

"What? They have gone? But it's still dark outside!" We were astonished at the way these people were pushing themselves. Since there wasn't much that we could do about them, and we knew where they were going, we collected our bags and had a good breakfast, after which we set out once more.

As we drove along the highway, the sun came up over the mountains. The view was breathtaking and the forests looked almost magical.

"What is the name of this mountain pass?" asked Tanya. I looked at our road map and found that it was called the Kop Pass, situated on Mount Kop.

"The pass is quite high. I am sure it must be closed during the winter," I guessed.

"Why do you say so?" asked Tanya, sounding amused at my random speculation.

"Look at the mountains around us. It is Autumn and they are already snow-capped. Just think how much snow there would be in the middle of winter." I gestured out of the window towards the towering, majestic peaks.

"You are quite right. The last time I was here on a mission, I heard talk that they were going to build a tunnel through Mount Kop since most trade comes to a standstill because of the snow, but so far, they are still planning— typical bureaucracy and red tape." Tanya laughed.

We drove along the picturesque highway for a few hours, towards Sivas, via Trabzon, where we caught a glimpse of the historic Black Sea. It was another picturesque tourist destination that we had to resolutely pass by. *"Maybe one day..."* I thought wistfully.

"I want to have fun on this journey, even though I know we are on an extremely serious mission," I told Tanya.

"Now what are you up to?" she asked amused.

"Nothing ominous, I can assure you. I just want to have an ice cream safari." I laughed at Tanya's face.

"What is that?" She asked, trying to concentrate on the steeply curving mountain road while looking incredulously at me.

"Don't worry, my love. We are just going to eat ice cream in every town we pass through. We can later compare what ice cream we liked the most. I will keep a log in my notebook."

Tanya laughed outright. "Well, this is better than playing a continuous game of 'I Spy.'"

"What do you mean?" I giggled as I poked her in her side. "Are you already bored with our road-trip?"

Tanya just laughed, but she stopped at a large ice cream parlor in the next town, which was called Bayburt.

The vendors were in their element, holding out cones of ice cream to the customers. In the last moment, they would flick their wrists so it seemed the cone had fallen, but it would then appear in their other hand. It looked as if the balls of cold sweetness were stuck onto the waffle. When we received our order after even more shenanigans, I realized why.

"This ice cream is different from the Irani one," I said. "It's a bit chewy and more compact."

"No wonder it didn't fall off with all the horseplay and jostling." Tanya smiled.

"Well, I had fun in there and it is a plus point for them in my notebook. Let us continue our safari," I said in a faux British accent.

We drove as long as we could without nodding over the steering wheel and were able to reach Sivas just as we had planned. The city was busy and confusing, and we had no clue where to go. Unfortunately, there was nothing marked on the map.

"Why don't we ask someone at a gas station?" I suggested.

"Good idea. We need to fill up our tank too."

We found a gas pump after asking a couple of pedestrians where to go. Tanya went into the office to pay the bill and to ask about a hotel nearby. She was grinning from ear to ear when she came out.

"There is a three-star hotel nearby called *Sivas Hotel Nevv*. The man in the shop said it was small but highly recommended because..." Tanya broke off and began to laugh. She knew the more she created a mystery about the hotel, the more agitated I would get. Therefore, just to tease me, she just shook her head and said, "You will find out when we reach there."

"I will smack you with this useless map... you...you..."

"Ok! Ok! Don't get your panties in a twist. I will tell you!" Tanya couldn't stop laughing even when she held up her hands to protect herself from being smacked. Not that I would have done that anyway.

"Sivas is famous for its hot springs, and this hotel is built on an ancient one and boasts of a spa. I thought that we could go and have a look, and then we could spend an hour there before dinner. They also have massages and Turkish baths." Tanya narrated parrot-like what they had told her at the gas station. I laughed at her monotonous tone of voice.

"Well, let's go then. We have a spa to explore," I said happily.

We found the hotel easily. It looked nondescript from

outside, but it had a faded old-world ambience inside. We checked in at the massive marble counter that seemed to dwarf the woman standing behind it.

"Would it be possible to have Turkish baths and use the hot springs at this late hour?" I asked, hardly able to conceal my excitement at the thought.

Nisrin, as her nameplate said, smiled and said in quite passable English that the springs were open to hotel guests twenty-four hours, but the attendants were there for just another two hours, so if we wanted to use the facilities we had to hurry up.

"Please book us for half an hour from now. We would like to see our room and freshen up first," Tanya said with a smile.

"Definitely, I will tell the attendants to wait for you." Nisrin wrote in a book and then picked up the phone to talk to someone. "It is done," she finally said. "You have appointment for thirty minutes from now. Here is your room key. Enjoy your stay with us and the spa." She smiled as if she knew something we didn't. Well, we didn't since this would have been the first time at a spa for both of us.

We found a brochure in our room that had the history of the hotel's spa with some glossy pictures in it. We hurried to the lift and pressed the button that said 'spa.' It took us deep down underground, which was a little disconcerting. Tanya sensed my disquiet and held my hand.

Stepping out of the lift once it stopped, we entered the spa through ornate double doors. We stood stock still as we looked around in amazement. The massive underground room was within a cavern. It was more like a grotto whose walls were glistening. I wasn't sure whether it was the rock face or the humidity that made it look that way. The roof was supported by eight marble columns that were ancient but seemed sturdy. There was a large steaming pool right in the middle of the cavern which was fed by stone spigots carved in the shape of lion's heads. The water gently flowed from the open mouths of these wall sculptures. Six rooms were cordoned off with curtains to one side and we noticed marble platforms through the gaps. We couldn't see anyone and the place looked eerie even though it was well-lighted.

"Helloooo...!" I called out tentatively.

"Yes, yes, Madam, I coming!" came a voice from one of the rooms. An attractive, slightly overweight middle-aged woman followed by a younger woman who was visibly pregnant came out of one the rooms. Both women were wearing colorful traditional Turkish clothes, and each held clean, folded cotton wraps that they handed to us.

"I Dinez. I wait you. You wear, then you come to room," said the older woman. "This girl Ozlem, she no speak Inglis," she said with an apologetic smile.

"That is all right. I speak Turkish," said Tanya. There were smiles and looks of relief all around after that, and we were ushered into the room that Deniz indicated. There were two ornately carved but ancient-looking marble slabs that were raised from the ground with marble gutters below them so that the used water could flow away. On one side was a cupboard that held a collection of oils and scrubs which I presumed were to be used on us. I shivered in delighted anticipation.

We were then asked to strip completely and lie face down on the marble slabs. I felt shy undressing in front of strangers, but Tanya had no such qualms, so I just copied her and lay down as I was asked to do.

"The brochure says that this spa was built by the Romans at the time of Pompey the Great. Its healing powers are the quantities of bicarbonate, calcium, and magnesium in the waters. Can you imagine that we might be lying on the same slab that Pompey lay on?" I told Tanya as I read from the brochure while my masseuse was mixing some oils in a receptacle.

"Ewwww! Gross!" she said while laughing out loud. "Relax, Sarah, and enjoy the experience."

"What will happen now?" I asked while looking warily at the women's preparations.

"From what I have heard from my colleagues who have been to such spas, we are to be washed and scrubbed for at least forty-five minutes with a rough handwoven washcloth called a *kese,* followed by a foam wash and a massage. After that, we can soak for a while in the hot springs' water." Tanya turned then to Dinez and asked, "What is the temperature of the spring water?"

"Thirty-two degrees Celsius," she answered promptly.

Dinez told to us relax after which we were scrubbed, rubbed, and kneaded by both women. I was sure a layer of skin had been sloughed off, but oh, the feeling of exhilaration afterwards was phenomenal. Once we lowered our nude selves onto the stone benches that were underneath the surface of the pool fed by the hot springs, we were positively languid and relaxed.

"No stay too long or fall sleep," cautioned Dinez. "Heat make thirsty or faint. Fifteen minutes good. I come fetch."

She was quite firm but went away and let us have a few moments of quiet privacy.

"I feel like I am floating on a cloud. I haven't been so relaxed in ages." Tanya closed her eyes but held out her hand to me and pulled me into her arms. I lay my head on her shoulder, reveling in the closeness.

"I think I saw an advertisement for a Turkish bath in Knightsbridge. Obviously, there won't be a hot spring, but we could indulge in pampering ourselves occasionally," I said in a sleepy voice.

"Uhuh," said Tanya, agreeing with me.

Just as Tanya leaned towards me for a kiss, we heard a scream shatter our peace. Startled, I jumped up to investigate, but that was a mistake because my head began to spin. "Whoa!" I said as I stumbled against one of the marble pillars. I held on for a few moments and once I got my balance back, I wrapped myself in one of the voluminous towels that Dinez had put on the side of the pool for us and walked rapidly towards the room where the scream came from.

Ozlem stood there looking with a surprised expression at her legs, which were streaming with moisture and blood. Dinez was unsuccessfully trying to get her to lie down on one of the marble slabs in the room.

"Baby come early. Not now time!" Dinez seemed just as agitated as Ozlem.

"Since when has she been feeling uncomfortable?" I asked Dinez.

"Not big pain, just little pain from morning," she told us. "Now big pain and water break."

"Why was she working at such a strenuous job near her

time?" asked Tanya. She was clearly uncomfortable but stayed steadfastly there with me because she knew that we had unwittingly stumbled into another one of my medical "side-bars."

"Husband soldier, dead in Kurdistan," said Dinez sorrowfully. "She alone, need money, so work. I help little."

"Can you call an ambulance to take her to the hospital?" I asked. "In the meantime, let me examine her. I am a doctor."

"Doctora? Doctora! Yes! *Alhamdolillah!*" Dinez was relieved, and the worried look on her face gradually faded away and was replaced by the resolute expression of efficiency that a person gets when they know exactly what to do in certain situations.

We finally got Ozlem to lie down and as I examined her, Tanya and Dinez gathered clean towels and boiled some water. I felt a twinge of guilt... Ozlem must have already been having labour pains when she was scrubbing and massaging me, because her uterus was already fully dilated and I could already see the head of the baby. Poor woman must have been suffering in silence without giving us an inkling that she was uncomfortable.

"Dinez, don't call the hospital now. It is already too late; the baby is nearly here..." I broke off when I heard Ozlem moan in pain. I realized the baby was already in the birth canal. Supporting her from below, I asked Tanya and Dinez to rub her back and prop her up with pillows.

"Push, Ozlem! Push!" I yelled as a contraction squeezed her uterus.

"*Itmek! Itmek sevgili!*" Dinez shouted with me, and Ozlem pushed with all she had to the point of exhaustion.

The baby was delivered quite easily for a primigravida within the next ten minutes, and I cut the cord with scissors that Tanya assured me had been boiled, and tied it with some silk that Dinez handed me. After cleaning the little one and examining her, I gave the baby to Ozlem and soon she was snuggling in her mother's arms.

"Congratulations! *Tebrikler!*" We all hugged Ozlem, and Dinez, a mother of three, helped her put the baby to her breast to start to suckle. There were happy tears all around. Dinez was especially grateful because she had come to love Ozlem just like her own daughter.

"I hope you will take some days off now," I said looking at Ozlem but knowing that she didn't understand me.

"No worry, Doctora. Ozlem go my house. I look her. Then after bring baby here for work. No problem!"

Once we were sure that the mother, baby and surrogate grandmother were all right, we said our farewells and went up to our room. The journey that day, the Turkish bath, and the following excitement had made us very tired. We were more than ready to fall into bed after a light meal.

"You did good, Sarah. Have I told you how proud you always make me? Even though I do make fun of your 'side-bars,' the way you react efficiently in emergencies is amazing."

I reached up and wound my arms around her neck and whispered, "Thank you..." Then we kissed until we had to forcibly separate for a breath of air.

Tanya

. . .

Even though we slept deeply, my agent's senses were still subconsciously alert. Sometime in the early hours of the morning I heard a scraping sound come from the door and warily opened one eye. There was a strip of light shining in from the corridor and I saw a shadow move as I heard something being pushed under the door.

I carefully disentangled myself from Sarah's sleepy embrace and walked cautiously towards the door. I quietly twisted the knob to open it, but there was no one to be seen in the long corridor.

I picked up the note and unfolded it.

"*There is pizza at the reception,*" it said. The note had been typed and printed out with a dot-matrix printer, with the holes on the sides of the page still intact. For a moment, I was nonplussed. What did this mean? Who had sent this? Then I remembered 'pizza' was a code word that Andy and I used when we were on our missions together. Looking towards Sarah and seeing that she was still fast asleep, I quickly dressed and made my way to the reception.

There was a sleepy receptionist behind the counter who perked up when he saw me come out of the lift.

"Ms. Kareem, there is somebody waiting for you in the coffee shop." He pointed in the direction of a corner of the lobby that was cordoned off to create a coffee shop, where breakfast was already being served to early travelers. "But before you go there, I was told by Dinez from the spa to give this hamper to you. Shall I send it to your room?"

What a nice gesture. The hamper was a round, flat handwoven basket that had fruit, *simik,* a Turkish sesame pretzel, and a couple of boxes of Turkish Delight in it. Sarah would be pleased. There was also a note which just said, "Thank you!"

"Yes, please, send it to our room."

Entering the coffee shop, I didn't find anything unusual or anyone familiar until I saw someone sitting at a table right at the back of the room attacking a plate of eggs and beans.

"Andy! What are you doing here?" I was so happy to see my work partner. "I hope you have ordered a carafe of coffee, because waking me up so early in the morning is not very nice. You know I tend to growl when I haven't had my regular morning dose of caffeine." I laughed.

"Sit down, please. I have ordered coffee and breakfast for you. Sarah will be sent her breakfast to your room."

"Thanks. Let me call Sarah from the house phone so that I can wake her up and let her know that her breakfast is on the way. I will also ask her to start packing."

When I came back after talking to Sarah, there was a plate of eggs and beans just like Andy's at my place. I was ravenous since we had had hardly anything to eat the night before.

"You are looking good, relaxed even. Maybe you should bring Sarah on all your missions." Andy laughed at his own joke.

"Hmph... what brings you here? Are you finished with your Afghan mission?"

"No, I have orders to help you get to Istanbul and then I must return. Apparently, the smugglers recognized you in Erzurum, but one of our undercover agents who are with the smugglers said they lost track of you. You are constantly in danger if we have no mode of contact with you, and you know it's not safe to use the phone lines. Headquarters wants you to report to them every alternate day, so they have instructed me to bring you a satellite phone so that there can be a two-way communication between you and them."

"I was feeling a bit lost being out of touch, but so far we have managed..." I started to say.

"Tanya, no one is saying that your work so far hasn't been absolutely stellar, but you will agree that being in touch with headquarters, especially in case you are in trouble, increases your confidence and obviously your safety factors."

Andy was right. All Interpol agents needed backup if things didn't go well, and so far, even though we were unscathed, it would have been nice to know that help was near.

Andy handed me a leather case in which there was a satellite phone. As I examined and familiarized myself with it, I noticed the difference between a regular cell phone and this one was the thick antenna.

"Let us go to your room. I am sure Sarah must be ready by now. You can call the boss and give him a report of what has happened so far. The information headquarters have received so far is sporadic since some of it was from us and some from undercover agents who couldn't contact you if they wanted to make sure their cover wasn't blown."

I finished the last of my coffee and we walked towards the lift. There was a poster advertising the hot springs and Turkish bath we had indulged in the night before.

"It's a pity that we don't have much time. I would have liked to check out the springs," said Andy wistfully.

"They were relaxing. Sarah and I spent some time there last night." I smirked.

"Of course, you would," he countered with a mock scowl followed by a wink and a grin.

We knocked on the door in case Sarah was still getting ready, but she opened the door dressed in her jeans and sweatshirt.

"Andy!" she said, delighted to see him. "What brings you here? I thought you were lusting after the ladies in blue *burqas.*" She laughed.

"I have brought a satellite phone so that you can be in contact with our head office." He turned to me with a smirk and said, "Well, what are you waiting for? Try it out; the boss is waiting to hear from you."

While Sarah and Andy chatted, I called Mr. Humphrey. He picked up after two rings.

"Agent Kareem... Tanya! I was waiting for your call. Andy tracked you down... very good. Now we will be able to send help for you in case you need it."

"Thank you, Mr. Humphrey. We are aware that the smugglers are en-route to Istanbul, but we need to go to Ankara to legitimize our travel documents."

"Didn't Andy tell you? He has already done that. He has new British passports for you and Dr. Sarah with the legitimate visas and stamps of entry into Turkey. You can now go directly to Istanbul and not waste precious time by diverting to Ankara. He has also procured a British carne du passage for your car along with British number plates. How you managed to get a car in your name in Iran is beyond me, but I am sure your written report when you get back will be very interesting to read."

I gave him a quick summary of what had happened so

far and told him about the addresses we had and where we thought the children were being taken.

"Not only do we have addresses for hideouts in Istanbul, but also in Sofia, Bulgaria, and Zagreb in Croatia. I hope we don't have to go there because the country is still at war with Serbia and it could be dangerous."

"You are right, if it comes to the point that the trail leads you to Croatia, I want you to stand back and let our agents there continue. You and Dr. Sarah have done a very good job so far and both of you will get commendations for it, but I don't want you to deliberately be in danger. Afghanistan was unfortunate because you were forced to go there because of the hijacking."

"I understand. We will keep you informed of our moves." With that, I switched the phone off. I didn't want to be tracked and had decided to switch it on only in the evenings or when I needed to talk to headquarters.

"Andy, I believe you have another packet for me?" I asked him.

"Yes, I have given your new passports and car papers to Sarah. When we check out, let us drive out of town and then I will help you change the number plates on your car."

"Thank you. I am relieved that we will be reaching Istanbul much earlier than planned." Andy knew about Sarah's psychic abilities, so we told him about her seeing the smugglers hide the children. He was surprised but took it in his stride quite well.

"We need to be on the road. As I told you before, I will only be with you until we reach Istanbul, and then I must go back to Herat."

Andy whistled in admiration when he saw our car. "This

is one hell of a gift!" he said as he walked around examining it like the car enthusiast he was.

Sarah opted to sit in the back since Andy's bulk wouldn't have fitted there, especially as the front seat had to be folded so that the back passenger could climb in. The highway to Istanbul beckoned us and we were soon on our way.

CHAPTER 19

"Here I come, Constantinople... oops, sorry, Istanbul!"
~S. Magedin

SARAH

Now that we were able to focus properly on our destination, the car seemed to eat up the miles. Tanya planned to enter the outskirts of Istanbul by early evening, and I was glad that we had Andy along to share in the driving. We only stopped once to stock up the massive cooler Ali had given us with sandwiches, fruit, and drinks. We also changed our car's number plates from Turkish to British to legitimize our cover in Turkey as British tourists. We didn't want to waste any more time and it was a relief just to think that we would finish this mission and go home soon... fingers crossed. *One never knew with our luck,* I thought as I smiled inwardly. We always seemed to turn straightforward journeys into adventures, and though it was frightening at the time, it was also a lot of fun to be working with real agents to save children.

Tanya and Andy spent most of the journey discussing the case. I was lulled to sleep by the motion of the car, but I piped in whenever I was awake and when it was relevant.

"We were informed that most of the children are taken to the Children of Mercy orphanage in Zagreb, from where they are sold to adoption agencies or child pornographers, depending on the demand."

"Why don't we just go straight to Zagreb then?" I asked.

"Because we need to help the children who are incarcerated in Istanbul. Moreover, we need to find solid proof that the orphanage is involved. So far, we just have circumstantial evidence," explained Tanya.

"We hope that we can find the proof in Istanbul, and then we will pass that on to our European agents and they will handle the case from there," said Andy.

"Why don't the police just go and arrest the men while we are on our way to Istanbul?" I asked. "After all, Mr. Murphey said we had to gather information and not engage with the smugglers."

"If we send in our men, it might trigger an international incident since the smugglers have been clever enough to hide the children in one of the busiest tourist neighborhoods. This has to be handled delicately, so we are to find out the best way to rescue the children, find proof, and then have the men arrested without creating a furor." Andy sounded frustrated. "If it were up to me, I would liaise with the local police and storm the place at night, but the red tape would take so long that the smugglers and the children would be long gone before the teams were in place. Our orders are then to act now and explain later...." Andy turned back to grin at me.

"Why are these private and illegal adoption agencies so popular?" I asked.

"Because they just charge a lump sum that is lower than the legal procedures, and arrange the paperwork for the prospective parents, who are not even aware of the nefarious ways the children are procured. They genuinely believe that the children are orphans and that they are providing a home to children in need," said Tanya darkly.

"Pakistani children from the Northern areas look very European with their fair skin and light eyes, so they are very much in demand," Andy added.

"Curses on Alexander the Great, who brought the Aryan gene to our area," I said heatedly. If the 'business' was so lucrative, I shuddered to think how many children had been taken from their parents. We used to hear radio and television announcements regarding missing children. Never before were they so poignant as they were now when we were painfully aware of their plight.

While mulling over our situation, I hardly noticed the beautiful landscape that we passed, but I noticed the children dressed in traditional Turkish garb waving at us from the roadside and shouting *"güle güle."* I hoped no one thought them cute enough to kidnap as I tried to shake the dark thoughts out of my mind.

Just as Tanya had planned, we saw the buildings and spires of Istanbul by early evening. I sat up straight, wanting to have my first glimpse of the ancient historic city. It was breathtaking. We were still on the Asian side, and the Marmara Sea was shining like a calm blue jewel on our left. The beaches were crowded with people taking advantage of the mild weather. I wished that we had time to dip our toes in that magnificent expanse of water, but we had important work to do and there was no time to be sidetracked. The traffic had increased by then, most probably because it was just the time when people went home after a day's work. Like in any major city in the world, it was the detested rush hour, which meant we could only inch our way slowly towards the Bosphorus Strait.

"Should we take the ferry or drive over the remarkable one-and-a-half-kilometer Bosphorus Bridge?" I asked. Tanya turned a looked at me with a smile.

"I see you are still gathering information... one and a half kilometer? That's impressive!" she exclaimed.

"What does the radio say?" asked Andy, who was driving at that moment. "You are the linguist here; you would understand what they are saying," he said while nudging Tanya's shoulder with his playfully.

Tanya leaned forward and fiddled with the controls of the FM radio in the car and finally found a station where they were giving live traffic information and commentary to the listeners. The announcements sounded like Double Dutch to Andy and me, but Tanya listened carefully and nodded.

"The traffic is congested and backed up at both places, so I suggest that we opt to inch along the bridge. No doubt it will be slow, but we will be spared the extra time that would be needed to embark and disembark at the ferry ports."

"Yes, that is a better option," said Andy. "We need to get to the European side of Istanbul, where the children are held captive. As soon as we check into our hotel, we should go and have a look around the area."

"I will come with you," I said.

"No, it's too dangerous," said Tanya and Andy in unison.

"And what we have gone through so far wasn't dangerous?" I replied.

"You are right, but we know that the smugglers are heavily armed, and I don't want anything to happen to you," said Tanya as she took my hand in hers and stroked it with her thumb.

"I can be a look-out and stay in the car to drive you away at short notice. I can be helpful to the team," I said almost sulkily.

"She has a point there," said Andy.

"Oh, all right. But you stay in the car. Whistle if you see or hear anything unusual. Just promise me you won't take any risks," Tanya said after mulling over the situation for a few seconds.

We found a nondescript but clean hotel near the *Taksim* area, where we last knew the children were held. While we washed off the dust of the road, we had room service send us a snack. As soon as we were ready, we went to the lobby to look for Andy.

"Ah! There you are! I was just about to send someone to fetch you!" said Andy with a smile.

Tanya made a rude noise and stuck her tongue out at him, causing him to laugh.

"Andy, since you know Istanbul better that us, why

don't you drive to the address we have and then Sarah can sit in the driver's seat and wait for us?" Instructed Tanya.

"Even at this time of the evening, the area will be crowded with tourists, so it won't be as if you are waiting for us in a dark alley. You will still have to be alert when you think you see someone you recognize. I said earlier that you should whistle, but now I realize that we will not be able to hear that over the hum of the crowd and the traffic. What do you suggest, Andy?"

"How about giving four short blasts on the car horn? It's loud enough. I am sure we would hear it from inside the building."

"Don't forget to activate your pendant," said Tanya. "In case I can't see you when we get out, I will track you by its signal."

The address we were looking for was a ten-minute drive from our hotel. It was a two-storied building on the main road, surrounded by a high wall with iron spikes on top. Diagonally opposite, we could see the minarets and the dome of the famous Blue Mosque. 'Hiding in plain sight' took on a new meaning that day.

I settled back into the driver's seat as soon as Andy and Tanya stepped out and walked stealthily into the side-lane that was on the right side of the boundary wall of the building. Tanya stopped to look back, sent me a flying kiss, and then disappeared into the shadows.

Tanya

. . .

I felt a mild disquiet leaving Sarah alone, but I knew that she would be an asset if we had to leave in a hurry. I was worried that someone might recognize and harm her. We had parked the car in the shade of a large billboard. It wasn't unusual to see a car parked that way in a city like Istanbul, and I made sure that Sarah's face was in the shadows.

Andy and I walked the periphery of the wall. It was about two meters high and had vicious looking spikes on top of it. There was a large main gate and a smaller one in the alley in the back.

"We should concentrate on the smaller gate," said Andy. "Let me go and examine the lock; in the meantime, go and take cover behind that dumpster beside it and keep a lookout in case anyone is coming."

I did as Andy instructed but I peered round the side of the dumpster and watched as he tried the lock. It had one of those spring mechanisms that lock the gate once it is pulled closed.

After jiggling the mechanism with his lock-picks, Andy looked over his shoulder and gave me the thumbs up sign. I quietly loped over to him and followed him silently through the gate. There wasn't much of a garden—just a strip of grass and some tired looking flowers that surrounded the wall of the house. The front door was locked, but we stealthily made our way to the back door. We were surprised that we didn't see anyone. The kitchen door had a glass window and as we peered through it, we noticed that it was dark inside.

"Can you see anything at all?" I asked.

"No, but the door is open. Let us be as quiet as we can," Andy said as he tried the door handle.

We held our weapons in our hands while we crept inside. There wasn't a speck of dust in the kitchen, and the fridge hummed as its compressor kicked in. I opened it and saw that it was well stocked. There was enough food there to feed a large family.

"Someone is definitely living here. Let's see what we can find in the other rooms." I gestured to Andy to go ahead.

We went from room to room, surprised that we didn't find any signs of them being occupied. In contrast to the kitchen, all of the furniture here was covered by a thin film of dust.

"This is strange," I said. "Are we at the right address?"

"We are." Andy sounded slightly offended that I would even ask that. "I studied the maps and the area in detail."

"Well, I don't want to be arrested for home invasion when a local family comes back home from vacation." I smiled to show that I wasn't blaming him for anything.

"We might find clues in the basement." Andy was clearly upset and wanted to find something to justify coming to this address.

"If the children were here, the smugglers wouldn't have had much time to take them away. We weren't very far behind them. Unless they had supernatural powers." I punched Andy lightly on the arm. I knew how he felt—this was frustrating.

We found the door to the basement in the pantry near the kitchen. The door handle was also dust free and I shone my torch around to see whether there was anything that would tell us what we wanted to know. As I trained the beam of light on the floor, I clutched Andy's arm.

There in the dusty floor were footprints. Many

footprints. Of adults as well as smaller ones that without any doubt belonged to children!

The basement door had well-oiled hinges, and there was no sound as we made our way down the stairs, following the footprints. Where was everyone? The basement was as dusty and empty as the rest of the house above. Where were the children? And where did the footprints lead to?

"This is strange." Andy stood there scratching his head. "Our first indication that someone was here, and it's leading us nowhere!"

"Look!" I pointed to where the footprints were going. "This is even stranger. The footprints are leading towards that wall on the right and then they disappear!"

We examined the area around the wall and noticed semicircular scrape marks on the floor.

"There seems to be a hidden passage behind that wall," I whispered, excited at the prospect of finding it. Since there wasn't anyone around, I switched the light on and saw that the empty basement was constructed of old stones that might have dated back to Roman times.

"We need to find a switch or a lever that will help us open the passage," said Andy.

"I wish Sarah was with us. She loves history and historic artifacts." I sighed.

"Sarah is much safer where she is. It was clever to convince her to be a lookout."

"You are right," I said with a smile. "It was just wishful thinking."

It took us nearly half an hour to find the hidden lever to open the passage. It was neatly fitted into a sooty alcove which I guessed was used to hold candles or lanterns in the olden days. It was a good disguise because it should have been completely covered with soot, but since it had recently been used, it was smooth and devoid of a thick layer of grime.

"Bingo!" whispered Andy with a grin on his face. There was a streak of soot on his forehead and nose where he had wiped them with his dirty hand. I couldn't help grinning because he looked just like a little boy who had been playing in the mud.

Andy pulled the lever and we watched in fascination as the wall silently swung open revealing stone steps that led downwards into a passage.

"Follow me and cover my back," said Andy as he stepped into the opening.

I went down a few stairs and must have tripped some mechanism because, to our dismay, the wall swung back into place leaving us in darkness.

"We didn't switch off the basement lights!" I said. "If anyone comes down, they will know that someone was there."

"Well, we are trapped now in this passage..." Andy sounded unsure, but then he shrugged and continued forward.

The passage was steep, and it went downwards for a few meters and then straightened, but we still didn't see any exits. After walking for another ten minutes, we saw a shimmer of light in the distance.

"Switch your torch off. We don't want to alert the smugglers. We are like sitting ducks here," I said.

We came to a heavy door that was made of thick wooden slats, making it possible for the light on the other side to filter into the passage. I looked through one of the slats and stepped back in astonishment.

"What is it? Are we in the right place?" asked Andy.

"Have a look for yourself," I said and stepped aside to let him look through the slats.

"But...but... that is the *Basilica Cistern*!" said Andy, just as surprised as I was.

"It is beautiful!" I breathed. "What is it exactly?"

"It is an underground cistern that provided a water filtration system for the Great Palace of Constantinople. It was built by Emperor Constantine and enlarged by Emperor Justinian."

"That's ancient!" The columns and arches over the quiet waters were awe inspiring.

"If I remember correctly, it is only 150 meters from the Hagia Sophia mosque. Maybe the children saw that dome?" Andy kept looking through the slats in the door as if he couldn't believe his eyes.

"It seems deserted now," I said.

"The last tour for the tourists ends at about seven pm. I know that because I caught the last one when I visited Istanbul in the summer."

"Let us go and have a look around. These ancient places usually have storage rooms and even large halls. I heard that Constantine tried to build a park down here, so there should be many other rooms or alcoves around." Andy carefully opened the door and peered out.

The cistern was fascinating, and the tall columns and arches gave the impression of a very high cathedral roof. Two of the columns sported massive medusa heads. I wondered why it all felt so familiar to me... I had never stepped foot there before.

"Isn't this amazing!" said Andy. "They filmed a scene from a James Bond movie here in the cistern." Ah! That was probably where I had seen it before.

As we walked alongside the pools of crystal-clear water, I heard a sound. More like a whimper. "The children, Andy! They are here!"

Andy stopped to listen and nodded. "I hear something too. Be careful."

As we neared a door that was set flush against an outcropping in the wall, we heard a whimper again. Andy whispered in my ear. "What do we do now? Should we take a risk and enter?"

Just as we were about to open the door, we heard a voice speak from within the room. "Agent Kareem, put your weapon down and come in with your hands on your head."

I gave Andy a startled look. What was happening? How did they know we were there?

As if reading our minds, the voice spoke once more. "Do you think a multimillion-dollar organization as ours won't have surveillance cameras around? We see you very clearly on our monitors. I wouldn't advise you to do anything rash because we have something precious of yours with us!"

"Sarah!" I shouted, terrified for her. "Are you there, sweetheart?"

"Yes! Don't worry about me; just take care of the children. They are in the next... mmmph!" Sarah's voice was abruptly muffled.

"As I said before we were rudely interrupted, put your weapons on the floor, kick them away, and then slowly open the door and come inside. Remember we can see you, so don't try to be smart. The life of your dear doctor depends on it."

Andy and I did as we were told. Sarah's life was at stake, and I didn't want to risk losing her.

We entered the room with our hands above our heads. The sci-fi looking console and monitors were incongruous with the ancient historical ambience we had just passed through. Every corner of the cistern was seen in the monitors, and on two of them we could see the children as they slept on their cots.

"Tanya!" Only because I knew Sarah so well could I detect a frisson of fear in her voice, but I was so proud of her as she sat up straight in the chair where they had tied her, trying not to show that she was affected by the men's rough behavior.

"Are you okay? Did they hurt you?"

"I am fine, but they have drugged the children like they did before. They are in a similar room a few meters away."

"Be quiet, doctor!" said one of the men who held a gun in his hand. He lifted his hand as if he wanted to slap Sarah, but before I could say anything, the man who was acting as their leader shouted, "Enough!"

Andy and I were roughly pushed into two other chairs and our hands and feet were bound with hemp ropes. Even though they didn't tie my hands too tight, the ropes chaffed my skin and soon my wrists were sporting red welts.

"Have you loaded the other children into the truck?" asked the leader. We had seen him with Farooq in Afghanistan, but we didn't know his or the other men's names.

"Yes, boss, we are ready to move out as soon as you give us the word," said the man who had been about to strike Sarah. I pointedly scowled at him, but it didn't bother him at all.

"You!" said the leader, pointing to a man in the corner. "Stay with these people. See that they don't escape."

"What do I do with them? They can't stay here indefinitely!" he said. He sounded disappointed that he was to be left behind.

"Just do as I say. I will telephone you with instructions as soon as we cross the border into Bulgaria."

"Okay, boss," he said sulkily and sat down on a stool in the corner while keeping an eye on us.

"We have most of the children with us; there are only ten of them in the next room. It is your responsibility to see that they are fed. If they get unmanageable, you know where the vials of morphine are kept." The leader winked to his disgruntled employee. "Don't let me down." With that, he turned around and left the room, followed by his other men.

"What do we do now?" Sarah whispered. "How do we get out of this situation? We are being guarded by a trigger-happy man who wouldn't think twice to shoot us." Tears started to roll down her cheeks.

"You are such a brave woman... I am sure the three of us can think of something." I tried to calm her nerves, but I wasn't very successful because I was just as anxious as she and Andy were.

We sat in silence for a while until the sound of a child crying came over the sound system.

Looking at the monitor, our captor gave an exasperated sigh and left the room without saying a word.

"Tanya, psst!" said Andy. "I have a slim blade hidden under the sole of my shoe. I will put my shoe near your hands, and you try to take it out. It's quite easy if you get a proper grip on the tip."

"Please hurry up. I don't want to stay here any longer," said Sarah.

Andy scooted over with his chair and put his foot on my lap. I thanked all that was holy that the men had tied my hands in front instead of the back. I pulled the blade from the sole, and soon all three of us stood up rubbing our wrists.

"Sarah, you hide behind the cupboard, and Andy, you stand on one side of the door while I stand on the other. As soon as the man comes in, I will hit him on the head with this heavy file that I found on the table. It won't hurt much, but it will disorient him long enough that we could tie him up and gag him."

Both of them nodded silently and took their positions. After what seemed like the longest ten minutes in history, the man walked in and did a double take when he saw that the chairs were empty. Just as he turned to walk out of the room, I smashed the heavy file on his head and he plopped down on the floor holding his head, visibly befuddled.

Things then happened very fast. Sarah and I tied him up while Andy called the Interpol liaison office in Istanbul and soon the place was overrun by men in uniform. The Turkish authorities were appalled that their historic Basilica Cistern had served as a covert command center for the smugglers. Ancient relics and buildings are sacrosanct for the Turkish people, and they weren't happy at all.

The children were taken by the local Child Protection

Services and we were assured that they would be properly taken care of, but we still had to connect the smugglers to the Children of Mercy orphanage in Zagreb. There wasn't a paper trail in this place that could have implicated them, so it was up to us to find proof.

CHAPTER 20

"There is nothing more deceptive than an obvious fact."
~ Arthur Conan Doyle, The Boscombe Valley Mystery
– a Sherlock Holmes Short Story.

SARAH

While Tanya and Andy were interrogated by the local police, I gave the Interpol liaison officer, Agent Argyll Thomas, a detailed description of the men and the vehicle they were driving. He had been assigned with following the truck, and he wanted to be on his way as soon as he could..

"Dr. Shah, I would suggest that you rest before you travel again. You have been through an ordeal, and I have a feeling we will be meeting the kingpin of this whole organization soon."

"Thank you for your concern, Agent Thomas. I will

leave for the hotel when Agent Kareem has finished with the local police. I do hope she isn't in trouble." I was concerned since we had entered the country illegally.

"Don't worry, Doctor, our agency has arrangements with local law enforcement all over the world. Especially when such important cases are involved." He winked and stood up. He gripped my hand in a firm handshake, tipped his hat in an old-worldly fashion, and left the room.

Having nothing else to do but wait for Tanya and Andy, I started to look around the room. Most of the files had already been removed by the police, but I still wanted to see whether anything had been missed. Since nothing was found in the main room, I quietly left to go the room where the children had been kept. Maybe I would find a clue on the off chance that no one thought that the children's room would have anything of interest except for the cots they slept on.

The room was in disarray as the children were taken away as soon as they were discovered by the authorities. Only a little blankie and a forlorn cheap doll were evidence that the children had been there.

I sat down in the sole chair in the room and looked around. It seemed futile—there was nothing of interest. I was getting bored so I started to count the ancient stones that made up the wall in front of me. It was a quirk of mine to count things when I wanted to focus or was stressed. There were thirty-six stones to a row.... but the twelfth row had thirty-eight stones, and yet the walls looked symmetrical. Was this just a medieval fluke in construction? Or was there something hidden behind the stones?

I got up to look closer and saw that there were minute, microfine gaps in between the stones. Someone had moved them and fairly recently! I pulled the chair to the wall and stood on it to try to pry one of the stones away from the wall, but they did not budge. I tried for over half an hour but made no progress whatsoever. Then I thought that if the wall in the other room could open with a lever and a hidden switch, then maybe there was a secret alcove in this wall as well. I pressed a few random stones, but nothing happened. I stepped off the chair and was about to turn away, disheartened, when I noticed that one of the stones was smoother than the others. I climbed once more on the chair, leaned over and pressed the stone firmly. Then I heard a loud click to my right. A panel swung open revealing an alcove with two shelves. On the top shelf were currencies from at least five countries, and the bottom shelf was stuffed with folders and files. I had found a veritable treasure! I hoped that the information in the files would help us put the investigation to rest. We needed to rid the world of these people who profited from the pain of parents and children.

I put the files back as they were, closed the panel, and then went back into the control room, where the others were. I heaved a sigh of relief when I saw that the monitors had been switched off. If nobody had noticed what I had been up to, we would have some time to read through the files before the local authorities became aware of them and took them away. Tanya and Andy looked as if they were winding down their discussions with the police, so I waited until they were finished. They shook hands cordially and walked over to where I was standing.

"Stay back; let them go," I whispered to Tanya.

"Why? What's wrong?" She looked concerned.

"Are they going to leave any officers here?" I asked Andy.

"I don't think so. They have taken most of what is available here. Someone will come to decide about the surveillance equipment. There was talk about handing it over to the tourist department. They can monitor the safety of the visitors to the cistern this way, and it won't cost them much since the best possible equipment is already installed here," Andy said with a short and terse laugh.

"I am going to mock-faint. Tell them you are making me lie down on one of the children's beds until I feel better. They can lock up the command center if they want to. It's important. I will tell you about it later...after they have left," I whispered to Tanya as I stumbled against her. It was easy to slowly slide onto the floor with my eyes closed and my limbs limp. Andy scooped me up in his arms and Tanya opened the door while proclaiming loudly that she was taking me to lie down next door.

I must say that they acted well. Tanya picked up a piece of discarded cardboard and started to fan me once I lay down while Andy went to look for some water to drink.

I heard him talk with the police in hushed voices and finally heard them say goodbye. Andy came into the room and locked it from inside. He had a bottle of chilled water in his hand which he had probably bought from one of the kiosks on the surface.

"Now tell us what this drama is all about," said Tanya.

Instead of answering, I got up and pressed the relevant key stone and enjoyed the look of surprise on her face when the hidden door swung open.

"We don't have much time. Take one of the pillowcases and stuff the files into it. Take the money as well. We will give it to the authorities with the files once we are done with them," Andy instructed.

"Dr. Sarah Shah! You are amazing!" Tanya reached out to hug me close and kiss me almost senseless.

I couldn't stop smiling. Maybe this was the breakthrough we needed?

Instead of leaving the citadel the usual way, we left the way Tanya and Andy came in. Tanya thought that was better since our car was nearby and no one would see that we were lugging two full pillowcases with us. We managed to reach our hotel without anyone seeing or apprehending us. All these underground passages and hidden doors made me feel as if I was in a live Enid Blyton mystery... I laughed at the thought, thoroughly enjoying myself.

Tanya

I thought that we would be exhausted after our ordeal, but the thrill of finding the hidden files was very exciting, so all three of us stayed up late reading the papers Sarah had found.

For once, we had solid leads and evidence that Farooq's group was heavily involved in the smuggling. We even found the name of a person that was almost deferentially mentioned in the files...Vladimir Jovanović. His name popped up many times in the documents.

"Vladimir Jovanović... where have I heard this name before?" asked Andy to no one in particular. I could see that his mind was working at high speed. After being quiet for a while, he suddenly jumped up, startling Sarah and me.

"Vladimir Jovanović! Of course! He is well known to Interpol. He is a drug smuggler and a gun runner. I don't think the agency realizes that he is into human trafficking now." Andy was agitated. "We need to contact headquarters! We have enough proof here that he is involved in the smuggling ring that supplies children to his adoption agency."

"Andy," I said quietly to calm him down. "Do you think that these papers are enough? Any slick lawyer could help him refute that. Most of the papers here are neutrally worded. They could be legitimate transactions with the adoption agency."

"Tanya is right. The only people these papers implicate without any doubt are Farooq and his gang. This Jovanović guy is very clever."

"I believe the last the Agency heard of Jovanović he was in Sarajevo. I wish I could go with you, but I have to go back to Herat." Andy said while looking down at the papers. "I will let the Agency know where you are, but you need to leave early in the morning."

"I have decided to leave the car here and fly to Croatia," I said. "Would you arrange for it to be sent to London for me please?"

"Won't the gang be on the lookout for us if we arrive in a commercial flight?" Sarah asked.

"You are right. I will charter an air taxi from Istanbul to Sofia, Bulgaria. If anyone is watching us, they will think that we are going in the wrong direction."

"I will ask Stepanov, our Bulgarian agent, to meet you

there and give you an update if there is one." Andy was all business now. "You can charter a plane from Sofia to Sarajevo incognito since you won't need passports to travel to Croatia from Bulgaria."

I picked up the hotel phone and asked the operator to put me through to an air taxi company. They had the number on hand. It seemed that many people visiting their hotel had used the services of the company. Booking a flight for two people on a small four-seater plane was easy and we were set to go at six in the morning.

"You do realize that booking through the hotel phone is a definite way to let the others know where you are going," said Sarah.

"Yes. That is why I booked the flight to Sofia International Airport, but once we are over Bulgarian airspace, I will ask the pilot to land on *Dolna Bania*, one of the smaller airports on the outskirts of the city," I said with a grin.

"Hmmm... devious." Sarah smiled.

Sarah and I spent the next hour copying the names and addresses mentioned in the files, and then handed the originals over to Andy, who would send them with the diplomatic pouch to London. We said our goodbyes and got ready for bed. Tomorrow promised to be busy, and I still had to formulate a solid plan in my mind. Sarah and I would most probably be brainstorming during the flight.

There was something bothering me. I just couldn't make out what it was. It was like an irritating song stuck in my head when I didn't know the words to it. I tossed and turned most of the night as my brain churned over the information we had gathered.

We left as scheduled for the small airport from which we were to take the air taxi. I kept looking behind us to see whether we were being followed.

"What is wrong, my love?" asked Sarah as she reached out to hold my hand. She knew that was the best thing to calm me down.

"I really don't know, but I have this feeling of disquiet that is getting more and more acute. I feel as if we are being followed."

"Do you trust Andy?" asked Sarah.

"I do. After all, he is my partner. If we don't trust each other, it could cost us our lives on dangerous missions." As I spoke, my feeling of uneasiness increased. Was Andy honest with us? He had all the files with him, and we had no proof except hand-written notes with addresses and names on them. If the files disappeared, we wouldn't have a case against Farooq or Vladimir Jovanović. I thought I should have kept some files with me.

As these thoughts were racing through my mind, Sarah reached out once more and asked, "Why are you upset? What are you thinking?"

"I was thinking that I was a fool not to keep at least one file with us." I didn't mention Andy. I didn't want to upset her in any way. We were in the last leg of our investigation and I wanted it to be as smooth as possible.

Sarah smiled and then tried to stifle a giggle. I looked at her as if she had lost her mind. "What on earth?" I asked.

As she continued to giggle, she lifted her sweatshirt and showed me the file that she had tied around her waist. No wonder she was sitting so stiffly upright.

"I didn't feel very comfortable either. I kept on getting

the sense that everything was not as it seemed, so when the two of you were discussing one of the files, I slipped this one under the mattress. I didn't tell you about it because I thought you might get upset that I acted upon one of my 'feelings' again."

"I have learned to respect your 'feelings,' my love. Thank God for them!" I took the file from her and leafed through it. It was the one that had the most information about the adoption agency and Farooq's involvement.

"I knew that you trusted Andy completely, but I kept getting negative vibes from him. I guess I kept tamping them down, since it was Andy, and like you I didn't want him to be a traitor. I think he somehow was able to block the negative vibes from himself since he knew of my psychic abilities. I am so sorry I didn't follow my intuition." Sarah hung her head.

I hugged her and gave her a kiss on the top of her head. The taxi driver was watching us through his rear-view mirror, and I didn't want to give him a free show. I just tightly held onto Sarah's hand and blessed God that I had such an enterprising and intelligent partner in my life.

We still didn't know whether Andy was involved with the smugglers, but I was glad that we had at least one of the files.

The flight to Sofia was uneventful and the pilot gladly agreed to land on the smaller airstrip since it wasn't very busy and that meant he could refuel and fly back almost immediately. We took a taxi to the middle of town and had our breakfast in a pretty roadside café near the *Ivan Vazof* National Theater.

I used the public telephone at the café to call Stepanov,

our local Interpol liaison agent. For one moment, I nearly didn't want to call him because he was the one that Andy had arranged for us to meet in Sofia. How much could I trust him? Was he really 'kosher' or was I just being paranoid?

After I dialed his number, I heard the bell ring a few times and was just about to hang up when I heard a curt voice say, "*Kakvo?*"

"Stepanov?" I answered, not sure if I had the right number.

"*Da, Stepanov tuk!*"

"My name is Agent Tanya Kareem. I believe you have some information for me?"

"Ah, yes! Agent Kareem. I was waiting for you. Tell me where you are, and I will come and give you the information that you need."

Even though what he said was innocuous, there seemed to be an undercurrent of menace in his voice. Was I just being hypersensitive? Even if I was, I wanted to be certain that he was on our side. I gave him the name of the restaurant which was diagonally opposite to the café where we sat. After I hung up, I sauntered over to our table and spoke to Sarah in a low voice.

"Stepanov is on his way, but I don't have a good feeling about him either. I think we shouldn't trust anyone at the moment." I sighed and ran my fingers through my already tousled hair. "I have told him to meet us at the restaurant across the road. I want to observe him when he arrives."

"Let us sit by the window then. The table near the door is ideal if we want to make a quick getaway," said Sarah. "Do you know how he looks? Will you recognize him?"

"Yes, I will. We have annual conferences at the head office, and the local representatives of the member countries are supposed to attend. It's usually a big affair. I think I told you about that before." I smiled at Sarah, knowing she was a bit absentminded at times.

"Ah, yes, you did. That's the day when you dress up formally and come back the next day," she said acerbically.

"Yes, that's the day." I laughed. "And no, nothing sinister or illegal happens there. We are just put through meeting after meeting, and after dinner all that we can do is fall asleep in the rooms that the agency arranges for us."

"I know. I would have liked to come along, but on a subconscious level I know that I would be as bored as you would be if you attended my medical conferences." Sarah smiled while reaching over to squeeze my hand affectionately.

"Look, there he is..." I pointed Stepanov out to Sarah. He was a short, overweight man with a toupee, and a red nose. He wore his pants under his protuberant beer belly and had a small handgun in his hand. He was looking inside the picture windows to see whether he recognized anyone sitting at the tables. That was enough proof for me. Stepanov was Andy's friend and seemed just as dirty.

"Is there a back exit?" I asked a passing waitress. She nodded and pointed towards the back near the restrooms. I tipped her and asked her to say that she hadn't seen us if anyone asked. Nodding, she pocketed the generous tip and moved on as if this conversation hadn't happened.

"Hurry up; let's go." I pulled Sarah along with me. My heart was pounding as adrenaline rushed through my body. I could see fear on Sarah's pale face as well, but she didn't say a word. She just held on to me and ran alongside. We were lucky that we didn't have to go far and caught a taxi just a few meters from where we emerged from the café. We passed by the restaurant and ducked down in our seats, but not before we saw Stepanov standing there scratching his head with a puzzled look on his face.

"Where do you want to go?" asked our taxi driver in English. My relief at being able to communicate easily with him must have been evident on my face because he laughed and said, "My name is Alexei. Here in Bulgaria, students are given the option to learn either French or English in school."

"You must have had a very good teacher because you speak English very well," Sarah said.

"My wife is English, and we have been together for twenty years now, so yes, she is an amazing teacher and an amazing person." We could hear the love he had for his wife in his voice.

"Well, Alexei, we need to charter a plane to Belgrade. Can you take us to an airport where we could hire one?"

"I can take you to the *Dolna Banya* airport. They have good air-taxi services there."

"That is too far away. Do you know of any airfield nearby?" I asked. I didn't want to drive seventy-five kilometers again. We needed to make a quick getaway, and I was sure that Stepanov had figured out we had entered the country via *Dolna Banya*.

"Okay, let me think..." After a few moments, Alexei thumped on his steering wheel and exclaimed, "Why didn't I think of it! My cousin Vlad works at the *Ihtiman* airport. It's just forty-five kilometers away, and they also have air taxi and charter services."

"Then let us go to *Ihtiman* airport," I said, pumping my arms in mock victory while trying to hide my anxiety by copying his jovial mood.

Vlad turned out to be the station manager of the small airport and he made us sit and have a cup of coffee while he arranged for our flight. He soon came back with the flight papers for us to sign.

"Vlad, we are being chased by bad men, and we need to get home as soon as we can. Would it be possible to make a fake booking to London in case anyone came and asked where we had gone?" I batted my eyelashes at him, playing a helpless female. It seemed that chivalry wasn't dead because he nodded and left the room again.

When he came back, he had similar papers in his hands to sign for a London trip. "I don't like doing this, but since you are here with my cousin and you are ladies in distress, I am helping you."

We thanked Vlad and Alexei. I tipped both of them quite generously when they escorted us to the waiting plane. They didn't want to take the money, but when I insisted, they sheepishly pocketed the money with a smile.

The little plane took off smoothly and, after a short uneventful one-hour flight, we landed on a small airfield just outside Belgrade.

CHAPTER 21

"I've always felt that life is a novel, and part of it is written for you, and part of it is written by you. It's up to you to write the ending, ultimately."
~ Lynn Johnston

SARAH

The crackle and static from the plane's intercom woke me up from my fitful nap. "If you look to your right, we are now flying over Belgrade," announced the pilot.

I eagerly looked out of the window. Even though it was a bustling metropolis, I saw there were still some shabby and nondescript buildings—probably remnants from the socialist era that was dissolved a couple of years back when

Yugoslavia broke up into six republics: Bosnia and Herzegovina, Croatia, Macedonia, Montenegro, Serbia (including the regions of Kosovo and Vojvodina), and Slovenia. I had flown to Ljubljana in Slovenia many times because they had a good international airport, and it was just an hour's drive over the border into Austria where I used to visit my relatives, but this place was very different from the cheerful Slovenian capital.

I was wondering why Tanya arranged for us to fly here because all the clues we had collected so far pointed either to Zagreb or to Sarajevo, but then I knew that she might do something like this to avoid Andy and Stepanov. It was a bit of an inconvenience, but in this situation, it was also wise.

Once we landed at the airport and bid farewell to our pilot, Tanya pulled me aside.

"I am going to use the glamor medallion Ali gave me. Everyone would be on a lookout for two women travelling together. No one would look twice at us if we acted like honeymooners," she said with a smirk and a lascivious wink. I giggled at her expression and nodded. It made sense, and since we didn't need our passports, we could fly to our other destinations undetected.

"I am going into that unisex restroom at the end of the hall to change. Wait outside for me. Keep a look out in case you spot any familiar faces," Tanya instructed.

I sat down on a bench near the restroom and spread our bags in such a way that no one else could sit down next to me. I was lost in thought when Tanya came out of the restroom, and I ignored her since I didn't recognize the man she had turned into. Due to her medallion's glamor, she had short blonde hair with a dark five o'clock shadow on her chin and looked quite Slavic. For a moment, I was bewildered. Only her voice assured me that it was my Tanya standing in front of me, and not a total stranger.

"Well, will I pass?" asked Tanya as she turned around and modeled her new self to me.

"Of course, you will! What a good idea to look like a local. No one will even think that you are the intrepid Agent Tanya Kareem of Interpol." I laughed.

"We won't stay long. Let us go and look for a café or restaurant and have some lunch. After that, I will book a flight to Zagreb. If Andy finds Alexei or Vlad, he will hopefully think that we are on our way to London. Fingers crossed."

I walked over to the information desk, where a smiling young lady in uniform was handing out brochures and talking to passengers. I had to wait for a few minutes, but after a short while, she turned to me with an enquiring expression on her face.

"Hello. How can I help you?"

"Hi, we are in transit and wanted to eat something other than what is available at the fast-food stands at the airport. Do you have any suggestions?"

"Yes, of course. Would you like to eat local or European cuisine?" she asked.

"We would like to experience some Serbian culture for the short time we are here," I said with a smile.

"Then I have just the place for you to go." She pulled out a brochure with a flourish and pointed to the name with a ball point pen. "This is *Restoran Jovanje*. It has European and Serbian cuisine, and it's just two kilometers away. You can take a taxi there, and if you tell the taxi driver to come back and pick you up after your lunch, you can be back at the airport in time for your flight."

"That sounds perfect, thank you," I said, taking the brochure from the woman.

Tanya was standing nonchalantly against a pillar, giving the impression of a long-suffering boyfriend waiting for his girlfriend. I walked over and told her what the woman had said, and she agreed that it would be interesting to visit that restaurant, so we caught a taxi and got there within a few minutes. Just as the woman had advised, we asked the taxi driver to come back to fetch us within forty-five minutes.

"Why aren't we going to Zagreb right away?" I asked Tanya. "It is not like you to dawdle over lunch no matter how interesting the place."

"You are right, my love. Coming out of the airport in disguise and then going back and booking the flight for Zagreb will show us if anyone is following us. A friendly conversation and even a little bribe can give us a lot of information if we ask the right questions."

I nodded in agreement and started to look at the extensive menu.

"Order something for me; you know what I like," Tanya said before getting up abruptly.

"Where do you think you are going?" I asked her a bit sharply. I didn't want to be left alone in the restaurant.

"I am going outside to see if I can connect with Mr. Humphrey. We were supposed to report in every other day. He will be concerned since he hasn't heard from me for two days now."

With that, Tanya left to go and stand in the sun outside. I think she wanted more "mileage" on her medallion; that's why she gave the impression of a man enjoying the weak autumn sun while making a call.

When the food came it smelled delicious and I started to eat the appetizers since I saw that Tanya was still deep in conversation with whoever was on the other side of the telephone line. She did turn around once and wave to me but continued to talk while gesturing wildly with her hands.

"Our suspicions about Andy are real. Apparently, he has been under observation by Interpol since they caught some unverified and misleading messages transmitted from Afghanistan." Tanya looked upset when she came back inside and sat down at the table. She liked Andy as they had been friends and partners for over ten years. "I am lucky that I wasn't sent with Andy to Afghanistan or I would have been under investigation as well."

"What exactly did Mr. Humphrey say?" I asked.

"Let us eat our lunch; it is getting cold. I will tell you everything on the way to the airport."

Having our suspicions verified depressed us, and the food that was smelling so delicious before, now tasted like sawdust. Finally, we stopped pretending to eat and Tanya signaled the waitress to bring us the bill. We were off to the airport in the taxi that had conveniently decided to wait for us.

Tanya

. . .

This whole journey was turning into a melee of betrayal and mistrust. People I had worked with for years were suddenly traitors. It was quite discombobulating. I wasn't sure what to do or who to trust. I wanted to talk to Mr. Humphrey, but I didn't know if I could trust him. On a hunch, I opened the back of the satellite phone and took out the battery. My suspicions were realized when I found a transmitting device just under it that was smaller than a thumbnail. We were being tracked! My calls had probably been recorded as well, if I understood the technology right. I prised it out with my fingernail and crushed it under the heel of my shoe, then I called Mr. Humphrey.

"Tanya! Where are you? I have been worried!"

"A lot has been going on, Sir, but first, tell me, have you received anything via the diplomatic pouch from Istanbul?"

"No, I haven't. Was I supposed to?"

"I requested Andy to send you the files we found in Istanbul." This was proof that Andy was not on our side anymore.

"I haven't heard from Andy in days. You say he was with you in Istanbul? What on earth was he doing there? He was supposed to go back to Herat!"

"Well, for one, he gave me the satellite phone to keep in touch with you. I thought you knew that, but I found a micro-transmitter in it just before I called you."

"Be careful, Tanya, this has become a dangerous mission and I am not happy that the two of you are there alone." He sighed deeply. "Andy has been under surveillance for a while. We believe he has gone over to the other side."

"What would you like us to do?" I did not want to go

back home with things unfinished, and I guess he realized that as well.

"We got to know from our intelligence cell that Vladimir Jovanović, one of our suspects, flew into Sarajevo this morning. I would suggest that you go directly there."

"How do you know about Vladimir?" I asked suspiciously. It would be the icing on the cake of betrayal if Mr. Humphrey was also a dirty cop. My heart started to sink.

"Don't sound so wary. I am on your side. We have had an eye on Vladimir for a while, and I suspected that you were going after him given your journey's trajectory."

I heaved a loud sigh of relief. Mr. Humphrey chuckled and continued. "Agent Max Millonig will be there to meet you at the airport. You can trust him. I believe you met him in London a couple of years ago."

"I did," I said, but I still sounded worried.

"I can vouch for Max, but I appreciate that you want to be cautious," said Mr. Humphrey.

After a short pause, I decided to trust my boss and said, "Sarah managed to hide one of the files. We have it with us. Before we charter a flight to Sarajevo, I will fax the documents it contains to you from the airport business center."

"Perfect. We can start going after the individuals named in the files as soon as we get the information from you."

"Sir, you need to get hold of Andy as well," I said quietly.

"I understand that you are upset, Tanya. Hell, he was your partner and confidante for so many years. I understand how betrayed you must be feeling. Don't worry, we will find him."

After a few more polite platitudes, I said goodbye and switched off the phone. I didn't want to take any chances even after destroying the transmitter.

On the way to the airport, I updated Sarah with what Mr. Humphrey had said. Sarah was also upset since she had liked Andy and could not think of any reason why he had betrayed us and the children we were supposed to protect.

"It all comes down to economics, I guess," said Sarah sadly. "He must have been paid very well to betray us."

I just nodded. It felt as if my best friend had died. Well, in a sense he had, because I doubted that we would work together or see each other ever again.

Once we reached the airport, Sarah told me to go and book a flight to Sarajevo.

"If I go and fax the documents and you book the flight, we will be finished much quicker and then we will have some time to plan what we will do when we reach Sarajevo." I agreed and gave her the confidential fax number of Mr. Humphrey's office, after which I strode over to the chartered flights counter while Sarah followed the signs to the business center.

We met in the main hall after half an hour. Sarah gave me the thumbs up sign as she walked towards where I was waiting for her. When she reached me, I took her arm and escorted her to the lounge. Our flight was supposed to leave within an hour. I was worried that I might revert to my true self, but there was sunlight streaming through the windows in the lounge, so I held up my wrist with the medallion to it, feeling the low vibration it made when it recharged. That would give me at least another hour or so of my disguise.

Sarah and I sat together giggling and laughing like a couple on their honeymoon. Anyone looking for two women would not have found them. At least that was one consolation. Soon our pilot came to tell us that our flight was ready for take-off.

CHAPTER 22

"Honesty is for the most part less profitable than dishonesty."
~ Plato

SARAH

Off we went on what I hoped was the last leg of our journey. We were exhausted. We were living on adrenaline highs, hurried meals, and sporadic sleep. I thanked my lucky stars that both of us were fit enough to sustain this abuse to our bodies, but we hoped this would only last for a short while. After all, we were human and needed to rest as much as anybody else. We were travelling through places that people would give anything to visit, but we were just giving them cursory glances while we sped through them, our eyes only on our goal—to catch the smugglers and liberate the children. I would definitely insist on a holiday once we were through with putting ourselves through the wringer.

We landed in Sarajevo after a short one-hour flight. Tanya was happy that there still was enough sunlight to recharge her medallion. She wanted to stay in disguise at least until we checked into our hotel.

We waited for over an hour at the airport for Max Millonig, but we could not find him anywhere. Tanya was worried, but after waiting fruitlessly, we decided to go to the hotel as planned and then inform Mr. Humphrey about Millonig's no show.

Our hotel was ironically called Old Sarajevo Hotel. I fell in love with the old-world ambience and the antiques that were strategically placed all over. The first thing I did while Tanya was having her shower was to read the complimentary brochure in the room. It was fascinating since we hadn't traveled to this area before.

"Do you know that due to its long history of religious and cultural diversity, Sarajevo is sometimes called the 'Jerusalem of Europe,'" I called out to Tanya.

"That is interesting," she called back. "Why is that?"

"Because it is one of a few major European cities to have a mosque, a Catholic church, an Eastern Orthodox church, and a synagogue within the same neighborhood. Isn't that fascinating?"

"What does your brochure say about our hotel and its surroundings?" asked Tanya. "I need to know exactly where we are so that we can plan our next move towards the smugglers and Vladimir."

"Well, it says that the neighborhood we are in is called

Baščaršija and is near a busy, historic central bazaar area with Gazi Husrev-Beg's Mosque, City Hall and Bosnian cafes and eateries nearby."

"To cut a long story short, you mean we are in the center of town," said Tanya with an indulgent smile as she emerged from the bathroom rubbing her hair dry. She looked once more like my gorgeous Tanya and not a male copy of the original.

I unfolded the brochure completely and noticed that there was a tourist map printed on the other side.

"Look, this seems like a fairly simple map with all of the areas and neighborhoods marked prominently on it. Where is the address that we have for the smugglers?"

Tanya rummaged in her bag for Farooq's notebook and leafed through it. "The area mentioned in the address is Konjic."

"Let me check..." I said absently while tracing the roads on the map with my index finger. "Ah! Here it is! Apparently, it is considered a separate town, but some still think of it as a suburb of Sarajevo since it's only an hour's drive away from the city. From what I can see here, it's also just as close to Montenegro, so for a business like Vladimir's, I would think that it is a strategically placed area. They can access or escape to either one of the cities."

"Hmmm," said Tanya with a frown. "That would make it even more difficult to catch them if we don't have any back up. Where in heaven's name is Millonig?"

"Let us get ready to go to Konjic. We can wait a bit more for him, but don't you think that we just need to find the address and gather information? Maybe Millonig was delayed and couldn't contact us." I tried to placate Tanya before I jumped into the shower. Since we had planned to stay out well after dark, we wore black jeans and black sweatshirts to blend into the shadows if we needed to. We even had black caps that we would put on when we got near our target.

"I am calling down to the concierge to find out whether we can hire a car while you are getting ready. I will also order something from room service. What would you like?"

"Something light please," I called out, my voice muffled by the shower as I washed my hair.

I heard Tanya speak on the phone and then, all of a sudden, she sounded agitated. Before I could stick my head out of the bathroom and ask her what the problem was, I heard the door of the room slam and her footsteps hurry down the corridor.

After a short while, Tanya still hadn't come back, but a waitress brought our food on a heated trolley and uncovered the dishes with a flourish. There were two kinds of eggs, some grilled chicken, and a large breadbasket with different types of rolls and croissants. The piece de resistance was the enormous platter with cold cuts and cheeses. My mouth watered just to look at that delicious spread. The waitress offered to serve me, but I told her that I would prefer to wait for my partner. She put the covers back on the hot dishes, nodded, and smiled as she left the room.

I wondered where Tanya had rushed off to...

Tanya

. . .

Max still hadn't shown himself and I was getting worried. Either he was also involved with the smugglers or he had been detained by them. Whatever the reason, we were vulnerable until Mr. Humphrey could arrange backup for us. I didn't want to worry Sarah, but it did not look good. We were in Bosnia for the first time in our lives and didn't know anything about the country. We would have to depend on our wits. The first thing I did was to check whether the transceiver for Sarah's pendant worked. I usually checked it off and on, but I needed to be sure that it was functional in case we were separated.

The concierge was not very helpful. He said that there was a harvest festival in the city, and none of the car rental agencies had any cars for us to rent. That was very frustrating, and I think he detected the desperation in my voice.

"You can hire a motorcycle or a moped. They still have those available," he said in a condescending tone, as if he was doing me a great favor. "Why don't you come to the lot behind the hotel? We have a few there, so you can have a look and decide whether you want one or two vehicles to go sightseeing."

Making a noise that sounded like a frustrated growl, I rushed out of the room. I met the concierge on the ground floor and we walked briskly to where some motorcycles and mopeds were parked.

"The mopeds are fun and can be ridden by anyone who knows how to ride a cycle," he said. "They aren't so noisy as the heavier motorcycles and are preferred by the tourists because of their maneuverability."

"Let me check them both and I will let you know what

would be suitable," I growled at him. The concierge, whose name was Abdul, was taken aback because, to be fair, it wasn't his fault that there were no cars available. In his mind, he was actually doing me a favor by helping me with the bikes.

The motorcycles were rickety, rusty affairs and there was no way that I would even give them a test run. Nevertheless, Abdul kick-started the one motorcycle that was least decrepit-looking and it roared to life while belching black smoke from its exhaust pipe. If we took this one, we might as well have hired a big brass band to announce our arrival to the smugglers.

"This is too loud!" I shouted over the rattling cacophony. "Is there anything quieter?"

"There are the mopeds. They are much quieter, but they only seat one person at a time." To demonstrate, he hopped onto one of the mopeds and started it. The sound was definitely not as loud, but it had an annoying high-pitched buzz, just like a giant mosquito.

Abdul looked pleased and I just rolled my eyes. "All right, you win," I said. "You take one and I will take the other to the front of the hotel carpark. My friend and I will use them to go on a sightseeing tour after we have eaten."

I had to bargain to pay a reasonable price for the rent of the mopeds. The vendor wanted to take advantage of the fact that there was a dearth of transportation during the festival, but with Abdul's help, I managed to bring the cost down to a fairly reasonable price.

After parking the mopeds in front of the hotel, Abdul went back to his post at the reception while I tried to contact Mr. Humphrey on the satellite phone. It took me a while to get connected, since it was the weekend, but after playing a frustrating half an hour of phone tag, I got Mr. Humphrey at his home.

"I wasn't expecting to hear from you until tomorrow. Is everything all right?" he asked, his voice tinged with concern.

"We are in Sarajevo, and we still haven't been able to contact Millonig. I am getting concerned. Has he also joined the ranks of the smugglers?"

"That is strange. I talked to him just this morning, and he had assured me that he would be meeting you at the airport."

"We waited for over an hour, after which we went and checked into a hotel." I didn't want to give our exact location to Mr. Humphrey in case his phone was tapped or ... the thought crept repeatedly into my mind... was he trustworthy?

"I understand what you are going through, Tanya," he said as I paused as if he was reading my mind. "If I was in your shoes, I would be suspicious of me too, but believe me when I say that I am on your side."

"Thank you, sir, that is a relief," I said warily, still not quite sure, but deciding to take his word at face value. "What do we do now? We have an idea where the address is and were going to do a recce of the area tonight. However, we do feel vulnerable because we don't have any backup whatsoever here in Sarajevo."

"Keep your phone on for a while. I will try to find out what happened to Millonig. If I can't get hold of him, I will try to find out which agents are nearby and can come to help you as soon as possible. Stand by and I will call you back within an hour." With that, Mr. Humphrey switched his phone off.

Sarah must have been worried since I had just run out without saying anything to her, so I went back to our room instead of waiting for Mr. Humphrey's call downstairs.

"Where did you rush off to?" Sarah stood there, visibly annoyed, with her arms folded across her chest.

"I am sorry, love." I sighed and hugged her. "Things are getting so frustrating, and we are here without any backup. I am worried, especially since you are with me. To top that all, there are no cars for rent in the whole city!"

"How is that possible?" said Sarah as she leaned back and looked up to me from our embrace. "This isn't such a backward city that there would be a shortage of transportation!" She looked incredulous.

I smiled at her indignant expression and explained. "There is a harvest festival going on, and the whole city is celebrating. Many tourists have also come from all over the world. The concierge said that we were lucky that we snagged the last room available in the hotel." Sarah heard the weary frustration in my voice that I unsuccessfully tried to hide from her.

"How are we going to get to Konjic if there are no cars available?"

"That was one of the reasons I ran out of the room. The concierge has arranged for mopeds, and I had to hurry up in case those were taken as well."

"Mopeds?!?!" Sarah was astonished. "Do you realize that they are noisy? We might as well announce our arrival."

"You are right, but the heavy motorcycles were in bad shape and much louder than the mopeds. The advantage these mopeds have is that they have pedals and can silently move along if the motor is switched off."

"Could you talk to Mr. Humphrey?" she asked.

"I did. He is concerned, but he will try to get us some solid backup before we go to Konjic. He will call me back within an hour. Till then, let us eat something and then rest. As soon as we hear from Humphrey we can leave."

"We will have to be very careful... mopeds aren't very fast." Sarah was still worried, and rightfully so.

"I am certain that once Mr. Humphrey has arranged for our backup, there will be faster modes of transportation available to us." I tried to reassure her, but how could I be convincing when I was worried myself?

We sat down and started picking at our food. None of us was very hungry. I was idly wondering what we should do with the leftovers when I had an idea.

"Do you have any strong sleeping pills in your medical bag?" I asked.

"Yes, I do, but what do you want to do with them?"

"It's just a thought... If Vladimir has a secure stronghold, then it is possible that he might have dogs that roam the periphery of the house. If we grind the pills and mix them with our leftovers, we could put the dogs to sleep." I grinned. I knew Sarah hated any sort of narcotic drugs, even if they were needed to tame animals, but sometimes drastic measures were needed, and she understood that.

Sarah made a face that showed her displeasure. "Much as I don't like drugging any living being, I do think that is a good idea."

Just then my satellite phone rang. It was Mr. Humphrey.

"Yes, sir?" I said as I punched the on button.

"No one can get hold of Millonig. It seems he has inexplicably fallen off the face of the earth. As I told you before, I had spoken with him and he was on his way to meet you. I fear that he could have been captured by Vladimir's men. Anyway, I have tasked some agents to look for him, but in the meantime, two other agents will meet you in Konjic." He sounded tired and I nearly felt sorry for him. "Go to the railway station, where you will meet two agents, one woman and one man, in a red Mercedes. You are to go up to them and ask when the next train to Koblenz is due to arrive."

"Koblenz?" I laughed.

"Well, I had to think of an out of the way place." He sounded amused as well. "They will answer, 'I don't know about Koblenz, but the train to Budapest has already left.' You will know that they are our agents when you hear that."

"We are on our way, sir. I will call you again later. For now, I am switching my phone off."

Sarah and I gathered our backpacks, in which we had packed our basic survival gear that included water, flashlights, and ropes. My backpack also held a small grappling hook. It was unwieldy, but it was better to be prepared than be sorry later.

Sarah had driven mopeds when on holiday, so it didn't take her long to get a hang of the light motorized cycle. It took us over an hour, but we finally saw the large red and white neon sign indicating that we were near Konjic railway station. I motioned to Sarah to stay in the shadows while I looked around for a red Mercedes. I found it parked under a tree a few meters away from the main entrance of the station.

I knocked on the driver's window and waited until he lowered it. I cleared my throat and asked the coded question.

"Can you please tell me when the next train to Koblenz is due to arrive?" I felt slightly foolish.

"I don't know about Koblenz, but the train to Budapest has already left," he answered with a smile and opened the door to step out of the car. I stepped back in alarm.

"Relax, Agent Kareem. We are on your side. My name is Agent Amer Bajrovic." He smiled while holding his hand out in greeting. The woman also stepped out of the car and introduced herself.

"Nice to meet you, Agent Kareem. My name is Nadja Salatic. We were told by headquarters to meet you here and provide as much assistance as we can to you."

"Thank you. I understand that there is a public holiday due to the festival, and you were informed to meet us at a short notice, however, I do appreciate your coming here."

They were dressed similarly to Sarah and me, which was reassuring, because that meant they were ready for action if it was required.

Looking towards where I left her, I signaled Sarah to come forward from the shadows and introduced her to the agents.

"Since we are going to be working together, let us address each other by our first names. I know that our surnames can be a mouthful," said Nadja with a smile. We readily agreed because she did have a point.

We all sat down in the car together to discuss our next moves.

"We have been keeping an eye on Vladimir Jovanović for the past six months but haven't been able to get any concrete evidence about his activities," said Amer. "Now, with your new evidence, we hope we can take him into custody. It is frustrating when you know that he is the one who is creating havoc and can't be arrested because international legal systems need proof."

"We know that he has motion sensitive lights and alarms around the periphery of the house, and where there aren't such lights, he has Doberman dogs patrolling the area. They are fierce and have been trained to kill," said Nadja.

"We thought that might be the case, so we spiked our dinner leftovers with sleeping pills and thought that we could feed them to the dogs," said Sarah.

"We have something very simple in the trunk of our car. Come, have a look." Amer could not hide the laughter from his voice. We climbed out of the car and walked to the back. There were strange sounds and scratches coming from the trunk, which wasn't completely closed.

"I know this is very simplistic, but we noticed that the lights were very sensitive to any form of motion. Therefore, I have gathered a few cats and rabbits in the trunk. When we get near the house, we will release them where the sensors are, and the lights will go haywire." Nadja giggled and I couldn't help smiling too.

Amer spread a blueprint on top of the car. "Have a look at this. We got the blueprint from the town's development committee. Usually, these documents are confidential, but we had means to get them." He laughed while he wiggled his thick eyebrows like Groucho Marx. We pored over the diagram and memorized the exits. It was imperative that we didn't run around like headless chickens once we were inside the building. Time was of the essence, and we needed to get in, get as much information as we could, and then get out again. After that, whatever happened would be dealt with by the local as well as Interpol authorities. I wished we could have done more... but we had our orders.

"Sarah, you take the spiked dogfood and feed it to the dogs. They are usually in the inner fenced in area where there aren't many lights. They probably have the dogs there to cover their cameras' blind spots." Amer was all business now.

"Nadja and Sarah hide behind the hedges there," he pointed them out on the blueprint, "and release the rabbits and the cats at two ten-minute intervals. If we let all of them go at once, it will look suspicious."

"Well, once they see the animals more than a few times, they would get suspicious anyway, but that is when we will need to be ready to move out," I said.

Amer nodded in agreement and continued. "Nadja, once the lights start fluctuating the first time, you will follow me and Tanya into the building." He pointed to a door that was the farthest away and least likely to be heavily guarded. "This door will lead to a short corridor, and the second door to the left, next to this small conference room, is supposed to be Vladimir's office." Amer pointed out the rooms on the blueprint.

"Sarah, since you are unarmed, you keep an eye on the dogs, and keep releasing a cat or a rabbit at ten-minute intervals. It is dangerous for you to be inside in case we are discovered and they start shooting at us. We don't want you caught in the crossfire." I was relieved that Amer was the one to tell Sarah to stay outside. If I had suggested it... I didn't want to think what she would have said to me.

"I know, I know." I could hear the mixture of resignation and frustration in Sarah's voice. "I will do as you say and try to be as close to the car as possible and be ready to drive us away."

I went over to her and hugged her close. "If anything happened to you, I would never forgive myself," I whispered in her ear. "Please be safe. We will be out as soon as we can. Keep the satellite phone with you and call Mr. Humphrey for help in case of emergency. Just press number one and the call will go directly to him."

Before we left, Amer then signaled Nadja to start placing the initial rabbits and cats over the fence. Showtime!

CHAPTER 23

"Alone we can do so little; together we can do so much."
— Helen Keller

SARAH

Nadja had decided to stay back with me and we watched as Tanya and Amer loped away and were swallowed into the darkness. Thereafter there was an eerie stillness. We could hear each other breathe, what is more, the sounds of the chittering night animals and the occasional meow from the basket in which we held the cats were strangely terrifying.

"The chain link fence is electrified. How will we pass the animals over?" I asked Nadja as my apprehension rose by the minute... no, make that seconds. She grinned and held up rubberized wire clippers and rubber gloves.

"Haven't you ever been a scout? 'Be prepared'...that is a wonderful motto to teach prepubescent do-gooders."

Giggling along with her, we turned our focus to the fence and counted the time when the guards passed the place where we were hiding.

"These men are like clockwork. They pass by this area at regular intervals. That means that we have a ten-minute window to clip the fence and send in the animals." Nadja prepared herself by pulling on her rubber gloves.

"The lights come on when they pass by here, and then switch off within twenty seconds. We will therefore be working in the dark. I suggest you also wear your rubber gloves so that you aren't accidently electrocuted if your hands graze the fence." Nadja was all business now.

I pulled on the gloves, and we waited till the next guard passed by. As soon as the lights went off, Nadja jumped up, darted towards the fence, and quickly cut a hole in it big enough to shove a cat through.

The cat just sat there for a while, smoothing its ruffled fur. We tried to make her move by making shooing sounds, but for a few frustrating moments she just sat there grooming herself. Finally, she got up and with an arrogant swish of her tail walked towards the building. The lights immediately switched on and were accompanied by the clanging of an alarm. Since the alarm hadn't gone off before, we deduced that the guards had a fixed route that prevented the alarms to be activated.

We watched from our hiding place as the guards ran towards the cat and stopped in surprise. They spoke amongst themselves and then made faces of disgust while one of them picked the cat up by the scruff of its neck and walked off.

"What did they say?" I asked Nadja.

"They were disgusted that it was a cat and now they are going to have a look where it came from."

Since the grass where we had cut the hole in the fence was very tall and it hid the breach, we were confident that it would take them some time before they found it. We waited another fifteen minutes, and this time sent a rabbit on its kamikaze mission. We had the same response as before, but this time we had to sidle a bit back into the underbrush because the guards were looking at the periphery with much more intensity. We were sure that they would see the breach if they swept the grasses away, but, to our surprise, they didn't.

"I don't think that they feel the animals are a serious threat to their security." Nadja giggled in my ear.

We sent another cat and rabbit into the compound, after which we retreated and went to sit in the car to wait for Amer and Tanya.

"That was exciting," said Nadja. "I hope our little diversions helped the others get into the building."

"I am worried. It all seems so dangerous." I started to bite my nails, a habit I had completely stopped when I was a child.

"Ah! But that is why we are Interpol agents." Nadja looked at me with a smile. "The whole adrenaline rush, the danger, the adventure, are all that excite a good agent, and we thrive by them."

"Yeah, yeah, I know," I grumbled. I knew those feelings

so well. They were the same that Tanya felt before she would go on a mission.

Another cat and rabbit were sacrificed over the fence, and then we decided that we should stop completely because from the increasing agitation of the guards, it was getting obvious to them that the hapless animals hadn't wandered into the compound on their own.

We sat in silence for a short while. The tension was so thick that one could have cut through it with a hot butter knife. What were the others doing? Were they alright? I was just about to voice my concerns when we heard an explosion towards the back of the building and, after a few beats, the clanging of the alarm again. All of a sudden, there was pandemonium with people running and men shouting. What in heaven's name was going on? *Please God let Tanya and Amer be safe!*

I wanted to run towards the fence to see what was happening, but Nadja pulled me back. "Are you trying to get captured?" she hissed angrily in my ear. "Stay here. I am going to climb up that tree to find out what is going on."

While I hid behind a small grassy knoll, Nadja swiftly climbed up a large oak tree that was growing nearby. I was surprised that she wasn't discovered with the precarious way she leaned over to see what was happening in the compound.

"I can't see anything from here!" she whispered. "Maybe if I climbed a bit higher?"

"NO!" I said to her desperately. "Come down. If we are caught, we won't be able to help the others."

She shrugged in resignation and dropped gracefully down onto the mossy ground where I was standing.

"What do we do now?" I asked her. "That explosion sounded ominous."

"Let us wait for a while. Let the chaos die down. Then we can go over to the other side to investigate..."

"I think not!" said a harsh male voice in accented English.

We turned around and found ourselves looking down the barrel of an assault rifle.

"Get up!" barked the man. "The boss wants to see you. How dare you try to blast your way into the compound?!?"

They thought that we were the intruders, and that meant there was still hope for Tanya and Amer.

Nadja and I looked at each other but didn't say a word. We just meekly got up and walked along the path while being periodically poked in the back with the rifle. As we stumbled along, I covertly put my hands in my pocket and pressed number one, which Tanya had told me was the speed-dial number for Mr. Humphrey.

Tanya

Sarah seemed comfortable with Nadja, but I still didn't want to leave her out there with the distinct possibility that she could be caught. The idea to activate the lights and alarms was brilliant, but the guards were not stupid. A few times could be overlooked, but if they saw too many animals, they would get suspicious and start to look beyond the fence for intruders.

Amer and I crouched down and loped to the back of the enclosure. Here the fence gave way to a high concrete wall.

There were lookout towers on the corners, and the top of the wall had iron spikes embedded in it. A searchlight was sweeping the periphery on regular three-minute intervals. It was strange to see that this part of the compound had a distinctive military appearance.

"Why is this area so heavily fortified while the front of the compound only has an electrified fence?" I whispered.

"This part of the compound is hidden in the woods. I'm not sure, but the fence could be to show the local authorities that there is nothing going on here and is just for the personal security of the owners." Amer gave the impression that he was just as puzzled as I was.

"We don't have much time. Either we try to outrun the searchlight and hop over the wall in record time, or we blast our way in. But that will alert them to our presence."

"Do you have your satellite phone? I gave mine to Sarah to call Mr. Humphrey in case of an emergency."

"Yes, I do. Let me call and let him know what we are about to do. We would need back up immediately." I thought that Amer looked worried. However, there was something in his demeanor that made me uncomfortable. Oh well, it might not be anything. Maybe I was just sensitive after being betrayed by two of our agents.

"We were promised back up, so I think they are just waiting for a green signal from us," I reassured him. "Let us set explosive charges on the left wall just below the observation tower there. When the guards are distracted, we can climb over the wall on the right side and run to the building," I suggested.

Amer looked at me with admiration. "I hadn't thought

of that," he said. "I was just going to blast through and force my way in. That's actually a brilliant idea!"

"Let me hoist the grappling hook up onto the right wall while you set the charges with a one-minute timer. That will give you enough time to reach me and we will be able to climb over with no one noticing us," I instructed.

Amer melted away into the darkness so stealthily that I hardly heard him move away. Just as I was about to step towards the wall, I heard the bushes rustling behind me and I saw an armed man step into the clearing near the wall. He just stood there looking around while he lit a cigarette and seemed to be in no mood to move. I needed to get rid of him, and quick. Otherwise, he would alert everyone when the explosion took place. I crept behind him and hit the back of his head with a stone that I found nearby. I took care not to hit him too hard since I didn't want to have the responsibility of having taken his life. He crumpled on the ground and moaned, and I saw that he was semiconscious and mildly disoriented. I clapped his own handcuffs on his wrists and gagged him with a bandana that he had tied around his neck, after which I pulled him into the bushes to hide him.

After that small interlude, I hoisted the rope with the grappling hook on top of the wall and waited behind a tree for Amer to set the charges. I kept a lookout for any further unusual movement or activity. After a few minutes, I saw him running back towards where I was. As soon as we heard the explosion, we swiftly climbed up the wall and used our backpacks as cushions to clamber over the spikes on top. Just as we had predicted, everyone's attention was towards the left wall, and we managed to slip into a conveniently unlocked door unseen.

When we entered the building, I pulled Amer into the nearest room, which happened to be a rest room. That was good—there wouldn't be any surveillance cameras there.

"I am sure they have cameras everywhere. We have to be careful or we will be caught before we have gathered any evidence to incriminate Vladimir."

"What do you suggest we do?" he asked.

"The cameras usually focus on the upper parts of whoever is passing in the corridors, so if we stay low, we can avoid them and spray black paint on the lenses as we pass by. That will give us a few more minutes to look for Vladimir's office... and before you ask, I have two cans of black spray paint in my backpack," I said with a self-satisfied smirk.

Before we left the restroom, we cocked our ears to listen whether there was any sound coming from the corridor. Amer opened the door a crack and looked out. It seemed to be empty.

"There is a camera right in front of the door. I will take a chance and quickly spray it, and hope that the guards are still focused on the commotion we started outside."

Signaling that I understood, I stepped aside as he sidled into the corridor and jumped up to spray the camera with black paint. Then I joined him and we crouched down as we loped towards where there was a large wooden door with a sign that said 'security.'

Amer pointed at the door and signaled that we should go in. He silently counted till three with his fingers and we burst into the room, where we saw two men manning the twelve monitors.

To say they were surprised was an understatement. We knocked them on their heads with the butts of our guns and tied them up, taking care to gag them with their own socks, one of whose I was happy to say was smelling quite ripe.

"Look!" I pointed to one of the monitors. "That seems to be Vladimir's office—the one with the head of the stuffed reindeer mounted on the wall."

"Aren't those women Nadja and Sarah?" asked Amer as he pointed to one of the other monitors, where we saw that they were being herded along the corridor.

"Oh, God! Yes! They caught them!"

"Let us increase the volume of that monitor to hear what they are saying."

"How dare you bomb your way into our compound?" said the man who seemed to be in charge. "What do you think you will achieve by that?" he continued in a heavily accented English.

"Wait! What? You think we had something to do with that?" asked Nadja. "I hope you realize that the explosion was on the opposite side of where we were."

"Then what were you doing in the woods near here?" said the man as he roughly pushed both of them into Vladimir's office.

"We were out for a drive and heard the commotion. We are just tourists and don't want any trouble." Sarah was talking in a quasi-German accent. Just like her mother. Clever. It would be easier to believe her if she was German and spoke like them instead of in her usual British/Pakistani accent.

We watched in dismayed fascination as Vladimir entered

the room from another door, half hidden by the cloud of cigar smoke that spewed from him.

"Ah, Dr. Sarah Shah! How nice to finally meet you! You can drop the accent now. I know who and what you are." He laughed out loud and looked pointedly towards the cameras.

"And I know what scum you are!" Sarah retaliated angrily.

"Tsk, tsk, temper, temper," said Vladimir with a laugh.

"You find that funny?" said Sarah. "You play with the lives of young children, and that amuses you?" She spat at him. Sarah wasn't a person to get angry so quickly. She usually was even-tempered and would explode only when it was the last straw, so seeing her go against Vladimir was awe-inspiring. I am sure even her own mother couldn't have stopped the tidal wave of anger billowing from her just then.

"I am but a businessman fulfilling a need in a niche market," said Vladimir while paring his nails with a switch blade. "That I am paid well for this service is just a happy coincidence." He laughed and then turned towards the cameras set on the wall.

"Agent Kareem, if you can see and hear me, you would be wise to come to this room. Otherwise, I wouldn't be responsible if anything happened to your dear friends here." He gestured with his smoldering cigar towards Nadja and Sarah.

"Don't you dare touch her!" I shouted, even though I knew he couldn't hear me. I turned around to leave the room and ran straight into the muzzle of Amer's gun. I was so surprised that he took my gun without any resistance from me and tucked it into the waistband of his pants.

"Et tu, Amer?" I said dismayed. "Who can one trust nowadays? This is getting to be ridiculous!"

"Well, it's all a matter of economics, as Sarah said. We need the money and Vladimir is quite generous to those who work for him." He chuckled while he pushed me out of the door with his gun boring into my back like a dark reminder that any false move could have me bidding farewell to the world as I knew it.

"And Nadja? Is she also part of this?" I asked, worried more for Sarah than my own self. She had been alone with Nadja for quite a while. "When I told you to call Humphrey, you called Vladimir instead?" I was outraged.

"Ah, they did say you were intelligent. This is the first spark of intellect that I have seen so far." Amer chuckled evilly. "Now go on. No sudden moves. You don't want your little doctor to get hurt, do you?"

In my opinion, in the short while that I got to know Amer, I didn't think he was as vicious or soulless as Farooq. Maybe I could still talk him out of making the biggest mistake of his life. On the other hand, I felt like beating him up, but I first had to try the diplomatic way, as Sarah usually advised. I looked over my shoulder to Amer and saw a strange expression on his face, as if what he was doing wasn't on his agenda and he didn't like it at all. There was still hope, I thought to myself.

"Amer, are you married?" I asked.

"What a random question! What has that got to do with your situation?" he mocked.

"I just wanted to know whether you have any children," I asked quietly while I cautiously turned around to look at his face.

"Yes, I do!" he barked while he poked me once again in my back with his gun to make me look forward instead of at him.

"I am sure you love your children, but have you thought of the deep loss the parents feel when their children are kidnapped and sold off?"

"These children are orphans and are getting into good homes with well-to-do adoptive parents. They have a better life than the one they would have living in mud huts in the mountains," he said sarcastically.

"Really? Is that what Vladimir feeds you?" I sneered. "Do you realize that he profits much more from child prostitution and pornography than the adoption schemes he has going on?"

"That is a lie!" Amer screamed. "We are helping orphans, not exploiting them!"

"If you believe that then you are dumber than I thought," I mumbled. Suddenly, I felt an inexplicable wave of rage come over me. I turned around and punched him on his nose. I must have channeled all of my anger and frustration into that punch because I felt the crunch of the bone as his nose broke while blood spattered on the walls, and damned if my hand didn't hurt excruciatingly. "You are the scum of the earth! You don't care what happens to those innocent children, do you? As long as you get paid! You disgust me, Amer, you are lower than a cockroach's belly!" I screamed at him.

Amer stood there holding his nose trying to stem the flow of blood, and he had a horrified expression on his face as he looked almost fearfully at me. He was shocked by my unexpected assault and outburst. He looked down at the ground and was quiet for a while, as if he was thinking and mentally struggling with what I had just said.

"What proof do you have?" he finally said as he leaned against the wall trying to prop himself up to avoid passing out.

"When we stormed into the surveillance room, I noticed that the men were watching kiddie porn. I switched it off when we were tying the men up, but I could swear that I recognized a couple of children from the camp in Afghanistan." I sneered at him. I was deeply disappointed that my colleagues were involved with such a disgusting organization.

"Show me..." he said. "And if you are lying, then God help you!'

We swiftly turned back the way we came, and when we entered the security room once more, I walked over to the video console. I pressed the button I had switched off earlier and started the sickening video. I turned my back since I couldn't watch the disgusting exploitation of innocence, and Amer must have only looked at it for a few seconds before he exploded with an explicit curse word and switched the video off.

After a slight hesitation, he took out his satellite phone and dialed Mr. Humphrey's number.

"Mr. Humphrey, this is Amer. We need backup immediately." Then he switched off the phone and gave me back my gun. "If I know Humphrey, he already had our backup ready to go. Let us move towards Vladimir's room. They will be here soon." With that, we walked the way we came, only this time once more as colleagues rather than adversaries.

Before we left the room, I ejected the incriminating tape from the video player and tucked it into one of the deep pockets of my pants. This was evidence and I didn't want there to be any chance for it to be destroyed or "lost."

As we reached Vladimir's office, we heard the sound of gunfire in the compound, and within minutes, the corridor was filled with men and women in combat gear and bullet proof vests. I think Vladimir's room must have been soundproofed since there didn't seem to be any reaction to the chaos outside, and anyone who would have alerted him was already in custody. I signaled to everyone to be quiet and knocked on the door before I entered the room.

"Ah, Agent Kareem. At last, we meet face to face," said Vladimir with a smug look on his face as he waved me to into the room.

The first person I looked for was Sarah. She was standing near the window, but one of Vladimir's goons had a gun pointed at her while another was holding her firmly by her upper arm.

"Are you alright?" I asked in Urdu. "When I give you the signal, go and hide behind the cabinet near the door." She smiled and nodded.

"Ah, ah, ah, Agent Kareem, let us speak in a language we all know..." Vladimir started to say when all hell broke loose. I pushed Sarah towards the cabinet while I took cover behind one of the heavily padded sofas in the room. Mr. Humphrey's men burst in and immediately took hold of Vladimir. His men were simultaneously disarmed, and it only took a few minutes for the Interpol agents to gain control of the room. We were fortunate that the element of surprise had ensured that Vladimir was arrested without even a shot being fired. Once he had handcuffs on his wrists, the rest of his men surrendered like lambs to the slaughter.

"You can't do this to me!" shouted Vladimir angrily. "I know people in high places! I will get my revenge! Just you wait, Agent Kareem! You will regret this!" We heard him continue to rant and shout random threats as he was frog-marched down the corridor.

I went over to the cabinet behind which Sarah was hunkered down and, without any thought that there might be an audience, hugged and kissed her soundly. She was my life... and if anything had happened to her, I would have never forgiven myself. She was in the middle of this melee because of me, and it was unthinkable if she was hurt in any way.

"We must go and look for the children. And we need to gather any information at hand before any of Vladimir loyalists tries to be clever and makes everything disappear."

Amer was talking to Nadja in one of the corners. I could see that they were arguing. Finally, Nadja looked at Amer quizzically and then nodded. Both walked over to where I was standing with Sarah and the leader of the task force.

"We have discussed our situation and our unfortunate involvement with Vladimir, and in exchange for information and insight into the operation, we would like to request for leniency."

"That is something only Mr. Humphrey can promise you, but I can assure you that I will put in a good word for you when the time comes."

"That is good enough for now," said Nadja. "We were told that there is a hidden cellar which has been furnished as a dormitory for the children. One of the men I got friendly with also told me that there was a lower level where there are supposed to be studios where we now believe that child-pornography was filmed or photographed. Believe me when we say that we didn't know anything about that. We just thought that Vladimir was running a lucrative adoption ring, and the studio was to take photographs of the children for the prospective parents."

Somehow, I believed her, but only time would tell once the actual investigation was underway. It was mind-boggling how far flung the net of this heinous operation was cast. Maybe we had just scratched the surface, but we were happy that the main lynch pin, Vladimir, had been arrested.

All four of us quickly explored every room in the building until we came to a room that was bolted from the outside. When Amer opened the door, we saw what looked like a well-stocked storeroom. What was unusual was that in the farthest corner was a padlocked door. "I think this is it!" exclaimed Amer. "Now where is the key?" He looked around as if it would be conveniently hanging on a nail near the door.

"I doubt that you will find the key since most of the people that were here have been arrested," I said. "We might have to break open that door."

Sarah looked around and spotted a pickaxe leaning against the wall. She hefted it in her hands and struck the padlock a few times, after which it broke into two.

"Good job, Sarah!" I said with a smile. "Where did you learn to do that?"

"Oh, here and there." She laughed. "I used to lose the keys to my hostel room, and I would borrow the pickaxe from the gardener to break my locks. Nothing to it," she smirked while blowing on her nails and polishing them on her collar.

We turned towards our task at hand. We opened the now unlocked door and walked down the well-lit stairs. As we reached the lower level, we saw that the whole open space of the basement was covered with rows of cots. The layout was similar to what we had seen in Tehran. There must have been more than eighty of them. On each cot, there slept a child of every possible size, age, and race. Their ages must have ranged from a few months to a few years. Keeping an eye on the children was a martinet of a woman who looked up in surprise from the book she was reading as we walked in.

"Who are you?" she asked in a coarse Croatian accent.

"We are the police," said Amer. "Put your hands up where I can see them."

She complied immediately. She didn't seem combatant or confrontational, and Amer handcuffed her to an exposed pipe on the wall.

"How do you get to the lower level?" Amer asked the woman, who was now cowering in her chair.

"What lower level do you mean? This is all there is," she said with a tremor in her voice. We questioned her for a few minutes but didn't get any further. Either she was very tight-lipped, or really didn't know anything.

A little girl who must have been about five years old was listening to us intently sidled up to me and pulled at the leg of my pants. She looked exhausted. Her hair was matted and there were dark circles under her eyes, but her expression was innocent and angelic... maybe even a bit forlorn. My heart went out to her. "Bad mans take us there..." she said as she pointed towards a cupboard that was flush against the opposite wall. "Make I do bad tings..." she said with tears in her eyes.

I looked towards Sarah, instinctively knowing that her eyes would be full of tears in sympathy for the little tyke. "Sarah, you stay here with the children. Check the ones who are awake. That is what you were brought here for, isn't it?" I said kindly. She swallowed convulsively, took a beat to compose herself, and then nodded.

"What is your name, little one?" she asked the girl while taking her hand and walking away towards the infant cots in the room. I didn't hear her answer, but I saw how the child leaned towards Sarah as if she was trying to draw some positive energy from her.

"Don't worry, little one. We will get you out of this hell hole as soon as we can," I muttered under my breath.

Amer had a haunted look on his face. "I really didn't know, Tanya. I swear..." He looked sorrowfully at Sarah's and the little girl's departing backs. He was already at the cupboard and with Nadja's help pushed it away to reveal an open doorway behind it. I couldn't resist looking back with a scowl at the woman, who cringed further into her corner if that was even possible. There was a switch on the wall near the doorway and by flipping it on, the stairway and the room below became well lighted with rows of tube-lights.

Just as we expected, this area was like a movie set with props, cameras, and lights spread all over the room. There were little cubicles furnished with child sized beds that were covered with ornate frilly bedding in garish colors, as if they were trying to replicate adult brothels. It was more than a person with compassion or a conscience could bear. It might have been my imagination, but the atmosphere in the room was heavy, as if the sorrow of many exploited children had leeched into the walls and created their own means of haunting anyone who would come into the rooms. Heaving a heavy sigh, I picked up the video tapes and CDs that I found in a cabinet hidden behind a large projection screen. Following my lead, Nadja and Amer also started to fill the garishly ornate pillowcases that would have been more at home in a house of ill repute. We found a mother lode of files and videos that could put everyone involved behind bars for years on end. It was such a relief that we had what we had set out to find. I had to hide the tears that had sprung in my eyes from my colleagues. They were tears of relief that we had caught the perpetrators, but most of all tears of sorrow for the young and innocent lives that were adversely affected by all this just for the sake of power and money.

We hauled our cache upstairs and, to my surprise, found Mr. Humphrey there talking to Sarah, who waved and smiled at me as she turned and walked up the stairs and out of the room. He had a few men and women with him who were busy dressing the children in warm clothes and taking them upstairs. Each child had a folder with them—pink for the girls and blue for the boys.

"Hi, Mr. Humphrey!" I was happy to see him. "Where are they taking the children?"

"They have been declared wards of the state and I am sending them back to England. We will try to find their parents and repatriate them as soon as we can. In the meantime, they will be taken care of physically and psychologically. Those children who are of school age will be sent to school as well." Mr. Humphrey sounded quite pleased with himself.

"But what about those children who really are orphans? What do we do about them?" I was worried that they would be exploited by someone else.

"They will be cared for by the child protection services and placed in foster homes with intent to adopt. Until they are permanently settled, we are committed to their education and care." Mr. Humphrey squeezed my shoulder to reassure me. "Dr. Sarah is doing a wonderful job. Before each child is taken away from here, she is giving them a thorough check-up and creating the folders you see with them. That will help us tremendously and save a lot of time."

"Where has Sarah gone?" I asked while looking up towards the door where she had disappeared.

"She has set up a clinic in one of the rooms upstairs and is working from there. There seem to be a lot of medical supplies and equipment that the smugglers must have kept here for the children. It is working to our advantage now."

I peeked into the room where the children were being examined. To my surprise, one child was sitting on Sarah's lap while another was hanging on her back with her arms around her neck as she wrote in one of the folders. It was such a cute picture that I regretted not having a camera to capture it.

Sarah looked up, smiled, and went back to what she was doing. I knew that it would be some time until she was finished, so I went back to Mr. Humphrey and we started to interrogate Nadja and Amer. They were just as horrified as we were by the child porn part of the business and couldn't say much about it, but they were a font of information about the child adoption schemes.

According to them, there was a network of adoption agencies spread worldwide that were owned by Vladimir. Parents who wanted to adopt a child would send in their requirements to him, that is... the age, sex, race, hair color, eyes, etc., and they would be sent the specifically requested child within a turnaround time of one month. By the time the child reached the agencies, the adoptive parents would already be waiting there, and they would take the child away almost immediately, albeit for a very high price. And of course, there would be no waiting period like it happened with legitimate agencies. It was a pay to order business. Preying on human suffering and profiting from it.

As we sat there talking, I became aware of a furtive movement from the corner of my eyes. "Get down!" I shouted as I flipped the table over to provide cover for Mr. Humphrey, Nadja, and Amer. There was a sudden burst of gunfire from an automatic rifle aimed specifically towards our Croatian colleagues, probably to stop them from talking to us. As I dived over the table to help them, I felt an excruciating burning sensation in my left lower leg—I had been hit! As I fell, I hit my head on the corner of the table and blacked out. My last coherent thought was for Sarah. I prayed fervently that she was safe.

When I regained consciousness, I was in a hospital and Sarah was sitting next to me, holding my hand and looking very worried. "Where am I? Are you alright?" I asked groggily while squinting at her.

"Oh, thank God you are awake!" exclaimed Sarah. "You have been unconscious for the past three days. We were getting worried, because you had a severe concussion and had lost a lot of blood through your injury." Sarah started to cry. I knew that it was a deep sense of relief that I was awake that made her cry. Even though my arms felt weak, I put them around her as she sobbed while leaning her forehead beside me on the mattress.

"What happened? I know I was hurt, but what happened after that?"

"Amer saw you fall and he reacted immediately. He and Nadja shot the gunman down. Unfortunately, one of the stray bullets caught Nadja in the jugular vein, and she died instantly," said Mr. Humphrey, who had just walked into the room.

"I heard the shots being fired, but one of the agents held me back. I was furious and so scared for you. Rightly so, but I thank all that is holy that you are still alive," said Sarah. "Afterwards, when the shooting stopped, I ran down the stairs and nearly fainted when I saw you unconscious and injured. I don't know how I did it, but my inner physician kicked in and I tried to staunch the blood and make you as comfortable as possible until the ambulance came and took you to the hospital." From her tone of voice, I could feel what a devastating strain that had been on her, and yet she was so brave that she had soldiered on.

"Sarah is being very modest. The paramedics said that if she hadn't provided first aid, you would have lost too much blood and wouldn't have survived because one of the bullets had severed an artery in your leg." Mr. Humphrey smiled at Sarah while she shyly looked away. "You have really been through the wringer with this case, Tanya," Mr. Humphrey continued. "I want you to go home as soon as the doctors allow you to travel, and then take at least two months off after you have recovered and just relax. I know that you have a lot of leave days pending."

"Thank you. I definitely shall. Sarah and I have decided that we will stay at home and be homebodies for a while." I laughed, happy at the thought of going home once more.

"Both of you will receive a commendation for the work you did. If I can, I will also try to bring this to the notice of Her Majesty the Queen."

"We were just doing our job, but it definitely is nice to be appreciated," I said with a smile. Sarah and I were looking forward to a quiet time... although if all went well, our life was about to be turned upside down in a very pleasant way very soon.

EPILOGUE

SIX MONTHS LATER

"When you reach the end of what you should know,
you will be at the beginning of what you should sense."
~ Kahlil Gibrán, Sand and Foam.

SARAH

Finally, we were home. There was a feeling of peace that had settled over us like a comforting soft blanket. We felt once more that our life was complete. Tanya and I had come a long way from our tentative journey of friendship in Nawabshah to being life partners in England. And what a journey it had been! The adventures, the exhilaration of the highs, and the heartbreaks of the lows added only to strengthen our love for each other and helped us bring our family together.

Looking out of the picture window from my kitchen, I quietly observed the center of my universe, and there was such satisfaction and a deep sense of peaceful belonging in that lush corner of our well-maintained garden. Tanya was taking advantage of the summer weather and was napping in our hammock, Hana snuggled in the crook of her left arm and Dania fast asleep on her right side with her leg and arm flung over Tanya's middle. Just like I always do. It was amazing how the little ones picked up our mannerisms. They were so similar to the two of us that one of us could have given birth to them.

We finally had our little girls with us. It had been a long and difficult time for all of us, but the effort was well worth it. Our family was now complete. I never thought that we would become mothers, but God had been good to us.

As I continued to take deep pleasure in observing that domestic tableau in the garden, I felt someone come and stand next to me.

"She looks content, doesn't she?" Razia said.

"All thanks to you, dear friend. You were a great help." I turned and smiled at her while gesturing silently towards the teapot. Razia picked up a colorful ceramic mug and poured some tea for herself. She had constantly been a good friend of ours and we would always consider her part of our family. Tanya and I loved her dearly and she was the sister neither of us ever had. She felt the same way about us since she was also an only daughter with two brothers, who in her early life had been extremely cruel and abusive to her. She knew how attached we had become to the babies she had helped rescue from the Afghan camp. It was love at first sight for Tanya and me, and just to let them go with Razia was painful even though we knew they were safe. As soon as she and Gulab reached Pakistan over the Afghan mountains and the

Khyber Pass, Razia contacted Mr. Humphrey and told him about the little girls and our intent to adopt them. They researched the adoption procedures of Pakistan as well as the UK and concluded that since the girls didn't have any known guardians or next of kin, it would be easier if Interpol took them to England as wards of the state, and then we could initiate the adoption process. There was a lot of red tape involved, but Razia and Tanya's brother, Shahnawaz, helped on the Pakistani side. Mr. Humphrey and other Interpol colleagues of Tanya helped expedite things on our end.

"Bless you, Razia; you risked your life for us and the babies. We will never forget that."

"And I will never forget how you saved my life all those years ago and protected my twins, so we balance the mutual admiration society." She laughed.

After Vladimir was arrested in Croatia, we traveled to Pakistan, where Tanya had decided to recuperate. Razia was once again our host since we didn't want to go to our own families. It was our time to rest, and we needed love and encouragement to heal our shattered souls, not the negativity and hate that we were sure we would get from Tanya's family or my Ammi. We didn't realize that at the time, but Tanya's injury had caused some nerve damage that led to partial paralysis of her leg. After harrowing physiotherapy sessions and sheer will power, Tanya could walk again, although she still had a nearly imperceptible limp that got pronounced when she was tired. Mr. Humphrey offered her a job at the London Interpol headquarters to train agents and promoted her to head the South Asian cell. It was a desk job, but Tanya said she was happy with that because now she would be able to spend more time with us... her family. However, I sometimes saw a wistful faraway look in her eyes.

"I heard you met the Queen!" said Razia. "How was that? You must have been so excited... I saw the two of you on the news, but the clip passed by so quickly that when I blinked you were gone." She smiled.

"I was shaking with nerves and had to practice curtsying for days." I laughed and demonstrated a perfectly regal curtsy while spreading my arms out wide.

"What about Tanya? Did she curtsy too? That must have looked funny." Razia started giggling.

"That would have been hilarious!"

"You mean she didn't curtsy? She disrespected the Queen?" Razia tried to look outraged, but still continued to giggle.

"No, not at all. Tanya wore her formal police uniform with full regalia and all of her medals shining on her chest. She was told that she could salute and then bow to the Queen. I think it was much more dignified than my clumsy attempts to genuflect, although after practicing, I managed a passable if not a graceful ballerina class curtsy." I raised my nose in the air, but I spoiled the faux snobbish effect by laughing.

"Show me the medals you were presented with." Razia couldn't come to the award ceremony with us because one of her twins was sick at the time, but she was as excited for us as if she had received the medals herself.

"Well, both of us were awarded the George Cross, which is the highest civilian award conferred by the Queen on civilians for acts of gallantry or courage in circumstances of extreme danger. We didn't expect anything, and just to meet the Queen would have made our day, but to get such a high honor is absolutely mind blowing." Razia was impressed. She knew the importance of the award and was proud of us.

"That beats the Pakistani President's Pride of Performance Award I got..."

"No!" I flicked her with a dishtowel. "Never say that. You received the highest award from Pakistan. You should be very proud!"

"I am! I am!" she said holding out her hands in a conciliatory manner while laughing at my fierce defense of her award.

Just then the front doorbell rang, shattering the peace of the afternoon with its loud ding-dong. "I wonder who that could be," I said more to myself.

"It could be Adam. He left about an hour ago and said he had something to do."

"Why is he ringing the bell then? He usually comes via the back gate when he knows that we are in the garden."

Razia just shrugged and turned away, but not quick enough to hide the smirk on her face. I knew how tight lipped she could be if anyone told her to keep a secret, so I didn't say anything, but I sighed and went to open the door.

"Adam, why are you... Ammi!?!" To my surprise, my mother was standing on the threshold with Adam.

"Are you going to invite me in? Or are you just going to stand there with your mouth open catching flies?" said my unusually cheerful mother.

"What...? How...?" I stammered as I stood aside to let her in. Adam shouldered his way into the house and straight away took her suitcase to the bedroom on the ground floor.

Oh, so that was why he and Razia had been working in the room that morning! They were getting it ready for Ammi! I guided her into the living room because I didn't want her to meet Tanya. Not just then. I needed to know why she had come all the way from Pakistan to visit us after all this time. Ammi never did anything without an ulterior motive.

As soon as she sat down on the sofa and was comfortable, my mother began to speak.

"I wanted you to know that I love you and I regret to have wasted so many years pushing you away. I am so proud of you and the life you have made for yourself. I am also proud of your partner, Tanya. I heard of the awards both of you were given and watched you meet the Queen on television. I just couldn't stop talking to my friends about my two daughters." She looked down at her hands and was quiet for a few moments, then she looked at me once more with tears in her eyes. "Please forgive me, daughter," she said in a small, almost inaudible voice.

I think I must have resembled a goldfish with my mouth soundlessly opening and closing. Ammi took my hand in hers and pulled me gently to make me sit down next to her. "The more I talked to people about your lifestyle, crazy exploits, and how proud I was of the two of you, I realized that you have chosen the perfect partner for yourself. You both love each other and are there for each other in every possible way. That is the sort of relationship everyone looks for and you are lucky you found that with Tanya. Therefore, I came to personally bless you...both of you."

I continued to be tongue-tied, but my tears were streaming down my cheeks. They were tears of relief and joy. I felt as if a weight had lifted from my shoulders. My life force was balancing itself, and I felt energy the color of rainbows swirling joyfully around me and reaching out to the people I loved. Tanya must have felt my energy beckoning her, just like it usually did, and I felt rather than heard her walk silently behind me and put a comforting hand on my shoulder. She had Hana in her arms while Dania toddled along beside her, hanging on to her leg. As she bent over to look at me, she noticed my tears and reacted defensively.

"What...?" she started to say in a loud voice.

"No, no, it's okay, Tanya!" I put my hand on her arm to calm her down. "Ammi has come to give us her blessing. These are tears of joy." I laughed as she tried to clumsily wipe my tears away while juggling Hana on her hip.

"We didn't know you were coming, Mrs. Shah, or we would have picked you up from the airport." Tanya was a bit embarrassed by her spontaneous reaction to my tears.

"I asked Adam not to say anything. I wasn't sure what my reception would be... and didn't I tell you a few years ago to call me Ammi?" she said with a smile.

"Sorry, Ammi," grinned Tanya. "Would you like to meet your granddaughters?"

"Are these the little girls? Oh, they are beautiful. The little one looks just like you did, Sarah, when you were a baby! Look at those beautiful curls!" Ammi held out her arms to take Hana from Tanya.

"Our elder daughter is Dania, and the little one is Hana," I said. Ammi leaned over and kissed a shy Dania on her cheek. Dania had toddled over to her and looked at this new face in wonder, her pink bow lips forming a little 'o.' As Ammi rocked Hana in her arms, she looked at Tanya.

"Would you mind if I spoke with Sarah alone? It's nothing confidential, but I do want to repair our relationship and get to know these cuties, and I am sure there will be more good news soon."

"That's a good idea," said Tanya. "Why don't you all go and sit in the garden, and I will bring you a nice cup of tea..."

"I prefer coffee, and I would like to have something to eat—the airline food was exceptionally plastic and tasteless on the flight."

"One cup of coffee and a snack coming up. Razia, come help me." Tanya turned to go to the kitchen. As I watched her walk away, I recognized the stoic way she held her back and shoulders. I knew my life partner was hurting. Not because of us or anything that was said, but because she missed her mother. It was only recently that she had confessed to me how deeply felt the void in her life. Even though I knew she was happy for me, Ammi making peace with us must have struck a chord.

Just then the doorbell rang once more. I heard Tanya call out that she would get it as I walked out into the garden.

After a few moments of silence, I heard the sound of glass shattering, and I ran inside to see what was happening.

There she stood as if in shock while her brother and mother stood on the threshold with their luggage. Tanya had dropped the mug she had been holding, and it was lying shattered on the floor with coffee splattered on the walls. She was trying to speak, but I could see that she was overcome with emotion and the words would not come out. I took over; otherwise, they would have been standing at the door for a long while.

"Salam, please come in," I said to our unexpected guests.

I escorted them to the living room and let Tanya take over from there while I again joined my mother in the garden and noticed the self-satisfied smirk she had on her face.

"How did you know?" I asked, remembering her enigmatic announcement just a few moments before.

"We met them at the airport. Shahnawaz asked us not to say anything, but I couldn't resist dropping a hint." She smiled while handing Hana over to me so she could pick Dania up and cuddle her.

Tanya's mother came to greet us, and I was surprised that she came over to hug me. Ammi smiled and held Hana up for her to see.

"Meet your grandbabies, Mrs. Kareem," she told Tanya's mother.

"Please, we are family; call me Zeba. Mrs. Kareem makes me sound as if I am a possession of that man. It is liberating to be so far away from his cruel and toxic presence." Ma looked much younger as she smiled at the babies. I hadn't realized what an eloquent and well-spoken woman she was. Tanya told me later that she had a master's degree in English Literature and had been a teacher before she married and was oppressed by her husband.

Could life get any better? We had our family with us, all three generations together. It took a few long and sometimes bumpy journeys to reach here, but they were worth the effort and heartache because we had achieved ultimate peace... for now...until the next adventure.

Tanya

. . .

I opened the door nonchalantly, expecting a tradesperson or a friend. I was so shocked when I saw who stood there... I nearly fainted, and the coffee cup that I had in my hand fell from my lifeless fingers, breaking into pieces.

"Ma? Shahnawaz? What are you doing here?" I asked in a hoarse voice. My mouth became inexplicably dry, and I just couldn't speak easily.

As I was rooted in shock, we remained standing at the door, and I was grateful that Sarah had heard my cup shatter. She came over and had the presence of mind to bring our guests inside. At the back of my mind I irrationally thought that I had to remember to clean the coffee splatters later or Sarah would be annoyed with me.

As soon as they were seated in the living room, Shahnawaz started to speak rapidly, as if he wanted to have his say without being interrupted.

"I had to bring Ma; he was killing her..." he said with a catch in his voice. "I should have taken her away years ago, but I was a coward, and poor Ma had to suffer because I didn't have the courage to face our father and take her away from his toxic presence. It was just too much to see how he treated her, especially when I was admitted in the hospital when you came to Karachi. When he saw you there, he kept on physically punishing her as if it was her fault that you were in the country. The last straw was when he pushed her and she struck her head against the doorjamb and had to be admitted in the hospital for a severe concussion. Ma was unconscious for three days." Shahnawaz was visibly disturbed as he spoke. Ma pulled his sleeve and tried to make him stop talking, but he went on. "The doctors scanned her and found multiple old fractures, including one in her forearm that was badly set and caused her a lot of pain. The orthopedic surgeon had to break it again under anesthesia and reset it."

"Well, it was a painful procedure, but I am grateful that my arm doesn't hurt anymore," said Ma while experimentally flexing and extending her arm. She looked anxiously at me as she spoke. "Daughter, please forgive me for the pain we caused you so many years ago. I am also sorry for barging in over here and disrupting your life..."

I bent down and hugged my much shorter mother. "Don't say that. You don't know how many times I have dreamed that you were here with us, and I was in your arms. I have missed you so much. Please, please don't go back to him. You will always have a place to stay here."

Both of us had tears in our eyes and we held each other as if we would never let go.

After she had greeted everyone and cooed over her new grandbabies, I settled Ma in our other guest room. Shahnawaz was going to stay with Adam and Gulnaz because we didn't have enough space to put him up with us. Maybe we would need to get a larger house in the future if there would be more visitors and we were all going to be here together? I wanted Ma to stay with us permanently. I hoped that she would agree to that. She wouldn't want to go back to a life of abuse and unprecedented disrespect. Sarah and I had discussed this once before and she agreed that if Ma was willing, we would have her as a permanent house guest.

As I looked out of the window overlooking our lovely garden, I saw Sarah, her Ammi and Razia playing with our daughters, while my brother Shahnawaz was sitting at a table with Adam and Gulnaz deep in discussion. It must have been a pleasant conversation because they were all laughing and smiling. *Our daughters!* Just to say that sounded so strange...and yet these two little humans, Dania and Hana, had wangled themselves into our hearts and completed our lives in ways that were beyond compare. It was as if we were destined to be part of each other's lives. They were truly our heartlines.

When I was thrown out of my father's house, I thought that I had reached the depths of human despair. I had even contemplated to end things there and then. If my aunt hadn't taken me in, taken care of me and helped me with my education, Lord knows I might have either been a vagrant on the streets or even dead. To become a scholar of law and order was just a dream in those depressing days where I deeply felt the loss of my mother. I was only eighteen years old, and in Pakistan, where children live with the parents till they marry or move away for their studies or their careers, I was just a baby. I sometimes wondered what my father wanted me to do all alone. Did he ever love me? Oh well, I had better shove away these maudlin thoughts out of my mind because my life was now ideal. I had a wonderful family and partner, and a prestigious career where I had earned the respect of my peers through sheer hard work and dedication. The impossible had now happened and my mother and my brother were here, in my house. I wouldn't have thought that likely before.

"What are you thinking about, my dear girl?" asked Ma as she entered the room and walked up to me, taking me by my arm affectionately. "You have been staring out of the window lost in thought for a while now."

"I was just thinking about the past. How far we have

come since..." I didn't want to elaborate, but my Ma knew what I was about to say.

"I wish I could go back and make things right for you and for me, dear heart," said Ma sadly.

"No. That's exactly what I was thinking about. All the pain and heartache were worth it. It made me stronger, and I wouldn't have met Sarah if I had stayed home. My present family is my source of strength, and I wouldn't have it any other way."

Ma hugged me and we walked arm in arm out to join our family in the garden, which was bathed golden with the evening sunshine. It looked almost magical with the vivid colors and the play of dancing sunrays. But then, everything looks brighter when one is happy.

Sarah was ecstatic that I wouldn't have to go undercover or on overseas assignments anymore. I still would have to travel, but that would be for corporate affairs and training. How much trouble could one get into with all of the fuddy-duddies around? Only time would tell. But then...one never knows with our luck.

RELATED TO THE NOVEL

Child smuggling or trafficking is defined by the United Nations as the "recruitment, transportation, transfer, harboring, and/or receipt of a child, which includes kidnapping of a child for the purpose of slavery, forced labour and exploitation. " (References can be seen on the UN, WHO, UNICEF and ILO websites). Small children are predominantly trafficked for the purpose of adoption. High demands by well-to-do people create a niche market that is filled by this heinous practice. However, adoption is not the only reason why children are sold to unscrupulous people.

It is sad to know that every year more than 300,000 children are taken from all around the world and sold by human traffickers as either slaves, for child pornography, or high-end adoptions. (Data on file at the International Labor Organization (ILO).

Thankfully, now the trafficking of children has been internationally recognized as a serious crime as it exists in every region of the world, and which often has human rights implications. There are many organizations worldwide that have helplines and means of helping women and children in dire situations. While I was researching for hotlines, I found many well-known organizations and their websites, but their hotlines were not always very easily accessible. The websites were there predominantly for soliciting donations and creating awareness. Therefore, I was pleased when I came across the list of hotline numbers given below.

Human Trafficking Hotline:

Phone: 1-888-373-7888.
Email: help@humantraffickinghotline.org.
Text: text HELP to 233733 (BEFREE)
Online chat: www.humantraffickinghotline.org.
National Hotlines for the European Union:
https://home-affairs.ec.europa.eu/policies/internal-security/organised-crime-and-human-trafficking/together-against-trafficking-human-beings/national-hotlines_en

The Child Helpline in Pakistan, at the Child Protection Welfare Bureau:

1121 provides prompt assistance and support to children subjected to violence, trafficking, exploitation, abuse, and neglect. It is also utilized for dissemination of information and guidance in respect of child rights.
NSPCC: https://www.nspcc.org.uk/keeping-children-safe/our-services/nspcc-helpline/

AUTHOR NOTES AND GLOSSARY

"BADLANDS"

The journey of Agent Tanya and Doctor Sarah in **Bloodlines** takes them deep into Pakistan's "Badlands." This area, known as the FATA (Federally Administered Tribal Areas) and later renamed as Pukhtunkhwa, is located along Pakistan's north-western border with Afghanistan, and consists of seven autonomous agencies. The Badlands notoriously have their own laws and traditions, which is why they have been left more or less alone by the different governments, which just had their representative political agents in each district, since the British separated this area from India in 1893 by the 2,500-kilometers-long (1,553 miles) Durand Line. To enter legally, one had to go through a whole rigamarole of permits and paperwork, and that explains why our team had to go in under the cover of night. The only place that offered some sense of safety was the Kohat air force base.

This beautiful part of Pakistan is bordered by the Hindu Kush mountains and is famous for the Khyber Pass, where a multitude of conquerors have entered ancient India, including Alexander the Great. Many areas have been likened to Switzerland and Austria and considered maybe even more beautiful because of their raw ruggedness. There were places where Sarah wanted to stay longer and explore, but the adventure and the chase of the story didn't give her much time to do so. Maybe next time?

I am lucky that I was able to travel to nearly every corner of Pakistan because of my parents' wanderlust and my father's job, so when I write about any of these places, I just close my eyes and travel there while my fingers start to move on my keyboard on their own volition. Therefore, I do hope you enjoy reading ***Bloodlines*** as much as I have writing it.

CHAPTER ONE

Congenital hydrocephalus:

Congenital hydrocephalus is a build-up of excess cerebrospinal fluid (CSF) in the brain at birth. The extra fluid can increase pressure in the baby's brain, causing brain damage with mental and physical problems.

Gojra: a small agricultural town in Punjab, Pakistan

Consanguinity: Two individuals that are "blood relatives" or "biological relatives."

NICU: Neonatal Intensive Care Unit

ESP: Extra Sensory Perception

CHAPTER TWO

MRCPCH*:* Member of the Royal College of Paediatrics and Child Health

Forced Marriage Unit*:* The Forced Marriage Unit was set up in the UK in 2005 and provides support to victims as well as expert training and guidance to professionals. It is jointly run by the Home Office and Foreign and Commonwealth Office. In 2011, they dealt with over 1400 calls in relation to forced marriages.

CHAPTER THREE

Ammi: Mother.

Baba: Father.

Shalwar kameez: A pair of light, loose, pleated trousers, usually tapering to a tight fit around the ankles, worn by women from Pakistan typically with a kameez or tunic (hence the two together being a *shalwar kameez*).

Chapter Four

Mazar of the Quaid: Mausoleum of Mohammad Ali Jinnah, the founding father of Pakistan.

Pushto, Sindhi and Punjabi: Local regional languages spoken in Pakistan.

Pathan: Person from the North of Pakistan who speaks Pushto.

CPR: This is an emergency procedure consisting of chest compressions often combined with artificial ventilation to manually preserve intact brain function until further measures are taken to restore spontaneous blood circulation and breathing in a person who is in cardiac arrest

Reiki: This is a form of energy healing, a type of alternative medicine. Reiki practitioners use a technique called palm healing or hands-on healing through which a "universal energy" is said to be transferred through the palms of the practitioner to the patient to encourage emotional or physical healing.

Defence Society: or Defence Housing Authority (DHA) is an upscale residential neighbourhood located within the Clifton Cantonment of Karachi. It was originally established as a residential town for retired military personnel by the Army in the mid 1950s, however, currently the majority are civilian families that reside in this town.

CHAPTER FIVE

Dadi: Usually, a term used for paternal grandmother.

AK47 rifle: This is officially known as the Avtomat Kalashnikova and is a gas-operated assault rifle that is chambered for the 7.62×39mm cartridge. Developed in the Soviet Union by Russian small-arms designer Mikhail Kalashnikov, it is the originating firearm of the Kalashnikov family of rifles.

C-130 Hercules: The Lockheed C-130 Hercules is an American four-engine turboprop military transport aircraft designed and built originally by Lockheed. Capable of using unprepared runways for take-off's and landings, the C-130 was originally designed as a troop, medevac, and cargo transport aircraft.

Kohat: is a city that serves as the capital of the Kohat District in the North of Pakistan. It has a well-established air force base there.

Parachinar: is a small Pashtun town which is the capital of Kurram District in the province of Khyber Pakhtunkhwa. It is situated on a neck of Pakistani territory west of Peshawar, that juts into the Logar and Nangarhar provinces of Afghanistan

CHAPTER SIX

Salam: Shortened form of the Islamic greeting Asalam alaikum which means peace be upon you. The shortened form loosely translated means peace.

Bell AH-1 Cobra: is a single-engine attack helicopter developed and manufactured by the American rotorcraft manufacturer Bell Helicopter. A member of the prolific Huey family, the AH-1 is also referred to as the HueyCobra or Snake.

CHAPTER SEVEN

Mingora: is a city in the Swat District of Khyber Pakhtunkhwa, Pakistan. Located on the Swat River, it is the 3rd largest city in Khyber Pakhtunkhwa and the 26th largest in Pakistan

Cutaneous Horn: is a type of lesion or growth that appears on the skin. It's made of keratin, which is a protein that makes up the top layer of the skin. The growth may look like a cone or horn, and it can vary in size. The name comes from the growth sometimes resembling an animal's horn. It is a skin condition that is more common in older adults.

Mullah: is an honorific title for a Muslim mosque leader. The term is also sometimes used for a person who has higher education in Islamic theology and sharia law.

Kishan Gul Mountain Trail: A steep and treacherous trail leading to remote little villages and scattered dwellings in the mountains of Parachinar.

CHAPTER EIGHT

Peritonitis: is an inflammation of the peritoneum — a silk-like membrane that lines your inner abdominal wall and covers the organs within your abdomen — that is usually due to a bacterial or fungal infection.

CHAPTER NINE

Meconium: is a new-born baby's first poop. This sticky, thick, dark green poop is made up of cells, protein, fats, and intestinal secretions, like bile.

Political Liaison Officer: Intermediary official between the Government of Pakistan and the Tribes in the area.

CHAPTER TEN

Chaddar: a large sheet-like cloth used as a head covering (and veil and shawl) by Muslim women and covers them from head to toe.

Peshawar: is the capital of the Pakistani province of Khyber Pakhtunkha. It is the sixth largest city in Pakistan. Situated in the broad valley of Peshawar east of the historic Khyber Pass close to the border with Afghanistan, its recorded history dates back to at least 539 BCE, making it the oldest city in Pakistan and one of the oldest cities in South Asia.

Darra Adamkhel: is the main town of the Kohat District of Khyber Pakhtunkhwa. It has gained fame and notoriety for its bazaars packed with gunsmiths and weapons merchants. The town consists of one main street lined with multiple shops, while side-alleys and streets contain workshops.

Halal: Halal is an Arabic word that translates to "permissible" in English. Or kosher.

CHAPTER ELEVEN

Sahib: A term used especially among the native inhabitants of colonial India when addressing or speaking of a European of some social or official status. Nowadays its used as a form of respect e.g. Doctor Sahib.

Multan: is a city located in Punjab, Pakistan. Situated on the bank of the Chenab River, it is Pakistan's 7th largest city and is the major cultural and economic centre of Southern Punjab. Multan's history stretches deep into antiquity.

CHAPTER THIRTEEN

Lahore: is the capital of the Pakistani province of Punjab and is Pakistan's second largest city after Karachi. It is the 26th largest city in the world. Lahore reached the height of its splendour under the Mughal Empire between the late 16th and early 18th century and served as its capital city for many years.

Mughal: A member of the Muslim dynasty of Indian emperors who originated from Afghanistan and established by Babar in 1526.

Parathas: Golden-brown in colour, flaky and layered, a paratha is a type of Indian/Pakistani bread that is typically consumed for breakfast.

Sargodha: is also known as the City of Eagles. It is one of the few planned cities of Pakistan. It is an agricultural district, wheat, rice, and sugarcane being its main crops.

CHAPTER FOURTEEN

Bibi: A name of Farsi and Persian origin, means "young lady of the house".

Imam: The person who leads prayers in a mosque and conducts religious ceremonies like weddings and funerals.

CHAPTER FIFTEEN

Oma: A term of endearment for grandmother in German.

Reich: The term is derived from the Germanic word which generally means "realm," but in German, it is typically used to designate a kingdom or an empire, especially the Roman Empire.

Führer: a tyrannical leader. In this book pertaining to Hitler.

Heil Hitler!: used by the Germans or their supporters during the Nazi regime as a greeting or an acclamation of the supremacy of Hitler.

Deutschland über Alles!: Germany above all: German unity above factionalism. A common Nazi slogan in WWII.

CHAPTER SIXTEEN

Gestapo: abbreviation of Geheime Staatspolizei (German: "Secret State Police"), the political police of Nazi Germany. The Gestapo ruthlessly eliminated opposition to the Nazis within Germany and its occupied territories and, in partnership with the Sicherheitsdienst (SD; "Security Service"), was responsible for the roundup of Jews throughout Europe for deportation to extermination camps.

EPILOGUE

PLAB: The Professional and Linguistic Assessments Board (PLAB) test provides the main route for International Medical Graduates (IMGs) to demonstrate that they have the necessary skills and knowledge to practise medicine in the United Kingdom (UK).

Kismet: 'this comes from the Arabic word 'qisma', which means "portion" or "lot." The word Kismet was borrowed into English in the early 1800s from Turkish, where it is now used as a synonym of fate.

ALSO BY SHIREEN MAGEDIN

The Journeys Series:

Book 1: Lifelines

Book 2: Bloodlines

Book 3: Heartlines

ABOUT SHIREEN MAGEDIN

Dr. Shireen Magedin is a practicing pediatrician who has studied in Pakistan, England, and Ireland. She has always had psychic abilities, and in the beginning they scared her, until she received guidance from trainers and connected with people who had similar abilities, thus knowing she wasn't alone. Connecting psychically and intuitively with her patients has helped her hone her medical skills.

She lives with her cat Pompi (aka Madam Pompadour) and enjoys visits from her daughter Sharmeen, son Nadir, and daughter-in-law Mariam.

Connect with Shireen

Official Author Site
https://shireenmagedin.com

Email
https://shireenmagedin.com/contact-us/

Facebook
https://www.facebook.com/groups/shireenmagedin

ABOUT AUSXIP PUBLISHING

www.ausxippublishing.com

AUSXIP Publishing publishes quality fiction and non-fiction with strong female characters that inspire, strengthen and enrich the soul. Stories that build up, create a sense of achievement and most importantly to entertain.

AUSXIP Publishing Newsletter
https://newsletter.ausxippublishing.com

AUSXIP Publishing Store:
https://store.ausxippublishing.com

Facebook:
https://facebook.com/ausxippublishing

Twitter:
https://twitter.com/ausxippublish

Printed in Great Britain
by Amazon